He's one human caught in a tangled maze of theft, politics,
magic, and blood.
In other words, it's just another night.

MIDNIGHT LABYRINTH

Benjamin Vecchio escaped a chaotic childhood and grew to adulthood under the protection and training of one of the Elemental world's most feared vampire assassins. He's traveled the world and battled immortal enemies.

But everyone has to go home sometime.

New York means new opportunities and allies for Ben and his vampire partner, Tenzin. It also means new politics and new threats. Their antiquities business is taking off, and their client list is growing. When Ben is challenged to find a painting lost since the Second World War, he jumps at the chance. This job will keep him closer to home, but it might just land him in hot water with the insular clan of earth vampires who run Manhattan.

Tenzin knew the painting would be trouble before she laid eyes on it, but she can't deny the challenge intrigues her. Human laws mean little to a vampire with a few millennia behind her, and Tenzin misses the rush of taking what isn't hers.

But nothing is more dangerous than a human with half the story, and Ben and Tenzin might end up risking their reputations and their lives before they escape the Midnight Labyrinth.

MIDNIGHT LABYRINTH is the first book in an all-new contemporary fantasy series by Elizabeth Hunter, author of the Elemental Mysteries and the Irin Chronicles.

PRAISE FOR ELIZABETH HUNTER

Praise for Midnight Labyrinth...

This marvelous story is part caper, part mystery and part political skullduggery as an attempt to do a good deed backfires spectacularly. Although this is a stand-alone book, Hunter's legion of fans will be thrilled to find a number of familiar characters included in the tale. ...Primarily a caper novel, it is also jam-packed with character revelations and sometimes painful growth.
—*RT Magazine*

Familiar and pulse-driving motifs readers have come to expect from Hunter, supplemented by a mystery-driven plot.
—Kendrai Meeks, *author of the Red Hood Chronicles*

Praise for Elizabeth Hunter...

Elizabeth Hunter's books are delicious and addicting, like the best kind of chocolate. She hooked me from the first page, and her stories just keep getting better and better. Paranormal romance fans won't want to miss this exciting author!
—Thea Harrison, *NYT* best-selling author of the Elder Races series

The Staff and The Blade is a towering work of romantic fantasy that will captivate the reader's mind and delight their heart. Elizabeth Hunter's ability to construct such a sumptuous narrative time and time again is nothing short of amazing.

—ReaderEater.com

"Elemental Mysteries turned into one of the best paranormal series I've read this year. It's sharp, elegant, clever, evenly paced without dragging its feet, and at the same time emotionally intense."

—Nocturnal Book Reviews

"Hunter has created a magnificent world of amazing characters entangled in a web of deceit, danger, loss, power, politics, and love that will have your heart racing time and time again."

—Cross My Heart Book Reviews

MIDNIGHT LABYRINTH

AN ELEMENTAL LEGACY NOVEL

ELIZABETH HUNTER

Midnight Labyrinth
Copyright © 2017
Elizabeth Hunter
ISBN: 978-1976211935

Cover by: Damonza
Edited by: Anne Victory
Formatted by: Elizabeth Hunter

 Created with Vellum

For every reader who ever asked,
"So are you going to write a Ben and Tenzin book?"

Reader, I decided to give you five.
I hope you enjoy the first, and I thank you for your patience. I've
been waiting to write this book nearly as long as you've been
waiting to read it.
With much love, EH

To be trusted is a greater
compliment than being loved.
—George MacDonald

1

_____

He chased his quarry up the ladder, launching himself onto a gravel-strewn roof in Hell's Kitchen. Ducking under a broken scaffold, he followed the dark figure who threatened to elude him. She was half his size, dressed in a black hoodie and leggings. She moved like a cat in the dim, predawn light.

She was getting away.

He ran left, skimming the side of a cinder block building before he leapt across a narrow vent, using longer legs to his advantage. He landed hard, rolled in a single somersault, then took to his feet in one smooth movement. He could feel gravel in the small of his back, and his arm was bleeding from the bite of a rusted ladder, but he kept running.

He was gaining on her. He scanned the landscape as he'd been taught, mentally calculating the most efficient way to get from his position to hers.

His lungs pumped in steady rhythm. In-in-out. He pulled in the humid air and tried not to choke. He'd been running at seven thousand feet the week before. His thin black shirt stuck to his skin. Grey light filtered over a city that still clung to the memory of the previous day's heat. New York City in July. Another day; another sauna.

The small figure scrambled up the side of a building—sticking to the stained brick like a spider—then she disappeared over the edge and into nothing.

He wasn't concerned for her safety.

He found the lips of the bricks she'd used to climb. He wasn't as fast as she was. He was forced to take his time crawling up the side of the building, finding each fingerhold and jutting brick to move his body up the wall. From a distance, he'd appear to be sticking too. He felt a fingernail tear, but he didn't pause.

Hoisting his body over the edge of the wall, he kept himself low and scanned the urban landscape. Water towers and rusted fire escapes mixed with recently gentrified gardens and sleek patio furniture.

She was barely visible in the distance, leaping from the top of one building to the next.

He ran after her, but he knew it was futile. She'd gained too much ground during his careful climb. She disappeared over the side of another building, and Ben knew he'd lost her.

Panting, he followed her tracks, not allowing himself to slow down. He leapt over the edge of a familiar building and jumped fire escape railings five stories down until he hung on the last rung of the old ironwork.

Ben Vecchio closed his eyes and did three rapid pull-ups, pushing his muscles right to the edge of exhaustion before he gave them a break. He had a runner's build, but he was six feet tall. Moving a large frame quickly would always be a challenge. He dropped to the ground and jogged down West 47th Street to the deserted playground. The gate was locked, but he easily jumped over.

She'd taught him that trick early.

A small hooded figure perched on the top of a red-and-green

play structure. Still breathing deeply, Ben jumped to the first platform and squatted in front of her.

"Believe it or not, you are getting faster," Zoots said.

"That wall nearly killed me." With the adrenaline waning, Ben was starting to feel his hands.

"But you made it up. That's a ten-foot brick wall, and you climbed it."

"Slowly."

"But you climbed it," Zoots said. "Remember, I grew up here. I know every inch of those roofs. I have the advantage."

He shook his head. "Doesn't matter. I have to be faster."

It had to be more instinctive. He wouldn't have the luxury of running in familiar places.

Zoots rolled her eyes and pulled out a cigarette. "Whatever, man."

When he'd first moved to New York, he'd watched. There were parkour and free-running groups, but they were cliquish and Ben was a beginner. Though he'd been drilled in martial arts and weapons training since he was twelve years old, parkour was new to him. It was only the lightning-quick reflexes of a girl he'd met a few years ago that had attracted him to the practice. She'd moved inhumanly fast.

Of course, she hadn't been strictly human.

Ben was. The sweat dripping into his eyes proved it. He wiped it away and sat next to Zoots.

He'd found her by watching. She wasn't part of the group, but they knew her. She was the one they wandered over to talk to when they were practicing. Zoots was tiny—barely five feet tall—with a slight figure. Her skin was pale under her hood. Her hair was short and her eyes were dark. She came out in the early morning and at night. He'd never seen her in the middle of the day.

It had taken Ben weeks to figure out who she was and what

she was to the runners in Central Park. If the young *traceurs* in the park had a guru, it was Zoots. She claimed to be self-taught from YouTube videos, but Ben suspected that Zoots was like him. He'd been running since he could remember, mostly to get away from trouble. She was just better at it.

Zoots ran everywhere, and she was a loner. She'd ignored Ben for weeks until her curiosity got the better of her. She'd talked to him, and he'd eventually hired her. He wanted to learn parkour, but he wasn't interested in joining any group. Zoots nodded and told Ben to meet her at Hell's Kitchen Playground and to bring two hundred bucks cash.

So he did.

She finished her cigarette, flicked off the cherry, and carefully tucked the butt into a tin she kept in her pocket. "Same time next week?"

"Yeah."

"You've been doing this for six months now. You know the basics. You sure you want to keep paying me for lessons?"

Ben raised an eyebrow. "You trying to get rid of me?"

"It's your money, man." She smiled. "I just spend it."

"I need to be faster."

She eyed him. "That's practice. You're twice my size; you gotta figure out your own style. Tall means longer legs and longer arms, but it also means more meat to move."

"I'll keep paying you if you keep teaching me."

"Like I said, it's your money." Zoots narrowed her eyes. "You told me once you needed to learn this for work."

"I do." His fingers itched for a cigarette. He'd stopped smoking when he was fourteen—his uncle could smell the slightest trace of cigarette smoke—but he still wanted one occasionally. Especially when people started asking personal questions.

"But one of the guys in the park said you were in antiquities or something."

Damn nosy kids. "Yeah."

Zoots frowned. "You jumping roofs at the museum or something?"

Ben couldn't stop the smile. "I work for private clients."

"Huh." She nodded. "So... you're into some serious Indiana Jones kinda shit, huh?"

Ben rose and raked a hand through his hair. "Don't be ridiculous. You think I'd look good in a hat?"

He caught the quick flush on her cheeks before he jumped off the play structure and walked toward the gate. "See you next week, Zoots."

"Later, Indiana."

BEN CAUGHT the train to Spring Street station, then walked toward Broadway and his favorite café. He sat at the picnic tables outside Café Lilo and watched the growing rush of pedestrians filling the sidewalk. He read a newspaper someone had left behind while he drank coffee and devoured a bagel.

There was no typical crowd at Café Lilo, which was one of the reasons Ben liked it. Stockbrokers, dog walkers, young parents, and college kids all frequented the family-owned café. A few tourists came in, but it wasn't a flashy place. Morning delivery and sanitation trucks competed in the narrow streets while a growing crowd of taxis and hired cars dodged between them, heading toward Lower Manhattan.

He flipped to the Arts section of the paper and made a few notes about gallery openings. An auction announcement. A charity gala sponsored by some outfit called Historic New York. A new surrealist exhibit opening at the Museum of Modern Art.

His sunlight quota met, he headed back to the building on Mercer he was still renovating. He'd called the massive, unfinished penthouse home for two years. Both stories had finished floors and the semblance of rooms. The roof garden was a work in progress.

He nodded at the silent doorman, who was known for discretion more than amiability, and took the elevator to the top floor. He had two full floors of the building. He pushed the button for the living area on the top floor, bypassing his office on the floor below.

The loft was home. It was his office.

Finely honed reflexes were the only thing that saved him from the three-inch-thick book that dropped from the loft overhead.

The loft could also be a death trap.

He glared up. "What are you doing?" There were books—his books—scattered on the floor under her loft. "Tenzin, what the hell?"

Another book fell flat on the floor to his left.

"Stop throwing my books!"

A dark head poked out, cloaked in carefully placed shadows that protected her from sunlight. "Did you move my swords?" She held out another book, narrowed her eyes, and dropped it.

"Cut it out!" Ben shouted. "And no, I did not move your swords. I swear, Tenzin—"

"Are you sure?" A small figure floated out of the loft like the proverbial angel of book death, arms stretched out with two of his massive art books in her hands. "Are you sure you didn't move my swords?"

Damn pain-in-the-ass, stubborn wind vampire.

Ben glared at her. "I did not..."

Oh shit. He had.

"I told you," she said.

"One sword, Tenzin! *One.* Sword." He held his hands out, ready to rescue his books. "Do not drop those books."

Tenzin hovered over him, a pissed-off, flying demon with a pretty round face and a sheet of black hair falling around her. She looked young, but she wasn't. She was one of the most ancient elemental vampires on the planet, born on the northern steppes of Asia thousands of years before. She was also Ben's partner.

And a book abuser.

She wouldn't have tried it when she'd been working with his uncle, Giovanni Vecchio. Of course, Giovanni was a rare-book collector and a fire vampire who would have seriously wounded her if she tried.

Tenzin narrowed her eyes. "It's not nice when someone messes with your stuff, is it?"

"I didn't damage your damn rapier! The way you had it placed, it almost took out my eye every time I left the downstairs bathroom. So I moved it. I didn't drop it on its hilt from a height of twelve feet!"

"It wouldn't have taken out your eye if you weren't looking at your phone all the time. You should watch where you're going."

"You're making me mental." His hardbacks were still suspended in the air. "Please put my books down. I'll tell Giovanni you're abusing them if you don't."

Tenzin had been friends with his uncle hundreds of years before Ben had been born, and they'd worked as assassins for a time. Tenzin wasn't afraid of his uncle, but she found Giovanni's disapproval annoying.

She floated to the ground, still staying in the shadows, and handed him the books. "There. Don't move my stuff again."

"Then don't put it where I could do myself permanent

bodily injury, Tiny. Not all of us can regrow body parts if we lose them."

She cocked her head and looked at him. "That is a very slow and painful process, even for vampires."

"And since I'm human, not an option for me. Please don't put your swords in places that will gouge out my eyes."

"Fine." She bent down and picked up a single book. "Here."

He took the book and ignored the dozen on the ground. "Thanks."

Tenzin smiled, all ire forgotten. "You're welcome."

Then Tenzin flew back up to her loft and disappeared.

Ben looked at all the books on the floor. "Do you have any more up there?"

"Yes. Do you want me to—"

"*Don't* toss them down." He took a deep breath. "Hand them down please. After I put these away." He picked up two more books. "Any calls or emails while I was out?"

"No calls."

"But did you check your email?"

"No." She sighed. "I wish you'd never made me an email account. It's not the same as letters."

"I know that, Tenzin, but it's how the modern world communicates. And if you don't check it every day, your inbox will take over the world."

"Is that why you take your phone to the toilet?"

"Yes," he said. "Now check your messages."

Tenzin flew down and picked up a magazine from the coffee table. "Cara, check my email."

A polite, artificial voice filled the living area. "Checking electronic messages for Tenzin." There was a soft hum before Cara said, "You have six new messages."

"Read subject lines."

She complained about it, but Ben was continually amazed

by how quick Tenzin was with technology. She'd had limited access to the electronic revolution until an immortal tech company in Ireland came out with the Nocht voice-recognition program. Vampire touch wreaked havoc on any electronic gadget because of their amnis, the electrical current that ran under their skin and connected them to their elemental ability.

Wind and water vampires had bad reactions to electronics. Earth vampires could handle some gadgets a little better than others. Rare fire vampires like his uncle could short out the computer in a modern car just by sitting in the front seat.

No computers. No mobile phones. No iPods or tablets or new appliances.

But then came Nocht.

"Reading subject lines," Cara said. "From Beatrice De Novo. 'I need a recipe, don't ignore me.'"

"Delete," Tenzin said.

"You should at least write her back," Ben said.

"I don't cook from recipes, so that would be useless." Tenzin turned a page. "Next message."

Cara read, "From Blumenthal Blades. 'Desirable saber for your Eastern European collection.'"

"Save," Tenzin said. "That sounds promising."

Ben shelved three more books. "Because you definitely need more swords."

"I always need more swords."

"From Viva Industries," Cara read. "'All-natural male enhancement from Asia.'"

Tenzin laughed. "That's what he said."

It took Ben a second to realize Tenzin had actually made a joke, then he grimaced. "Delete!"

"I do not recognize voice signature for the current account," Cara said. "Shall I log out Tenzin?"

"No," Tenzin said. "Delete 'All-natural male enhancement,' Cara. Next message."

"From Jonathan Rothwell. 'Confirming details for upcoming travel.'"

"Save," Tenzin said quickly, glancing at Ben. "I'll read that later."

He kept his eyes on his bookshelves. "You going to Shanghai?"

"I haven't decided yet."

Ben tried not to react. Jonathan Rothwell was the personal secretary for Cheng, an honest-to-goodness vampire pirate who ruled Shanghai. He was also Tenzin's ex... something. Former lover? *Current* lover? Ben had met Cheng on the very first job he and Tenzin had done together four years before, but he still didn't have an answer.

It's none of your business. Ben said, "We don't have anything on the schedule, so whatever you want to do."

Ben decided to reorganize the art section of his bookshelves. He'd had the hardbacks arranged by color, but Tenzin had screwed it all up. He might as well reorganize according to style and period.

Tenzin called, "Cara, next message."

"From René DuPont. 'Think about it.'"

Ben's head popped up and his eyes went wide. "What?"

"Cara," Tenzin called, "move that one to the folder labeled René."

"You have a folder labeled René?" Ben asked. "A *folder*?"

Tenzin shrugged. "Know your enemies and know yourself."

"He tried to kill me last summer in Scotland. Several times."

Tenzin squinted. "Did he *really* try to kill you though? I mean, you did steal a sword from him," she pointed out. "A really valuable, legendary one."

"One," Ben said, "I didn't steal it from him. He stole it

from me after I found it. I just took it back. And two, he wanted that old vampire to drain me, so yes he tried to kill me."

"Your points are valid." She flipped through the magazine.

"Thank you. What does he want?"

"I don't know. Do you want his email address?" Tenzin looked up. "He often sends me funny jokes. You might find them amusing."

Ben blinked. "René DuPont, thief for hire and the vampire who tried to *kill your partner*, sends you spam emails and you don't mind?"

"You know, I don't think he was serious about killing you," Tenzin said. "That's just his sense of humor."

Ben was half-tempted to ask her to forward René's "funny jokes" just to find out what a sociopathic immortal thief found funny.

Then he remembered he lived with Tenzin.

René DuPont was part of a clan his uncle had strong ties with, so Ben didn't want to pick a fight unless he had no other choice. He and Tenzin had come off their last confrontation with René looking like the winners and the reasonable party.

Ben smiled. René probably loathed that as much as he loathed Ben.

Or as much as he wanted Tenzin. René hadn't been shy about expressing his admiration in that direction.

"You know what?" he said. "Never mind. Seeing that name in my inbox would just make my head explode. Tell me if you think he's going to be in the US or if our paths are going to cross. That's all I ask."

"Okay. Cara, next message!" Tenzin yelled.

"From Novia O'Brien. Copied to Ben Vecchio. 'Monthly meeting at Bat and Barrel?'"

Ben looked up. "Better read the whole thing. She's been

trying to pay off that favor for six months. She and Cormac are getting annoyed."

"I don't care," Tenzin said. She dropped the magazine and flew back up to her loft. "It was a pair of opera glasses, but it wasn't an easy retrieval. I'm not willing to waste a favor so they can mark it off their ledger. Let them be annoyed. Cara, read message."

Cara read, "Good evening. Would love to meet and touch base with the two of you when you have a free night. Gavin's new pub is getting good buzz. Saturday night at eleven work for you two?'"

Ben waited for Tenzin to look at him. "We need to throw them a bone."

"I don't understand the idiom," Tenzin said. She turned her eyes and stared at the opposite wall, swinging one leg back and forth on the edge of her room.

"Yes, you do," Ben said. "Don't play dumb. Throw them a bone. Let them pay us back."

She shrugged. "I don't need anything from them right now."

"It was two days' work at the most—"

"And I refused to let them pay us for that reason," she said.

"The O'Briens are a huge clan," Ben said. "They're independent, and they don't like owing people."

She smiled. "Well, they owe us now."

"I know you live for racking up favors," Ben said, "but we live here at their pleasure."

Tenzin laughed.

The vampires in charge of the great city of New York were the O'Briens, a clan of earth vampires who'd taken over the city in a violent coup and held it for a century through numbers, wise bribery, and clever manipulation.

Ben and Tenzin had moved to New York with the understanding that Tenzin—a highly powerful and connected vampire—would demonstrate no ambition that would challenge the current vampires in charge. She would also use her influence and connections in Asia to increase foreign trade.

"All I'm saying," Ben said, "is that unless you want cause an intercity incident, piss off a powerful earth vampire clan, kill a bunch of people, and take control of the city—which obviously you could do if you *really* wanted to—we should probably just meet with Novia and let her do something nice for us so her sire feels better."

Tenzin dropped from her room and hung upside down, her face level with Ben's. Talking to her like that was always disorienting.

That was, of course, why she did it.

"Is there something you need?" Ben asked.

"I'm hungry."

"Doubtful." He'd seen her drink a tall glass of blood three days ago while she was binge-watching a British reality show. At Tenzin's age, she didn't need much blood to survive.

Nevertheless, she glanced down at his neck and licked her lower lip.

"Don't piss me off, Tenzin." That was *not* their agreement. They were partners. He wasn't food.

"Novia said she wants to meet at Gavin's? Why Gavin's? There are too many humans there."

And Tenzin couldn't be around humans too often. Unlike most vampires, her fangs never retracted, which could lead to some awkward staring in the wrong places.

"Gavin pays the extra tribute to have neutral pubs in every city," Ben said quietly. "Novia is leveling the playing field, making the effort to accommodate your status. We should meet her."

Tenzin narrowed her eyes. "You meet her first. Tonight."

"Fine." Massaging egos was all part of the vampire package.

Tenzin flew back to her room and Ben continued organizing his books, mentally composing the email he'd send to Novia.

Ben Vecchio might have been born in the Bowery to good-for-nothing human parents, but he'd been raised and mentored from the age of twelve by his adoptive uncle, a fire vampire of fierce reputation and a deep desire to be left alone. Ben knew more about immortal politics than most vampires. Their world operated on a carefully balanced network of allegiances, loyalties, family ties, and favors. It was feudal, but it worked.

Most of the time.

TENZIN WATCHED him as he slept that afternoon.

Shining boy.

The lines around Ben's mouth and eyes had deepened. Not much. But he'd grown from the young man she had known and into the man he would become.

Even so, he was her shining boy, eager to fix problems, fight battles, and seek treasure. He'd dragged her to this metal city and made her a nest in the sky, quick to reassure her of his plans.

It will be brilliant. It will be fun. We'll get rich. Well, I'll get rich and you'll get richer.

Tenzin smiled.

Ben would go to the meeting with the young vampire and charm her into a solution both Tenzin and the New York hierarchy could live with. He'd negotiate with smiles and debate with quips. Ben was both her partner and her better half. He was one of the few humans who'd ever understood her, and possibly the only one who'd never feared her. Even her own sire feared her.

Not Ben.

He picked and poked at her as a hobby. He antagonized her

and did it with a smile. She pushed him just far enough to drive him crazy. Why?

It was fun.

Their partnership was good. He was finding his way and meeting his people. Making connections and learning the ways of their world. He had time as long as she was with him. As long as she watched. His human experience would only add to the being he would become.

Of course, he did have that white knight tendency.

She'd have to fix that.

White knights had a tendency to get their armor bloody, and *that* could not happen.

Not until it was time.

2

The Bat and the Barrel, newest whiskey pub in the Bowery, was the kind of place where privacy was treasured, quiet conversations could still exist, and everyone kept their eyes to themselves as they sipped some of the finest cocktails available in Lower Manhattan. It was populated by the rich, the ambitious, and the immortal.

Carefully curated blood donors of all ages, sexes, and ethnicities drifted among the tables, serving drinks. Though Gavin Wallace's pubs were open to humans, only the vampire clients and the humans who worked for them knew that the servers were available to sample. A discreet reservation and the human who served your martini could also be your dinner.

If that was your thing.

Ben watched as Novia O'Brien, favored daughter of Cormac O'Brien, brushed a thumb over the cheek of the handsome server she'd fed from in a private room. The server's smile was easy, and Ben had a feeling the young man was a frequent partner. Novia gave him a little wave as she walked into the main room.

She was attractive, as most vampires were. Her skin was the

color of sunbaked clay, her hair a riot of red-tipped corkscrews. Her bloodlines were Caribbean, but her loyalty was to the Irish vampire who'd sired her. She was young, around Ben's age when she'd turned, and looked to be in her early twenties. In reality, she was probably around thirty or forty. Still young for a vampire, but rising quickly in the hierarchy because of her drive and connections.

"Hey!" he said as she sat. "Long time, no see. How's it going?"

"Very well. How are things in California? Have you talked to your aunt and uncle lately?"

Ben had been raised mainly on the West Coast, where his aunt and uncle lived in wary alliance with the vampire lord of Los Angeles. Novia could have been fishing for information, but Ben's gut told him she was just treating him like a fellow immortal and asking after his clan.

"Everyone's doing great. It's hot this summer. Really hot. Everyone's asking how I survive without a pool."

"I wish." Novia plucked at the green silk blouse that matched her stunning eyes. "I'm relieved I don't have to walk the city during daytime. I miss the sun occasionally, but not the heat."

"And yet even with this summer, tourists are still pouring in."

New York wasn't just an international city for humans. It was a vampire mecca as well. The city that never slept was very attractive to vampires who could only operate at night. The business of immortal life had to be accomplished between dusk and dawn for vampires, which wasn't as easy as it might seem.

Tenzin was so old she no longer had to sleep, but she was far from normal. And even Tenzin was limited by daylight.

Novia sipped a glass of red wine. "How's your partner? I haven't heard anything that indicates mayhem lately."

"Then I must be doing my job right." It was well known that Tenzin was the muscle and connection in their operation and Ben was the social animal. He tasted his scotch and soda. It was excellent, but he wouldn't expect anything less from one of Gavin's pubs. "Tenzin is doing well. Sends her apologies for not making the meeting."

"She didn't want to see me?"

"She was busy tonight," he said. "Maybe we can set up a meeting for later this week. How's Cormac?"

"Cranky," she said. "But that's normal for my sire."

"Anything we can help with?"

"No, it's family."

Ben raised his eyebrows in question, and Novia rolled her eyes.

"It's not really a secret," she said. "Ennis is being... Ennis."

The O'Briens were a clan. And if Cormac was the level-headed and mostly legal leader of it, Ennis was the under-handed little brother who liked others to clean up his messes. Ben understood the dynamic between the two, but he chose to keep out of it.

"So your dad didn't want to come for a drink?"

"He was busy tonight," Novia said. "Maybe we can set up a meeting for later this week."

Ben tapped the edge of his glass and smiled. "Touché."

"I'm tired of hearing him complain about this," Novia said. "Please, Ben. You'll be doing me a favor if you can think of something. She refused the cash we sent. Twice."

"We did offer to comp you the occasional job for your cooperation and generous welcome to Manhattan."

"And we agreed to no comps, but only the interclan rate for services," Novia said. "You know why my dad and uncles are cautious about accepting favors. Free work is a favor."

And favors in the vampire world were subtle power plays.

Who was owed and for what could quickly become a bargaining chip.

Ben mulled over the problem as he finished his drink. "What if..."

Novia raised her eyebrows.

"What if we consider the Rochester job a gift from Tenzin? I was barely involved. It could be a gift, not a favor?"

Novia nodded slowly. "A gift to the new landlord, so to speak?"

"Exactly."

"So if it's a gift... Cormac could offer a gift in return?"

"Tenzin would never refuse a gift from an ally. She's too old-fashioned. Would that satisfy your sire?"

She narrowed her eyes. "I believe so. We may need some guidance on what would be acceptable."

"There's a shop in New Orleans that caters to discreet collectors. I'll forward you the number." Ben was glad he'd filed away the name of the shop who had emailed Tenzin about the new saber.

Face saved on both fronts.

Favor negated.

Balance restored.

And a beautiful woman on the other side of the table.

Ben smiled. "Now that business is finished, can I buy you a drink?"

∾

IT WAS after two in the morning when Ben strolled out of the Bat and Barrel and turned right on Grand. Heavy flirting with Novia O'Brien and two more whiskies had gone straight to his head, so he decided to take a walk. He unbuttoned the second button of his dress shirt and let the night air cool his neck as he walked toward home. Novia had left a half hour before for another meeting. Ben's workday might have been drawing to a close, but hers was only starting.

He was halfway back to his apartment when he spied someone walking on the opposite sidewalk. It was a short woman with a familiar—and very unexpected—head of curls. He glanced at her. Looked back.

Ben stopped in his tracks, waiting for the woman to walk under a streetlamp. When she did, he couldn't believe his eyes.

"Chloe?" he said, his voice slightly raised. No need to frighten the woman if he was wrong.

The woman stopped and turned toward him with wide eyes.

"Chloe Reardon, it *is* you," Ben shouted with a laugh.

"Ben?" The woman's wide eyes turned from surprise to delight. "Ben!"

He leapt across the deserted street, ran toward her, and picked her up in both arms, hugging her to his chest. Then he swung Chloe around like a hero in an old Hollywood flick.

"Oh my God," she said. "You're crazy. Put me down."

"What are you doing here?" He didn't care how loud he was. He lowered her and smacked a kiss on her full lips, cupping both her cheeks in his hands. "You look exactly the same. *Exactly* the same!"

Her light brown skin might have been paler than when she'd lived in California, but the scattered freckles he adored still covered her nose. Her hair was cut in the same riot of curls she'd worn proudly in high school, a cheerful rebel among the pin-straight blondes.

Chloe was speechless, but he could tell she was pleased. Round brown eyes with thick lashes looked at him with delight. Her smile was enormous.

"I can't believe you're here," she said. "You said you'd never come back. Why are you in New York? Are you visiting?"

"Come on, you can't hold a guy to the shit he says when he's a seventeen-year-old kid," he said. "I live here now. I have a place in SoHo."

"No!"

"Yeah. I gave in and headed home. Kinda. How are you doing? You took off and left everybody wondering. What are you doing?"

She shrugged. "The same."

"Are you dancing?"

"Trying." She looked down and bent her leg up; a thick black brace was wrapped around it. "I tweaked my knee a few months ago, but I'm mostly healed now. The doctor says it's nothing permanent." Her smile was a little bashful. "No one back home really thought I was going to walk onto Broadway, did they?"

"I was hoping." He flicked her nose. "I tried emailing. You dropped off the face of the planet. What happened?"

She opened her mouth, then closed it. She let out a laugh. "Oh man. This is not a conversation to have when I'm dead on my feet after dinner service. Can we meet for coffee when I'm not half-asleep?"

He couldn't help it. Ben hugged her again, picking her up off her feet and making her laugh. "I missed my girl," he said into her hair. "I know you had to break up with me because you were too smart to stick with your high school boyfriend, but did you have to disappear afterward?"

"Ben." She hugged him back. "You're taller, but you smell the same. Did you know that? I missed you too."

He put her back on her feet. "Give me your phone."

Smiling, Chloe reached into the heavy shoulder bag she carried. "Don't trust me not to disappear again?"

"Maybe." He took the phone she held out and put his number in, dialing and hanging up so he didn't lose her again. "I tried getting your number from your mom when I knew I was moving here, but—"

"They try to pretend I don't exist." The forced cheer was brittle. "They harassed me for about two years to come back, but I think they've given up now."

"They're idiots."

"They're not." She shrugged. "They're my parents. You know."

"Yeah, I know." He leaned down and kissed her cheek. "Damn, I needed this. I need a friend here."

She bumped her shoulder against his arm. "You got one, Benny. Always. We promised."

Ben was actually fighting tears. He'd been afraid he'd never see her again. Chloe had been his first love. His first *everything* when it came to girls. Two misfits in their private high school. Two kids who'd never fit in and always wanted bigger things. By the time they'd graduated and broken up, they were more friends than lovers. When he'd lost touch with her, it felt like missing a limb.

"I missed you," he said again.

A cautious look came to her eyes. "I'm not... I have a boyfriend, Ben. I hope you're not thinking—"

"No." He smiled and put a hand on her cheek. "That's not it. Not anymore. I'm just... really glad to see you, Chloe. It's hard to meet people you can trust in this city."

A knowing look came to her eyes. "Yeah, I know what you mean."

A yawn overtook her, and Ben yawned in reaction.

"Okay," he said. "Clearly we need to pick this up when we're more awake." He looked in the direction she'd been walking. "I'll walk you home."

She put a hand on his chest. "It's cool. I'm over by the Delancey Street station, so we're in opposite directions. It's close."

"Don't care." He hooked his arm through hers and steered them south. "We can catch up a little while we walk."

She looked like she was going to protest but thought again. She knew him well enough to know it was useless to object. Letting a friend—especially a small female friend who didn't have fangs—walk home at three in the morning through the Lower East Side was not going to happen.

"Fine," she said. "But you have to tell me why the heck you're here when you told me once you'd seen everything you ever wanted to see of New York City."

"Did I say that?" He scratched his chin. "I don't remember saying that."

"Dude, it was one of the reasons we broke up."

"*Dude.*" He smiled fondly. "You can take the girl out of California..."

"Ha ha." She started down the sidewalk. "I know. They tease me about it at work."

Ben pried cautiously as he walked her home. Like most struggling performers, Chloe also worked other jobs. She had a waitressing position at an Italian Restaurant in Little Italy. She worked as a theater usher at one of the bigger venues in Midtown. She'd been dating the same guy for two years, and they'd been living together for over a year.

"Tom?"

"Tom."

"Is it short for anything?" Ben asked. "Tom seems so... boring."

She frowned. "Says the guy named Ben?"

"It's all in how you wear the name, gorgeous." He winked at her. "Seriously though, I can't wait to meet him. I'm sure he's great. Well... not as great as me, but I know you must be resigned to that."

Chloe sighed. "We'll have to shield Tom from the truth."

"I'll try not to rub it in."

"What can I say? I caught you on the upswing. I probably couldn't keep up with you now. It's better this way, Benny."

"Couldn't keep up with me," he muttered, bumping her shoulder. "That was never the problem."

TENZIN PAUSED MIDFORM, her sword lifted over her head. "Chloe?"

"Yeah, Chloe." Ben moved deliberately into the next form, and Tenzin followed his lead. "My girlfriend through most of high school. You don't remember her?"

They were practicing slow tai chi forms with *jian*, hiding from the midmorning sun in the lower level of the penthouse. The windows in the lower floor were completely blocked, so Tenzin always had access if she wanted to work or train. Ben had started tai chi at age thirteen. Tenzin had started training him on the sword a few years later. Though both were proficient, they practiced regularly to keep up their form.

Tenzin was frowning. "Were you already with her when we met?"

Most days Ben couldn't remember a time when he hadn't known Tenzin. In reality, he'd met her when he was fifteen.

"I think we were just friends then," Ben said. "We started dating when I got back from Italy."

"And you broke up after school ended?"

"She wanted to go to New York and be a dancer." He swept the sword back in a smooth motion Tenzin mirrored. "I had other plans."

Tenzin shook her head. "I don't understand."

"She was accepted at UCLA, but she didn't want—"

"No, I don't understand why you just saw her again." Tenzin chided him, "Friends who have known you since childhood are rare and should be treasured. You have retained contact with most of your former lovers. Why not her?"

"Can you do me a favor and not call my ex-girlfriends 'former lovers?' It seems too..."

"What?"

"French. I don't know." He thrust his *jian* forward, his left arm raised. "Just don't call them *lovers*. And I lost touch with Chloe because her parents cut her off."

Tenzin dropped her sword arm. "They did what?"

"They cut her off. She went to New York with nothing but a little savings her grandmother had given her. They took her phone, her computer, her car, everything."

"They took her things and allowed her to move across the country with nothing?" Tenzin bared her fangs. "They are cruel and unloving people."

He shrugged. "They were definitely harsh. Both of them were doctors who came from pretty humble backgrounds, so they didn't have patience for Chloe's dancing. They thought it was an extracurricular activity to put on your college application, not a career. I imagine they thought if she started out with nothing, she'd fail faster and come home."

"They were foolish people," Tenzin said, picking up the routine again. "Is Chloe a good dancer?"

"Very. She studied ballet, modern dance, tap dance. I loved watching her. She was amazing. I'm sure she still is."

"Dance is one of the oldest arts," Tenzin said, sweeping her arm to the side as her sword lifted, "used to express truths too delicate or complex for spoken language. Some religions use dance as a form of worship. Communal dance was a bonding activity in the oldest civilizations. Chloe's parents were fortunate to have a daughter who was gifted in such a way."

Ben smiled. "That's beautiful, Tenzin."

She could be so harsh. Ben thought about all the times she'd inadvertently—or completely advertently—offended someone with her bluntness. Then at the most unexpected moment, Tenzin would turn around and say something so compassionate or eloquent it made his heart ache.

"What is she doing now?" Tenzin asked.

"She's working at a restaurant and as an usher."

"She's no longer dancing?"

"I think she is, but she's recovering from an injury."

"Ah."

They passed the next ten minutes in purposeful synchronicity. Ben loved sparring with Tenzin, but something in his soul that morning needed the quiet meditation of moving with her, not against her.

"There was something else going on," Ben said.

"With Chloe?"

He nodded.

"What—"

"I don't know." He pushed his left arm out, holding his sword arm completely still. "But my gut is telling me there's something going on with her. Something that's stressing her out."

"The injury?"

"She's an athlete. Injuries are expected." He stepped to the right, his hips shifting to balance his heavier upper body. "No, it's something else."

"You have good instincts," Tenzin said. "Follow them and you'll figure it out. When are you seeing her again?"

"We were talking and she mentioned that surrealist exhibit opening at MoMA this Friday. The same one Novia told me about. Chloe is a huge fan of one of the artists they're featuring, so she wanted to go. Which is perfect because I didn't want to go by myself."

Tenzin curled her lip. "Surrealists."

"Just because you don't understand an artistic movement doesn't mean it's not worthy of attention."

"As long as you don't make me go with you."

The corner of his mouth turned up. "See? Aren't you glad I ran into Chloe again?"

BEN ALWAYS DRESSED up for evening events in museums. It didn't matter that most men his age would come wearing casual jackets with a bohemian aesthetic. He'd been raised by Giovanni Vecchio, bastard son of an Italian nobleman, elegant immortal assassin, and respected scholar.

When Ben picked up Chloe in the car he'd hired for the evening, he wore an understated summer suit he'd had tailored near Piazza del Popolo in Rome by a family who'd been making his uncle respectable for two hundred years. His bright blue shirt was open at the collar, and a patterned pocket square decorated his chest.

Ben looked good, and he knew it.

There was a tiny part of him that hoped Chloe's boyfriend would be there even though she'd said Tom was working. Ben was competitive; he recognized the feeling for what it was. He wanted to win, not win Chloe back.

He leaned against the car and looked up to her window as he sent her a text.

I'm here. You ready?

A moment later, her head popped out from the third-floor window and she grinned. "I knew it."

"Knew what?"

"You'd be dressed up. It's a good thing I shop vintage. Let me put on my shoes and I'll be right down."

When she walked out the door, she was wearing a bright green band around her curls that complemented her halter-neck sundress and orange sandals.

He leaned down and kissed her cheek. "Prada?"

"It's so annoying that you know that," Chloe said.

"I have been dragged on too many shopping trips by my female friends in Rome not to recognize a Prada sundress when I see one." He opened the door. "Shall we?"

Chloe winked. "Thanks, Romeo."

He noticed them as she stepped in the car. Four small bruises on her shoulder.

Ben's skin went cold, but he calmly shut the door and walked around to the passenger's side. As he got in, he slid across the seat and put his arm around Chloe; his thumb gently brushed the shoulder where the bruises marred her skin.

"What happened?"

She looked up with wide eyes. "What?"

"Bruises on your shoulder." He tried not to overreact. Maybe she was training with a new partner for a dance routine. Dance was physically demanding work and bruises happened.

"Oh." She smiled. "It's nothing. I nearly fell down the basement steps at the restaurant carrying too many dishes. One of the guys grabbed my shoulder and stopped me from falling. Probably saved my life. Must be from that."

Too smooth. She hadn't hesitated a moment giving the reason for the bruises because she knew they were there.

"Hope they don't hurt," he said, keeping his arm around her as the driver pulled into traffic.

"You know I bruise easily," Chloe said. She stared out the window, but he could see her reflection as they passed under a streetlamp. Was her smile brittle? Forced? Did her eyes carry the sad and yet hopeful expression he remembered his mother wearing for most of his childhood?

Seven years ago, he would have been able to tell. Now he didn't know.

Ben kept his arm around her.

He didn't know. But he would.

3

_____

"**A**re you bored?"

"No." Chloe tapped her museum map against her bottom lip. "Are you not enjoying this?"

"I'm kind of bored."

"How?" Chloe turned to him. "How can you be bored? You wanted to see this exhibit. The presentation is beautiful, and we haven't even gotten to the Samson pieces yet. Calm down; you're acting like a puppy that needs to pee."

She turned back to the Magritte she'd been looking at, the two lovers' kiss thwarted by the shrouds that covered their faces.

Masks and disguises. It seemed to be a theme for the evening. Ben had seen quite a few vampires mingling in the crowd, acting like humans to attract their prey. They were easy for Ben to spot, though he knew most humans would hardly look twice. He wandered to a clutch of them staring at a lean bronze sculpture of a man with extraordinarily long legs.

They reminded him of cats with their languid eyes and predatory manner, scanning the crowd like the predators they were.

Immortals were as vain as the average human, and some

could be remarkably superficial. Just as they preferred to surround themselves with beautiful art, good music, and luxury, they also liked being surrounded by pretty people. They were attracted to the glittering and the beautiful. They were fascinated by art and science.

Ennui was an eternal complaint.

At any given gallery opening or gala, vampires would congregate. They'd look for the beautiful humans to feed from and use for sex. They'd keep any with interesting ideas or unusual talent close by to allay boredom.

Ben saw one trying to chat with Chloe.

"What perfume are you wearing?" the pale young immortal said. "I know I recognize it."

"Really"—Chloe was trying to distract him—"I'm not wearing any perfume. I'm sure you must have me confused with someone else."

"I don't think so." The vampire was hovering over her shoulder; tension radiated off Chloe. "Are you here with someone?"

She looked around and sighed in relief when she caught sight of Ben. "Hey."

Ben walked up to the vampire, invading his personal space and muttering, "*Hoc propter vos non est sanguis.*" He said it low enough that the vampire heard him and paid attention. The vampire looked European, and Latin was still a lingua franca in the immortal world.

The young one narrowed his eyes and his fangs grew long behind his lips. "Do I know you?"

"I don't think so," Ben said. "But if you're involved in rare books, you might know my uncle. He's a collector on the West Coast."

"Oh?"

"Giovanni Vecchio."

The vampire grew paler and melted back into the crowd.

Chloe stared at him. "So that wasn't weird at all."

"What?" He put a hand at the small of her back and tried not to notice Chloe avoiding his touch. He stuck his hands in his pockets. "So which one was the artist you were raving about?"

Ben had been asking casual questions about Tom all night, and he could tell Chloe was annoyed. Maybe she thought he was jealous of her new boyfriend. Maybe she thought he was just being an ass. She knew Ben was competitive.

They walked into the next room, and an older woman who looked like a docent struck up a conversation with Chloe, asking about her dress. Ben wandered away after checking the immediate area for vampires. He strolled through two galleries of abstract sculpture until he came into a room that piqued his interest.

The canvases were large and boldly colored. The style was crisp and realistic. No still lifes with melting apples here. These canvases were bold landscapes and crowded scenes filled with figures. Looking closer, he glanced at the label.

Le Marché Nocturne.

Oil on canvas.

Emil Samson, 1933

Ben looked back to the painting. *The Night Market.* It was almost a bucolic scene. A village market bathed in a bright half-moon. Tidy stands selling fish and produce. Buyers wandering among stalls. But on closer inspection, the crowd was... macabre. A little girl ran with her arms held out in front of her; her mouth spread in a smile, but the child had no eyes. A woman led a donkey up the cobblestone street, the animal dripping blood from its mouth, its hooves leaving a red trail. A farmer weighed onions, and behind him, a demon tail flicked from beneath his apron.

Weird. And kind of awesome.

Samson. *This* was the artist Chloe had mentioned. Ben

wasn't familiar with him, but as he examined each painting, the crowd in the room grew thicker, the voices louder. This section was clearly an anticipated feature of the exhibit. He glanced at the program he'd been handed and flipped to the back page.

Emil Samson (1908-1943), celebrated Jewish painter of the surrealist school in Paris, was thought to be confined to a few surviving works and photographs of his paintings until this previously lost collection of early canvases was found and loaned anonymously last year.

Admired by his contemporaries, he was known for the insertion of the subconscious in otherwise ordinary scenes. His work, particularly his Labyrinth series, gained him international attention at an early age.

Samson was killed in Drancy internment camp in 1943 during a confrontation with camp guards. His work was labeled as degenerate art by the Nazi party, and much of it was destroyed. The current exhibit was made possible by a generous donation from Historic New York and surviving friends of the artist.

Ben walked through the exhibition, finally understanding all the buzz. Recovered art always felt more exciting. Even Ben, who'd spent countless hours in museums and galleries around the world, felt his pulse pick up as he wandered. The room had filled with chattering clutches of excited admirers whispering over each painting. Photographs were strictly prohibited, but he saw a few respectable folks grabbing cell phone pictures behind their wineglasses. The energy in the room was palpable.

But then there was the woman.

She sat on a bench in the center of the room, back straight, eyes going back and forth between two canvases that sat side by side on the longest wall. Crowds blocked Ben's view of the paintings, but the young woman didn't seem to see the people. She stared through them, her gaze distant.

She'd been crying.

Ben felt someone bump his arm.

"I see you found the best room," Chloe said. "Isn't Samson's work amazing? This is so cool."

"She doesn't seem to think so." Ben nodded at the crying woman.

"Hmmm." Chloe narrowed her eyes. "How do you manage to find a damsel in distress even at an art museum?"

"It's a talent."

"It's something."

The woman appeared to be around Ben's age or a little younger. Early twenties. Her skin was a pale cream and her hair the color of bittersweet chocolate, sleek and twisted in a knot at the base of her skull. Her face was a Botticelli Madonna, but her eyes were red. Her cheeks and lips were flushed.

"Well," Chloe whispered, "I have to say that is the prettiest crying woman I've ever seen."

Ben bit his lip to keep from smiling. "Don't be a brat. She's genuinely upset."

"I can tell. But when I'm upset, my nose gets swollen and snotty and my face turns red. It's not very pretty."

"I know. I remember."

Chloe's elbow landed in his side. It hadn't gotten any softer over the years.

"Moved by art or tragedy?" Ben said.

"Can it be both? The painter was killed by the Nazis because he was Jewish. Most of his work and his family were destroyed. It's a tragic story even if you're not a fan of his paintings."

"True."

"Are you going to talk to her?" Chloe said.

"I think so." He cocked his head. "Italian?"

"You and your weird thing about nationalities."

"It's languages more than nationalities." He glanced at Chloe. "Should I try Italian? It might be charmingly disarming."

Chloe examined the woman again. "French. No one wears scarves like French women."

"Oh, good eye," he said. "You may be on to something there."

Chloe patted his arm. "Go and comfort her, Romeo. Make sure you get her number. If you give her yours, she's too emotionally distraught to keep it."

"Good call." Ben started to walk away, then he turned. "Is this weird?"

"Me giving you advice about picking up crying women?" Chloe scrunched up her face in that way he found adorable. "Kind of? But not really. Just don't be a toad. If she wants to be left alone, leave her alone."

"Okay." He nodded. She was right. It *was* weird. But his whole life was weird, so that bit didn't bother him much.

Casually, Ben walked over to the bench and sat next to the woman, staring at the two paintings on the main wall as he relaxed for a moment. He glanced at her, saw her looking before she looked away. He smiled and crossed his arms, bringing his hand up to his chin and idly stroking his thumb over his lower lip.

The woman sniffed delicately, and Ben saw his opening.

Reaching for the linen handkerchief he kept in his pocket, he held it out to her. "*Mademoiselle, un mouchoir?*"

A faint smile through her tears. "*Merci.*" She reached for it and dabbed her eyes. "How did you know I was French?"

"Just a feeling." She didn't have much of an accent, but Chloe was right. Definitely French. "My name is Ben. Are you feeling all right? Can I help you?"

"I am fine, I assure you. I'm..." She shook her head and

motioned around the gallery. "Emotional, I suppose. A bit over-whelmed by all this."

"You're a passionate lover of Samson's art then?"

"I am." She smiled. "I'm very passionate about his art."

He smiled back and angled his legs toward her. "But that's not the whole story, is it?"

She offered Ben her hand. "I'm sorry. You told me your name was Ben, but I didn't introduce myself. My name is Emilie."

"Nice to meet you, Emilie. That's a beautiful name."

"Thank you. I was named for my great-grandmother's twin brother, Emil Samson."

"So your family, is it involved in the exhibition?" Ben had recovered from the shock and moved closer to Emilie on the bench. She wasn't leaning away from him.

"I'm afraid not."

"That's surprising. You'd think they'd ask the artist's surviving family for—"

"Some of his paintings?"

"Maybe. Or sketches. Family pictures. Things like that."

"I doubt they even know we exist. And it wouldn't matter if they did. We have nothing." Emilie gestured around the room. "These all come from private collections."

"Samson left no paintings with his family?"

"He did," Emilie said. "Of course he did. But Emil wasn't the only one arrested. My great-grandmother, Emil's sister, was taken to the camps with most of the family. Her daughter, my grandmother, was sent to a convent to be raised in secret. My great-grandmother did survive, but when she returned there was nothing left. Everything had been stolen or destroyed."

Ben frowned. "That's horrible. Surely there's some recourse for her. She has birth records?"

"She does, but..." Emilie shrugged. "It doesn't matter now. Emil sold much of his work—he was quite well-known—so these could easily have come from a legitimate collector who simply hid the paintings so the government could not destroy them. Perhaps an heir found them. Perhaps they simply felt the time was right. They remain in an anonymous collection, so it's not for me to say."

Ben glanced at the two paintings Emilie had been staring at. "These two, are they special?"

Her eyes went wide. "Are you saying you don't know the story of the Labyrinth Trilogy?"

The majority of the crowd had drifted to the front gallery where a string quartet was playing and wine was being served. Ben remained with Emilie, enjoying the quiet of the Samson room. He sat with his arm along the back of the bench, casually letting his fingers brush against her shoulders.

She was beautiful, interesting... and she was a mystery. He wouldn't have left unless he was dragged.

"The Labyrinth Trilogy?" He shook his head. "No."

Her face lit up. "There were three paintings Emil worked on from 1930 to 1933. He did do some other, smaller pieces in that time, but the majority of those years was spent on the Labyrinth. He considered them a single work. They were his masterpiece. Fascism was rising in Europe. Anti-Semitism was becoming more and more virulent, even among the artistic community. My grandmother said that Emil wrote to his sister, Adele—my great-grandmother—many times during that period. He'd been tormented by dreams of being caught in a labyrinth, unable to find his way out."

Ben was transfixed. Emilie was a natural storyteller, and her voice enchanted him.

"All around Emil was darkness. He could hear monsters and creatures around him. He could smell their stench, my grandmother says, but he could not see what chased him. So he decided to paint it." Emilie motioned to the painting on the left. "*Le Labyrinthe Crépusculaire. Twilight Labyrinth.* Emil painted a woman—my grandmother says the figure is Adele— walking into a maze at twilight. The moon is low in the sky, and there are eyes peeking through the hedges. Do you see them?"

Emilie rose and took Ben's hand. They walked to the painting and leaned in.

"Do you see?"

"I do."

Eyes peered through thick hedges. At first glance, they appeared to be leaves, but on closer inspection they were definitely eyes. Bloodshot eyes. Cat eyes. Snake eyes. The woman stood at the entrance of the labyrinth, her neck bared to the elements and her diaphanous dress clinging to her legs. She was barefoot, as if she'd walked through long grass to reach the dark green maze.

"There is so much detail," Emilie said, her hand floating over the painting. "I'd only seen pictures before this, and they were so small. I could look at this for hours."

"Are those fangs?" Ben cocked his head and squinted.

"Fangs or thorns," Emilie said. "We have no way of knowing what monsters are hidden in the maze." She took his hand again and drew him to the right. "And this is the final painting, *Le Labyrinthe de L'aube. Dawn Labyrinth.* See, the woman is out of the maze now. The monsters have retreated. She has survived, but barely."

It was the same woman, but now her dress was torn and bloody. Her feet left bloody prints in the sand at the maze's entrance. Her long hair hung loose and tangled, half obscuring her face. Her lip was bleeding, but a phantom smile lurked at the corner of the woman's mouth. She had a secret.

Ben's heart raced. "Where is the last?"

"This is the last."

"No, you said there were three. A trilogy." He looked around the room. "Where is the third one?"

A haunted look came to Emilie's eyes. "*Labyrinthe de Minuit. Midnight Labyrinth.* That one is lost."

"Lost?" His eyes went wide. "Just... lost?"

"Sadly, yes. We will never know what happened to Adele at midnight. The few pictures we have are very unclear. My grandmother remembers her mother describing it, but—"

"If these survived, then it's possible the other exists too."

There was that look again. It was so like the mysterious woman's half smile in the painting that Ben's heart skipped a beat.

"Perhaps," Emilie said. "I suppose you're right. It might have survived." Emilie walked back to the bench and sat. "You see, the Labyrinth Trilogy was never sold. Emil kept them for himself, but during the International Exposition in Paris in 1937, his friends pressured him to display them together. Just once, they said, the public should see his masterpiece. Pictures were taken. Tickets sold out. The three paintings became a sensation."

"And then?"

"And then nothing. After the exhibition, they went to private collections. My uncle was forced to move, and so he sent these two to friends for safekeeping."

"And *Midnight Labyrinth?*"

"To his sister." Emilie stared at the space between the paintings. Her voice went low and grim. "But then the Nazis came and everything was lost."

Ben sat next to her. "Are you sure?"

"Of course I'm not sure." Her voice held a bite. "We're not sure of anything except that most of the family died and all the art was lost. Probably destroyed. Possibly stolen." Emilie's eyes filled with tears. "I'm sorry. This is why I was upset when you first saw me."

"Don't apologize for being upset over horrible things. That just means you're human." He was intrigued, enthralled, entranced. By her and by the paintings. "I want to see you again."

She smiled through her tears. "Ben—"

"Let me have your number. Please. I promise I won't be a nuisance, but you're upset and I really want to see you again. Away from here. We'll do dinner. Coffee." He had to know more. About her and the paintings.

Emilie's mouth opened, but before she could respond, a gentle chime signaled the museum's closing.

She stood. "We need to go."

Ben stood too. "May I have your number?"

She was flustered, glancing at the door. "I don't know."

Ben heard footsteps coming and reached for Emilie's hand before she could escape. "Please."

"Ben?" It was Chloe. "Are you still... Oh!" She smiled brightly. "Sorry to interrupt, but the museum is closing."

Emilie wiped her eyes with Ben's handkerchief. "My apologies. Is this your—"

"My friend," Ben said.

"Just a friend," Chloe said. "Promise." She stepped into the gallery. "Sheesh, Ben, she's still crying. You used to be better at comforting a girl."

"Ha ha."

Chloe walked to Emilie and held out her hand. "Hi, I'm Chloe. Why don't we visit the restrooms while we can? I have some drops for red eyes that work wonders."

"You're so kind," Emilie said with a watery laugh. "And I promise, Ben wasn't making me cry. It's something entirely unrelated."

"No problem. I have some cream for the puffiness around your eyes too."

"Oh, I must be a mess."

"No, you're great." Chloe patted her arm. "Seriously, you have the prettiest crying face I've ever seen."

He watched them walk down the hall, Chloe's powerful and curvaceous figure next to Emilie's gentle, willowy shape. Chloe looked over her shoulder and caught him staring at their asses. She raised a sardonic eyebrow, but he only shrugged.

What could he say? He had a type. And that type was female.

Ben sat on a bench by the entrance, waiting for the two women to leave the bathroom. A few guests were still trickling out, but the lobby was mostly empty. He heard the click of heels on the ground and looked up to see Chloe coming toward him.

"Hey," he said. "Everything come out all right?"

She wrinkled her nose. "You are such a boy."

He smiled and rose from the bench, folding his suit jacket over his arm as his eyes turned back to the women's bathrooms.

"What?" Chloe asked.

"What do you mean, what?"

"Aren't we ready to go?"

"Aren't we waiting for Emilie?"

Chloe frowned. "She left before me. Said she'd find you. I had to fix my hair and she seemed flustered, so..."

"Dammit," he said, his eyes sweeping the lobby. "Are you serious?"

"No, Ben. I routinely lie about random stuff like strangers leaving the bathroom." She held out her hands as if to say, *Really?*

How had he missed her? He'd been watching for them, but maybe he'd been relying on spotting Chloe's vibrant presence and Emilie managed to slip away. He was getting rusty again. He started toward the museum store, but Chloe grabbed his arm.

"Sorry, Benny, but this one's a no. If she wanted to give you her number, she would have."

"She didn't have time in the gallery. I wonder if there's a guest list with—"

"Nope, you are not being weird about this," Chloe said. "Did you ask her for her number?"

"Yes, but—"

"And she didn't give it to you?"

"She was upset."

"Ben." Chloe put her arm around him and steered him toward the front doors. "She would have made sure you had it if she was interested. Stop. She ditched you. It happens."

"Not to *me*."

Chloe laughed. "Well, it looks like I was present for yet another first."

Ben pouted. "This one wasn't as fun as the other firsts."

"Speak for yourself, Romeo."

"Hey!"

Chloe kept walking. "Just drive me home, Ben. I'm dead on my feet. Plus, if I get in too late, Tom will have a fit."

"Hmmm." Ben took Chloe's hand and escorted her to the door, thoughts of Emilie, the Labyrinth paintings, and Nazis mixing with a sneaking suspicion in his gut that something about Chloe and Tom's relationship was very, very wrong.

4

She hovered behind the water tank on the building across the alley, hiding in the shadows as she watched him. The crystal-blue pool glowed in the darkness, and sleek modern furniture surrounded it. There was a bar and a pool house on the roof, and music poured from discreet speakers placed around the pool. It was the perfect setup for a party, but Gavin Wallace was only entertaining one human woman.

Entertaining might have been too strong a word.

Gavin was bored. He carried the look of a vampire who'd been alive long enough to try everything he'd always thought he wanted in his mortal life and found eternity wanting. The only thing particularly admirable about him in Tenzin's eyes was that Gavin was Scottish and cursed with great imagination and vigor. He was also conventionally handsome and very self-assured. She imagined human women were probably attracted to him even without the use of amnis to lure them.

But in Tenzin's eyes, he was an adolescent. He was a wind vampire like her, but he'd only started flying a few years before. She knew nothing about his origins, nor was she interested. She was stalking Gavin for one reason only: he was a friend of Benjamin's.

She flew closer, enjoying the cool night air above the sweltering concrete gorges of the city. Tenzin didn't care for cities, but she'd come to terms with New York. Unlike Los Angeles, New York was vertical. It was possible to fly above human notice in Manhattan. In a single leap, she could vault over traffic and the noise of modernity and be in the clouds. In minutes, she could be over the ocean.

Yes, New York suited her much better than Los Angeles.

She landed in the shadow of the pool house and allowed her amnis to spread, infusing the air with her scent and presence.

Gavin's hand paused kneading the woman's hips and his eyes lit with interest. "Leave," he said quietly.

The human woman was incredulous. "What?"

Gavin moved her off his lap and stood, zipping his trousers and tossing her a towel. "Leave." He watched while she wrapped the towel around herself. "You're amusing, but there's something I need to attend to. Veronica will call a car for you downstairs."

The woman pouted, and Tenzin wondered if she'd had one of the modern surgeries to enlarge her lips. Modern masks were endlessly fascinating. Cosmetics had reached new levels of sophistication, and body modification was accomplished so subtly that most times Tenzin could hardly detect it.

Humans had always modified their appearance; vampires could not. Tenzin had no idea how old she was in mortal or immortal years, but to most people, she probably appeared to be in her late teens or perhaps her early twenties. Her friend Beatrice told her Tenzin's age depended on her hair. Longer hair made her younger-looking. Shorter hair made her older.

Fascinating.

The woman with the enlarged lips was delaying her departure from Gavin's roof. She stomped around dramatically, angling for his attention. It didn't matter; he'd spotted Tenzin in the shadows and was staring at her, his hands hanging casually in his pockets.

She could feel the tension coming from him.

The human finally departed the roof with some parting shot about how Gavin was missing something.

Ridiculous. The human hadn't made any particular impression on Tenzin. She doubted Gavin would miss her. He was an adolescent, still seeking stimulation by pushing boundaries and seeking experience. Of course, if he was going to survive past his next century without walking into the sun, he'd have to adjust his perspective.

"What are you doing here?" Gavin said.

"Watching you." Tenzin walked out of the shadows, and Gavin's amnis spiked the air. She paused in her approach. "You don't currently have anything to fear from me."

"*Currently* being the operative word. Hello, Tenzin."

"As long as you have no plans to betray or take advantage of any of my people, we have no quarrel."

"Your people?"

"Benjamin. Beatrice. Giovanni. My sire." There were various secondary connections springing from those four primary loyalties, but naming all of them could get complicated.

"Three of those people, I consider friends. The other is a vampire so ancient the gods probably bow to him. So no, I have no plans to betray or take advantage of your people."

"Excellent." Tenzin sat on one of the lounge chairs. "Then we have no quarrel."

Gavin sat across from her, elbows casually braced on his knees as he considered Tenzin. "Can I get you something to drink?"

"No, thank you."

"Then we come back to my original question: Why are you here?"

"Ben is pouting."

Gavin blinked. "He... What?"

"He's pouting. I think it has to do with a woman he met when he went out with Chloe the other night."

Gavin held up a hand. "Stop there. He met a woman when he went out with Chloe? Who's Chloe? Do you mean Novia?"

"No, he met Chloe when he went out with Novia."

Gavin shook his head. "How a single human manages to charm so many mortal and immortal women, I'll never understand."

"It's Ben," Tenzin said. "Women like him because he likes women."

Gavin said, "I like women."

"And some women like you." Tenzin toed the panties the human woman had forgotten toward Gavin. "But not for the same reasons. What are you complaining about?"

"Nothing," he said. "So Ben met a woman when he was out with another woman who he met when he was out with yet another woman. Why is this my business?"

Tenzin cocked her head. "Do you not know Chloe?"

"Should I?"

"Weren't you and Ben friends when he was younger? Chloe was his girlfriend in school."

Gavin leaned forward. "Tenzin, when Ben was sixteen, I was interested in him because he was disarmingly mature, an excellent fighter, and his uncle was an assassin who owed me a favor. I saw his potential and enjoyed corrupting him to piss Giovanni off. I wasn't interested in who his girlfriend was at school."

"Huh." Tenzin shrugged. "Neither was I. I didn't remember Chloe until he reminded me. He's brooding."

"Ben is brooding over Chloe?"

"No, over Emilie."

Gavin pinched the bridge of his nose. "I'm not even going to feign understanding."

"You need to call him and meet him for a drink," Tenzin said. "Drink alcohol together and... bond."

"Bond?" Gavin said.

"I saw someone reference this on a daytime television show."

Gavin opened his mouth. Closed it. Finally he said, "Tenzin, are you arranging playdates for Ben? I don't think he'd appreciate that."

"No. I'm telling you—who claim to be his friend—that there is something wrong with him."

"And?"

Tenzin did not understand why Gavin was being willfully obtuse. "He is brooding. Do you understand?"

"I understand that, but why don't you..." He sat up straight. "He won't tell you why he's upset?"

"Of course not," Tenzin said. "If he'd tell me why he's brooding, why would I come here and talk to you? I don't have any interest in you."

"I consider that an accomplishment." Gavin reached for a glass on a side table. It smelled like whisky. "I'll call him and ask him to help me with something at the pub next week."

"You need his help at the pub?"

"No," Gavin said. "But I have a cock, Tenzin. I'm not going to call Ben and tell him we need to cry into our drinks together. He'll come to help me, and I'll find out why he's 'brooding,' as you say."

Tenzin smiled. "Excellent. You're far more clever than I thought you were."

Gavin said nothing, but his eyes didn't appear friendly.

"You're helping one of my people," Tenzin said. "So I'll offer you advice. You should listen to it, because I'm older and wiser than you."

Gavin said nothing, but his eyes went from hostile to blank.

"This life you're living—with the rich houses and numerous women, the driving ambition to make money—it is not sustainable for eternity. You'll die," Tenzin said. "I would estimate within the next twenty years."

His eyes widened. "What are you talking about?"

"You're unhappy. Unless you look for some kind of meaning in this life beyond yourself, you will die. And you'll die by your own hand."

He was silent, and he didn't look away from her. Tenzin could see his mental battle. Gavin didn't want to believe her, but he did. She wasn't telling him anything he didn't know already.

"And what do you suggest?" he asked quietly. "If I want to survive."

"Two things. Don't be afraid to die," Tenzin said. "I've died many times. Tried on lives and abandoned them. Died again. Lived again."

"You're telling me if I want to live, I need to die?"

"You'll understand when you let yourself think about it. The second thing is people. You need to find your people."

"Humans? I have humans."

Tenzin shrugged. "Humans. Vampires. People. Find the ones worth living for."

Gavin raised the glass to his lips. "Your advice is noted."

"You're welcome."

He couldn't stop the low chuckle. "You're a legend for a reason, Tenzin."

"I know." She stood and jumped into the night sky. Gavin would meet with Ben. Then maybe Ben would stop brooding.

BEN WALKED into the Bat and Barrel at two a.m. on a Sunday night. The bar had closed at one, and he saw Gavin behind the bar, polishing glasses in his shirtsleeves. Ben went in and sat down across from him, watching as Gavin set two tumblers on the glass shelves behind him, then turned to a battered wooden case at the end of the bar.

He pulled two cut glass tumblers from the case. They weren't anything like the fine crystal glasses Gavin's customers were served. These were scratched, and Ben knew there was a chip in the lip of one.

These were Gavin's own, and he didn't pull them out except for friends.

Without a word, the Scotsman pulled a label-less bottle from the cabinet beneath the bar. "How've you been?" he asked, pouring two fingers in each glass. "Water?"

"Please."

"Sparkling or still?"

"Still and cold."

"As you like." Gavin brought a small carafe to the bar, along with Ben's drink, before he turned and took his own. "Cheers." He held out his glass to Ben.

"Cheers." Ben added a touch of water and tasted. "It's good."

"It's bloody perfect," Gavin said. "It's not good."

"Whose is it?"

"Mine."

Ben raised an eyebrow. "Didn't know you'd bought a distillery."

Gavin shrugged. "Had to find the right opportunity. This was the right one."

"Where—"

"Scotland. Other than that? None of your business." Gavin smiled. "Enjoy."

"Thanks." Ben tasted the whisky again. It *was* bloody perfect. He suspected it was an island whisky, but he wasn't expert enough to say with assurance. "So what did you need help with?"

"Nothing." Gavin set down his glass. "Or something."

"That's... specific."

Gavin watched him, and Ben could see the wheels turning behind his eyes. He liked Gavin. Trusted him to a certain extent. But the man was conniving. He was a thief and a con. He manipulated people as if they were pieces on a game board. Maybe Ben should have disliked him for those reasons, but he didn't. He understood Gavin.

"There was something I needed your help with, but it's been taken care of," Gavin said. "Now there's something else for which your particular skills might be very useful."

Ben sipped his drink. "Which is?"

"Keeping bloody Tenzin off my back and uninterested in me."

Ben set his glass down. "Explain."

"She thinks you're brooding and wants me to find the reason," Gavin said. "I could stalk you or use amnis to comb through your brain—"

"Not if you want to continue being my friend," Ben muttered.

"Noted," Gavin said. "Which is why I'm simply asking what's got your knickers in a twist." He finished his whisky and turned to grab the bottle. "Damn, this is excellent."

"My knickers aren't twisted, but thanks for asking after them." Ben was tempted to hold out his glass, but if he drank too quickly, Gavin wouldn't need to use amnis to get him talking. Ben could be a chatty drunk.

"Wrong," Gavin said. "She said you're brooding, and I can see it all over you." He waved a hand. "You won't stop thinking about it until you talk to someone, and you don't want to talk to Tenzin because it has to do with a woman. Or women."

Ben narrowed his eyes. "How do you know—"

"You talk to Tenzin about everything," Gavin said. "Except for women." He leaned on the bar. "You can think about why that is on your own time, but for right now, talk to Old Uncle Gav and tell him what the trouble is."

Ben shook his head. "I don't know what you're—"

"You were a much better liar when you were young," Gavin said. "You're getting soft."

"I didn't trust you when I was young."

"You shouldn't trust me now." Gavin took a sip of scotch. "Much. I have my limits."

"Which apparently don't include intruding on a friend's privacy."

Gavin grinned. "Right you are. Now, what's the name Tenzin mentioned? Was it Chloe?"

Ben's mind went into overdrive. "What do you know about Chloe?" Had he mentioned her to Gavin before? Chloe knew nothing about the supernatural elements of his life. She'd met his uncle and aunt—she'd even met Tenzin on numerous occasions—but she had no idea what vampires were. Ben was very, very careful about the boundaries he'd erected. Gavin should not have known about Chloe.

"Listen, Gavin—"

"Chloe was your girlfriend in school, eh? You trying to win her back?"

"It's not like that. We parted as friends. We're still friends. She's got a boyfriend now."

Gavin's keen eyes must have picked up on Ben's misgivings.

"You don't like the boyfriend. If it's not a question of jealousy, then there must be something wrong with him."

Ben flicked a finger over his lower lip and considered Gavin. Gavin wasn't Tenzin, but he was resourceful. However, if he involved Gavin, Chloe would be exposed to the immortal world.

The Scot was a friend, but he was also a strategic thinker. Gavin didn't have a sire that Ben knew of. He had pubs all over the world. He had property in every major city, and he'd acquired it quickly. The vampire survived the way he did because of carefully constructed and leveraged alliances and deals. Gavin, at the end of the day, was a deal maker. His words, not Ben's.

"If I tell you," Ben said, "I want a promise that you won't tell anyone about Chloe. She's not a part of our world."

Gavin shook his head. "Not the way it works."

"It is for her," Ben said.

"No, it's not," Gavin said. "I think you forget you're not a vampire sometimes. You don't have an aegis. You canna put people under your protection. That's not the way it works."

And Tenzin wouldn't do it. Ben didn't even want to ask. Tenzin had her people, but she hadn't used a formal aegis since her last human assistant had died. If she needed formal protection for someone, she used her sire's aegis. To put someone under her own aegis implied a level of intimacy and responsibility that Tenzin wasn't willing to give to any but a very, very few.

"You're still under your uncle," Gavin said carefully. "Any deal you make with a vampire is in that context. But this girl—"

"She's mine," Ben said. "She's my friend. I don't care if that doesn't hold weight with the O'Briens or even my uncle. *You* need to know that Chloe is my friend. If I tell you about her and any harm comes to her because of a vampire, I will consider it a personal betrayal."

Gavin paused, his glass halfway to his mouth. Then he carefully nodded and said, "Fine."

THEY MOVED to the tall wingback chairs in the corner by the gas fireplace. There was a trunk between them, serving as a coffee table, and Ben set his drink down.

"At first, it was subtle things. Chloe's always been a very affectionate person. She's a hugger. She doesn't hug anymore. Not like she used to."

"People change."

"There are bruises," Ben said. "She brushes them off, but I know what they are."

Gavin's nostrils flared. "The boyfriend?"

"I think it has to be. If it was a stranger who hurt her, I'm sure she'd report it. But a boyfriend?" Ben shook his head. "She's loyal to a fault and doesn't like asking anyone for help. She's also struggling with money. I think he pays most of the bills. He does something in finance, and she's a dancer. She doesn't make much, even with a second job. And her parents have cut her off because they don't approve of her life here."

Gavin frowned. "She's a dancer? Exotic?"

Ben almost spit out his scotch. "Ballet, man. Ballet and modern dance."

"Then why'd her parents—"

"Because they're assholes who wanted her to become a doctor or something. That's not the important part. Chloe has bruises, and I don't buy the excuses."

"Have you asked her?"

"She always has a reason. A fall. Someone who saved her from falling. A doorjamb when she wasn't wearing her contact lenses—"

"But you doona believe her," Gavin said. "Is she typically a liar?"

"She's not a liar."

Gavin said, "But you think she's lying."

"It's not the same thing."

"No," Gavin said, leaning forward. "You need to understand this, Ben. Everyone lies. We all do it, and we all do it for roughly the same reasons. Vampire. Mortal. We lie because we're ashamed, we want something we doona have a right to, or because we're afraid. So what you need to discover with your little Chloe is: Which one is it? Ashamed, greedy, or scared?"

Ben thought about that. It wasn't greed. Was it fear or shame?

Both?

He closed his eyes. "If her boyfriend is abusing her—and I'm not honestly sure he is—then it could be both fear and shame."

"But you're not sure?"

"No."

"Easy." Gavin sat back in his chair. "I'll put one of my security people on her. Don't worry, it isn't a favor. I'll send you the bill."

Ben blinked. "You think we should spy on her?"

"Yes." Gavin set down his empty tumbler. "If it's nothing and she's just going through a clumsy streak, then she'll never be angry at you for accusing her boyfriend of abuse. If he is hitting her, you'll know for sure and you can take care of the situation. Or have one of my people do it."

Ben tapped his chin. If Chloe ever found out, she'd be pissed. Of course, the whole point was that Chloe was never going to find out.

Never.

"Okay," Ben said. "You have a human in mind? I don't want some burly guy who's going to scare her. The last thing she needs is to think she has a creepy stalker with everything else going on."

Gavin gave him a withering look. "Do I look like one of the O'Briens? I'm not a gangster, my friend. I'll put one of my female guards on your Chloe. She's very skilled and very subtle. Your friend will never know she's being watched."

"Okay." Ben nodded. "That could work."

"Of course it'll work. Here, have a drink." He poured two more inches of whisky in Ben's glass.

"Thanks." Ben added a bit of the cold water and enjoyed the warmth of the liquor sliding down his throat. Scotch had never been his drink of choice, but when he was with Gavin, he drank whisky with no *e*. "This is good."

"I know."

He could feel the amber liquid going to his head. He closed his eyes and rested his head on the side of the chair, drifting in the early morning hours.

Gavin said, "You know, it's interesting to me."

"What is?"

"Tenzin was wrong about something. That doesn't happen often."

"More than most people think," he muttered.

Gavin continued, "She said you weren't brooding about Chloe, but you were."

"I wouldn't call it brooding. I—"

"She said you were brooding over someone called Emilie," Gavin said, watching Ben carefully.

Ben froze.

"Who's Emilie?" Gavin asked with a smile. "Do I need to follow her too?"

5

Ben stormed into the loft an hour before dawn. Tenzin heard him stomp through the kitchen.

"Tenzin!"

She popped her head out of her room. Ben was angry. He didn't look bonded at all. He was supposed to be relieved and most likely a little drunk.

Gavin Wallace was a... What would they say in Scotland? There were so many inventive Scottish insults she'd learned the last time she was there she could barely keep them straight.

Bampot. Gavin was a definite *bampot*.

He was supposed to make Ben stop brooding, not make him angry.

"What?" she yelled. "I'm busy!" Tenzin had discovered when Ben was angry, it was better to put him on the defensive. "You leave books and notebooks and papers lying everywhere, then go visit your friends. I had to clean up your stuff. You made a mess in the kitchen, and you didn't—"

"Stop trying to pick a different fight," Ben said. "Why did you tell Gavin about Emilie?"

Tenzin made her eyes wide. "Who?"

"Don't play dumb. Emilie. The girl from the museum."

"The one you're obsessed with?"

He put a hand in his hair and tugged. "I am not obsessed with her, Tenzin."

"You've been brooding."

"I am obsessed with a painting. I'm annoyed with Emilie."

"Oh!" Tenzin said. "Why didn't you say so?"

"Because it's none of your business. And you shouldn't have told Gavin. Now he knows I'm looking into a job, and I don't want him—"

"A job?" She flew down to the dining table, which was covered with books about World War II and surrealism. "For what?"

"A painting."

"What painting? We don't do paintings."

"We don't do paintings *yet*." He flipped open a book and pointed at a grainy photograph. Tenzin saw a maze and a figure standing at the entrance, but the details were too difficult to make out.

"This is the only time they were displayed together," Ben said. "It's called the Labyrinth Trilogy."

"Isn't that a movie?"

"No, it's—"

"I'm pretty sure that's a movie. A very odd movie."

"Can we stay on topic, please? The Labyrinth Trilogy was a series of three paintings by Emil Samson. They were thought to be destroyed, but two survived. The third... I don't know. I can't tell yet."

"So this is what you were obsessed with?" Tenzin asked. "Not the girl?"

"The girl was interesting, but..." He scowled. "Why did you tell Gavin I was brooding?"

"He's your friend." Tenzin flipped through the book. "I

thought he could make you stop brooding. I don't understand surrealism."

"No?" He turned the page in the book she'd been looking at. "I've always enjoyed the dreamlike nature of surrealist art." He picked up another book. "But I agree, it can be a little weird. Samson's paintings were good though."

"Maybe I need to go to the museum." Tenzin made a face. "Because I don't get it."

"I'll check night hours this month." He continued to flip through books.

"Paintings," she muttered. "There isn't much money in paintings."

He snapped a book shut. "What are you talking about? Paintings go for millions at auction."

"Only if they're desirable or you have a buyer looking for something specific. They're... trendy. Fashionable. They have no intrinsic value like gold or jewels or silk." She flipped through a book titled *Lost Treasures of World War II* and wanted to laugh. Many of the "lost" treasures of the humans had simply disappeared into immortal hands. Oleg, the fire vampire, had a treasure trove in Russia.

"I cannot imagine having everything I owned, even my name, stripped away from me," Ben said.

"Can't you?" Tenzin could. She put down the book. "The war was an awful time. I didn't hear much news then—I was in Tibet—but the little bits that encroached on me were bad."

"Emilie's family..." Ben rubbed his face and went to the sofa. "Maybe I am a little obsessed."

"With her?"

He closed his eyes. "I don't know. I'm definitely obsessed with the story. How many families had that happen, Tenzin? How many families were impoverished and had all their possessions, all their history, stolen?"

"Many," Tenzin said. "Millions. Humans are unspeakably cruel to each other."

"And vampires aren't?"

She shrugged. "I know very few vampires who kill without purpose, and when we kill, it's usually more efficient. Humans are far more cruel than vampires."

He looked as if he'd counter—this was an old argument—but he didn't. "Getting back to the painting," he said, "I understand what you're saying about intrinsic value, but—"

"Oil on canvas is oil on canvas, whether it's Rembrandt or a five-year-old." Tenzin sat next to him.

He shook his head. "I refuse to get into this again. You don't care about paintings. I get that. But this painting—the missing one—wasn't just a painting to Emilie's family. The artist was her great-grandmother's brother. This had sentimental, not just financial, value."

"So?"

"So..." He shrugged. "What if we could help them?"

"For money?"

"No, not for money."

Tenzin sighed. *Oh Ben.* He really did love a damsel, didn't he?

"The woman ran away from you," Tenzin said. "She didn't want help."

"I hadn't offered help," Ben said with a smile. "At that point, I was just trying to get her number. She was cute."

Tenzin raised an eyebrow. "But it's the painting you're obsessed over. Not the girl?"

"There are plenty of cute girls in the world." He reached over and tugged a lock of her hair. "But there's only one *Midnight Labyrinth*."

"Until you find it," Tenzin said quietly, "and it's reproduced on postcards and cheap hotel art all over the world."

"You're such a romantic." He looked at her. "But I think I have to try."

"Because of the girl?"

BEN THOUGHT ABOUT THE QUESTION. *Was it about the girl?*

The girl who sprang to mind wasn't the one Tenzin was thinking of. He wanted to find Emilie, yes, but the girl he was obsessed with was the girl in the painting, the one who had survived the labyrinth and the monsters. She was the one who intrigued Ben the most.

He wanted to see the monsters.

"It's a challenge," he told Tenzin. "Lost art from World War II. A painter who achieved renown only after his death, partly on the strength of his story. Though I'd point out that this recent show at MoMA has spurred definite murmurings among the collecting community. I'm seeing lots of subtle activity online from people looking for Samsons and trying not to be noticed."

"Do we know anyone who owns some?" Tenzin asked. "Does Giovanni? Might be a good time to sell."

"These things go in streaks. They can be trends as much as anything else."

"*More* than anything else."

"Are you hungry?" he asked, picking up the laptop that was sitting on the coffee table. "I'm hungry."

"That was not a statement, it was a question," Tenzin said. "I'll make you something, but it won't be fancy."

"You're the best, Tiny." He went online and jumped art-collecting websites and message boards for a few minutes as Tenzin went to the kitchen to make him food.

Within minutes, the smell of frying onions and carrots drifted into the room. He could hear the sizzle as she put something in oil. Tenzin was an amazing cook, and she cooked enough to keep leftovers for days.

Ben sorted the books that had been helpful and left them on the large library table near the bookshelves. It doubled as a dining room table on the few occasions they had company, but he and Tenzin usually ate at the low coffee table in the living area, sitting on cushions around the table.

Within minutes, she placed a large bowl of vegetable korma in the middle of the table with two bowls of rice next to it.

"Eat," she said. "Art later."

"Uh-huh." Ben put the book down and joined her.

It would probably surprise most humans and vampires, but Tenzin prayed before she ate. Or she said something. She didn't do it in public, but at home she lifted her hands, palms up, and murmured something in her old language before she ate. Was it an invocation? A blessing? An expression of gratitude or a curse against anyone who might try to poison her? He had no idea.

"Gavin is bottling his own scotch now," Ben said.

"That sounds like it would be exciting if you liked scotch."

"You like scotch."

"Occasionally." Tenzin spooned two generous ladles of korma over Ben's rice. "You're not brooding anymore."

"One, it's not brooding. It's thinking. And two, I have a rough plan, which helps."

"A rough plan for what?" Tenzin furrowed her eyebrows. "The painting could take months of work. Finding pieces like that can be more maddening than satisfying."

"I wanted to start with the current owners of the two existing paintings. The ones at the museum. I'll investigate them, find out how they collected the paintings, then look into the acquisition."

Tenzin picked at her food. "They don't have it, and they have no idea where it is."

"Why do you say that?"

"Because they'd already have it, wouldn't they?" she said. "Two of the three? Collectors are collectors whether they collect coins or paintings. They've looked for the third painting. I can guarantee you that. Probably put considerable funds into it."

"Then we investigate where they've looked and check out where they haven't. At least we'll be able to conserve some of our time."

"We?" Tenzin asked. "Our?"

Ben raised his eyebrows.

Tenzin asked, "Who's paying for this, Ben?"

He opened his mouth. Closed it.

Tenzin continued, "Because this is time and money."

"We don't have any other jobs right now."

"It's a waste of our time and resources."

"We have the time, and I won't pull company funds for this," Ben said. "I'll fund this on my own if I have to."

Tenzin thought for a long time. She ate most of her small portion before she answered. "Fine," she said, "but if someone calls tomorrow and says they need us to fly to Guam to dig up a seashell and they're willing to pay us for the privilege, you have to drop the Labyrinth thing."

"*Midnight Labyrinth*," he said. "That's the name of the painting. That's what we need to find."

Tenzin paused. "Okay, that is a cool name for a painting."

"It's really cool."

"What did Gavin say about Emilie? Has he heard anything about these paintings?"

"We didn't talk about Emilie," Ben said. "I managed to brush him off, but I'm sure he knows I'm hiding something."

"If you didn't talk to Gavin, where were you for so many hours?"

"Do I need to tell you?" Ben glanced at her.

"I suppose not."

Ben smiled internally. She looked like a little kid pouting. Tenzin was nosy and wanted to know everything. That didn't mean he told her, but he did try to keep her informed. How had she put it once?

If I don't know where you're going, how am I expected to track down your murderer if you're killed?

Oh, Tenzin.

"I *was* with Gavin most of the night, but we were talking about something else."

"Not Emilie?"

"No." Should he tell Tenzin? If Chloe's boyfriend was hitting her and Ben told Tenzin, the boyfriend would end up dropped fifty miles offshore from a distance of a hundred feet in the air. Ben wasn't sure he wanted that on his conscience, even for an abusive asshole.

"If I tell you, you have to promise not to overreact and kill anyone."

Tenzin crossed her arms. "Would this be in perpetuity?"

He considered this. Tenzin was literal. If you made a bargain or agreement with her, you needed to be very, very specific. "If I tell you what Gavin and I were talking about, you cannot bring any harm to either of the parties involved for a period of no less than six months. After that, we may have to reconsider."

She nodded. "Very well. Tell me."

"I'm not sure, but I think Chloe's boyfriend might be hitting her."

TENZIN FELT the black void creeping into her mind. "Who is he?"

"Not yet," he said firmly. "Tenzin, I'm not sure."

She pushed back the void, but she could feel it whispering on the edge of her mind.

Tenzin didn't have many rules. Most human morality was too changeable. But using violence against those weaker than you was a simple matter of scales.

Violence against an opponent of equal strength? Honorable. The scales were balanced.

Violence against someone weaker or less skilled? Dishonorable. The scales were unbalanced.

Since Ben would not nurture a relationship with a naturally violent person, it was most likely that Chloe was the victim of unprovoked violence from her partner.

That was unbalanced.

"That's what I was talking to Gavin about," Ben said. "I'm not sure, which is why you can't hurt him. I may be paranoid. Gav's putting one of his guards on Chloe and tracking her during the day. If she finds out, she'll be pissed."

"She'll be dead if he hits her the wrong way," Tenzin said. "One hit at the wrong angle. That's all it can take sometimes. If you care about this woman, you should kill this man and do it quickly."

Ben let out a low breath. "You are scary as shit when you're pissed. Do you know you're hovering off the ground?"

Tenzin looked down and realized he was right. She'd been sitting at the low table in the living room, enjoying her meal. Now she was floating a foot and a half above the floor, eyes level with Ben.

"She can come here," Tenzin said. "She'll need a place to stay."

He gave her a skeptical look. "You want a human who

doesn't know anything about our world to move in with us? How do you not see that as a bad idea? I was thinking I'd help her find a place of her own."

"But then she would be alone," Tenzin said. "She could become depressed and frightened thinking about her boyfriend. She might return to him."

"The one who hit her?"

Tenzin stayed silent. Intimate abuse was complicated, and Ben didn't understand it. Another reason he should have told Tenzin about this man far earlier.

A stray thought entered her mind. "She doesn't know about vampires?"

He shook his head.

"I thought you'd known her for many years."

"I have."

Tenzin asked, "Is she untrustworthy?"

"What?" He frowned. "No, of course not. She's very trustworthy."

"Greedy then. Stupid?"

"None of those things!"

"Then why not tell her?" Tenzin said. "Then she will know about us. You can be honest with her, and she will be a better friend."

"And she'll be put in danger."

"Knowledge does not equal immediate danger."

"It did for me," Ben said.

"You're not everyone." She tapped his bowl with the edge of her spoon. He needed to eat more. She had plans to train with him later. "You were adopted by an assassin—"

"Rare-book dealer."

Tenzin laughed. "He was an assassin far longer than he's been a book dealer. As I said, you were adopted by an assassin in

65

the middle of an attempt to upend an immortal dynasty. That is not the normal course of things."

"True or not, Chloe will be safer if she doesn't know anything about vampires."

Tenzin shrugged. "She's your friend."

"Yes, she is." He started eating again. "Gavin is putting a guard on Chloe. Once I know what I'm dealing with, I can take the appropriate steps."

"And what do you think those will be? Why don't you let me or Gavin deal with it? Me, preferably."

He raised his eyes. "She's one of my oldest friends. She's alone in this city, and her family has disowned her. I will take care of it, Tenzin. Don't get involved unless I ask for your help."

In moments like this, she was reminded how formidable Ben would be when he was finally ready to discard his mortality. He was young, but life had forged him to be protective, particularly of the women in his life. He wasn't showy; he never would be.

But his hand was as firm as his resolve.

Tenzin took another bite, then handed the rest of her bowl across the table.

Whoever Chloe's boyfriend was, she pitied him.

6

That night, Ben ran over the rooftops with her voice in his head.

Faster.

He ran and launched himself halfway up the side of the chimney, fingers finding holds more quickly than they had the night before. Within seconds, he'd scaled it using his fingertips and toes. He leapt off the chimney and landed on the rooftop across the alley, rolling into a ball before he sprang to his feet and kept running.

Faster, mortal.

On the next landing, he felt the skin on his palms split and bleed. Could he actually smell the blood, or was it his imagination?

He licked his hand, tasted iron and sand, and worked out the gravel that had embedded itself in the cut with his teeth. He spat it out as he ran.

Faster.

Faster.

BEN WAS READING the newspaper at Café Lilo on a sunny summer morning. It was Friday, and he had plans to visit the museum the next night with Tenzin. He hadn't made much progress on finding the true owners of the existing Labyrinth paintings. The exhibition was put on by the very private Historic New York organization, whatever they were. He'd managed to find records of galas they'd sponsored, but no actual information about the organization. There was no office address. No record of buildings owned by HNY. Their phone number led to a polite voice and a mailbox. Their website only contained information about their current exhibitions and past galas, but nothing about the leadership of the organization.

What were they?

He heard someone sit across from him at the picnic table, but he didn't look up. The picnic tables were communal seating. If it wasn't a full table, you were expected to share. He glanced up when he finished his article and found a pair of clear brown eyes staring at him.

Ben blinked. "Emilie?"

"I love this place." She smiled. "You come here?"

He narrowed his eyes. "You *ditched* me."

Emilie groaned and put her hands in her face. "I was being weird. I'm sorry."

Ben couldn't help but smile. She was wearing a loose summer-yellow sundress—the day already felt like a scorcher—her hair was pulled to the side in a messy bun, and a straw fedora covered her hair. She was cute as shit, and he couldn't help it. He forgave her immediately.

Still, he had to play with her. "Being weird? Or overwhelmed by my charm?"

She laughed. "Yeah, that must have been it."

"It's okay. It happens to a lot of women." He picked up his

coffee and rested his lower lip on the edge of the mug. "I try to control my magnetism to set them at ease, but it doesn't always work."

Emilie picked right up on the game. "So really you should be the one apologizing."

"You're right." He set his coffee down, lifted her hand, and kissed the knuckles. He smelled a hint of turpentine on her hands. "I'm sorry, Emilie. I hope you'll forgive me for your over-whelming attraction. To me."

"Are you always like this?" She was trying to stifle the smile, but it wasn't really working.

"Yes."

"Forewarned is forearmed?"

"Is this a battle?"

She pursed her mouth a little. "Isn't it always?"

"Only if you've been playing with the wrong men." He forced lightness to his voice. He hadn't received a report from Gavin last night, and he was debating whether he should call Chloe or not.

"Hey, what was that?" Emilie lifted the hand he held and smoothed her fingers between his eyebrows. "Everything all right? I really do apologize."

"Yeah, it's fine. Another friend's troubles on my mind. Sorry. So you were being weird at the museum. I didn't think you were weird."

She picked up her own coffee. Black with a hint of foam at the top. "I was more than a little emotional. It was the first time I'd seen the paintings outside of family pictures. So... over-whelming."

"You mean it wasn't all my charm?"

"Not all of it." She smiled. "That was just a bonus to the evening."

Oh, she could kill him with that smile. "So, if I asked for your number today…"

She slid a piece of paper across the table. "My email is on there too."

Smiling, Ben picked up the paper, punched in the numbers, and called her. "There. Now you have my number too."

"But I don't have your name." She held out her hand. "Emilie Mandel. I don't think I caught your last name the other night."

Instinct battled with caution. Real name or fake? "Ben Vecchio," he finally said.

"New York Italian?"

"Born and bred." That part was true, even if he wasn't Italian. With his name, most people assumed, even though his blood was an even split between Lebanese and Puerto Rican. But he *was* born and bred in New York. "I was born in the Bowery, actually. So I'm not very far from home."

"Wow. Have you always lived around here?"

He shook his head. "Moved to Southern California when I was young. I've traveled a lot for family and work reasons. But New York still feels like home." Kind of.

"Well, it's nice to meet a native. I was born in Paris but moved to the United States to be with my grandparents when I was quite young."

"No parents?"

She smiled. "Complicated."

He nodded. "Yeah, I get that." His were complicated too. They were both alive. He was pretty sure of that. Sometimes he even thought he caught a glimpse of his father driving a yellow cab.

But did he want anything to do with them?

Not a chance.

"So when can I take you out?" Ben asked, changing the subject. "A cup of coffee isn't going to be nearly enough time to get to know you."

She cocked her head, and it was adorable. She was a fairy princess and the girl next door. The girl next door if you lived in a little town in the south of France.

"Do you like music?" Emilie asked.

"I do."

"I'm going to the free concert in the park Saturday night. Want to join me? We can take a picnic."

"Damn, I'd love to." He really would. "But I made plans with a friend to take her to your uncle's exhibit at MoMA on Saturday—she says she doesn't get surrealism—and I don't like canceling on friends."

Emilie nodded. "Fair enough. I don't like friends canceling on me, so I can respect that. Maybe dinner next week then?"

"Sounds perfect. Wednesday night? There's an Indian restaurant in the Village that also has live music on Wednesday. Does that sound good?"

"Music and dinner? Sounds perfect." She stood. "I should really go. I'm going to be late already, and I hate being late."

"But what were the chances?" He rose with her. "In a city this big?"

"Exactly." She smiled again, and it was as bright as the morning. "I can't believe I saw you here."

Ben grabbed her hand and kissed the knuckles again. "It must be meant to be."

She laughed, pinched his chin, and waved as she walked away. "Goodbye, Ben. You really are far too charming."

"No such thing."

Ben watched her walk away. The newspaper he'd been reading caught the breeze and fluttered off the table. Whistling, he bent to pick it up and put it back on an inside table. His dark mood had lifted, and it was all because of a girl wearing a bright yellow sundress and a smile.

~

BEN DIDN'T RETURN home until nightfall, and Tenzin was already gone. He opened the carton he'd picked up at the food truck and poured it into a bowl, blowing on the fried tofu and spicy noodles. "Cara, turn on the television please."

"Which program would you like?"

"International news. BBC or CNN."

Without another word, the news clicked on, the volume already tuned to his preferred level. He grabbed a beer and his noodles before he walked to the couch and toed off his shoes. He'd been sitting only a few minutes when a knock came at the door.

"Cara, pause program." The news went silent. Who could be knocking at the door? Visitors were rare because very few people knew where he and Tenzin lived. "Entry camera wide angle."

A clear picture popped up on the television screen.

It was Chloe. Ben had forgotten he'd given her his address. But why hadn't she called? Something about her posture pinged Ben's internal alarms. "Cara, zoom entry camera."

Ben cursed when he saw her face. Chloe's eyes were purple and starting to swell. Her lip was bloody. He dropped his food on the table and rushed to the door. "Cara, unlock entry."

"Entry unlocked."

He heard the click as he reached the door. He pulled it open and stared at Chloe's battered face. She stared straight ahead, her expression a total blank.

"Cara, call Dr. Singh." Shock battled with rage, but Ben

knew she didn't need his reaction spilling over the trauma battered into her face. He gently took her hand and pulled her into the loft. "Hey, Chloe."

She didn't speak, but she walked in without resistance. Her posture was pliant, but she moved stiffly.

"I'm glad you came here. You're safe now. I'm going to take care of you, okay?"

For a heartbeat, Ben was back in his mother's bedroom, shaking her shoulder and waiting for her to move.

"Chloe?" Childhood memories battled with adult anger. "What do you need?"

Chloe didn't say a word, even when he sat her at the kitchen counter and lifted her chin so he could examine her face. His phone rang, and he considered ignoring it but... "Cara, who's calling my mobile?"

"The mobile caller is Gavin Wallace."

Cursing quietly, he pulled out his phone, keeping Chloe's hand in his. "Gavin?" he answered. "Your guard—"

"Called me minutes ago. Did she arrive at your apartment safely?"

"She did."

"Audra called me as soon as she realized Chloe was leaving the apartment. She didn't have your number, but when she told me her condition and which direction Chloe was walking, I assumed she was heading to your place and told Audra to keep her distance and make sure nothing further happened to her."

Ben glanced at Chloe, who still hadn't spoken. "Is there anything else?"

"I'm holding him in the basement. One of my men went in after I received Audra's call. I am assuming you'll need to call me back."

"I need to focus on more immediate things at the moment."

"Understood." Gavin went silent for a moment. "Ben, I'm sorry we dinna prevent this."

It wasn't part of the job to guard Chloe, just to follow her. Even knowing that, Ben battled anger. "I'll call you later, Gav."

"Very well."

Ben set the phone down and took Chloe's other hand. "Cara, is Dr. Singh on the way?"

"He responded to the page three minutes ago. A car has been sent to his location. Estimated time of arrival here, fourteen minutes."

"Thank you." Ben tried to catch Chloe's eye, but her stare was still blank. Her eyes were both turning purple, and a vein had burst in one side, spreading a red film over the corner of her eye. Ben saw red welts rising on her throat in the shape of large fingers. He took a deep breath and kept his cool. "Hey Chloe, I need to know if you can talk, okay? I can see he had his hands on your throat—"

"I can talk," she whispered.

"Good." He squeezed her hands. "That's good."

"But I didn't scream," she said. "I never screamed."

He forced himself to be quiet and listen.

"I should have screamed the first time, but I was so shocked." Her voice was hoarse, but talking didn't seem to be painful. "Why didn't I scream later, Benny?"

He resisted the urge to hug her. "I don't know."

"I was so stupid."

"You are not stupid."

"But I was. I am."

"Was I stupid when my dad beat me up?" he asked. "Or was I just stuck?"

She fell silent as tears slipped down her cheeks. Ben rose and went to the kitchen sink, wetting a washcloth to clean her face. He dabbed at her lip. "Hold this here." Chloe pressed the cold washcloth to her mouth as he went to get an ice pack.

As much sparring as he and Tenzin did in the apartment, he had enough supplies to stock a small medical office. He broke two packs and took them to her, urging her to the sofa so she could lie down and ice her face.

Minutes later, he heard a knock at the door. He left Chloe in the living area and opened the door for the doctor. Arjan Singh was a young Sikh doctor and a friend of Giovanni's who'd moved to the United States to work for the O'Briens after his discharge from the British armed forces. His posture and bearing marked him the formidable soldier he'd been, but his kind eyes and calm demeanor were innately trustworthy. He was wearing a dark blue turban that night that matched his linen shirt. Ben hoped Chloe would be at ease with him. If not, Ben had no doubt Arjan could suggest a discreet female physician.

"Benjamin, my friend, it is good to see you. I came as soon as I could. What is the emergency?"

He ushered Arjan into the loft. "A friend of mine has been very badly beaten," he said quietly. "She's not saying much, but I believe it was from her boyfriend."

Arjan's expression didn't change. "And she did not want to go to the hospital?"

"I didn't ask," Ben said. "She walked out and came here, so I didn't want to push it."

"There might be no need for her to be admitted, but I will have to examine her to be sure." He glanced at the couch. "If there are signs of head trauma—"

"There are."

Arjan nodded. "Let me perform an initial exam. We will decide after that."

Ben nodded and walked to the living area. Chloe still had

the ice packs over her eyes. "Chloe, the doctor's here. Dr. Singh is a friend of my uncle's. Is it okay if he examines you?"

She shrugged.

"Do you want me to leave?"

She stared at the wall. "Yeah."

Arjan said, "Chloe, it is a pleasure to meet a friend of Ben's, even in these circumstances. My name is Arjan Singh. I am a physician and a friend of Dr. Vecchio's. I'm originally from London, but I am fully licensed to practice in the United States, and I specialize in emergency medicine. Do you have any questions for me?"

She shook her head.

"Can you sit up? Or is it too painful?"

She pulled off the ice packs. "I need a hand."

Arjan's expression didn't change as he helped her sit, even when he saw her face. "Now, I am only suggesting this if you feel comfortable with me as your physician, but if you'd like more privacy, we can use Ben's bedroom. If not, I am happy to examine you here."

She flinched when she tried to stand. "The bedroom is okay."

"Give me your hand, and I can help you up." Arjan set down his medical bag and took Chloe's hand. "Ben tells me you're a dancer."

"I don't want to talk right now."

"That's fine," Arjan said.

"Where's your room?" she asked quietly, turning to Ben. "Do you have... a robe or something? It's mostly around my face, but he punched other places too."

Ben swallowed his anger and nodded. "It's down the stairs. Can you make it, or should I—"

"I can make it."

"I brought a gown with me," Arjan said. "Let me get you

settled and you can put it on. I think you'll be more comfortable in bed."

"Okay." Chloe was wooden. Ben led them to his room and waited in the hallway until Arjan came out.

"She's putting on the gown," the doctor said in a low voice. "This is a friend?"

"My girlfriend from high school." Ben raised a hand. "Nothing like that anymore, but we're still very close. She's important to me."

"Will she contact any human authorities? The police? Social services?"

"I don't know."

"Did you know this was happening, Benjamin?"

Ben could hear the subdued anger in the doctor's voice. "I suspected. I wasn't sure."

Arjan was judging him. Ben could tell.

"Does she have anywhere else to go? Her parents—"

"She can stay here," Ben said, all thoughts of getting Chloe her own place abandoned. "We've got plenty of room. She'll stay here. Her parents aren't an option."

The doctor gave him a quick nod before he tapped on the door. "Chloe?"

"I'm ready."

Ben grabbed Arjan by the shoulder. "She doesn't know about... you know."

The doctor's eyebrows went up. "And you want her to stay here?" His voice dropped to a whisper. "How long do you think you'll be able to keep Tenzin a secret?"

That... was going to be a problem.

BEN PICKED up the phone hours later when Chloe was sleeping. She'd flat out refused to go to the hospital when it was suggested, but Arjan was fairly confident she had no serious head trauma. Her injuries looked horrible, but she'd heal quickly. The doctor had given Ben pain medications to help her sleep, bandaged the broken ribs he felt, and ordered Ben to keep her eyes iced. He'd also ordered Ben to wake her every three hours just to be safe.

Ben called Gavin at two a.m.

"He's still here," the Scotsman said. "Pissing himself in the basement."

"Let him go," Ben said.

Gavin was silent.

"Let him go home," Ben said quietly.

"Are you sure about that?"

Ben grabbed the bloody washcloth he'd cleaned Chloe's face with and put it in the sink. Then he dumped his forgotten food and straightened the cushions on the sofa. Tenzin still hadn't made an appearance, but that wasn't unheard of. Sometimes she'd be gone for days.

"Send Audra to the apartment," Ben said. "Have her grab anything that looks like it might be Chloe's. Move her stuff out so he can't touch it. Pictures. Anything with her handwriting. I want her to disappear from his life, do you understand?"

Gavin said, "I'll send Audra and another guard right now. Shall they take her things to your apartment?"

"Take them to the pub. I'll get them later." The fewer people who knew where he lived, the better. "After the apartment is cleaned out, I want you to let him go."

"Ben—"

"Don't tell him anything," Ben said. "Just let him go. I want him scared for a few days."

Gavin sighed. "I forget how cold you can be sometimes."

"Make sure he doesn't leave town," Ben said. "Other than that, don't touch him."

"Let me take care of this. Let me or Tenzin—"

"No."

"Ben—"

"I want him holed up in his apartment, scared shitless," Ben said. "I want him in his safe place when I come for him."

7

B en heard Tenzin land on the roof. "Gavin, I need to go."

"I'll let you know when it's done."

"Thanks." He hung up the phone.

Tenzin walked in and took a deep breath, her eyes narrowing immediately. "That is not your blood."

"Chloe's."

She bared her fangs. "The boyfriend made her bleed?"

"Yes."

"Then we will make him bleed."

He put a hand on her arm. "One, making him bleed is my job, not yours. Don't argue, you know I won't budge on this. Two, Chloe is here, sleeping in my room. Dr. Singh came by and cleaned her up. Bandaged her ribs. She needs time to heal, so she needs to stay here for a while."

"Very well."

"Which means you need to be human for a while."

"Not possible."

"Tenzin—"

"No." She threw off his hand. "Is she in your life? Why are you hiding things from her if you trust her?"

"She's already had one shock." He sighed. "I'll consider telling her, just... give her a break before she gets the next shock, all right? She may not even want to stay in New York. If she wants to go home, I'll take her home, but for now can we just be a little bit human? For me?"

Tenzin was silent.

"Please."

"Fine," she said. "I'd like to point out that I've never asked you to be a little bit vampire for me."

"I'm not in a joking mood, Tenzin."

"I can tell." She stared at him. It wasn't an angry stare, just a persistent one.

"What?" he asked.

"It's not your fault she was hurt."

He didn't say anything. Ben walked to the bar and poured two fingers of scotch in a glass.

"It is not your fault she was hurt," Tenzin said again. "You don't control the world."

"I should have listened to my gut."

"And done what?" Tenzin asked. "Dragged her out of her home like a Neanderthal? Lectured her?"

Ben swallowed half the scotch and enjoyed the quick rush of heat. "I don't know. Maybe."

"Have some respect," Tenzin said. "She came here because she knew it was a safe place. Don't ruin that."

He looked at Tenzin and said quietly, "He's not going to touch her again."

"I have no doubt about that, but be smart. Don't try to order her around for her own good. Don't be a fool."

"Sometimes women go back." His own mother had. Over and over and over. She went back when Ben's dad hit her. She went back when Ben's dad hit him. It didn't matter. His father would knock on the door and she'd let the bastard in.

"Women go back because they don't have options," Tenzin said. "Give her options and she won't need to go back."

"Done." He finished the scotch and set the glass on the bar. "I need to go to Gavin's to get her things. I'll be taking the truck. Can you stay here with Chloe? Wake her up every few hours. Change her ice packs."

"I can do that."

"No flying."

She planted both feet on the ground. "If you insist."

"I do."

"Can I assume we're postponing our visit to the museum tomorrow?"

He worried his lip with his front teeth. He really didn't want to wait another week to take Tenzin to the museum. He knew she'd be as hooked on the mystery of the Labyrinth paintings as much as he was... as soon as she saw them. But with Chloe at the house, he didn't trust anyone but Tenzin or himself to stay with her.

"We'll wait until next week." He suddenly realized he hadn't seen Tenzin since he'd seen Emilie again. "Did I tell you I ran into Emilie at Café Lilo?"

Tenzin frowned. "Had you mentioned to her that you go there?"

He shook his head. "Just a coincidence, I guess. She apologized for taking off at the museum, and we made dinner plans for next week. Can you believe it?"

Tenzin was still frowning. "Maybe?"

He rolled his eyes. "Don't be paranoid. I'm keeping the date. I'll see if I can get any more information from her about the Labyrinth paintings or this Historic New York outfit." He felt lighter just thinking about dinner with Emilie. Did that make him a bad friend? He hoped not. What were the chances he'd run into a girl like that again?

Tenzin asked, "So you hadn't mentioned what neighborhood you lived in or anything?"

"Is it that hard to believe I'd just run into her again? Manhattan isn't *that* big, Tenzin. I ran into Chloe, didn't I? Sometimes even New York is a small world."

TENZIN DIDN'T TRUST COINCIDENCE. She was still thinking about the chances of Ben running into this girl hours later as she sat in his room, staring at Chloe's bruised face. She'd woken the young woman with a gentle nudge, roused her to consciousness, and replaced the ice packs over her eyes before Chloe drifted off again.

Dawn was approaching, and the girl was still sleeping. Ben's room wasn't light safe. Tenzin would have to leave soon.

Chloe opened her eyes with a short gasp. She stared at Tenzin with blank eyes.

"Chloe?"

The woman's breathing changed, but she didn't speak. Tenzin kept to the shadows in the corner of the room. Not only was it more comfortable, but she was trying to conceal her fangs from Chloe. There was no hiding them unless she mumbled.

"Do you remember me? I'm Tenzin, Ben's roommate. We met when you were in school."

She whispered, "I thought I was dreaming."

"You're not."

"You look exactly the same." She blinked rapidly. "Did you wake me up last night?"

"I did. We needed to change your ice packs."

"Where's Ben?"

"Getting your things," Tenzin said. "I believe he'll return soon."

"I had so many strange dreams last night." Chloe closed her eyes and turned her face into the pillow. "Ben was arguing with someone about being a human. Then he turned into a bird and flew out the window."

Note to self: keep voices down when arguing.

Tenzin said, "It sounds like the doctor gave you the good drugs."

"I should call the police." Chloe wasn't looking at Tenzin. She was staring at the wall.

"We can if you want to." Tenzin really didn't want to call the police. "Do you want to?"

It took a long time for Chloe to answer. "Not really."

"Then why should you call them?" Tenzin rose and took the melted ice packs and the towel they were wrapped in.

"Because..." Chloe sat up. "It's illegal to beat someone up. They would arrest him."

"Perhaps. But will the police beat him up and publicly shame him for his treatment of you?"

"Does this look like Medieval Times?" Chloe frowned, then winced. "Of course not."

"Will they deal with it swiftly, or will the courts drag the case out for months and years?" Tenzin knew how the modern system worked. Justice came slowly. Too slowly for her taste.

"I don't know." Chloe's shoulders slumped. "I don't think he's been arrested before. But he shouldn't just get away with—"

"Let Benjamin deal with it."

Chloe hesitated.

"You know I'm right," Tenzin said. "You know Ben can handle your boyfriend. You're a smart woman with good instincts."

"Tom is not my boyfriend," Chloe said, pointing to her face. "Can't you tell? That's what prompted all this. I broke up with him."

Tenzin gave her a piercing stare. "This wasn't the first time."

Chloe went pale. "No. Just the worst."

"Let Ben deal with Tom."

"It's not his job."

"He's your friend. You're one of his people. It's his job."

Chloe squinted at Tenzin. "I remember you from LA. You really do look exactly the same."

Tenzin shrugged, trying not to let her self-protective instincts spike. Vampires were secretive by nature, and Chloe was perceptive. "I guess I have good genes."

"Your hair was shorter then."

She raked a hand through the long strands. "I'm thinking about cutting it off again. Something more modern—updated," she added quickly. "More... stylish." If she was going to play human, it might be easier with less hair.

"I have a friend who's a stylist. Maybe we can call her." Chloe winced again. "If she's still speaking to me."

"Does she work at night?"

"Yeah, I think so. Why?"

"I'm..." What could Tenzin say? Eventually Chloe would notice she never went into the sun. Tenzin didn't want to explain vampire combustion. "I'm allergic to sunlight."

Chloe's eyes went wide. "For real?"

Tenzin nodded.

"I've heard of that. It's really rare."

"It is. I'm the only one in my family who has my condition." That was the absolute truth.

"That's crazy," Chloe said.

Tenzin frowned. "Did someone tell you I was crazy?"

"Uh..." Chloe stammered. "I didn't mean... The disease, I mean. It's crazy that you're allergic to sunlight."

"Oh." She nodded. "Yes, it's very inconvenient. Which was why I was asking about your friend working at night."

"I know she used to work at least one late night a week, but I haven't talked to her in a while." Chloe forced a smile. "She didn't like Tom. Tom didn't like her much either."

"Let me guess," Tenzin said. "He didn't like most of your friends."

"He didn't like any of them. He got me fired from my last restaurant job because he pissed off the owner, who used to be a friend of mine." Chloe plucked at the blanket covering her legs. "And I'll probably lose my current restaurant job too. The owners know Tom's dad. That's how I got the job."

"Can they do that? Fire you for breaking up with him?"

"I don't know, but I don't want to work there. His parents come in all the time. They never liked me anyway." Chloe curled her lip. "They clearly didn't want their son dating anyone who wasn't lily-white, especially if she had to work at a restaurant to pay her bills. Sometimes I think I stayed with Tom just to keep pissing them off." She touched her fingers to her swollen cheek. "Stupid."

"No, contrary."

Chloe asked, "What?"

"You were being contrary. Not doing what others expect. Contrary is not stupid," Tenzin said. "Going back to him would be stupid though."

"I'm not going back." She pressed her lips together.

"It's not the first time you've said that, is it?"

Chloe shook her head. "I thought he loved me. He said he did, and I believed him. My friends, none of them understood. Eventually... I just had Tom."

"Until Ben came back."

"I guess." Chloe shrugged. "I should have left him a long time ago."

Tenzin didn't say anything. What could she say? She'd once loved someone who was violent with her. She was violent with him too. None of it had ended well, but at the time...

"Emotions are produced by chemical surges in the body, which we have little control over," Tenzin said.

"What?"

"Emotions are produced by chemical surges—"

"I heard that part," Chloe said. "Are you trying to say I didn't really love Tom? Or that he didn't love me?"

"No." She cocked her head. "Maybe?"

Chloe narrowed her swollen eyes. "Ben always said you were weird. I told him he was being rude."

"No, I'm very strange to humans."

"To humans?"

"To *other* humans. People," Tenzin said. "Other people. Because I'm... a person who doesn't like many people. And people don't like me."

Chloe said, "I'm not trying to be rude, but I can see that."

"It doesn't bother me."

"At all?"

"No." She glanced at the window. "I don't need many people. I have Ben. Giovanni. Beatrice."

"I have Ben," Chloe said with a rueful smile. "I guess now I just have Ben."

"And me," Tenzin said. "You have me too."

"You don't even know me."

"I know Ben cares for you more than he cares for most people. I know you're important to him. So you're important to me."

"Wait." Chloe blinked. "Are you and Ben...?"

"Are we what?"

"You said you were his roommate." Chloe looked around the bedroom. "I guess I assumed..." She started to get out of the bed. "Sorry. I shouldn't have assumed. I know you're older than him, but that shouldn't matter. Why should that matter? You're not *that* old. My memory must be playing tricks on me. I'm so sorry."

Tenzin frowned. "I have no idea what you're talking about. Get back in bed."

"But isn't this your bed? I can use the couch upstairs. I don't want to take your bed."

"No. I have a loft in the living area upstairs. And the couch in the living room is very uncomfortable. I don't know why he bought it."

Ben's room was on the bottom floor of the apartment, next to the training area. If Tenzin was going to play human, she'd need to get a ladder for her loft. That was annoying.

Chloe was sitting on the edge of the bed. "I'm confused. You and Ben aren't...?"

Tenzin frowned, trying to understand Chloe's confusion.

"It's just the way you talk about him, I thought you were together," Chloe said.

"We are together. Well, not at the moment because he's getting your things. But we live together."

"But you don't share a room?"

"No." Tenzin finally understood. "We don't have sexual intercourse, if that's what you're wondering about."

"Oh." Chloe's face went red. "Sorry. This is awkward."

"Why are you apologizing? I've heard he's an excellent sexual partner, so I'm not offended you thought I would choose to have sex with him."

Chloe looked at the ground and let out a long breath. "This is a really weird conversation."

"Is it?"

～

BEN WALKED into the Bat and Barrel two hours before dawn. There were four moving boxes in the corner along with two suitcases and a heavy purse. Either Chloe didn't have many things, or Gavin's people hadn't collected all of them yet.

Gavin was sitting at a table, staring at a framed picture of Chloe with a tall man who had his arm around her. Ben recognized Tom from the pictures Chloe had on her phone.

"This is Chloe?" he asked.

"Yeah. And that's the asshole."

"She's lovely." Gavin swiped his thumb over Chloe's cheek before he carefully set her picture down. "I'm genuinely sorry, Ben. I wish I'd told Audra to keep closer. We knew—"

"We knew he was maybe shoving her around." Ben took the picture frame, extracted the photograph from the back, and carefully tore Tom from the picture. "We saw bruises, Gav. Nothing like what he did to her tonight."

"If you need any help—"

"I won't."

"If *she* needs any help then. I owe her a favor."

"You don't owe her anything," Ben said.

"Let me be magnanimous, old boy." Gavin shot him a rueful smile. "I don't come by the opportunity very often."

How about that? Gavin Wallace was acting like a human for once.

"I'll let you know if anything comes up," Ben said.

Gavin nodded.

"Is that everything?" Ben nodded to the boxes in the corner.

"Yes. Audra said there was very little evidence of her in the apartment. Most of her things appeared to be in one closet."

"Bastard."

"I'd very much agree."

"I have the truck. Can you help me carry this stuff out?"

Gavin nodded and took off his coat, folding it over the back of the chair. "What does she do?"

"Chloe?"

"Yes, for work. What is her profession? You told me she was a dancer, but that she had a second job."

"Waitress. She works at a family place in Little Italy."

"Will they give her time off?"

"Don't know." Ben hoisted one box over his shoulder.

Gavin was already carrying a box and one of the suitcases. "She can have a better job here if she likes. I'll pay her more and the hours would be flexible."

Ben gave him a hard look. "The last thing she needs is some vampire biting her."

"Not all my servers are on the menu," Gavin growled. "Some of them doona even know what we are."

Likely story. "I'll keep it in mind."

"Just let her know she has options should she want them."

Should he be concerned how much attention Gavin was paying to Chloe? Most likely, the old vampire was just feeling guilty. As much as Gavin liked to pretend he was a hard case, Ben knew he was loyal and highly generous with the few people he considered friends.

Ben dropped the box in the bed of the truck and said, "You know, I don't need help with the asshole, but I do have another project."

Gavin raised an eyebrow. "Work related?"

"Maybe. Haven't decided yet."

"Sounds interesting."

Gavin liked interesting. He was an easily bored creature, and once the excitement of opening a new place was over, he typically moved on to the next project. It was one of the reasons he had so many bars around the world.

"This new project might keep me busy for a while," Ben said.

"What do you need help with?"

"Have you heard of Historic New York?"

"Know the name, not clear on the details. They haven't been on my radar."

"Keep your ears open," Ben said. "If you hear anything, I'd appreciate if you passed it along."

"Does this have to do with some little art project of yours?"

"Something like that."

"Fine." Gavin walked back in the pub to grab another box. "I'll keep my ears open."

TENZIN HEARD the door slam upstairs. Thank the gods. Chloe looked nervous, and Tenzin was clearly very bad at acting like a human. Also, the sun was almost over the horizon.

"Ben's back," Tenzin said as she stood. "I'll send him down to check on you. I need to go... sleep." She didn't sleep, but she could meditate silently for a few hours. That would set the human at ease.

"Okay. Thanks again, Tenzin."

"You are welcome."

Tenzin walked upstairs and intercepted Ben as he was heading toward the stairway with a suitcase.

"Gavin's guard packed a bag for her. The doorman is arranging to bring the rest of her stuff up the service elevator. I just told him to put it in a corner downstairs. Is she awake?"

Tenzin nodded.

"Is she... okay?"

"From the way she's moving, her ribs are uncomfortable, but she didn't mention any sharp pain. She broke up with him, which is what prompted this beating. He's cut her off from most of her friends. And she is embarrassed because she thought we were having sex. I'm not sure why that embarrasses her. Other than that, she seems fine. Her eyes need more ice."

Ben opened his mouth. Paused. "There was a lot in that statement."

"You asked a very broad question."

"Fair enough. Give me a minute." He frowned. "Why did she think we were having sex?"

"I have no idea, but I told her we weren't. So if she wants to resume your sexual relationship, I would not be an obstacle to that."

He closed his eyes. "You didn't tell her that, did you?"

"No," she said. "I need a ladder."

"That's interesting, but I'm pretty sure we could manage without it."

"What?"

Ben was biting back a smile. "Why do you need a ladder?"

She pointed at herself. "Human, remember?"

He still looked confused.

"I need a ladder to get to my *bedroom*. So I can *sleep*. Like a *human*."

"Oh. Got it." He started back toward the stairs. "I'll order one and have it delivered. Until then..."

"Just keep her downstairs for a while."

"I will."

"And don't forget the ice."

Tenzin flew up to her loft and hid in the shadows just before the sun reached the windows of the apartment.

This was going to be a very long day.

———

8

He called Zoots early the next morning. "Can you fit in a run?"

"Now?"

"Yeah." He squeezed his eyes shut. "I'll pay you extra for last minute. I just need to burn off some shit."

She was silent for a beat. "I have an idea. Meet me at the usual place in a half an hour."

Ben dressed and jogged to catch the train. By the time he got to Hell's Kitchen, the sun had risen over the buildings and it was hotter than their usual running time.

Zoots was sitting on the swings at the playground. She rose when she saw him. "You want to get out of your head?"

"Yeah."

"Then come with me."

She took him down an alley and up a fire escape. Within minutes they were beyond curious eyes, standing on top of a building bordered by two taller brick factories.

"This one used to be taller," Zoots said. "I always wondered, so I looked it up at the library." She pointed to the buildings on either side. "All three of these were factories, but this one had a big accident or something. The top two stories were demolished and they built a new roof. But see? No windows on either side."

"Huh." Ben squinted at the two stories of solid brick that surrounded them. "Weird. But these are too high for a wall run."

"I know." Zoots clapped her hands together. "We're going to work on climbing."

Ben stared at her. "You can't be serious."

"'Cause I regularly joke about this shit?" She looked annoyed. "I lose you on the walls. Every time. You're fast as hell, especially for being so tall, but you gotta work on climbing or you'll never be fast enough for... whatever it is that makes you run."

"You lose me on the walls 'cause you're a freaking spider monkey."

"You think this shit comes naturally? I'm faster than you because I practice." She dragged an old mattress to the base of one wall. "Every wall is different, but practice helps. You can learn technique. Teaching yourself to look for the right kind of grips, understanding your balance when you're vertical. All that stuff."

Ben was still gaping at the wall.

"Trust me," Zoots said. "I watched a lot of rock climbers on YouTube. Those free climbers are fucking insane."

"Yeah. Are you listening to yourself? They're *insane*." Ben stared at her.

She shrugged. "But not really. There are tricks to it you can learn. This is just... urban rock climbing. Didn't you say you rock climbed in South America or something?"

"Zoots, I can't climb straight up a building. There aren't any windows; there aren't any fire escapes or pipes—"

"Yeah, you can. It's not flat; it's brick." She backed away from the wall, started the ascent as a typical wall run, but didn't reach the top. Instead, she stuck to the wall, paused a moment, then reached up and started climbing the surface like a spider. Ben was left gaping. She clung to invisible perches and swung from seemingly flat surfaces. When she got to the top, she pulled herself up, turned, and sat on the edge, swinging her legs. "See? Your turn."

DAYS LATER, Ben was still bruised from falling but feeling carefree as he sat at a low table at the Indian restaurant on West 8th Street. The sitar player was winding down in the corner, and he and Emilie had finished the tandoori chicken and saag paneer. They were sharing a pistachio ice cream, finishing their wine, and talking about cities they'd lived in. Ben regaled her with stories about Rome, while she offered playful childhood memories of Paris.

"Did you think about going back?" he asked her.

Emilie smiled. "To Paris?"

"Yeah. I mean, you're an artist—"

"Designer," she said. "My sketches are hardly art."

"Fashion design is art. Plus, fashion and Paris? It's a natural combination."

She smiled. "There's no fashion in New York?"

"Of course there is. I just mean... You know what I mean."

Emilie laughed as she poured more wine into his glass. "I could have gone back. I have a French passport and can work there. But New York is home. And the fashion houses in Paris... They are more traditional, in my opinion. I want to do something new. I think the opportunities in the States are easier to come by if you work hard. In Paris, it's all about who you know. What your connections are."

"You don't have anyone left there?"

Emilie shook her head. "Not in fashion. There are a few cousins. Some distant great-aunts and uncles. No one close."

"So you're a New York girl."

"For now." She coyly sipped her wine. "I am open to life and whatever comes my direction."

"That's a good attitude to have."

"And you?" she asked. "You haven't said what it is you do. I know you mentioned something to do with art, but you weren't specific."

Ben was always wary about giving too much information, but the public story wouldn't be enough for Emilie. Not if he wanted to get more information about *Midnight Labyrinth*.

"Well, I grew up with my uncle, who is a rare-books dealer."

"That sounds interesting! I love books." She blushed. "I don't have any valuable ones though. I mostly read e-books now."

"With Manhattan apartment sizes, I don't blame you. I love books too, but not as much as my uncle."

"So you don't work with him?"

"I do, in a way. I've always had an interest in art and antiquities. So what I do is kind of an offshoot of his business. If his clients are looking for a specific artifact or object... an Incan idol from Peru, for instance—"

"Wouldn't that belong in a museum?" Emilie asked with wide eyes.

"Not necessarily. Most countries have prohibitions on taking antiquities out of their territory, but that still leaves room for objects that are already on the market in private hands." He took a sip of the crisp Rhone white he'd ordered to complement the food. "I simply connect a buyer with the right seller. It's aboveboard." *Some of the time.*

"That sounds interesting." She frowned. "But I think there are some people who might try to take advantage."

"Of who?"

"Of buyers. Aren't there a lot of fakes out there?"

"Absolutely. You have to know your art and know the right experts to ask when you don't know."

"So you must know a lot about art history."

"I do. I love art history."

"Was that your major?"

"No. Political science actually."

Emilie laughed. "What?"

"Believe it or not, it comes in handy." He took her hand and played with her fingers. She wore a ring on her right hand, a single pearl surrounded by small diamonds and rubies. "This is beautiful."

"It belonged to my great-grandmother." She pulled her hand away and put it on her lap. "Family heirloom."

"From the Samson side?"

"No, from my grandfather's side." She sipped her wine. "I think you must be interested in my family, Ben."

He let her see the rueful smile. "Hard not to be in my line of work."

"Is that why you asked me out?"

"No. I asked you out because you are stunning in yellow."

She laughed. "And I didn't wear it tonight. Sorry."

"Don't be sorry." He glanced at the blue blouse that draped over her delicate cleavage. She'd paired it with a tangerine pencil skirt and heels that made her legs a mile long. "You look great in blue too."

"And orange?"

He glanced at her legs. "And orange. And purple. And every other color I can think of. I have a feeling you'd make a paper bag look good."

"I hope so. I hear that's a common challenge on *Project Runway*."

She was adorable. And clever. And fun.

Ben ignored the last of the ice cream melting in the bowl. There was something far sweeter he wanted to taste. He reached for Emilie's hand. "Come here."

He kept the kiss light, fit for a dimly lit corner of the restaurant, but with just enough heat to have the color rise to her cheeks. He pulled away, licked the flavor of sweet pistachio off his lips, and went back for seconds. This time, the tip of her tongue touched his, and he tasted the acid bite of the wine and the heady flavor of Emilie. Her taste. Her scent.

With a happy murmur, Ben pulled away, keeping her hand in his, rubbing her knuckles as he hooked his ankle around hers. "That was nice."

Her red-painted lips turned up in the corners. "Yes, it was."

"You taste delicious."

"It must be the wine."

"The wine is good, but not as good as you."

"You are very charming," Emilie said. "Did you know that?"

"Yes. Is it working on you?"

"It's been working since the first night we met. I wouldn't have met you for dinner otherwise."

A discreet server brought the check, and Ben snatched it before Emilie could look. "Thank you for joining me. I really want to do it again. Soon."

"Are you going to let me buy the wine like you said?"

"Not on your life."

"Ben!"

He smiled and kissed Emilie's knuckles before he glanced at the bill and grabbed cash from his wallet. He'd been raised by vampires, and cash was his habit. He'd never felt comfortable with credit cards. He didn't like anyone knowing what he was spending his money on.

"Tell you what," he said, sliding the leather check folder

back to the server. "Meet me for coffee tomorrow and I'll let you buy."

"You'll let me buy coffee?"

"Absolutely."

She shook her head, but he knew she was thinking about it.

"Meet me at the museum," Ben said. "There is something I want to talk to you about, but I don't want to bring it up tonight."

Emilie narrowed her eyes. "Why not?"

"I don't want there to be any confusion." He leaned over and brushed a kiss over the corner of her mouth before he whispered, "I am interested in your family. I am interested in your uncle's work. But I'm more interested in you."

HE WALKED BACK to the loft after hailing a cab for Emilie. She lived on the Upper East Side with her grandparents and preferred to go home alone, even after he offered to accompany her. It was a first date. Ben didn't push too hard. When he arrived back at the loft, it was nearly midnight. He expected Chloe to be asleep, but she wasn't. She was standing in front of the mirror in the training area, holding on to the back of a chair as she went through a simple ballet routine.

"How's the knee?" He leaned against one wall and watched her, making a mental note to install a barre along the mirrored wall.

"Feeling better than my ribs." She stopped and turned to him. "How was the date?"

"Nice." He grinned. "More than nice."

Chloe smiled, her face still a cluster of bruises though the swelling had gone down. "Did you make her pretty-cry again?"

"Absolutely not. She was smiling all through dinner."

"But you came back here?"

"Now, now, Miss Reardon. I am a gentleman and it was just a first date."

"I don't remember that slowing you down in high school."

He winced. "Give me a little credit for personal growth."

She laughed and started doing pliés again. "So, did you nail her down for a second date?"

"Coffee tomorrow at the museum."

"I'm giving you a mental high five." She lifted a slim arm over her head. "Good follow-through, Mr. Vecchio."

"Thank you very much. I'm being nosy, but did you check with Dr. Singh about exercising?"

"He said as long as I don't bend my torso, working on my knee wouldn't be a problem." She lowered her arm to bring it even with her shoulder and swept it to the side. "My shoulder is stiff, and lying in bed isn't doing it any favors."

"Just don't push if your body says stop."

"You sound like Tenzin."

Ben walked around the sparring area where Chloe was practicing. "We've trained together for a lot of years."

"As long as I've known you, I think."

"Probably."

Chloe stopped, a small frown forming between her eyebrows. "How old is she? I'm too embarrassed to ask."

"Join the club." He removed his jacket and tie, rolling up his shirtsleeves as he toed off his shoes. "I don't know how old she is either."

"Crazy."

"Yeah, she's a little crazy. We like her anyway." He tried to divert Chloe's attention. "You ever do tai chi?"

"Every now and then."

Ben moved into a slow tai chi routine next to Chloe. Both of them watched their forms in the long line of mirrors along the wall. It was soothing. Ben had a hard time not getting angry when he saw Chloe's bruises, so he focused on her knee. It was stiff, but it appeared she had full range of movement.

"This is a great area," Chloe said. "You're lucky to have this kind of space. Not too many lofts like this anymore."

"I am really, really lucky my uncle is rich." He smiled when Chloe laughed. It was good to hear her laugh. "But seriously, we looked for a long time before we found the right one. We both train a lot, so space was a priority."

"Still doing jiujitsu?"

"Jiujitsu. Judo. Tai chi. Wing chun. Tenzin works primarily in tai chi and wing chun, so that's what we practice down here. I go to a studio for judo and jiujitsu." They also practiced swords, daggers, and staffs in the training area, but Chloe didn't bring up the rows of weapons along the wall. Maybe she thought they were for show.

They weren't.

"I called my boss at the restaurant today," she said. "Shockingly, they found someone to replace me."

"Do you want to make an issue of it?"

She shook her head. "I'd rather not."

"Fair enough." He debated sharing Gavin's offer. The Scotsman paid a good salary and was a loyal employer. It wouldn't be fair not to tell Chloe a position had been offered. "I have a friend who's looking for servers at his bar. When you're ready to work again, let me know and I'll talk to him. He pays pretty well."

She let out a low breath. "It's going to be a while. I don't think anyone wants to buy cocktails from a girl with bruises all over her face."

"Hey." He waited for her to look at him. "When you're ready, he'll hire you. It's not about that."

She nodded.

"Besides, anyone who isn't blind can still see what's under there, gorgeous."

"Thanks."

It wasn't her face he was worried about. It was the defeated look in her eyes.

"Thanks for cleaning the kitchen, by the way. Tenzin says I'm the worst about doing dishes."

"It's the least I can do for stealing your bed." She glanced at him in the mirror. "Are you sure that futon was already ordered?"

No. "Totally. We've been meaning to create a sitting area down here for months." Or days. Whatever.

"I wish you'd trade with me. I hate knowing that you're sleeping on that thing."

"It's very comfortable. Don't insult my futon."

"If it's so comfortable, why don't you let me sleep on it so you can have your room back?"

He walked over and stood in front of her, putting both hands on her shoulders. "You're staying here until you get on your feet," he said. "You know my uncle and aunt. They'd kick my ass if I made you sleep on the futon, so don't argue."

"It's just—"

"And I love that you help out around the place, but please don't think you have to. You don't. This is your home too, Chloe. For as long as you need it. I know Tenzin agrees with me, so you don't even need to ask. As long as you replace the toilet paper when you finish a roll, we'll be fine."

He saw tears fill her eyes, but she brushed them away and nodded. "Only monsters don't replace the roll."

"Exactly."

She sniffed and kept wiping her eyes gingerly.

"Can I hug you?" Ben hadn't tried since she'd been beaten

up. The thought of her cringing from him was too painful. "I really want to hug you right now."

She nodded, and he enveloped her in a gentle and thorough embrace. She wrapped her wiry arms around him and squeezed hard. She was so strong. She was so tough. And Ben felt like he could draw breath for the first time in days.

"So what did you do today? Did you call your choreographer friend?"

She sniffed and relaxed her arms, but she didn't pull away. "Yeah. He's working on something right now, but it won't be ready for a few more weeks. He was excited to talk to me though. He offered to let me try out for a part when it's ready. If I'm all healed up."

"That's awesome news. Is a few weeks enough time?"

"I think so." She wiped her eyes. "You know, right after Tom kicked my knee, I thought—"

"What?" His heart spiked and his voice went cold. "What... what did you say?"

Chloe's eyes widened. "I thought you knew."

"You told me you injured yourself training."

Her cheeks went bright red. "I know. I told a lot of lies, and I'm sorry—"

"He kicked your knee?" The red was teasing the edges of his vision. "He purposely kicked your knee to keep you from dancing?"

Chloe's mouth opened, but she didn't speak. Ben didn't need to hear her answer to know what had happened.

He didn't know why her knee injury felt so much more hateful than any of her other injuries, but it did. Maybe it was because dancing wasn't just a hobby for Chloe. Dancing was who she was. She'd fought to be taken seriously at the studio in LA. Dancing was what she'd sacrificed her relationship with her parents for. It was what she'd given up her scholarship for.

He'd never seen her shine like she did on a stage. Never seen her more herself than when she was moving to the rhythm and swell of music. Tom would have known that. Would have seen that.

Killing Chloe's ability to dance would have killed the light inside her.

She put a hand on his shoulder. "He was jealous. I was dancing a routine with Henry, and he didn't realize Henry has a boyfriend and—"

"It doesn't matter how jealous he was," Ben bit out. "He didn't hit Henry, did he?"

"Don't go there." Chloe shook her head. "Ben, you're scaring me."

"Don't be scared of me." He put both hands on her shoulders and kissed her forehead. "You don't ever have to be scared of me, Chloe."

"Don't hurt him," Chloe said. "Don't give him the satisfaction of having you arrested. Because he will, Ben. He'll report you and—"

"He won't report me," Ben said. "Don't worry about me."

Records can be expunged. His uncle's voice was in his mind. *Money can do many things, Benjamin. That is why we accumulate it. Money is a tool. Keep yourself and your loved ones safe. That is your most important assignment.*

He unwrapped Chloe's arms from around his waist and walked to the door.

"Please." She was crying. "Ben, please don't kill him."

He paused and turned around, but he didn't say anything.

"Promise me," Chloe said. "If you have any love for me. Any respect. I know I can't keep you from hurting him, but don't kill him."

Ben could kill him. He'd killed in the past to protect the people he loved. He'd kill again if it was necessary.

"Please." Chloe's bruised face pleaded with him. "Promise me, Ben."

"I won't kill him," Ben said quietly. "I promise."

9

Ben called Arjan Singh as he walked toward the Lower East Side. Rats and stray dogs scuttled in the alleyways, but the streets were eerily quiet. He'd been putting off this call for days, but he'd known from the beginning he needed to make it.

"Ben?" The doctor answered on the first ring. "Is Chloe all right?"

"She's healing. She's strong. I'm going to ask you to do something for me that's not strictly ethical."

"My, my," the doctor said in his laconic British accent. "This must be the first time anyone has asked such a thing of me, Benjamin. I'm shocked. Heartily shocked."

"I'm going to ask you, and you have the option of saying yes or no."

"I should hope so."

The doctor could be flexible, but Ben knew he had a strict personal code of honor. Ben just hoped Arjan's code matched his own in this matter.

"You took a complete medical history of Chloe, correct?"

The doctor's voice was cautious. "I did."

"I don't need to know it all. Most of it is none of my business. But I want you to email me a complete list of every injury that bastard ever gave her. In detail. Do you think you can do that for me, Arjan?"

The doctor paused. "Let me call you back."

"Fine."

He walked quickly. Ben was crossing the Bowery when Arjan called him back.

"There is a list in your email inbox," he said quietly. "Be wise, Benjamin Vecchio. For though a sword must be drawn to protect the needy and anger is necessary for survival, a lack of discipline leads only to death in the spirit."

"I understand."

"I hope you do."

He walked toward the Williamsburg Bridge and turned left on Norfolk Street, then left again on Rivington, pausing when he reached the apartment where Chloe had lived in fear. He stood in front of the redbrick building and waited until all the lights went out, reading the email from Arjan while he waited.

There were bruises and a few cuts at first. Then...

Spiral fracture of the left radius.

Chipped front tooth.

Dislocation of right patella.

Torn meniscus on right knee.

Severe strain on the anterior cruciate ligament.

The list went on and on. Cracked ribs. Hair torn at the scalp. Most of the injuries were things she'd be able to hide until the most recent beating, but the evidence was there.

As a rule, Ben avoided violence. He had no hunger for it and no thirst to prove himself. He'd walked through too much real carnage to be fascinated by bloodshed.

But anger was necessary for survival.

And sometimes a sword needed to be drawn.

Ben wouldn't use a sword on Tom. He'd use his fists, the same weapons Tom had used on Chloe.

An eye for an eye.

A tooth for a tooth.

A torn meniscus for a torn meniscus.

The last light went out on the second floor. Ben walked to the green door facing the street, his lockpicks in hand. In seconds, he had the door open and was walking up the stairs. He passed an apartment on the right and went to the end of the hall, stopping at the last door on the left. The bay windows in the front of the building were dark and the curtains were drawn, but a low light gleamed under the doorway.

I want him holed up in his apartment, scared shitless. I want him in his safe place when I come for him.

Ben tried Chloe's key first. It turned, but the door didn't open. Tom was scared. He would have put in a deadbolt. Maybe a chain. Some other barrier locks. Fortunately, Tom's landlord probably frowned on altering the windows. Not waiting for anyone to wake, Ben walked back out of the building and quickly jumped up the fire escape. He climbed to Tom's window and, after wrapping his arm in his jacket, broke the glass on one window, clearing it in seconds.

He climbed over the couch and into the living room just as Tom was walking out of the bedroom in his boxer shorts.

"Shit!" The man cursed and ran for the door, but the series of locks he'd installed to keep Ben out also kept him from escaping.

Ben grabbed Tom by the hair and pulled his head back, punching his throat before he could yell and alert any of his neighbors. Then he dragged Tom to the bedroom, threw him on the ground, and shut the door, shoving a sturdy desk chair under the doorknob.

"Hello, Tom."

Tom rolled on the ground, his hands at his throat, gasping for air through his bruised windpipe.

"I'm a friend of Chloe's," Ben said quietly, "but you probably guessed that."

Tom was still gasping; his body was curled into a ball. He was a tall man and his muscle tone was good, but Ben had the feeling his muscles came from a trainer at the gym and not from any martial discipline. He had just enough skill to beat up a woman who was half his size.

"I promised Chloe I wasn't going to kill you. But if you think about reporting this—think about making any kind of trouble for her—if you even try to call her, Tom, then I'm going to make sure you're dead." Ben kept his voice low and calm. "I won't have to do it myself, so I won't be breaking my promise to Chloe. Do you understand?"

The smell of urine filled the air.

"Do you understand? Nod if you can't talk."

Tom nodded.

"Good. Now for a little history lesson. Do you remember the first place you hit Chloe?" Ben asked. "She does. She told the doctor. The doctor told me." Ben bent down, pulled Tom's head back, and slapped him hard on his left cheek.

Tom blinked in surprise and his eyes went wide with anger. "Who the fuck—?"

Ben slapped him again. "Don't talk. I don't want to hear your whining. Isn't that what you told her when she cried?" Chloe hadn't told Ben that part, but she'd told Tenzin, who thankfully had no sense of boundaries.

Ben smacked Tom with the back of his hand, hard enough to make the big man's lip bleed, then dropped him on the ground where his head thudded on the hardwood floor. "It's not fun to be treated like someone's punching bag. Is it, Tom?"

Tom spit out blood and shook his head.

"I want to make sure you know something," Ben said quietly. "This is not a onetime visit, Tommy. I'll be back. If you try to run, I'll find you. If you try to report me, I'll cut out your tongue. You can live without your tongue. They don't bleed as much as you'd expect. Did you know that?"

Tears had come to Tom's eyes. He was drooling blood and crying.

"Tonight I'm going to crush your knee the way you crushed Chloe's," Ben said softly.

Tom began to rock and groan quietly, shaking his head.

"You knew exactly what you were doing when you did that, didn't you, Tom? She's brighter than you. She's beautiful and special. And you're a little piece of shit."

"Please," he croaked. "Please don't..."

Ben lifted Tom's leg at the ankle and stomped his foot down on the knee, listening for the telltale pop of the tendons and kneecap as Tom's leg bent at an unnatural angle.

Tom screamed and Ben dropped the leg. He threw a pillow on Tom's face. "Stay quiet, Tom. I don't want to have to gag you, but I will."

The man sobbed into the pillow while Ben checked his knee. The injury was more severe than Chloe's, but then Tom wasn't a dancer. His knees weren't as valuable as Chloe's in the first place.

Ben wanted to leave Tom with one more memento from his first visit. He rolled the man to his back and remembered Chloe's chipped tooth. Ben ripped the pillow away from Tom's face and leaned one arm hard on his chest.

"Please," the man gasped. "Please, no."

"Did she say no, Tom?" Ben asked calmly. "Did she cry? I think she did. That's all for tonight, except for one more thing. Hope you have a good dentist."

Ben reached for a large chunk of polished marble sitting on

Tom's desk. He brought the paperweight down on the man's mouth, hitting him precisely on the front tooth, just hard enough to make his lip break open again and crack a tooth in half.

"That looks painful," Ben said, setting the marble back on the desk and squatting by Tom's shaking figure. "Now remember what I said. If you make any trouble for Chloe, I'll make sure you're dead. Stop crying. If she could handle these injuries, so can you."

Tom turned his head to the side and vomited. A little bit hit Ben's shoe. He stood and wiped the vomit on Tom's pillow before he took the chair from under the doorknob.

"Like I said, Tom, don't try to run or hide. I'll find you if you do."

Ben left the apartment the same way he came in, but instead of dropping to the street, he climbed higher, lifting himself onto the rooftop just as Tom began to scream in rage and pain.

He took a deep breath and jogged across the roof. It was cool that night, and he could use a run to clear his head.

10

"You're distracted."

Ben looked up from the double espresso on the table and forced a smile at Emilie. "Sorry. I was working late last night. Had to take care of something after dinner that took longer than expected. I probably should have postponed our date, but I didn't want to miss seeing you."

Emilie was wearing a long dress in a red bohemian print that day. The pleased flush in her cheeks almost matched her dress.

"When you put it that way, I can hardly be mad at you," she said. "So I'll be kind and offer to postpone if you'd like."

"No, I'll be fine." He downed the espresso in one gulp. "Caffeine cures everything."

She sipped her iced coffee. "Hot drinks on a hot day. I just can't."

He could already feel the heat and the slightly burned shots working their magic. "I'm good. I've never liked coffee cold."

"No? Is that an Italian thing?"

"My very Italian uncle doesn't even like coffee." His uncle didn't like much besides good scotch and rich blood. Maybe the occasional rare steak. "He likes the smell when my aunt makes it though. I think I started sneaking her coffee when I was twelve."

"You were raised by your uncle?"

Ben nodded. "Mostly. I was born here, but my parents split up when I was little. My mother... not the greatest. My dad was history. My uncle was pretty young when he took me in, but he was big on education. He took over when I was eleven. My aunt came along a little bit after that. They're still in LA."

"You're close."

Ben nodded. "Very."

"My childhood was similar," Emilie said. "My parents are also... not the greatest. They're together, but they're very self-centered. They travel constantly. My father's family is very wealthy. I was an inconvenience to them, so they left me with my grandparents."

Ben frowned. "I'm sorry."

"Don't be. My grandparents are wonderful." Her right dimple peeked out. "They did an amazing job, if I do say so."

He reached for her hand. "I would agree."

Her eyes flashed in pleasure. "So you wanted to talk about my family? About Samson?"

Ben shot her his best bashful smile. "Am I overstepping?"

She shook her head. "In your line of work, I think I'd be surprised if you weren't interested."

"Your grandparents—the ones here in the city—they're the ones who are related to Samson?"

"My grandmother is his niece. Her mother was Emil Samson's sister."

"But she never knew him?"

"Not really." Emilie sipped her coffee. "There are a few pictures of her with him as a baby—my great-grandmother was very close to her brother—but he died when she was quite young."

"But you do have pictures?"

Emilie nodded. "When my grandmother was left at the convent, she left quite a large trunk with the sisters. It contained many of our family documents, pictures, deeds. Things my grandmother might need if her family were all killed. We were fortunate that it was kept safe for us. And that my great-grandmother returned."

"I'll say."

"Many families were shattered. They had nothing." Emilie shrugged. "We didn't have property or art anymore, but we had our history. At least we had that."

"Are those pictures where you first saw *Midnight Labyrinth*?"

"They are." Emilie finished her coffee and set down the tumbler, rattling the ice as she talked. "I loved that old trunk. My great-grandmother obviously was proud of Emil. She kept newspaper clippings, gallery flyers. I saw the Labyrinth pictures from the exhibition flyer."

"But you'd never seen them before in person before the current exhibit?"

She shook her head.

"Emilie..." Now that it came time to offer, he hesitated. Would she interpret his personal interest as predatory? Would she understand he found the mystery of the painting as alluring as she was? "You know what I do for a living, correct?"

"You find art." She smiled. "Trust me, if I could afford to hire you—"

"What if I offered for free?"

Her mouth dropped open. "What?"

"What if I offered to find *Midnight Labyrinth* for you and your family? No charge."

She slowly shook her head back and forth. "But we don't... we can't—"

"I can't make any guarantees," Ben said. "I never can, though some jobs I'm more confident than others."

"It's been lost for seventy-five years."

Ben smiled. "Not the oldest trail I've followed, if you can believe it."

She still hesitated. "I'm just not sure what you get out of this, Ben. If we found it, I don't think my grandmother would want to sell. So there's no profit—"

"It's not about that," he said, leaning forward. "Emilie, do you trust me?"

She opened her mouth, but again, nothing came out.

"You barely know me," he said. "I get that. And I can't say my interest in this is purely academic."

"Then what—"

"It's the challenge," he said quietly. "I'm not sure if that makes sense to you, but for me, the challenge is as much of a draw as the reward. I want to know if I can find it. I want to see the paintings together." *And I want to see the look on your face when you see it.*

He didn't share that part. Too soon. But he was quickly becoming infatuated with her. It wasn't only her beauty, it was her humor and her generosity and her passion. He wanted to see her face when she saw the painting. He wanted to see her eyes when she was deep in concentration over her work. He wanted to watch that mouth part when he made her breathless.

Ben wanted her.

So did that mean he was going to spend time, money, and possibly favors among friends to impress a girl?

Yes. Yes, he was.

IT WAS midafternoon when he walked back to his place with

plans to visit Emilie's grandparents the next night. She'd agreed to let him look for the painting and agreed when Ben asked to meet her grandmother. Though Emilie was hesitant to get her grandmother's hopes up about finding the painting, she knew Ben needed cooperation.

"Chloe?" he called when he entered. "I'm... Wh-what is going on here?"

Ben came to a halt in the middle of the main floor. Yards and yards of fabric were unrolled around the room. It draped across chairs and sofas. In the middle was Chloe, draped in emerald green, with Tenzin kneeling at her feet, shiny silver pins clutched between her lips.

"Help me," Chloe said. "I'm not even sure what she's doing."

"Tenzin, what—?"

"I don't have any formal clothes," Tenzin said, not looking up. "Chloe is my height. I'm using her as a dummy."

"As a mannequin?" Ben put his messenger bag on the table. "She's nowhere near your size, Tiny."

"She's closer than you. And I have a feeling I'd have a hard time making you stay still for this."

Chloe's eyes were wide and she mouthed, *Make it stop!*

Ben nodded at her reassuringly. "And the reason you're not buying clothes is...?"

"I have all this fabric," she said around the pins.

"And the reason you're not hiring a seamstress is...?"

"I know how to sew."

"You do?"

Tenzin looked up and gave him a look that said, *Really?*

He sometimes forgot she'd lived in a time when you couldn't just run down to the corner store for bread or buy clothes off the rack. Tenzin knew how to do everything, from grinding wheat by hand to spinning and weaving cotton.

"Okay." He tried a different tack. "Why don't we get you a proper mannequin so that Chloe doesn't have to stand there getting pins stuck in her?"

"I haven't stuck pins in her. Not once."

"That's true, actually." Chloe gave him a pained look. "But my arms are getting tired."

"Can she put her arms down?"

Tenzin looked up. "I didn't realize you still had them raised. Yes, you're fine."

Chloe lowered them with a relieved groan.

Ben said, "Seriously, Tenzin, why don't we get you a mannequin? And what's with this sudden need for dress clothes?"

"Formal attire requested," she said, pointing to the coffee table.

"What?"

"An invitation from Gavin."

Chloe asked, "Who's Gavin? I love that name."

"He's a..." Tenzin looked between Ben and Chloe. "He's a friend of Ben's. And mine. He's odd like me."

"I don't think you're odd," Chloe said.

Ben and Tenzin both stared at her.

"Okay, you're odd," Chloe said. "But in a nice way."

Tenzin gave her a closed-mouth smile, probably so she didn't scare her with the two-inch fangs. "Thank you, Chloe. I also find you odd in a nice way."

"Thanks, Tenzin."

Ben wandered over to the coffee table, noticing the heavy cream envelope in the center. When he slid out the invitation, he saw the formal announcement at the top.

Summer Evening Gala
Historic New York

Rothman Ballroom
July 31st at midnight
Further directions upon acceptance

BENEATH THE GILDED LETTERING, Ben read, "guest of Gavin Wallace" and "formal attire requested." There was a small RSVP card and an envelope with no address. The envelope had been sealed in wax but not stamped by the post office. No, it appeared the invitation had been delivered by hand.

Historic New York was either very private, very old-fashioned, or very immortal. Possibly all three.

"When did this come?" he asked Tenzin.

"This afternoon."

"Day people," he muttered.

"What?" Chloe asked.

"Nothing." Someone's day person knew where he lived. Ben didn't like that. "Was there anything else in the mail?"

"I don't know. Chloe, turn right. No, my right. That was the only thing that looked interesting. There was a letter from Gavin, but it was addressed to you."

"And you didn't open it anyway?" Ben asked. "I'm so proud of you."

"I'm all about personal growth. Stop wiggling."

"I need to go to the bathroom," Chloe said. "I think my mannequin days are over."

"You haven't been doing this for days."

Ben walked over and lifted the pinned cloth over her head. "Enough, Tiny. She's not a doll."

Chloe scooted from under the fabric and rushed to the bathroom down the hall. As soon as she was out of sight, Tenzin took to the air, flipping end over end with her arms outstretched.

"Feel better?" Ben said, laying the green shell of a dress on the back of the couch.

"How do you stay on the ground all day?" She groaned.

"Because I don't really have any other options."

"That's not true and you know it."

Ben ignored the expected dig. Tenzin was constantly reminding him that he'd make an excellent vampire and that humanity was only slowing him down. He was used to it at this point, and he had no intention of changing. "You have to remember not everyone is as patient as me," he told Tenzin.

"You're right. Chloe is far more patient than you." She landed in front of Ben. "I want to keep her."

"She's not a pet, Tenzin."

"Neither are you, but I kept you."

He shook his head. "She's staying here until she gets back on her feet," he said in a low voice. "If she stays permanently, there'd be no way to keep things a secret."

"So don't keep them a secret," Tenzin said. "You know I think you're being ridiculous about this."

"If she knows about you—about everything—then she's at risk. Just like me."

"You run after risk, Benjamin. Don't kid yourself. Chloe would be as protected as any normal day person. Gio knows her. He'd put her under his aegis."

"Would you?"

She turned and started sorting her pins and tape. "I don't do that."

"Uh-huh." He looked at the unfinished dress along the back of the couch. "This color is beautiful. I'm getting you a mannequin."

"Fine."

"Do you even have a sewing machine?" He looked, bewildered, around the loft. There was fabric of every kind, but most of it was patterned. He saw elaborate patterns, silks, stripes of every color. "Where did you get all these?"

"I collect them when I travel. What do you mean, a sewing machine? An industrial machine? Do we have room for that?" She turned in a circle, surveying the loft. "I don't know if we have room."

"No, the small, personal-sized ones," he said. "Are you kidding? How do you not know about sewing machines?"

"I thought they were only in factories."

Ben shook his head. "How long were you living in that cave?"

"Long enough." She threw her scissors in a bag. "Let's keep Chloe."

"We'll talk about this later. I have a meeting with Emilie's grandparents tomorrow night."

She sighed. "So we're really doing this thing that's going to make us no money?"

"We have plenty of money," Ben said. "Come on, it'll be fun."

"Do I have to go with you to visit the old humans?"

Ben tried to imagine Tenzin meeting Emilie. "Uh... no. You can skip this one."

"Good. You should take Chloe."

"Why?"

"Because she's very smart and very observant. Plus she's patient and probably likes old people."

Ben patted Tenzin on the head. "Well, she likes you."

She reached up and snatched his hand, bending his finger back as he yelped.

"Everyone likes me." She dropped his hand. "I'm very *likable*."

Ben grunted and shook out his fingers. "Sure you are."

CHLOE DID COME with him on the trek to Emilie's apartment the next night. It was a hike from Lower Manhattan, but the minute the cool breeze and scent of the trees hit Ben out of the 190th Street subway station, he understood why people chose to live on the far north point of Manhattan. Emilie said her grandparents lived in a comfortable apartment on Fort Washington Avenue just south of Fort Tryon Park. It was a quiet neighborhood, especially after dark. Ben wondered if any vampires lived in the area. With the park close by, it would be an ideal location for an earth vampire who had to be in the city.

Earth vampires, as a rule, hated cities. The O'Briens were misfits in that regard. Most cities were run by water vampires with an affinity toward politics. His aunt was a water vampire. His uncle came from water vampires. Cities were no problem for them. For earth vampires, however, civilization could cramp the power they drew from the earth.

"Are you sure they're not noticeable?" Chloe kept peeking at the small mirrored compact she kept in her wallet.

Ben looked carefully. Again. "If someone was looking really closely, they'd notice. Emilie might notice. Her grandparents probably won't."

"And you're okay with me lying if they ask?"

He stopped on the sidewalk. "Chloe, it's your business. If you were lying to me about being hurt again, I'd mind. If you don't want to tell relative strangers a complicated story, that is your prerogative. Tell them you were in a car crash if you want. It's nobody's business but yours."

"Okay." Her voice was tiny.

"And mine." He started walking again. "And the people who love and care about you. And no, that does not mean I'm going to tell your parents."

"They wouldn't care anyway."

Ben had a feeling that was definitely *not* the case. Dr. Reardon would blow a carefully concealed gasket if he knew someone had beat up his daughter. However, Ben also had a feeling that Chloe's parents would see this as another excuse for her to leave New York. And since Ben was taking care of her and didn't particularly want her moving back to Los Angeles, it was a conversation he was putting off.

"How long have they lived here?" Chloe asked.

"Emilie's grandparents? I'm not sure."

"There's a big Jewish community up here, right?"

"I think so."

The street was dark and very few cars passed them. By the time they reached the address Emilie had given to them, the wind had picked up and the night was almost chilly.

"Feels nice, huh?" Chloe grinned.

He felt his heart thump in his chest. It was so good to see her smile. She was more like herself every day. In the back of his mind, he heard the crunch of Tom's knee under his foot. He put an arm around Chloe and guided her up the walk, pressing the button for apartment 202 when they reached the buzzer.

A man's voice answered, "Hello?"

It was a French accent, but heavier and low. Probably Emilie's grandfather.

"Is this the Vandine residence? I'm Ben Vecchio, Emilie's friend. And I have another friend with me."

"Hi!" Chloe chimed in. "I'm Chloe."

There was a short pause. "Let me ring you in."

The door buzzed open a second later. Ben and Chloe entered the nicely updated entryway and walked up the stairs to the second floor. The door to 202 was already opening.

"Hey!" Emilie stepped into the hall.

"Hey yourself." Ben leaned down and kissed her cheek. "You remember Chloe from the museum, right?"

"Oh hi! Yes." Emilie held out her hand. "How are you? I need to get the brand of those eyedrops you gave me. They were amazing."

"Oh right." Chloe's smile was forced. "Remind me before we go. Think I have some in my purse."

Emilie waved toward the door. "Come in. Do you like cake? My grandmother made cake and coffee. I couldn't have stopped her if I tried."

"Why would you try to stop someone from serving cake?" Ben walked toward the door and entered before Chloe and Emilie. It was a habit. While it might have seemed rude to most people, even a sweet old lady's apartment was unknown territory. Ben wasn't going to let Chloe enter any room if he didn't know what was waiting for her. They might not have been human manners, but they were vampire ones.

"Emilie?" An older woman with silver-grey hair entered the room speaking French. "*Est-ce que vos amis boivent du café?*"

"We'd love some coffee," Ben replied in French.

Emilie's grandmother smiled and spoke in English. "How lovely. Did you study French in school? Your accent is quite good."

"Thank you. I've traveled extensively with my aunt and uncle, so I speak a little. I'm afraid asking for coffee is about as fluent as I get."

"No matter." She waved to the sofa. "Please sit. My husband was ready for bed when you rang. I hope you won't consider him rude if he retires."

Ben said, "Of course not."

He and Chloe sat on the couch while Mrs. Vandine, who was an extremely handsome woman in her seventies, sat across from them on a chaise. Her posture was ramrod straight, and she was dressed in a stylish button-down shirt in coral red with a chunky necklace peeking out from the collar. Silver-grey hair was swept into a twist at the base of her skull, and simple diamond studs twinkled in her ears. It was easy to see where Emilie acquired her style.

"I made one of my mother's cakes," Mrs. Vandine said, picking up a knife and cutting into a bright yellow cake drizzled with a white glaze. "It goes very well with coffee."

"It looks amazing," Chloe said. "Thank you for having us."

"When Emilie said she'd met a young man who might be able to find my mother's painting, I admit I was skeptical. Why do you have so much confidence that you can find it, Mr. Vecchio? After all, we have looked." She put thin slices of cake onto delicate china plates, then handed them to Emilie.

"Please, call me Ben. And I don't know if Emilie told you this, but I find antiquities for my business. I was trained by my uncle, whose passion is finding and dealing in rare books and manuscripts. So I've been doing work of this sort for quite a long time, even though I'm young."

Emilie handed him a fork and a piece of cake. It smelled heavenly.

"How old are you?"

"I'm twenty-five," Ben said, taking a bite. He was actually twenty-four, but his identification said twenty-five. "This cake is wonderful. Thank you."

"Emilie, the coffee should be ready." Mrs. Vandine smiled. "You are quite young, aren't you Ben?"

"I am. But as I said—"

"Where would you even start?" she asked. "I cannot imagine."

"I'd start where most of these types of investigations start," Ben said. "In the library, going through auction catalogs. Reading old newspapers. Most beginning work on a case is pretty mundane. Lots of busywork and checking off boxes. I do have a few sources here and in London who are particularly attuned to the art world."

Emilie came back with coffee in a french press and poured it into eggshell-thin demitasse cups she put in front of Ben, Chloe, and her grandmother.

"Thank you," Ben said, lifting the cup to his mouth. It was steaming hot and very rich. He burned the edge of his tongue when he sipped it. "I'd also like to look into owners of the other two Labyrinth paintings. It's possible they have some information about *Midnight Labyrinth*."

Mrs. Vandine looked at Emilie. "I thought you said the owners were anonymous?"

"They were," Ben said drawing her attention back to him. "But anonymity is often a very public secret when you know the right people to ask. I have some contacts with Historic New York, who cosponsored the surrealist exhibit at the museum. I plan on starting there."

Mrs. Vandine looked at Emilie. "We donate to them, don't we?"

"I think so, Grandmother."

"They do so much for the city." She lifted her own coffee cup. "And your friend? Is she part of your business as well?"

Ben glanced at Chloe. "My partner would like to hire her, but Chloe's just keeping me company tonight."

Chloe smiled at Ben. "She does not. Tenzin would hardly—"

"She does. Tenzin's the one who suggested you come tonight, so make sure you're taking notes."

Emilie took a seat and reached for her cake. "Who is Tenzin?"

"His partner," Chloe said. "She's the muscle. He's the pretty face."

"I beg your pardon," Ben sat up, trying to look offended. "I also have muscles. And a pretty face. I have both."

"And charm, I think," Mrs. Vandine said with a twinkle in her eye. "If you have turned my Emilie's eyes to you, you also have charm."

Emilie murmured something too fast for Ben to catch, but it made her grandmother smile.

"I like this idea," Mrs. Vandine said. "I don't know if it will amount to any new revelations, but I am willing to let you look through our pictures and letters if you like. We don't have any money to pay you, but—"

"This would be solely at my own expense," Ben said, winking at Emilie. "If I could dig into your family history a little more, I'd be grateful."

Emilie and her grandmother exchanged a cryptic look. Finally Emilie said, "What would you like to know?"

11

Tenzin stared at the small screen mounted to the wall.

The human said, "This is unusual for you."

"I know."

The face on the other end was blurred, but the voice was familiar. Tenzin's face would be blurred on his side too. It was the way Ben had set up her amnis-resistant tablet so that Tenzin could make calls in the relative privacy of her room.

"Are you sure?" her art buyer asked.

"Quite sure."

"Very well." She saw the blurred face look down. He was writing something on a legal pad. "I'll let you know what I find."

"Private sellers are going to be the most desirable. The gossip has already started on the East Coast."

"I'll see what I can do and email any leads. You're sure of this budget?"

"Yes."

A hint of laughter. "I never thought I'd see the day."

"And Emmanuel, if I hear about this tip spreading to any other clients—and I will hear—I will kill you," Tenzin said. "Do you understand?"

The laughter stopped. "Have I ever betrayed you?"

"There's a first time for everyone. Don't let this be yours." Tenzin used the stylus to end the call.

She checked her email. There was a follow-up email from Blumenthal Blades.

Damn. She'd waited too long to decide on the saber and someone else had bought it.

Another email from René.

DEAREST TENZIN,

I miss you so. The Paris lights are calling you. Won't you answer? We could have a marvelous time in the city. France is ripe fruit waiting to fall these days, and I do know how you hate being bored.

Speaking of fruit, I have a joke for you.

"How do you make an apple turnover?

Push it downhill."

Isn't it amusing? Write me back when you can.

Your constant admirer,

René DuPont

SOMETIMES RENÉ's jokes were funny. Sometimes they were just bad. This was the third apple joke he'd sent her, and none of them made sense. Was this current one a threat?

She used the stylus and touched an arrow button at the end of the message. She thought it might be a voice message of some kind—René would sometimes send those—but instead a low-plucked bass sounded from the house speakers and a lazy song about taking a walk on the wild side filled the loft. She listened to it for a moment. The rhythm was nearly hypnotic, but she couldn't make sense of the lyrics. She briefly debated forwarding the message to Benjamin to see if he could make sense of it, but instead she moved it to the *René* folder. Her email program closed and the loft fell silent just in time to hear the quiet churn of the elevator. Ben and Chloe were almost home.

Perfect.

A few moments later, Tenzin heard them chattering in the entryway and took to the air, floating in the middle of the living room, reading the manual for her new sewing machine. It was past time that Chloe was made aware of vampire life. Tenzin would have to take matters into her own hands since Ben was being stubborn.

The door opened.

"No," Chloe said with a laugh. "Because when she stopped serving coffee, I just wanted more cake. It's a vicious..."

"Chloe?" Ben asked.

Tenzin looked up. Chloe's eyes were locked on her. She waved. "Hi. How was the meeting?"

The girl's face went pale a second before she fell over in a faint.

CHLOE HEARD the voices before she opened her eyes.

"—that on purpose!"

"Of course I did. You were never going to."

"It is not your place to tell my friends about my other life. I am the one who—"

"Don't be so selfish," Tenzin snapped. "She's my friend too."

Oh, that was nice. Tenzin could be so odd, Chloe was never sure quite what the other woman thought of her.

The other woman.

Who floated.

Chloe's eyes fluttered open. The light was too bright, and someone had laid her on the couch. Had she hit her head when she fell?

"She can be your friend," Ben said, "but she was my friend first—"

"Are you five now?"

"—and you should *not* have decided to tell her, especially not like that!"

"Well, it was direct."

"She passed out from shock."

Chloe started to sit up. "She's kind of awake now."

Ben rushed to kneel next to her. "Hey. How are you feeling?"

"I'm... okay."

God, he was so great. Why couldn't she have just stayed in love with Ben Vecchio and married her high school sweetheart? Her life would have been a lot easier if that had happened. Sure, by the time she and Ben broke up they were already more friends than boyfriend and girlfriend, but she could have worked with that. He was handsome as sin, smart, and funny. He had his own business. He was self-assured and a great friend. He was also pretty great at sex—even as a teenager. He was probably so much better now.

He was a catch.

And he was staring at her intently. "Do you remember anything... weird?"

She closed her eyes. "I think we might need to call Dr. Singh again. I don't want to be a pain in the ass, but I'm pretty sure I had a hallucination before I passed out. There might be some head trauma from before. I don't know. Is that weird?" She rubbed her eyes. "I hate feeling like I'm putting everyone out, but if I'm seeing things like—"

"Like women floating above the ground?"

Chloe looked up. Tenzin was there. Floating. Above the ground.

And she was smiling.

And... there were teeth. Very long, curved teeth.

Spots danced across her vision again as Chloe closed her eyes.

She decided to lay herself down this time. She really didn't want to hit her head.

"Dude!" Ben shouted, jumping to his feet. "Tenzin, cut it out! Stop doing that."

"We're all going to laugh about this someday. It's going to be hilarious."

"Well, it's not hilarious now. We're never going to convince her it was a hallucination if you keep doing that."

Chloe muttered, "I'm pretty sure I'm dreaming. I'm dreaming, right?"

Ben pressed his lips together and pointed at Chloe's back.

Tenzin wasn't sure what he wanted her to do, but he had that pointy, judgmental face that made her want to hoot with laughter and antagonize him more.

"What?" she asked.

Ben pointed at Chloe again but didn't speak. Then he waved his hand in front of his face before he touched a finger to his temple.

"What are you doing?" she asked. Was this a strange game of charades? It wasn't really the time for charades, even though she did enjoy that game.

"Amnis. Memory," he said through gritted teeth.

"I'm not going to use amnis to wipe her memory," Tenzin

said. "I don't want her to forget. You're the one who wants her to forget, so you wipe her memory."

"I can't do that, Tenzin; I'm not a vampire!"

Tenzin sat down next to Chloe on the couch. "No. No, you're not. Don't you wish you were right now though?"

"I hate you so much."

"No, you don't," Chloe muttered into the pillow. "Did someone say vampire?"

"Yes." Tenzin patted Chloe's back. "I'm a vampire, but I won't bite you. I promise."

Chloe kept talking into the pillow. "Okay sure. Why not? Ben, where's my purse?"

Ben was pacing the room, arms crossed on his chest and one hand gripping his hair. "Uh, why?"

"I need my phone."

"Why?"

"To call Dr. Singh, of course," Chloe said, her face still smashed in the pillow.

Tenzin watched with satisfaction as Ben realized that he was going to lose this fight. Chloe was going to learn about vampires and be part of their world. Tenzin kept herself from clapping with glee.

She didn't need to rub it in. He already looked defeated.

But she was so very pleased. Chloe was a delightful person. She was funny and smart, and Tenzin could really use another day person around the house. She was missing Caspar, Giovanni's butler. Not that Chloe would be a butler. Tenzin and Ben weren't as formal as Giovanni was. No, Chloe could be their day person and friend. She was perfect.

Ben was glaring at her. "Selfish," he hissed.

"What?"

"You are selfish." He uncrossed his arms and his eyes went

cold as he switched to speaking in Mandarin. "You did this for you, not her."

That was partly correct. But not entirely.

"I did it for you too," she replied back in Mandarin. "You need more people who understand you."

"And did you, *even once*, wonder what would be best for her? What she might want?"

No. Not that Tenzin didn't like Chloe, but Chloe wasn't one of her people. Not yet. Her blank expression must have given away the answer to Ben.

"Selfish," Ben said again. "Leave. I don't want to see you right now."

"Are you going to explain things to her on your own?"

"Yes."

"She might not believe you."

Ben glared. "I'll invite Gavin over. He already knows about her. I'll be needing his help to protect her anyway."

He preferred Gavin's assistance to hers? Tenzin curled her lip. "Now who's being selfish?"

Without another word, she flew out the rooftop door and into the night.

WHEN CHLOE finally opened her eyes, she turned over and saw Ben sitting on the end of the couch, her feet resting in his lap. He had a hand on the back of her ankles and was absently rubbing her bad leg. His face was a carefully controlled blank.

"Hey," she said.

"Hey." He rubbed a hand over her knee. "Is it feeling better?"

"A little more every day."

He nodded, but he didn't say anything more. Ben had

turned the lights in the loft down, but the dreamlike quality of waking was giving way to a clearer mind. She had seen Tenzin floating in the air. Floating like she was held up by strings. But there were no strings in the apartment.

Ben had not been shocked. He'd been angry. Chloe had seen teeth that came straight from a horror movie. Long curving teeth in the mouth of a woman of who didn't seem to age.

And somehow she knew. Maybe it was from the look on Ben's face. Maybe it was from a flash on the edge of her peripheral vision or the flutter in her belly when Tenzin stared at her too long.

None of this was a movie. None of this was a dream.

Chloe battled through the queasy feeling in the pit of her stomach. She'd never seen Ben more nervous.

"Do you know I still get stage fright?" she blurted out.

"Really?" Ben's voice was barely above a whisper.

"Really. Every time."

"You never look scared."

"It's an odd feeling. Not like real fear. There's excitement mixed in. I'm scared and excited."

"That makes sense." He was still rubbing her knee.

"You know, the first time I felt that, I was six years old. I was with my class and we were performing the swan dance from *Carnival of the Animals* by Saint-Saëns. Do you know that one?"

"I think so. Cello?"

"Yeah. I remember..." She felt the same pressure in her chest. The quickening of her blood and the faint prickle that ran along her skin. "I remember standing behind the curtain in my shoes and tutu. And I remember thinking, 'When this curtain opens, I will be a different person. Nothing will ever be the same.'"

"Chloe—"

"I was scared, but I was excited too." She looked at Ben until he met her eyes. "I have the same feeling now."

He opened his mouth, but nothing came out. Chloe had never seen him so unsure. Not even with her, and he was more honest with her than he was with most people.

"I always knew you hid things, Ben," she said. "I always knew there was more."

He took a deep breath. "There's a lot more."

She nodded because she wasn't surprised. Though she couldn't wrap her mind around the whole of it, *none* of this was a surprise. Ben was one of the most extraordinary people she'd ever met. He had secrets. He'd always had secrets.

She asked, "Your uncle?"

"*Not* my uncle."

She'd known. Yes, she'd known that. "But he loves you."

Ben nodded. "He took me in when I was eleven. I was a street kid here in New York."

"Why'd he take you in?"

He swallowed hard. "He needed... another person. They can't go out during the day."

Chloe's heart was pounding, but she forced herself to nod. "Okay."

He's not crazy. Ben is not crazy. Neither am I.

"The sun part is true," he said quietly. "A lot of the stories aren't. They don't have to... to kill to eat. They do have to drink blood though. They can't go out in sunlight, but they don't all sleep during the day. Tenzin is proof of that."

"Okay." The black spots were back, but she battled through the quick spike of nausea and focused on Ben. "Tenzin doesn't look any older than she did when you were in high school."

"No. I think she's looked the same for a few thousand years now."

Chloe's stomach dipped. "Thousand?"

"That's old. Really old. Even for them."

"Okay."

"Chloe, how you doing?"

She drew in a shaky breath. "I'm not crazy."

"No." He looked her straight in the eye. "You're not crazy."

"She can fly."

"She can. Not all of them can. The thing Tenzin mentioned. Amnis? It's like an electrical current that runs beneath their skin. And with that they can control an element. Wind, like Tenzin. Water, like my aunt."

"Your aunt?"

Ben nodded. "Earth. Do you remember my Uncle Carwyn?"

"The weird priest?"

"That's the one."

Chloe put her head in her hands. "Oh my God."

"Chlo—"

"Oh. My. God." She took deep, even breaths. "How many of them are there?"

"More than a few."

"Is your whole family... like that?"

"Like vampires?"

The word hit her like a hammer, and Chloe started to laugh. And laugh.

And laugh some more. Oh, this was not good. She'd hit her breaking point, and it was coming out as laughter.

Ben got off the couch and knelt beside her. "Chloe, you're not crazy."

"I know." She had tears in her eyes. "Are there werewolves too?"

He shook his head.

"Zombies? How about demons and witches? Mermaids?"

"Don't think so."

"So you grew up with an uncle who drinks blood for dinner and... what? Makes earthquakes or something?"

"No," Ben muttered. "He's a fire vampire, actually."

"Oh, *fire!*" She laughed some more. "That seems... likely."

"It is. Not common, but it happens."

She let her head fall back, still shaking with laughter. "Okay. Why not?"

"I'm going to call my friend Gavin over," Ben said. "He's..."

"A vampire?" Just saying the word made her burst into laughter.

It wasn't funny. She knew it wasn't funny. But Chloe had this dreadful feeling that the minute she stopped laughing, she would start to cry.

Vampires existed in the world, and she'd been sharing a house with one.

CHLOE WAS STILL LAUGHING like a crazy person when Gavin arrived.

The Scotsman walked into the apartment with one eyebrow raised. "Well, laughter is better than screaming."

"I've never done this before," he said. "It's been fourteen years since I found all this stuff out. I don't remember what I'm supposed to do. What am I supposed to do? Should I give her a drink?"

"To begin with, you can calm the fuck down, ya cockwobble," Gavin muttered. "Where's Tenzin?"

Ben took a deep breath. "I asked her to leave. I was pissed at her."

"Is she the one who told your friend?"

"Yes. For purely selfish reasons."

Gavin's eyes drifted to the quietly snickering Chloe. "Has she vomited? Passed out?"

"No and yes. She passed out once, hit her head, and she's been on the couch since then. There's been a lot of laughter."

"It's a common reaction of some humans to emotional stress," Gavin said. "She probably does the same thing at funerals."

"I do!" Chloe said. "Or I want to. That's awful, isn't it? My parents used to get so mad at me."

"No, it's not awful." The corner of Gavin's mouth lifted, and he walked over to the couch where Chloe was sitting. Her legs were drawn up, and she'd wrapped her arms around them. "Hello, Chloe. My name is Gavin Wallace. Congratulations. You've just learned something rather shocking, and you're not screaming or crying, which puts you far ahead of most humans. It's very nice to meet you."

"Hi." She hiccuped. "You're Scottish. I didn't know Ben knew Scottish people."

"He knows a few."

"It's nice to meet you too, I guess. You're all so beautiful. Tenzin's pretty. His uncle is like... I don't know. A supermodel. All the girls at school talked about it. And here you are and you're a... vampire." She snorted. "And you're really handsome too. Is that part of the package? Drinking blood makes you gorgeous? Has anyone told Hollywood?"

Gavin was clearly amused. "Not part of the package, but nice-looking humans do catch the attention of vampires. We like pretty things." The corner of his mouth turned up. "So I'd be careful if I were you."

"Are you calling me pretty?"

"Pretty is an understatement."

Ben walked over to the couch. "Watch it, Gav. I didn't bring you here to—"

"I know, I know." He pulled over a chair. "So, lovely Chloe, you've just found out that vampires exist in the world. In fact, there's one sitting right in front of you. Things are not as they seem. Bad things go bump in the night." He leaned forward and said quietly, "But you already knew that, didn't you?"

Chloe's laughter died. Ben watched Gavin closely. The minute he made Chloe uncomfortable, he was out the door.

She stared back, unshaken. "You're a vampire. Are you a bad guy?"

"Debatable."

She relaxed her legs, crossing them under her on the couch. "Are you dangerous?"

He cocked his head, clearly intrigued. "A better question. Yes, I am quite dangerous. But not to you."

"So you're not going to drink my blood?"

"No."

"Can you smell it?"

"Yes. It smells delicious. A little like tart apples."

Ben glared. "Gavin."

"Fine." The vampire took another deep breath, but he pulled away from Chloe.

She said, "So I smell good, but you're not going to drink my blood?"

"Do you eat any food you come across just because it smells good? If you're hungry, do you eat without control? Or do you eat at the appropriate time and only until you're sated?"

"Until I'm... sated."

"As do I," Gavin said. "The human stomach can hold roughly a liter of liquid at its normal size. I, once being human, have the same size stomach as you do. So even at my hungriest, I'm likely to only drink around a liter of blood. Do you know how much blood a healthy human can safely give without losing consciousness?"

Her eyes were wide, transfixed on Gavin. "How much?"

"Roughly a liter and a half. So even if I was very hungry, dove, it's not likely that I'd drink enough of your blood to harm you unless I *wanted* to."

Chloe blinked. "Oh."

"Though you might want me to keep drinking from you. A vampire's bite can be—"

"Gavin!"

The Scotsman cleared his throat. "Which is not to say that all vampires are nice people who respect others. Most of us are... morally ambiguous predators at best. But then most humans are too."

Chloe said, "You have a dim view of human nature."

Ben piped up. "He owns a chain of bars."

"Well," Chloe said. "That explains it. Food service will make anyone cynical."

Ben couldn't explain the fascinated expression he saw on Gavin's face, but it made him wary.

Not on your life, bloodsucker. She is not for you.

Chloe's eyes kept straying to Gavin's mouth as they spoke.

Gavin leaned forward. "Do you want to see them?"

Chloe's cheeks reddened. "Sorry, is that rude?"

Ben rolled his eyes. Most vampires loved showing off their fangs. They preened like peacocks. Gavin was no different. He smiled widely, flicking his tongue over the edge of one fang as his canines grew long in his mouth. All vampires had sharper-than-normal canine teeth, but most of them weren't extended unless the vampire was hungry, horny, or just showing off. Tenzin was the only vampire Ben knew of who couldn't make her fangs retract.

"Oh wow." Chloe cocked her head. "Are they..." She lifted her hand.

"Don't!" Ben snapped.

She drew her hand back as if she'd been burned. "Sorry. I didn't mean to... Sorry."

"No need to apologize." Gavin glared at Ben, but Ben shook his head firmly.

Touching a vampire's fangs was intimate. Ben knew they were highly sensitive. Chloe touching Gavin's fangs was roughly equivalent to copping a feel, something Ben knew Chloe wouldn't do to a strange man she'd just met.

"*Cavete*," Ben snapped in Latin. *Careful. She's not yours.*

Gavin's pale cheeks were ruddy when he sat back in the chair. He ignored Ben and lifted a hand to stir the air, making Chloe's curls bounce in the breeze he created.

"What are you doing?" she said with a smile.

"I'm a wind vampire. I'm playing with the air."

"That's so strange. It feels just like the wind but... more."

Because Gavin was using amnis. So the wind that brushed across Chloe's face was as tangible to Gavin as it was to her. He might as well have been caressing her skin with his fingertips. Ben glared at Gavin until the vampire caught his expression and the wind in the apartment died down.

"That was cool," Chloe said. "Can you fly like Tenzin?"

"I can."

"How old are you?"

"Don't ask that." Gavin cleared his throat and stood. "We can be touchy about our age because we don't like revealing weaknesses, and younger vampires tend to be weaker."

She nodded. Ben noticed with some relief that her laughter had died down and whatever spell Chloe had woven over Gavin was broken. The vampire walked to stand at the bar next to Ben and pulled out a card from his wallet.

"Chloe, it was a pleasure to meet you, but I need to go." He handed the card to Ben and said under his breath, "Have her call me about the job."

ELIZABETH HUNTER

Ben shook his head, more convinced than ever to keep Chloe far away from the vampire world.

"If you don't tell her, I will," Gavin muttered.

"Tell me what?" Chloe stood up.

"Nothing," Ben said as Gavin glared. "Thanks for the calm and measured explanation, old man."

"You're quite welcome, young Benjamin." Gavin flicked Ben's collar. "Do see to the matter I mentioned."

"I'll talk to Tenzin."

"She's not a child." Gavin turned to Chloe. "Chloe Reardon, it was a pleasure making your acquaintance. I look forward to our next meeting." With a nod, Gavin left, leaving Chloe staring at the door behind him.

"Are they all so..." The dreamy expression was back.

Ben cleared his throat. "What?"

"Um... I don't know." She shook her head. "Charismatic, I guess."

"Is Tenzin?"

"No." Chloe squinted. "Yes? There *is* something about her."

"Yeah, I know what you mean."

"I still have about a million questions."

"I know." He threw his arm around her shoulders and swiped Gavin's card to hide in his pocket. "Don't worry. I can answer most of your questions, and I don't have any fangs to distract you."

"That's... probably a good thing."

12

Ben could hear Mozart's Mass in C Minor in the background when he called his uncle's home in Los Angeles.

"How is my favorite nephew?" His aunt Beatrice answered the phone with a laugh in the back of her voice. "Your uncle is driving me crazy."

He smiled. She might have been named for Dante's muse, but his aunt looked like a cross between a Latina goth and a London punk with musical tastes to match. "Classical music rocking the house?"

"He's turned Mozart up to eleven, Ben."

Ben closed his eyes and couldn't stop the smile as he imagined his uncle darting like a madman around the library that took up most of the second floor of their mansion in Pasadena. "He must be on a new project."

She sighed. "We were hired to track down a rare book of hymns illuminated by a monk known for the naughty pictures he drew in the margins. It was supposedly destroyed in Ireland under Cromwell, but recent rumors have put it in Belgium."

"Everything Giovanni loves. Manuscripts, music, monks, fire, and naughty pictures."

Beatrice laughed. "Did you need to talk to him about something or were you calling to visit with your coolest aunt?"

The barb found its mark, and Ben winced a little. "To talk to you, of course."

"Liar," Beatrice said. "We haven't seen you in months."

"I know, I know." His aunt knew Chloe. In fact, Beatrice probably remembered Chloe better than Giovanni did. "There was something I needed to tell you."

"What's up?"

"Do you remember Chloe?"

"Chloe?" Her voice warmed. "Of course I remember Chloe. Did you find her? Is she still in New York? Is she dancing and living some marvelous, amazing life?"

Ben smiled. Trust his aunt to remember the important stuff. "Yeah, I found her. And yes, she's still dancing, but not full time. She had a knee injury. And... some trouble with a boyfriend."

All humor fled Beatrice's voice. "What was that?"

"I'm taking care of the boyfriend. Who is an ex now, by the way."

Beatrice was silent for a long time.

"She's fine now, B. She's going to be fine."

"How bad was it?"

Ben wavered between spilling his guts to his aunt and honoring Chloe's confidence. "It was bad. But we're taking care of it."

"Is Tenzin aware of what's going on?"

"Yeah."

"Okay." Beatrice let out a breath. "Is this what you need to talk to Gio about?"

"Kind of..."

"I'm not even going to try to guess what's behind that voice. I'll pull him away from his books."

"B?"

"Yeah?"

"Love you the most," he said quietly. She might have only looked a few years older than him since she'd turned into an immortal, but Beatrice was the closest thing he had to a mother. A real mother, not the woman who'd given birth to him.

She sniffed. "Love you too, Ben. I'm proud of you for taking care of Chloe."

"I should have—"

"Should-haves are ridiculous," she said. "Don't carry the world on your shoulders. That's not your job. Come see us soon. Bring Chloe. You know she's always welcome here."

"Thanks." He waited on the line and listened for the muttering that was his uncle being forced to the phone.

Like his aunt, his uncle was a mess of contradictions. He was an immortal legend who wanted to remain anonymous. A fire vampire descended from the ancient powers in the Mediterranean world who chose to live in the Americas. A five-hundred-year-old assassin who liked books more than killing and music more than the cries of his enemies. A cranky old man who looked like he belonged in an Italian fashion spread.

"You need to come visit your aunt, Benjamin." Giovanni's voice bit through Ben's musing. "She hasn't seen you in months."

Ben smiled. "I miss you too."

Giovanni wasn't the most sentimental man in the world. He was exacting, stubborn, egotistical, high-handed...

And he loved Ben fiercely.

"What's wrong?" his uncle asked. "Beatrice mentioned Chloe. I always liked that girl. Is she in trouble?"

"Nothing I can't handle," Ben said. "But she's been staying here for a while. And Tenzin took a liking to her. And..."

Giovanni uttered a Roman curse. "She told her, didn't she?"

"She claimed it was inevitable and Chloe would find out about vampires anyway, but—"

"She didn't ask you or Chloe, did she? She just assumed that Chloe knowing about our kind was the best course of action." Giovanni sighed. "How is Chloe? Do we need to attempt a memory— What am I saying? Tenzin would just tell her again."

"That's what I thought too. Chloe's doing pretty well. I put her to bed a couple of hours ago and she went right to sleep. I'm pretty pissed at Tenzin though."

"I don't blame you."

"I kicked her out of the apartment and called Gavin over."

"Gavin?"

"I figured dry sarcasm would go over better than manic glee."

Giovanni said, "That's a fair point. Do you trust Gavin?"

"To an extent. He was already aware of Chloe because of... something else. And he's independent of the O'Briens, so he has no reason to share information with them. Speaking of the O'Briens..."

"Ah." Giovanni must have clued in to the reason Ben was calling. "Chloe needs to be put under aegis."

"You know Tenzin won't do it."

"I'm tempted to push the point since Tenzin's the one who told her, but I know it's an exercise in futility. I'm happy to put Chloe under my protection, Ben. She's a wonderful girl. I don't suppose you and she have reunited in more meaningful ways, have you?"

"Sorry, no."

"An uncle can hope."

"What do I tell the O'Briens?"

"You tell them nothing," Giovanni said. "I'll contact Cormac and let him know you've hired an old friend who is under my aegis. I'll tell him she's a friend of the family and we needed another day person for the business. He won't put up a fuss unless she's acquired some kind of reputation in the human world."

"Anonymous twentysomething trying to make a go of it. Two jobs. Nothing high profile."

"Keep it that way. Notoriety isn't recommended. She will need to work with you in some capacity though."

A troubling thought reared its head. "Okay, but... are you saying she can't dance anymore? I mean, she's not super famous or anything, but she does dance professionally, and I don't want her to lose—"

"Is she going to become a prima ballerina?" Giovanni asked. "Profile in newspapers? Face on television?"

"Not likely."

"Then she's fine." Giovanni sighed. "Americans are profoundly ignorant of the arts. In this case, it will work to Chloe's advantage. What about you? Any jobs on the horizon?"

Ben smiled. "Well, there is this one thing. It's not a job, per se, but it looks interesting."

"It's too early for you to be doing pro bono work, Benjamin."

Ben bared his teeth at the phone. "Did Tenzin tell you something?"

"No, but I know you. Is there a damsel involved?"

"There's a painting involved," Ben said. "That's the main point. It's by a surrealist, Emil Samson. There's a trilogy of paintings, and the middle one has been missing since World War II. And... yes. There's a girl, but she's related to the artist and she didn't ask—"

"Let me get this straight," Giovanni said. "There's a missing piece of modern art. Part of a set."

"The middle painting in the trilogy. It's called the Labyrinth Trilogy and—"

"And there's a girl who needs your help."

Ben tapped a pen on the notepad by the phone. "Yeah."

Giovanni started to laugh.

Ben said, "It's not like we have anything going on right now. So taking time out to help Emilie isn't going to hurt anything."

"Emilie. She's French? Does she have an accent?"

Ben muttered, "Kind of."

Giovanni started laughing again.

"You can stop," Ben said. "Anytime now."

"It pushes every single button for you, doesn't it? Missing painting. Missing third out of a *set*. Pretty girl with an accent. I'm never going to convince you to drop this."

"She didn't ask for my help."

"Of course she didn't," Giovanni said. "Ben, you do have a type."

"Of woman? Hardly." He loved all women. Every single one of them.

"No, of job. Valuable art with a mystery attached? You can't resist."

Ben smiled. "I hate being bored."

"I know." Giovanni calmed down. "Emil Samson, you said?"

"Heard of him?"

"I've heard... something. I'll try to remember, but the name sounds familiar. It was recent."

"How about Historic New York? Does that ring any bells?"

"No. Have you spoken to Cormac or his daughter?"

"I don't want them to know I'm poking around. They have their own interests in the art world. Cormac's brother Ennis likes to pretend he's some kind of patron and collector, and Ennis is a pain in the ass. This doesn't need to have anything to do with them."

"Fair enough." Giovanni went silent for a moment. "Have you spoken to Caspar?"

"No."

Giovanni's butler still lived with Giovanni and Beatrice. He was married to Beatrice's grandmother, but both were retired.

"Caspar knows far more about the art world than I do. And he knows quite a lot about that era and work that went missing then. If you run into a wall doing research, try calling him."

"Will do."

"I need to go," Giovanni said. "I'll keep an ear out for any mention of that artist and let Beatrice know as well. And I'll call Cormac tomorrow night."

"Thanks."

"Settle things with Tenzin," Giovanni said. "She's cranky when the two of you fight. I don't want to get dragged into this."

"She's your friend."

"And she's your... partner. Or whatever the two of you are calling each other lately. Settle it, Ben. You won't be happy until you do."

And with that warning, the line went silent.

TENZIN FLEW BACK to the apartment and landed on the roof. Dawn was only an hour away, and she needed to get inside, but she hoped Ben was asleep. She didn't want to deal with his self-righteous anger at the moment.

But when she flew up to her loft, he was there, lounging on her floor pillows with his eyes closed.

"That ladder is turning into firewood as soon as possible," Tenzin muttered.

Ben's eyes opened. "Don't be cranky."

"I'm not the cranky one."

He let out a sleepy sigh and stretched his arm out. "You were gone a long time. Come here."

She settled next to him but didn't lie down. She didn't need to sleep, so she had no bed in her loft. She did have a pallet and large pillows to make meditation more comfortable. Ben was taking up most of the space with his excessively long limbs.

"I was mad earlier," he said.

"Yes, I may have sensed that with my superhuman powers of deduction."

"Don't start with me." He sounded more awake. "You were selfish. You were probably right too. But you were still thinking of yourself, Tenzin. Don't try to make this about me."

"Chloe is an excellent addition to your people."

"Did you stop to think—even for a minute—whether she wanted to be one of 'my people'? Or were you too excited to tell her?"

Tenzin turned to him. "Do you regret knowing?"

"About vampires? I didn't have a choice, Tenzin."

"Yes, you did. Giovanni wouldn't have forced you. You were a child. If you'd asked him to take you back to where he found you, he would have. He would have wiped your memory and you would have lived in ignorance."

Ben was silent.

"You know I'm right."

"I didn't have many choices then, Tenzin."

"But you do now. And every single time, you've chosen to be involved in our world. *Your* world. You could have stayed in LA and worked for Matt in human security. You could have gotten a job in business or in the government. You had the connections to do both. You chose to stay. You chose to live in the middle of it instead of staying on the edges."

His mouth was set in a line. "What are you trying to say?"

She turned and leaned over him, her face inches from his.

"You complain about your uncle being stubborn, arrogant, and high-handed, but you are *exactly* like him. You decided Chloe didn't need to know about us. You didn't consider her either. You decided, and that was that. You knew better than she did."

Ben gripped the back of her neck and pulled her face back, propping himself on one elbow to meet her glare. "I did know better. She didn't need to know."

"Maybe she wanted to. Did you ever consider that?"

His hand tightened in her hair, but he said nothing.

"She was with you, Ben. For years. You were never shallow or simple. Neither was she. What do you think she saw in you? The pretty face or the dark edges?"

"You didn't consider what knowing about the immortal world would mean for her life," he said in a low voice.

"And you didn't consider what ignorance would mean for her either." His hand relaxed in her hair. If anyone else had pulled her hair, they would be bleeding. But it was Ben. "Chloe will be fine. She has the information she needs now. She can be as involved as she wants to be, and she's under our official protection now. I'm assuming you already called Gio?"

Ben released her and lay back on the pillow. "Yes."

"Good." She lay next to him and put her head on his outstretched arm, using his bicep as a pillow. He was so warm and comfortable when he wasn't being overbearing. "I like Chloe."

"I know you do." He yawned. "I like her too."

"She'll be an excellent day person."

"She gets to decide, Tenzin. We'll have to pay her something because she's under Gio's aegis. But I'm not forcing her to stay if she wants to go."

"There's room to build another bedroom downstairs. I'll call the contractor in the morning."

"Tiny..." He drifted off, and she could tell he was falling asleep. "Gavin... he likes her."

Hmm. "That's interesting."

"It's not interesting. It's dangerous."

"Again with the you knowing what she wants instead of letting her decide."

He closed his eyes. "Don't care. She's not working for him."

"Did he offer her a job?" Tenzin smiled. That was *very* interesting.

Ben nodded. "Left a card."

She'd have to find it and give it to Chloe. Ben was being imperious again.

"Sleep," she said. "You can stay up here. I won't destroy the ladder until tomorrow." He'd been sleeping on that futon in the training area, and she knew it wasn't big enough for him. He really did have excessively long limbs.

Ben's hand went to her hair, playing with one of the braids she'd woven behind her ear. "Don't like it when we fight."

"But we do it so often," she whispered.

"You like it."

She did. "Sleep." Tenzin put her hand on Ben's chest and felt his breath moving in and out. "I'll keep an eye on Chloe."

BEN WAS STILL SLEEPING when Tenzin heard Chloe stir. She waited until the human walked up the stairs before she flew out of the loft. Chloe was already looking up.

"Wasn't a dream," Chloe said. "Got it."

"Ben's sleeping." She nodded to the loft. "Did you want breakfast?"

"Okay?"

"Was that a question?" Tenzin landed in the kitchen and

opened the refrigerator. "I can make you some eggs with tomatoes."

"That sounds good." Chloe sat at the counter, staring at Tenzin.

"I have cooked for you before."

"And you've eaten," Chloe said. "That's a little confusing."

"Ah." Tenzin nodded. "That's a fair point. Vampires do eat a little bit. Our stomachs like to have something other than just liquid in them. We can survive on blood alone, but food fills us up. And it tastes good. We still enjoy the sensual aspects of life, as humans do."

Chloe nodded. "*All* the sensual aspects?"

Tenzin smiled, and for once, she didn't have to hide her teeth. "Yes. *All.* Our senses are stronger than human senses—because of amnis, probably—so most of those sensual experiences we enjoy more than humans do, as long as they're the pleasant ones. We have sexual intercourse, though we can't produce children. We eat. Most of us sleep."

"But you don't. Ben told me you don't sleep."

"I wish I could, but I can't."

"Why can't you?"

"I don't know. It's related to my blood."

"Huh."

Tenzin could see the wheels turning in Chloe's mind.

"What is it?" Tenzin asked. "Just ask. If I don't want to answer, I won't."

"Do vampires need to pee?"

Tenzin burst into laughter, and Chloe's cheeks turned red.

"Sorry," she said. "That's none of my business."

"No," Tenzin said. "I'm sure so many humans wonder, but they don't ask. The answer is yes, but not very often. Our systems are very slow. That's why my hair grows slowly. My fingernails grow slowly."

Chloe cocked her head. "About your hair."

Tenzin poured the beaten eggs into the heated frying pan. "What about my hair?"

Chloe just shook her head. "You need help."

"I trimmed it a few months ago."

"I can tell. You have gorgeous hair, but you need it cut properly."

She frowned. "I don't—"

"That friend I mentioned a while ago? She's moved to a salon that's also a bar. They're open at night. I'll call her about fitting us in this week."

Tenzin was growing nervous. "Why?"

"Because you're beautiful, and your hair should be too." Chloe grabbed a notebook that was sitting on the counter. "I'll call her. Now, Ben said something about a job while he was hustling me to bed last night."

Tenzin found the card she'd retrieved from Ben's pocket and tossed it toward Chloe. "Gavin offered you a job, but we'll need you to work for us too. At least part of the time."

Chloe nodded and picked up the card. "Is this because I know about the vampire stuff?"

"Yes, but I think Gavin offered you a job previously."

"What?" Chloe looked at Gavin's card. "Why?"

"You can be my assistant," Tenzin said. "That will work out nicely."

Chloe tapped Gavin's card on the counter, then slid it in her pocket.

Good girl. Save your questions for Ben and Gavin.

"Okay," Chloe said, "about being your assistant... I'm not going to argue because I got fired from my last job and I need the money, but will I have time to dance too?"

"I'm likely to be a far more flexible employer than any human. If I need help with something, you help me. If I don't, your schedule is your own. If we need to adjust things, we will."

"Sounds fair." Chloe tapped a pencil against her lower lip. "I don't suppose I'll have medical insurance, will I?"

Tenzin frowned. "Of course you will. Giovanni keeps it for all his human employees, and technically we're an offshoot of his business."

"Oh my God, seriously?"

Tenzin didn't know why Chloe find that so exciting, but then Tenzin healed with an extra pint of blood. "I would recommend using Dr. Singh, however, for anything work related. He knows about immortals and won't ask inconvenient questions."

"Dr. Singh knows about vampires?"

"Of course. Also," Tenzin said, "if you're going to keep living here, we'll need to make some adjustments to the loft."

"*Am* I going to keep living here?"

"Do you want to?"

"I don't want to keep taking Ben's room. He's too tall for that futon no matter what he says. Maybe we can put up some dividers to create another room. Something like that."

Tenzin sighed. "See? This is why we need a day person. I have an excellent relationship with Cara, but it's just not the same thing."

Chloe narrowed her eyes. "Isn't Cara the voice-command program that runs the communications for the house?"

"Yes. She's great, but it's just not the same as having a human."

"Ooookay then." Chloe made a note on the notepad. "What would you like me to do?"

"Ask Cara for a listing of contractors." Tenzin stirred the eggs and added the tomatoes when they were almost finished. They were excellent tomatoes. She grew them on the roof garden. "Ben used one to do interior work already. We'll need to add another bedroom downstairs. Do you mind sharing a bathroom?"

"As long as Ben doesn't."

"He does bring dates home occasionally. Not often, but is that going to be a problem?"

Chloe waved a hand. "Been there. Done that. Don't need a T-shirt."

"Excellent." Tenzin slid Chloe's eggs onto a plate and across the counter.

"I do have one more question for you," Chloe said.

"Which is...?"

"All these weapons around the house." Chloe picked up a fork. "They're not for display, are they?"

"No. Does that bother you?"

"Only if you're not willing to teach me how to fight."

Tenzin reached over and stabbed a tomato. "This is going to work out perfectly."

13

"This is going to drive me crazy," Ben said, slamming back the scotch Gavin poured for him. "They're ganging up on me now. In my own house."

Gavin pursed his lips. "I'd be happy to take Chloe off your hands. It's the least I can do for a friend."

"You need to stop with the Chloe thing."

"Says who?" he muttered. "What are they doing?"

"Construction."

"Ah." Gavin refilled his glass. "That's enough to drive any man to drink."

"And Tenzin said I need to bring Chloe in on the painting job."

"Are you going to bring *me* in on the painting job? I did obtain those gala invitations for you; I ought to know what illicit activities I'm supporting. You're welcome, by the way."

"Yeah, how did you—?"

"I sponsored a table for the gala. I'm a benefactor of the arts now. They'll be asking me for charitable contributions for the next two hundred years." Gavin tasted his scotch. Added a little water. "I was allowed to invite seven other people. You and Tenzin are two. Chloe will be the third."

"She doesn't need to—"

"Yes." Gavin set his glass down on the bar. "She does."

Ben grew silent. "Are we going to have a problem about this, Gav?"

"She's not yours, Ben. You need to stop treating her as such."

"She's not yours either."

Gavin picked up his drink and sipped it. "A beautiful girl who likes to dance deserves a night at a gala where she can wear a gown and be treated like a queen. You'll introduce her to much of New York's immortal society and associate her face with you, Tenzin, and your uncle's aegis, which is not a bad thing for her safety. Plus her presence will keep the focus on the new girl instead of whatever mischief you and Tenzin are up to. So yes, Ben. She needs to be at the gala."

Damn clever Scotsman. "You planned that all out very neatly, didn't you?"

Gavin smiled. "Yes, I did."

"Fine. I'm bringing Emilie, so Tenzin and Chloe can go together."

Gavin's eyes glazed over.

Ben snapped his fingers in front of Gavin's face. "Cut it out."

He blinked. "Sorry. Just enjoying a mental scenario I'll never witness. You're bringing your human girl?"

Ben ground his teeth. "Yes. I'm bringing Emilie."

Gavin shrugged. "Fine. That makes four at my table. I'll tell them to put three random humans with us so your girl won't be uncomfortable." He fiddled with a toothpick on the bar. "Do you know what color Chloe is wearing?"

"No, and it's none of your business."

"I'll ask Tenzin. So tell me about this painting and why we want it? I haven't stolen anything in too long. I'm nearly respectable now. It's boring."

"We're not stealing it," Ben said. "We're finding it and retrieving it for its rightful owner, who is the family of the artist."

Gavin grinned. "So we're self-righteous thieves this time? Excellent."

"I'm telling you. We're not..." He shook his head. "We don't know where the third painting is. Not yet. But the other two are newly displayed at the surrealist exhibit at MoMA, which was sponsored by Historic New York."

"And you have what evidence that the third exists?"

"Gut feeling."

Gavin gave him a look. "Seriously?"

"Yes, seriously. Plus I think vampires are involved. Be honest. How many pieces of art conveniently ended up in immortal hands after the Second World War?"

"I don't know." Gavin's fangs fell. "How many priceless historic artifacts and artistic masterpieces have humans destroyed with bullets and bombs over the years?"

"I'm not trying to start a fight, Gavin."

The vampire shook his head and bit back on his temper. "Fine. We'll entertain this for the time being. Are the owners noted in the listing at the museum or online?"

"Anonymous. Private collection."

"Hmm." Gavin tugged at his lip. "Could be human or vampire. I'm guessing vampire since most humans like to preen."

"My thoughts too."

Gavin frowned.

"What are you thinking?" Ben asked.

"How big are they?"

"The paintings? I'd estimate... four by six feet unframed. They're large."

"Oil on canvas?"

"Yes."

Gavin rapped his fingers on the bar. "Look for the shippers."

"The shippers?"

"Yes. Who moved the paintings to the museum? They had to come from somewhere. Was it here in the city? Overseas? Two canvases that size are going to require a large crate. Look for the shipping company."

"Good idea," Ben said. "Great idea, in fact."

"Do you know anyone at the museum? Anyone who works there?"

"No," Ben said. "But Chloe might. She has a lot of dance friends who work at theaters, museums, stuff like that."

"Ask her. And I can ask around. Are you informing the O'Briens about this?"

"And risk them looking too closely? It's none of their business. From what I can tell, if Ennis O'Brien gets a hint of anything related to valuable art in this city, he'll stick his nose where it doesn't belong. No thank you."

Gavin chuckled. "You do like playing dangerously, don't you?" He clinked his glass against Ben's. "Watch out, young Vecchio. You're getting more and more like your partner every day."

CHLOE WAS STRETCHING out her legs when the front door opened upstairs. The minute she heard steps on the stairs, she knew it was Ben. He was heavier than Tenzin and made way more noise. Hell, now that Tenzin wasn't hiding her ability to fly, she snuck up on Chloe more often than not.

The lower floor of the loft was more training area than residence. One bedroom and a large bathroom had been built at the far end, and carpenters were framing out a second room for her in the other corner. The rest of the loft was taken up with mats, mirrors, and row upon row of weapons.

There was no sun shining through the high windows. There never was. They'd all been blacked out. From the hands on the clock, Chloe knew it was nighttime. An hour earlier, Tenzin had disappeared into the sky, and Chloe started practicing basic stretches and routine exercises to strengthen her knee.

"Hey," Ben said from the bottom of the stairs. "Can I join you?"

She had one leg stretched straight up toward her ear. "Are you saying you can do this too? I had no idea."

He smiled and toed off his shoes. The man was incorrigible. Far too charming for his own good.

And arrogant. And bossy.

Damn. She wasn't harboring any lingering feelings over the man, but did he have to be so appealing? It made it harder to stay mad at him. "How's your vampire friend?"

"Which one?" he asked.

"The one who's not your roommate. The one who offered me a job."

Ben groaned. "Who told you that? Please don't work for Gavin."

"Why not? I still have no idea what I'm getting paid working for Tenzin."

"She'll probably pay you a ridiculous amount of gold or something. Don't worry about money."

"Gold?"

"It's not a big deal. I can help you sell it."

"That is not reassuring." She lowered her leg. "You know, I made good money waiting tables."

"Yeah, because you're gorgeous and friendly. The same reasons you'd constantly be hit up at Gavin's pub to be a blood donor."

Her eyes went wide. "Blood donor? Tenzin didn't mention anything about that."

Ben looked slightly embarrassed. "Okay, you wouldn't have to be a donor. Gavin leaves it up to individual employees. But a lot of his servers supplement their income that way because it pays well."

"How well?" Wait, had she asked that? Chloe shook her head. "Ben, whether I take the job at your friend's place or not, the point is, you shouldn't have tried to hide it from me. You're not my dad."

"No, I'm not. Your dad is an overbearing asshole who never liked me. Also, we've had sex, so that would be wrong on many levels."

"And you're not being overbearing?" She stretched her other leg. She was barely feeling the pain in her kneecap anymore. Only at the end of a long practice session and first thing in the morning did it bother her.

Ben unbuttoned his shirt and stripped down to his undershirt. "If I'm overbearing, it's because I know this world better than you and I'm cautious. You're important to me, Chloe."

"Tom used to say that kind of stuff to me too." She winced as soon as the words left her mouth. That wasn't fair.

"Hey! Don't compare me to that asshole. I would never hit you."

"You're right." She lowered her leg. "That was over the line, and I'm sorry. But you have to admit, Ben, you're more than happy to control me. I'm sure you think it's for my own good, but—"

"It is for your own good. And before you start in on me

being sexist, I'd like to point out that I'd be just as concerned if it was a male friend in this world."

She crossed her arms. "From what I've seen, all your male friends are vampires."

"Maybe. Probably." He frowned. "Is that important?"

"I don't know," Chloe muttered, "but it seemed weird and I wanted to point it out."

He couldn't hide his smile. "Listen, this world..."

"What?"

"It's strange. And beautiful sometimes. Fascinating. Seductive. And it can be dangerous. Very, very dangerous. I know Tenzin explained all the reasons she went over my head and told you, but I had good reasons to keep you in the dark." He stood behind her and lifted her arms up, stretching her shoulders. "Good?"

"Good." It felt closer to amazing. It also gave her an idea. Ben was in great shape, but he was also tense as hell. She felt it in his shoulders every time he gave her a hug. "Have you ever done a dancing stretch routine before?"

"No. Should I?"

"It's the best stretch out there." She pulled him over to the center of the mat. "Take off your pants."

"What?" He laughed.

"You're wearing boxers or something right?" Chloe grinned. "You don't want to ruin your dress pants. Just take them off."

He unbuttoned with a flourish. "Chloe, if you wanted my pants off, all you had to do is ask."

She rolled her eyes. "Whatever, Romeo. Lie on the mat faceup, with your arms stretched out."

Chloe hopped up and went over to put on music, choosing a quiet piece by Arvo Pärt for viola and piano. Chloe couldn't remember the last time she'd seen Ben really relaxed. He worried about everything. He constantly wore a facade except for the few times she saw him talking or fighting with Tenzin. Every night he came home, she saw the weight on his shoulders grow heavier.

Time to ease up a little, Benny.

The resonant strains of the viola filled the room, and Chloe went to the center of the mat and lay next to Ben. She closed her eyes and tried to remember the routine she'd learned as a child. "Reach your right arm out, stretch as far as you can, then fold it across your body and reach for your opposite wrist." She turned her face and saw Ben following her movements. "Good. Hold it."

He held it. Then he stretched wide again and repeated the movement with the opposite arm, his eyes locked on her, following her movements.

"Bring your knees up to your chest."

He struggled with that one. His quads were probably tight.

"As far as you can," Chloe said. "We'll work up to this one." She curled into a fetal position, lying on her left side. "And stretch out…"

Ben followed each of her movements as she curled and stretched on the ground. They flipped over and pressed up, stretching hamstrings and calves. His breathing went from labored and tight to rhythmic and long.

"Right arm up. Kind of like warrior pose in yoga."

He followed her as they came to their feet, moved in sync with her as she shook out the last of the tension holding her from rest.

"Do you do this every night?" he asked as they returned to the floor and the simple stretches they'd started with.

"I try to." Chloe lifted up her right leg and flexed the toe up. "I sleep better when I do."

He let out a long breath. "Sometimes I don't sleep well."

"I think you *often* don't sleep well." She rolled over to him and smoothed a finger between his eyebrows. "You need to relax. Take care of yourself too."

Ben smiled sadly. "I used to sleep better. Before I came back here."

"Have you seen them?"

He shook his head.

Chloe knew she was one of the few people in the world who knew just how awful Ben's biological parents were. She might not have known about the vampires, but she knew about that. "Do you want to see them?"

"No." He sighed. "Yes. I don't know. Morbid curiosity."

"I get it."

"Do you want me to ask Gio about your mom and dad?"

She shrugged. "If you want to. I still talk to my aunt sometimes. I get the highlights. Or lowlights, if we're going to be accurate. They still sound like miserable people I don't want to spend my life with."

Ben reached over and tugged the end of a curl. "We're a pair, huh?"

"I get you, Ben. I always have."

"I know. I didn't tell very many people about my life. Now you finally know the whole of it."

"Maybe someone needed to," Chloe said. "Maybe that's why she did it."

Ben sat up. "Don't make her noble. I've made that mistake too many times, Chloe. Tenzin is... complicated."

Chloe sat up and wondered if Ben knew just how true that statement was.

She loved him, but he could be remarkably oblivious at times.

⁓

"For now"—Tenzin spoke to Chloe's reflection in the mirror —"we'll work on strengthening poses. Eventually we'll move up to combat training."

Chloe mirrored her position. "How long will that take?"

"Don't count the days. Focus on making your body as strong as you can. You're already in excellent shape and far above average flexibility. Focus on making your body strong. Focus on simple postures. Combat postures will flow from that."

"I don't want anyone to ever beat me up again," she said quietly. "Never." She could still feel the sting of Tom's slap on her face. Still hear the echo of her finger popping when he broke it.

"That may not be feasible," Tenzin said. "I don't know what your fate is. I can promise that you will not be defenseless. If someone hurts you, you'll be able to hurt them too."

Blunt honesty felt better than platitudes. "Fair enough."

"Good. Now I'm going to show you a posture, and I want you to hold it for a minute."

They practiced for a half an hour. It was slow. It was deliberate.

"I'm exhausted," Chloe said, slumping against a wall and drinking from a jug of water.

"Stillness can be more exhausting than movement," Tenzin said, squatting in front of her. "We'll stop here tonight."

Chloe nodded and kept drinking water. Every muscle in her body ached. "Were you a fighter?" she asked. "Did you learn this as a human?"

Tenzin laughed. "No."

"When did you learn?"

"Many years later." She turned to Chloe. "I was a victim for a long, long time. Then I wasn't."

Chloe had a feeling that Tenzin had outlived her attackers many times over. "Do you like it?"

"Not being a victim? Yes."

"No, do you like being a vampire?"

Tenzin frowned. "I don't know if anyone has ever asked me that. Do you like being human?"

"Yes." Chloe smiled. "I love sunshine and the smell of rain. I love the feeling of wind on my face. I love the sound of children at the playground."

Something Chloe had said made Tenzin blink. An instant later, she was standing by the stairs. "Come," the vampire said. "I'll make you food. The sun will be over the edge of the upstairs windows soon, and I want to cook."

Chloe followed her up the stairs. Tenzin, she'd learned, loved to cook. And she was a good cook. Chloe wondered what had set her off.

"Talk to me about your dress for the gala," Chloe said as Tenzin got out a bowl and some eggs.

Chloe had been informed the day before that she'd be going to a gala with Tenzin and Ben. Officially, it was an art fundraiser. Unofficially, it was an event heavily attended by immortal society.

That's right. Chloe was going to a vampire ball. Was she excited? Very. Was she nervous? Hell yes. She hadn't been to anything resembling an elegant party since she'd left her parents' home. And her parents' parties always filled her with dread and anxiety because she'd be surrounded by people she hated.

This party would be far, far different, but Chloe was short on evening wear and wondering if Tenzin had any suggestions.

"I'm making my dress," Tenzin said.

"But what does it look like?"

"You've seen it. I'm using the green silk."

Chloe dropped her water bottle. "Not the green thing." Oh no. No no no no.

"What?"

"Tenzin, you can't be serious."

She frowned. "What's wrong with my dress?"

"It's not really a dress. It's more like... a robe."

Tenzin shrugged. "And?"

It was probable that at some point in her very long life, the dress that Tenzin was making was perfectly acceptable evening wear. In fact, there was a certain elegance to the way the silk draped and the carefully sewn folds of fabric in the sleeves. Chloe was sure that sometime, somewhere, Tenzin's green dress would be the height of fashion.

But that place was not twenty-first-century Manhattan.

Chloe walked to her messenger bag and pulled out her notebook. "I'm calling Arnold."

"Who is Arnold?"

"He makes dance costumes and he's a genius. He can make dresses for us, but I need to call him right now. Also, you're getting your hair cut tomorrow night at ten o'clock. Do not fly away and leave me hanging. Breanna switched clients around to fit us in before the gala."

Tenzin had stopped moving.

"What?"

"You're ordering me around?" Tenzin asked. "For *dress* appointments?"

Chloe stopped writing and looked up. "I thought I was supposed to be your assistant."

"You are."

"Then yeah, Tenzin. I'm ordering you around for dress appointments. Do you want to fit in at this gala or not?"

"I don't care about fitting in."

"Fine, but..." How to frame this for a thousands-of-years-old predator? "Think of it this way. If you wear your green... dress to the gala, every person in the ballroom will be looking at you.

Do you want that?" It was just a hunch, but Chloe was guessing that Tenzin would much rather blend.

"No." Tenzin's lip curled. "I never fit in at these events. This is why I don't usually attend them. When I do go, everyone stares even if I keep my mouth closed. At my father's house, they bow. I hate the bowing."

Chloe knew she'd have to tread carefully. "I don't know anything about the vampire world, but I do—unfortunately—know about society. I'm guessing part of the attention you get at events is unavoidable." *Like the bowing. What was that about?* "You are a really powerful vampire, right?"

Tenzin nodded.

"But part of that you could probably avoid if you just looked more..."

Tenzin raised an eyebrow. "More what?"

"Modern." Chloe walked over carefully. "Style your hair." She lifted thick strands from Tenzin's shoulders. "You have, like, the world's most gorgeous neck. If you wore your hair shorter, you'd show it off."

Tenzin frowned, but she didn't injure Chloe, which Chloe took as a positive sign. "And if you wear clothes that are more modern—things that would blend in at a gala like this—you'd be *beautiful*, but not particularly noticeable. Do you know what I mean?"

Tenzin nodded slowly. "You're talking about field-appropriate camouflage."

Chloe blinked. "Uh... yeah. I guess I am."

Tenzin continued to nod. "You are modern. And stylish for this era."

"I like to think so."

"Therefore, you can teach me about appropriate social dressing as camouflage. Help me to perfect my human mask for this era."

Chloe said, "Something like that, yeah."

"I approve of this." Tenzin patted Chloe's cheek. "You are an excellent assistant. Just be aware I cannot alter my face to create large lips, though yours are very lovely and fit your face well. But vampires cannot have facial surgery."

"Okay?" *What just happened?* "You don't need plastic surgery," Chloe said. "Please ignore anyone who tells you that. You're already gorgeous."

"Thank you. Will I need to wear cosmetics for my disguise?"

Chloe examined Tenzin's pale face. It was very, very pale. "We probably want to add a little color. Breanna can help us out with that too."

Tenzin smiled. "You have an excellent team. I knew making you my assistant would work out well. If these are long-term associates, I'll pay them. Otherwise we can use their skills for this job, and I'll wipe their memory afterward."

Chloe cleared her throat and tried not to laugh. "These are long-term associates. We should probably pay them and not wipe their memory."

"Good thinking. There's no telling how many of these events Ben will force on me."

14

"A gala?" Emilie's smile was incandescent. "Really?"

"A summer gala to benefit Historic New York," he said. "The sponsors of the surrealist exhibit, remember?"

"Of course I remember," she said. "Ben, this is wonderful. Do you think someone who works there would know about *Midnight Labyrinth*? Know anything about Emil's work?"

"They have to know something. They included the two other paintings in the exhibit, didn't they?" He speared a raspberry and offered it to her. "I'm looking into a couple of other leads, but this might give us a much better idea of where we should be looking."

"If nothing else, we might eliminate some possibilities, right? So we're not wasting time?"

"Exactly."

She leaned over and kissed him, letting her lips linger. They'd come to Gavin's bar for a couple of reasons. One, Emilie had heard Ben mention his friend's pub. And two, Ben wanted to stake his claim on her before the gala. He wasn't a vampire, but he was well-known enough that most immortals would respect a human he marked as his own.

"So tell me." She played with his collar. "Will you be in a tuxedo for this gala?"

"Of course." His fingers slid from her shoulder down her back, lingering at the curve of her waist. "Will you be wearing a slinky dress?"

"Should I?"

"Definitely." He ran his nose along the delicate shell of her ear. She smelled like roses that night. "A very small, very slinky dress."

She laughed lightly. "Not too small, I think. We don't want to scandalize the proper people."

Or advertise his date. "Tenzin and Chloe will be coming along too. I hope you don't mind."

"Of course not. Are they dating?"

Ben almost spit out his drink. "Tenzin and Chloe?"

"What?" She smiled. "Sorry, did I get that wrong?"

Ben laughed. "Chloe is my ex-girlfriend from high school. And Tenzin is... Tenzin. No, they're not dating. But they are working with me to find *Midnight Labyrinth*. So Gavin was able to get them tickets too." He glanced across the bar. "Speaking of Gavin, we should say hi."

He nodded at the vampire who was holding court with two other immortals on the opposite side of the bar. One was an enforcer Ben recognized. He belonged to the O'Briens but didn't look like he was working. The other was a dark-haired woman with ruby-red lips, wearing a black veil—an honest-to-goodness veil—and a vintage-looking dress.

Ben didn't recognize her, but she moved a little too fast to be human. She was good, but he was guessing she'd been out of human company for a while. One of Gavin's servers sidled next to her and leaned down, letting the vampire sniff his neck before he led her to one of the private rooms.

Gavin wandered over, looking Emilie up and down with an

appreciative glance. "Benjamin," he said, letting Scottish brogue flow. "Good to see you. This must be the lovely fashion designer I've heard too much about. Evelyn?"

"Emilie." She held out her hand and Gavin took it in his.

"My apologies." He bent over her hand before he released it. "It's very nice to meet you, Emilie. I hope you've found my pub a friendly place."

"It's perfect," she said. "The music makes it private, but it's not too loud to talk."

"You've learned my secret to keeping people drinking here."

"I promise I won't tell."

Gavin's eyes twinkled. "I like her." He glanced at Ben from the corner of his eye. "Any news regarding the lead we spoke of?"

Ben shook his head.

"Very well. I have one other line I might tug, if you'd like me to."

"That might be a good idea." Ben played his hand along Emilie's neck. He loved how smooth her skin was. She'd undercut her hair, and her trimmed nape felt like velvet. "I'll call you later, shall I?"

"Do."

"Can you join us?" Emilie asked. "Ben tells me you're the one who found the tickets for us to the gala."

"Found?" Gavin raised an eyebrow at Ben. "Oh yes. They tumbled into my lap."

Ben asked, "Did you want me to share details?"

"That's quite all right."

Emilie asked, "Can we buy you a drink for being so generous?"

He smiled. "No, love. This hardworking publican has other guests to greet before he can turn in tonight." Gavin held her eyes. "But I believe we'll be sharing a table on

Friday, so if you'll save a dance for me, I'd consider my favor repaid."

Emilie's smile sparkled. "Of course. As many dances as you like."

"*Not* as many as he'd like," Ben said quickly. "I don't share that well."

"I'm afraid I have a few ladies waiting," Gavin said with a wink in Emilie's direction. "So I won't be able to monopolize your evening."

"Sounds good to me," Ben said.

"Vecchio, do say hello to the lovely Chloe, will you?" Gavin asked, straightening a cuff. "I'm saving my first dance for her."

Ben flipped him off as Gavin walked away with a smile.

Emilie looked between them, confused. "Is your friend interested in Chloe?"

"He knows it annoys me."

"But why?" Emilie asked. "He seems lovely. He has nice manners. Does she like him?"

"She doesn't know him," Ben said. "Or... not the real him. Gavin is fine, but he's got a few rough edges."

"And you don't?" Emilie gave him a reproachful smile. "How many of us know—really know—the person we fall for? That's part of the fun, isn't it? The mystery? The discovery? If you knew someone completely, I bet you'd lose interest."

"Do you think so?" He slid a hand around her waist and tugged her closer. "Are you saying I'm a mystery?"

"Of course." She leaned into him, running her fingers over his chest. "Aren't I? If you've already figured me out, I'm not doing my job very well, am I?"

Ben's hand slid down to cup her bottom. "I think there are still a few layers to tease me."

"Oh?" She lifted her chin. "Tease away. I think you're up for the challenge."

~

SHE WAS IN HELL. A hell designed by the devil's minion. This particular minion wore black glasses, black jeans, and bright purple hair spiked high on his head.

"I can't work like this." The minion pursed his lips. "Make her stop moving."

Tenzin barely managed to contain a growl before Chloe slapped a hand over her mouth. "Tenzin, the faster you quit wiggling, the faster this will be over."

She bared her fangs and let them scrape over Chloe's hand. The human yelped and pulled her hand away.

"Don't you dare," Chloe hissed. "Stop being a brat."

"He's poked me with pins three times. This dress is too tight."

"It is not, and Arthur poked you because you keep wiggling."

"I'm wiggling because he keeps poking me with pins!"

The door swung open, and Tenzin turned toward it.

"Stop moving!" the devil's minion yelled.

"Roast in hell!" Tenzin snapped. "Save me, Ben."

Ben had been leafing through the mail, but he stopped, grabbed his phone, and held it up. She heard the telltale click of his camera before she could escape.

"I don't know what's going on, but I'm sending that to Gio," he said.

"Traitor!"

"Uh-huh." He looked back at the mail. "Hey, Chloe. Who's that?"

"Hey, yourself," Chloe said. "Ben, this is Arthur, the miracle worker who's making our dresses in three days. Arthur, this is Ben."

"Arthur." Ben walked over and offered a fist to Arthur.

"Nice to have another guy around. I'm usually outnumbered."

Arthur bumped Ben's knuckles before he tugged Tenzin back to face him. "Stop. Moving. Or I will make you bleed."

Ben said, "Chloe, you wanted me to look at something downstairs?"

"Plans for the bathroom. Give me a minute."

The two humans went downstairs as Tenzin glared at her tormenter. Despite how annoying he was, she had to admire the human's single-minded focus. She submitted to the manhandling so she could get the costume fitting finished.

"I usually make my own clothes," she muttered.

"So Chloe said. What do you make? I'm assuming not formal wear."

"Not from this century."

"Formal wear is a very particular animal," he muttered through the pins in his mouth. "Though I have to say, you have a couturier's dream in this place. These fabrics are insane." Arthur glanced at the bolts and stacks of fabric behind them. He'd been delighted when Chloe told him he could work with any of it he wanted. He'd chosen an amethyst brocade with a chrysanthemum pattern for Tenzin, but he was pinning pattern paper to her at the moment.

"I make practical things," Tenzin said. "Fighting clothes."

Arthur stood and cocked his head. "Really?"

Tenzin nodded. "I have one coat that has room for a dozen blades."

Arthur's mouth dropped open.

"And one pair of pants that conceals a saber in the folds. It's very convenient."

"Oh my God. Are you for real?"

"Yes. Entirely."

Chloe swept into the room. "What's going on?"

Arthur pointed to Tenzin. "She has a coat with room for a dozen blades."

Chloe's eyes went wide. "Arthur, I can explain—"

"Explain that your friend is a complete badass?" He started pinning again. "Holy shit, Chloe, now I want to see how many daggers I can fit up in this evening gown."

"I will give you a bonus for each dagger you make a sheath for," Tenzin said. "Five times that bonus amount if you can fit a saber."

Chloe opened her mouth, but Arthur raised his hand before she could speak. Staring straight at Tenzin, he said, "This is some serious superhero shit, my friend. And I now consider it a personal challenge. I'm going to pretend I'm making this for cosplay and not ask any questions. How does that suit you?"

"Sounds to me like you've already earned your first bonus." Tenzin smiled at Chloe as Arthur went back to work. "I approve of this tailor."

"I'm so glad."

"I just had the best idea." Arthur went back to his sketch book on the table. "Tenzin, which arm do you hold a sword with?"

"Both. But I favor my right. And if you should share that information, it would not be to your benefit, young tailor."

"Right. Like I'm going to be sharing all this on Instagram." He started scribbling and wandered away as Tenzin stood stockstill on the platform Arthur had brought to work.

Chloe said, "Oh, now you're being patient?"

"He's going to add dagger sheaths to the dress. I can stand still for that."

"Good to know your priorities are in order."

"Dagger sheaths, Chloe. In an evening dress."

"Good." She sat on the couch and pulled out her phone.

"Are you still working?" Tenzin asked.

"Yeah."

"Finish and go stretch. You didn't stretch long enough after we practiced today. If you don't stretch before bed, you'll be stiff in the morning."

"Sure thing, mom." Chloe was still checking her phone. "That plumber still hasn't emailed me back."

"Why do we need a plumber?"

"I don't mind sharing a bathroom. I do mind sharing a sink." Tenzin shuddered. "Ben leaves an awful mess when he shaves."

"Doesn't he?"

"He needs to grow his beard back."

Chloe gasped. "He'd look *great* with a beard. He had a beard?"

"I'm not sure why he shaved it. It grows quickly."

Ben walked back upstairs. "What grows quickly? What are you talking about?"

"Your beard," Chloe and Tenzin said in unison.

Arthur looked up. "What's that?"

Chloe patted her chin. "Beard, Arthur. Facial hair?"

"Oh." Arthur pursed his mouth. "Yeah, you should definitely grow one. You'd have the dark, sexy bad-boy thing going on," he said. "I mean, more than you already do now."

Ben frowned. "You're a tailor? Do you alter suits?"

"No. I'm a *designer* who's going to put half a dozen daggers in an evening dress." He held up a hand to Tenzin, who clapped it like she'd seen humans do. "I *love* this girl. If you need a tailor, call my friend Nelson. He's ancient, but he's the best."

Ben cocked his head and looked at Tenzin draped in brown pattern paper. "You can put how many... You know, I don't think I want to know. Chloe, is Arthur making your dress too?"

"Yes! Tenzin gave me some gorgeous grey silk," Chloe said. "But Arthur will be making mine without daggers."

Tenzin said, "I'd rethink that. It's going to be more difficult to add them later when you're more weapons proficient."

The tailor's eyes went wide, but he muttered "cosplay, cosplay" under his breath and went back to drawing.

Tenzin floated down from her loft hours after Arthur had gone home and Chloe finally turned in. Ben was working at the table by the bookshelves, newspaper clippings and auction catalogs scattered around him.

"Are these the things from Emilie's grandmother?"

Ben nodded. "There's some letters. Some news clippings. But nothing concrete. I did track down the Nazi officer who was in command of the village where Adele lived."

"That was the artist's sister?"

"Yes, Emilie's great-grandmother."

"And you tracked down the officer, but..."

"Nothing. He was arrested by the Allies. Put on trial. Died in a military prison. There are no reports of property recovered."

"That just means there are no reports," Tenzin said. "Not that there was no property."

"If there were reports, where would they be?"

"France." She shrugged. "Probably."

"Who do we know in France?"

"That can look for us? No one. Terry's friend killed Jean."

"He killed Jean because Jean was dealing in Elixir." Everyone who dealt in the illicit vampire drug was marked for death. Now that a cure had been found for both humans and vampires—though details on that cure were sketchy—the danger of Elixir had gone down and rounding up suppliers was the hot new trend in vampire politics. Cormac O'Brien had killed one of his own lieutenants when he found him colluding with an Elixir supplier in the Baltic.

"France." Ben tapped his pen. "It's fractured. There's no central immortal government like England."

"True. But doesn't Gavin have a bar there?"

Ben nodded. "He has one in Paris and in Cannes."

"So send him. He could ask around."

"Are we sure we want him that involved?"

"Isn't he involved already?" Tenzin asked. "Ask him after the gala. I was thinking you'd jump at the chance to put an ocean between him and Chloe."

Ben's face turned grim. "That is a good point."

"I don't know why you find him so objectionable. He's your friend."

"Yes, which means I know how he is with women. And Chloe is like my..."

"You can't say sister. That would be wrong."

"She's my *friend*." He dropped his voice. "One of my best friends. And she just got rid of the asshole. She needs someone *nice*."

Speaking of the asshole, Ben was reminded that it was time to pay another visit to old Tom. He needed to break three ribs now that Tom's knee would be mostly healed.

"It's not your job to tend to Chloe's wounds," Tenzin said. "She's a very smart girl. Though I wish she'd reconsider the dagger sheaths for her dress."

"Focus, Tenzin."

She propped her elbow on the desk. "Get Gavin to ask a few questions in France. If we're being honest, the most likely scenario is that a thief or a vampire—or a vampire thief—"

"Which Gavin is. Or used to be."

"Exactly. Chances are, a thief stole the painting and it's hidden in some collection somewhere. Or Historic New York acquired it with the others, but they're hesitant to loan it because of provenance."

"Either way," Ben said, "someone with criminal ties like Gavin would be able to find it faster."

"Exactly. If nothing else, he could find the gossip."

"We'd have to pay him."

"No," Tenzin said. "*You'd* have to pay him. This is your job, remember?"

"Fine." He closed the auction catalog he wasn't really reading. "Speaking of gossip, have you heard any lately? Local gossip, that is."

Tenzin shrugged. "Who do I talk to?"

"Cormac O'Brien."

"True." Tenzin was oddly fascinated by the O'Brien clan's leader. "We had a drink last week. I think I'm going to steal his pocket watch."

"Why?"

"Because he likes it so much." She frowned. "I know that's probably not politically wise."

"Maybe instead of stealing his pocket watch, you could steal some *information*." Ben tried his most cajoling voice.

"Information is not as shiny as a pocket watch."

"I know that. But there was a new vampire at Gavin's. He had her nickname but nothing else."

"What's her nickname?"

"The Lady of Normandy."

Tenzin rolled her eyes. "I hate it when vampires get pretentious like that. Just use your name. No one is impressed by titles anymore."

"You're full of shit, O Commander of the Altan Wind."

"Whatever you say, Master of Iron in Lothian."

Ben and Tenzin exchanged looks that turned into wry smiles.

"Fine," he said. "I'd like to point out that mine is a ceremonial title given solely because I recovered that sword in Scotland, and I don't lead with it."

"I should hope not. I'll try to discover who this very mysterious lady might be. Is there any particular reason why?"

He shook his head. "Just want to know who's hanging out in my sandbox."

"Speaking of your sandbox, have you tried calling Novia about the shipping information?"

Ben blinked. "Huh?"

"Novia O'Brien. One of the bigger kids in the sandbox. Have you tried calling her and working your Ben magic?"

"Why would she know about shipping at the Museum of Modern Art?"

"I'm assuming she does because she's Cormac's right hand in the city. It's worth a try, don't you think? If she doesn't know, then she might know who would."

He pulled her close and kissed her forehead. "This is why I keep you around. You're brilliant."

"You keep me around because I'm rich and everyone is afraid of me."

"Hey." He pulled out his mobile phone. "Your money has nothing to do with it. I have my own money. I keep you around for the fear." Ben winked and Tenzin floated back up to her loft.

Novia's number rang twice before she answered. "Give me a minute to call you back."

"No problem."

Since vampires couldn't use most technology, they were reliant on voice-command systems like Nocht, which was what Cara ran on. Nocht was convenient. It could ring you in your car or your house. Some immortals even hired humans to carry around phones for them so they had the same access that humans did. What Nocht couldn't do was give you privacy.

Ben's phone rang a few moments later.

"In my office," Novia said. "What's up, my friend?"

He did his best to sound annoyed. Not a lot annoyed. Just a little annoyed. "Sorry, I have a boring business question. Can this night be over yet?"

She laughed. "I don't know if I can help, but I'm all ears."

"I figured you might know because you and Cormac are involved in arts fund-raising, right?"

"We're already going to the gala on Friday, Ben. Sorry, but our table is full. Ennis invited a bunch of his humans. Wants to impress them."

She sounded annoyed with her uncle, but not *that* sorry about missing a seat for Ben. He tried not to be offended.

"No, no," he said. "I'm at Gavin's table for this one."

"Excellent. I'll see you there."

"But what I'm needing is a shipper. I have a very... private client. Nothing that could cause problems, mind you, but she needs to get some things to"—he desperately tried to think of a probable city in Europe—"Luxembourg." That wasn't great, but he hoped Novia wouldn't ask too many questions.

"Luxembourg?"

"I don't ask questions, Novia. I'm just the lackey this time. Doing a favor for my uncle. The items she wants to ship are rather large."

"Shipping container large?"

"Crate large. But a sizable crate. Say... five tall by seven wide?"

"And how deep?"

"Shallow. The items are fairly flat. Perhaps two feet with internal packing."

"I'm getting a clearer picture now." Novia paused, and Ben heard her riffling papers. "I have a name for you, though I'm surprised you haven't used them before in your line of work."

"The kind of antiquities we recover are usually delivered in person. They're also usually smaller than this."

"Fair enough. DePaul and Sons. Let me give you a number. They're not listed."

"Thanks, Novia."

"Fair warning. I have not used them. But I know the museum and other similar establishments have. They are known to be most discreet."

Bingo. She rattled off the number and Ben jotted it down.

"You're a lifesaver."

"You're the first human who's told me that in a while."

Ben tried not to wince. "Save the human a dance on Friday?"

"You think you can keep up with this girl, Vecchio?"

"I sure as hell want to try."

Novia laughed. "I'll see you in a few days. I know my father is hoping Tenzin will be there. What's your best guess?"

"She will be." He thought of the chaotic fitting that afternoon. "I think she even has a new dress for the occasion."

God help us all.

15

"No!" Zoots yelled at him from the top of the brick building.

Ben was sure of his footholds, so he let his left arm dangle. "What?"

His fingertips and palms were bleeding. He'd fallen four times, and his ass hurt no matter how many mattresses Zoots piled up. He was just glad he hadn't tweaked his knee on the last fall. It had been close.

Zoots stared over the edge. "You're working yourself into that same dead end. You're going to run out of holds in two more moves."

"No, I'm not." Ben pulled a screwdriver from a side pocket on his cargo pants. "Because I'm going to make one."

Zoots started laughing, but Ben was fed up.

If he couldn't find a way up the damn wall by Zoots's methods, he'd cheat.

They could judge him when he reached the top.

Ben and Tenzin walked toward DePaul and Sons later that night. Ben needed information, but he didn't want anyone knowing he was asking after that information. Therefore, he needed a vampire.

They ducked into an alley that ran behind a brownstone building in Greenwich Village and aimed for a door that wasn't marked. The front of the building advertised nothing more than the name of the business. Pedestrian art filled the windows, blocking the view inside, and a small sign written at the base of the glass door said By Appointment Only. No phone number. Definitely no website.

Ben saw a sliver of dim light coming from beneath the door along with the distant sound of jazz. He debated knocking, then decided to go for his lockpicks. In a few seconds, he had the door open and Tenzin slipped inside. He immediately pulled out a scanner and swept the area for listening devices or video surveillance. It would be unusual for a business that catered to vampires to risk angering customers like that, but he didn't take anything for granted. No one needed to know he'd been there.

"Remember," he whispered to Tenzin. "We just want some questions answered."

Tenzin rolled her eyes and disappeared down the dark hall, shutting off lights as she went to hide herself. Ben heard gusts of wind, as if a window had been left open, and papers rustled to the floor somewhere in the darkness. A thump and a scuffle. He slowly worked his way down the hall, following the music as he continued to scan. As he scanned, he examined each room with his flashlight. Tenzin could work in the dark. He couldn't.

"Come back," Tenzin said quietly. "There's only one."

They hadn't expected any more, just as Ben hadn't expected any bugs.

He followed the sound of the music and the glow of distant light to a small office where an older gentleman was sitting in a swivel chair, green glass lamp illuminating an old rolltop desk. Tenzin's hand was pressed to the back of the human's neck. DePaul had a shiny bald head and a grey mustache. On the desk in front of him lay a ledger open to neat rows of numbers. A stack of receipts, all handwritten, sat to the side. No computer. Not even a mobile phone in view.

"Ask," Tenzin said quietly.

"Mr. DePaul?" Ben started.

The old man's eyes swam. "Who...?"

"Don't worry about who."

"Won't... like. O'Briens..."

The man probably had an existing agreement with the O'Briens, but if Ben and Tenzin did their jobs right, Mr. DePaul would never know he'd even been visited by vampires.

"You're in no danger," he said quietly. "All I want is information."

"Can't... discreet. Paid to not..." DePaul blinked, but Tenzin kept him in hand.

Ben said, "I need to know about the Samson paintings at the Museum of Modern Art."

"Which ones?" The human's voice was soft and wondering, as if he was talking to a child.

"The Labyrinth paintings."

"Four by six feet," he mumbled. "Natural wood crates. Deliver in the morning, Charles. On trash day..."

Ben filed each tidbit of information away, just as he knew Tenzin would be doing.

"Where did they come from?" she asked.

"France. Origin was... Caen."

Another connection to France. Ben asked, "When did they arrive?"

"Six months ago."

"Delivered to MoMA?"

"One crate to the museum. And one... to Rothman House."

Tenzin looked up. Ben's eyes widened.

"Rothman House?"

"Yes. Different... delivery. Same origin."

"How many crates total?"

"Two crates." Mr. DePaul sighed. "Seven paintings. Beautiful, beautiful..."

There'd been at least that many paintings by Samson in the museum, but not all had been borrowed from the same source. Of course, many of the donations had been anonymous. Whoever the mystery collector was, he'd amassed quite the Samson collection. There was no way of knowing which specific paintings had been shipped from Caen, but only two would have needed a crate as big as six by eight feet.

"Which paintings went to the museum?" Tenzin asked.

"Don't ask," DePaul said. "Paid not to ask."

It wasn't the right question, Ben realized. "How many paintings went to the museum?"

"Five. No... six on the manifest."

Leaving just one to go to Rothman House where Historic New York was hosting their gala. Ben's heart beat faster. "The crate delivered to Rothman House," he asked. "How big was that crate?"

The swimming confusion behind DePaul's eyes cleared for a moment until Ben saw Tenzin grip his neck harder.

"How big was the crate?" Ben asked again.

"Same," DePaul mumbled. "Same size. Five by seven feet and... five by seven feet. To Rothman."

Ben and Tenzin's eyes met over DePaul's head, and they both smiled. It was possible there was another Emil Samson painting just as big as the Labyrinth paintings. It was possible.

But it was also possible that *Midnight Labyrinth* was already in New York.

And they had an invitation to the house where it was being stored.

~

"What are you thinking?" Ben asked.

Tenzin leaned her elbows on the counter, staring into the distance while she sipped on the chocolate milk shake she'd demanded Ben fetch her from the Shake Shack in Madison Square Park. He'd barely managed to catch them before they closed.

This was not an unusual occurrence. Tenzin loved chocolate milk shakes.

"We need to bring Gavin in," Tenzin said. "All the way."

"But we have you."

"But we don't need me," Tenzin said. "If I disappear during the party, they will assume I'm stealing something. If Gavin is showering attention on Chloe and they disappear, no one will think twice. It's Gavin. They'll assume he absconded with Chloe to seduce her."

Ben did not like that idea. At all. "You want Gavin and Chloe to search the house?"

"They're the least likely to be missed. The most likely to be excused for other mischief."

"So you want to put Chloe at risk too."

Tenzin looked at him. "Gavin won't hurt her. He may have few scruples with human women, but he would never—"

"I'm talking about searching the house, Tenzin." He didn't even want to think about Gavin and Chloe flirting the whole night. Gavin wouldn't leave it at flirting. Ben knew that. Which meant...

"We'll go in after," he said. "You and me. We'll find access to the house another way. Another night."

Tenzin frowned. "That's ridiculous. Security will be most compromised the night of the gala."

"Are you sure? They'll have hired more security, Tenzin. They'll be on alert. They'll be—"

"Compromised." Tenzin was firm. "There's no way to completely secure a building when you willingly allow guests in. This is why I encourage your uncle to never, ever entertain. Their security will be spread thin, even with increased numbers. On the off chance Gavin and Chloe are noticed, they'll be able to excuse their behavior without giving the rest of us away. Ben, be reasonable."

There was nothing reasonable about how much he wanted to shield Chloe from danger. And Gavin. But he knew Tenzin was right.

"I'll talk to him. He already knows most of it. Just not the details."

Tenzin slurped her milk shake. "Historic New York."

"Have to be immortals."

"But what kind are they?" she asked. "What is their game? They've been sponsoring events and funding artists for decades according to your research. Is it all a front for moving stolen art?"

"It might be. Or they might have been fooled into thinking that the Labyrinth Trilogy was legitimately acquired. We have no way of knowing, but you and I both know that most vampires don't ask too many questions when they come across pretty things."

"True." Tenzin finished her shake and threw the cup in the garbage. "I still don't understand why they're hiding *Midnight Labyrinth* though."

"What?"

"They have the other two on display," she said. "Why not

the full set? And why display them at all? Who displays stolen art?"

Ben said, "The other two paintings were given to friends of Emil Samson. It's possible they were both legally bought."

Tenzin nodded. "They may be trying to cover their tracks and mock up some reasonable provenance before they display the full set."

"Not to mention how this attention has affected the market," Ben said.

Tenzin's head shot up. "What?"

Ben opened his computer and clicked on an email from Caspar. "Emil Samson is buzzing in the art world right now. The attention from the MoMA exhibit, the mystery of the missing third painting, the artist's personal story... Prices for Samson's work are going up fast. Even human auctions have caught on. The private market is going crazy, according to Caspar."

Tenzin's eyes caught that faraway distracted look.

"What?" Ben asked.

"There's something... It's all tied together."

"We're not worried about the private market," Ben said. "We have one job: retrieve *Midnight Labyrinth* for Emilie's grandmother. It's her uncle's work. It's her painting. We don't need to make this job more complicated than it is. We find the painting. You and I form a retrieval plan. We return the painting to Emilie."

"Fine," Tenzin said, still frowning. "But there's still something I'm not seeing."

"Well, see it quickly," Ben said. "The gala is tomorrow night."

She flew up to her loft without another word, leaving Ben at the kitchen counter.

Time to talk to Gavin.

∾

"LET ME GET THIS STRAIGHT," Gavin said. "You're giving me permission to steal the lovely Ms. Reardon away so you can charm the vampires of Manhattan without suspicion."

"Did you miss the part about searching for the painting?"

Gavin waved a hand carelessly. "I'm more than happy to find your painting, but I'm choosing to dwell on the part that is making me most excited for this previously dull evening."

"You know what? I've changed my mind." Ben slammed down the tumbler of scotch.

"No, no," Gavin said with a wicked smile. "No taking it back now."

"If you do anything to make her uncomfortable—"

"Ben." Gavin cut him off, his voice frigid. "Have you once known me to force my attention on a woman? Forget this is your friend for a moment and doona insult me."

Ben seethed, but he remained quiet.

"I know exactly what she's been through," Gavin said quietly. "I also know exactly how much you care for her. Stop with this ridiculous jealousy and—"

"I'm not jealous."

"Then what is it?" Gavin asked.

Ben took a deep breath. "I know you."

Gavin raised an eyebrow. "And?"

"And you're never serious about a woman. Not since Deirdre have you—"

"That is finished and doona bring it up again. I'm sorry I ever told you."

"I know you had feelings for her."

Gavin picked up his drink. "One does not simply recover from the loss of a mate to whom you've been blood-bound for five hundred years," he said carefully. "I hold no ill will toward her. My feelings are my own."

"That doesn't change the fact that Chloe isn't a vampire. She's human. She's young. And as far as I can tell, she's had two boyfriends in her life. Me and the asshole."

"I am not the asshole."

"I know that," Ben said. "But you're not exactly prime relationship material either."

Gavin smiled. "Ben, you offend me. And who said the lovely Chloe wants a relationship? The woman might want a bit of uninhibited fun."

"You think she's the fling type?"

Gavin set down his glass. "I don't know." He leaned across the bar. "And neither do you. So stop trying to lift your leg on her like an overeager pup. I've been dealing with the female sex far longer than you."

"Gavin—"

"Leave. It." Gavin finished his whisky. "Let it be, Benjamin. I'm through talking about this. Let's talk about the job."

He tucked his resentment to the back of his mind and focused on logistics. "I'm sending a car for Emilie. We're meeting at the loft. Do you want to meet there or at the gala?"

"Best not to look too unified," Gavin said. "I have a disinterested reputation to maintain."

"We'll meet you there then. You... flirt with Chloe." He gritted his teeth.

"Keep moving and don't stew," Gavin said.

"And eventually, after dinner, you two can slip away. Tenzin and I will remain in the ballroom."

"Who is she going to talk to?" Gavin said. "You know she has no filter."

"Cormac O'Brien, most likely. They're friendly and Cormac

hates formal events as much as Tenzin does. I'll circulate with Emilie and try to pick up anything I can about Historic New York and who they're connected to. Someone at the gala has to know."

"Of course they do, but will they tell you? Chloe and I will search the house while you're being charming in the ballroom."

"How will you get past the guards?"

"I'll manage," Gavin said. "Doona worry about me." He rubbed his chin. "This human girl..."

"Emilie?"

Gavin nodded. "Will anyone recognize her?"

"I don't know why they would."

"Because she's related to the artist," Gavin said. "It's possible that whoever stole the painting has researched the family. Do they have any money? Is there any reason they could be seen as a threat?"

"Her father has money, but her mother—the one related to Emil Samson—doesn't have any of her own and no particular interest in family history. I can't see anyone thinking of Emilie and her grandmother as threats. No money. No particular influence. If they marched up to a judge and told him the painting belonged to their family, they'd probably be laughed out of court."

"For your purposes, that's good."

"I told them I'd recover it for them. What they do after that is up to them." Personally, if it was Ben, he'd want the whole Labyrinth Trilogy, but one painting was probably enough for Emilie and her grandmother.

Gavin smiled. "Look at you, Benjamin Vecchio. It appears the white hat is finally acquiring a bit of dust."

"Not dust," he said. "Not for this job. On this one, my conscience is completely clear."

16

Ben was straightening his cuffs and waiting for Emilie's car to arrive. "Tenzin?"

Chloe had kidnapped Tenzin as soon as the sun set and taken her out to get hair and makeup done. Ben hadn't seen either of them since, though he'd seen their dresses when Arthur dropped them off the night before. Both were stunning and Ben was more than impressed by the man's talent. He'd created dresses that suited both women perfectly.

Chloe's silver-grey dress would wrap around her, displaying her stunning figure and long legs. The skirt flowed like many of the dance costumes he'd seen her wear. Tenzin's dress was a rich purple in a fabric that drew the senses. It was regal and classic while still being a little punk. He wondered if she'd even put it on. It wasn't anything like he'd seen her wear before. Tenzin chose utilitarian clothes for herself. She was practical. She was...

"Why were you calling me?"

Ben turned and Tenzin was at the top of the stairs. His mouth dropped open.

"What was it?" she asked.

Ben couldn't move. He wanted to touch. *Everywhere.*

Tenzin's hair was cut at a sharp angle around her face, the short layers and subtle makeup enhancing her cheekbones and flaunting her graceful neck.

Looking at the pale curve where her shoulder met her neck, Ben felt his mouth water and he had the distinct urge to bite. He pushed the desire to the back of his mind, but he couldn't ignore it completely. He wanted to sink his blunt human teeth into Tenzin's neck.

Not okay.

"You look beautiful," he said in a rough voice. "The dress is..."

"I like it." She smoothed her hands down the purple silk. "More than I thought I would. It's more comfortable than it looks."

The rich fabric of her dress clung to her slim curves, highlighting the dramatic cut of the material around her shoulders. The designer had managed to make silk look like armor. Decorative layers started at her shoulders, draping like blunt dragon scales and concealing the subtle knife sheaths Arthur had worked into the design. The rest of the dress was simple, contoured to her body except for a slit that ran up her left leg. He spotted a flash of silver on her thigh.

"I don't..." He had to clear his throat. "You might have to take the sword off for the gala."

She looked down in disappointment. "Do you think so?"

"Yeah."

"Oh well." Tenzin flipped back the slit of her dress, exposing her leg as she removed the slim, foot-long blade she'd concealed on her thigh.

Ben almost turned around to hide his reaction.

Damn you, Chloe.

His body had a mind of its own. He tried to think of something—anything—else.

He'd never noticed how Tenzin's eyes were the exact color of smoke. The line of that dress made her legs look miles long even though she barely came to his chin.

What was Chloe thinking? They wanted to remain low-key for the gala. In that dress, with her hair cut to enhance her neck, everyone in the ballroom would be staring at Tenzin.

"I still have about a dozen small dagger sheaths," Tenzin said with a grin. Her mouth was subtly colored. Her eyes had dark shadow on the lids. "Arthur is very talented."

"Uh-huh." Where was Chloe? Where was Emilie? "Are you ready to go?"

"Yes." She turned toward the stairs. "I think Chloe was nearly ready as well."

"Good."

"Your cuffs," Tenzin said, walking over to him. "Do you need help with them?"

Before he could protest, she'd lifted his arm and pinched his french cuff together.

"I can get it," he said. She was too near. Her scent was a combination of honey and some spice he couldn't place. He stared at the floor and caught a peek of her toe in a gold heel.

"Where is your cuff link?" she asked.

He reached in his jacket pocket and handed it to her.

"These are nice," she said. "Were they a gift?"

"Yes." He couldn't stop staring at her neck.

"Giovanni?"

"Filomena."

Her mouth turned up at the corner. "One of your Italian admirers. They do give the best presents." She held her hand out for the other cuff link and dropped his arm. He silently handed her the second gold cuff link and turned his head toward the stairs.

Damn you, Chloe.

As if drawn to his mental reproof, she appeared at the doorway. She caught his expression and her smile gave way to confusion.

"What?" Chloe asked.

"We're going to be late."

Tenzin said, "That's good. Nobody important comes to a party on time, and we're very important."

"We're not going to be late," Chloe said. "We're still waiting on Emilie anyway. Have you heard from her?"

Ben pulled out his phone and ignored the brush of Tenzin's fingers at his wrist. "She's almost here."

With sudden mortification, Ben realized that Tenzin knew exactly what his reaction to her was. She could hear his pulse. She could probably smell his arousal by the change in his pheromones.

Irritation quickly overcame arousal.

By the time the driver buzzed the apartment, Ben had himself under control. Under control and out from Tenzin's spell. His reaction was biological, more a reaction to the surprise than to her. After all, she was his partner.

That was all.

EMILIE REMINDED TENZIN OF A BIRD. A delicate little songbird with pretty feathers. She wore a dress the color of pomegranates cut to emphasize her collarbones and slim shoulders. She was a beautiful woman, and she stared at Ben as if he was the most handsome man in the room. Glancing around the glittering ballroom, Tenzin had to agree with her. Ben *was* the most handsome human in the room. There were a few vampires, however...

She let her eyes rest on one of Cormac's guards. He wasn't

her usual type, but the way his trapezius muscles swelled under his crisp white shirt invited her teeth. She was feeling hungry after scenting Ben's reaction to her. She knew it had irritated him, knew he liked to ignore the biological attraction between them, and that was perfectly fine with her. Entertaining any interest along those lines was far too complicated.

Tenzin was feeling exposed in the dress Arthur had designed for her, even though she liked everything about it except the need to wear a short heel. It was formfitting but not uncomfortable. The sleeve design reminded her of some of her favorite armor, which she knew was his intention. She'd seen him sketching the suits of leather armor in the apartment when he was drawing her dress. She liked the purple. She liked the way it felt. She didn't like the eyes it attracted.

Ben and Emilie were dancing in the middle of the floor. Chloe and Gavin were dancing a few steps away. Ben was glaring at Gavin like he wanted to rip his throat out. Gavin was smiling and charming Chloe, completely ignoring Ben. It was all quite amusing. Tenzin was delighted that Gavin had shown an interest in Chloe. She liked the human, so the more vampire protectors she had, the better. Chloe was the type of human who would attract immortals no matter where she went. There was a timeless quality to her beauty and age behind her eyes. Plus she was talented, and talented humans always drew attention. Gavin wasn't the only vampire looking at Tenzin's newest day person.

Tenzin smelled Cormac O'Brien approach her from behind. He carried the distinct scent of cherry pipe tobacco and leather. It wasn't at all unpleasant, and it matched his style, which was... unique. Normally Cormac wore a contrary combination of tweed jacket and ripped jeans with worn motorcycle boots. But that night he wore a tuxedo like the rest of the men. His hair had been tamed and he might have even trimmed his beard.

Same smell though. She would always recognize his smell.

"Hello," she said as Cormac came to stand beside her.

"Good evening," he said, glancing at her from the corner of his eye. "I like the hair."

"Chloe says it ages me in a good way."

He angled his head and examined her before he nodded. "I would agree."

"Thank you."

"For what?" He took off his glasses and cleaned them with the linen handkerchief he carried. The glasses were an affectation. Cormac's eyes were perfectly functional.

"For complimenting my hair. Chloe says my manners need updating."

"No need. I like your bluntness." Cormac offered her a narrow smile. "Chloe is your new day person, correct?"

Tenzin nodded. "I'm assuming that Giovanni called you?"

"He did." Cormac put his glasses back on and scanned the room. The way his eyes locked on Chloe, Tenzin knew he'd done a background check.

Which was fine. Beatrice was an accomplished hacker—despite her immortal nature—and had made sure Chloe's electronic trail was short and uninteresting. Cormac would find nothing that Tenzin and Ben didn't want him to find.

"She seems like a lovely girl."

"Ben has known her for years."

"Ah, yes. Your other human. Who is the woman he brought tonight?"

"A designer friend," Tenzin said. "And again, he is not *my* human." Tenzin had no humans under her aegis. She didn't want any.

"Whatever you say."

"I like the gala."

His eyebrows rose. "That's surprising. I don't. They're necessary, not enjoyable."

"Then why host them?"

"Because my brother insists, and my daughter convinced me it creates good will among the humans."

"Which brother?"

"Ennis."

Tenzin went silent.

"Don't," Cormac muttered.

"You're going to have to kill him, you know."

Cormac glanced around before he glared at Tenzin. "You need to stop saying that."

"It's true."

"It's not true, and you don't know anything about my family."

"I recognize the signs." Tenzin had killed all of her own siblings, but that wasn't any of Cormac's business. "You're a stable leader. He likes to provoke chaos. You've been holding him off for decades now, but eventually..."

"I don't know why I like you when you continue to threaten my own brother."

"*I'm* not going to kill him," Tenzin said. "You have to do that on your own."

"Can we change the subject please?"

"Fine."

"Good."

Tenzin searched for topics that could be classified as "small talk." She was terrible at chatting.

"Are nonprofits a good way to hide money?" she asked. "Historic New York. That's yours, right?"

"It's not *mine*, per se. It's funded by the clan and a few other individuals with deep pockets and good connections who sometimes need to invest funds in charitable organizations."

"And then?"

"And then what?" He narrowed his eyes.

"How do you launder the funds?" she asked. "I'm assuming that's why it exists."

The corner of Cormac's mouth turned up. "I don't know what you're talking about."

She smiled. "But you actually fund charitable events too."

"We have to. The odd gala here and there. Sponsored exhibitions at museums—those are easier because our kind tend to have trinkets lying around." He shrugged. "It's not bad. Nonprofit organizations require quite a bit of paperwork though."

"Hmm."

"If I were you, I'd keep your dragon hoard in untraceable gold and weapons." He flicked her shoulder. "Don't think I didn't notice the knives, Tenzin."

"I couldn't leave them at home." Her eyes went wide and innocent. "They match the dress."

Cormac couldn't stop the wry smile. "As long as you don't behead any of my guests, I don't have a problem with it."

Tenzin scoffed. "When have I ever...?"

Oh. Hmmm.

He raised an eyebrow. "A certain massacre in Rome springs to mind."

Rome? She'd been thinking about an entirely different dinner party, but hopefully Cormac hadn't heard about Chandigarh.

"I was provoked in Rome," Tenzin said. "You don't make a habit of provoking me."

"No, I don't have any interest in bloodshed before dinner."

Tenzin smiled. "Novia is a good influence on you. A natural diplomat. Far better than you."

"I know. The smartest choice I've made in the past fifty years was siring that girl."

Tenzin caught sight of Cormac's progeny. She was talking with a group of visiting vampires and their retinue. She was charming and friendly, but Tenzin caught the keen gaze. Novia O'Brien never let her guard down. She was taking in every word and gesture.

"She's an excellent vampire, Cormac. I would also be very proud."

"Thank you."

Her eyes dropped to the chain looping from his pocket. Cormac caught the look.

"Don't steal my pocket watch, Tenzin."

She sighed. "I really want to though. I'd probably give it back."

"No, you wouldn't. And if you were really going to steal it, you would have already taken it. Let's not cause a national incident for no reason, shall we?"

"Fine." She wondered if Gavin and Chloe had already made their escape. She couldn't see them dancing.

Cormac asked, "You're not stealing anything else from me tonight, are you?"

She glanced at him. "Me? I don't even know whose house this is. They might not have anything good to steal." She asked because she knew Cormac would expect it. "Is there a safe?"

CHLOE WAS DANCING with Gavin Wallace.

Again.

Chloe remembered him from the very first night, but he hadn't made the same impression he was making now. His hand was on her waist, and warm fingers clasped her hands. His feet were light as he led her in a foxtrot.

Gavin was an incredible dancer, and he'd monopolized most of her evening. Somewhere between the dinner and the dancing, she'd had a chance to walk around the ballroom with Emilie, who was mostly interested in the art hanging on the walls and the dresses of the guests. She swooned over the vintage ball gowns. Chloe bit her tongue and didn't mention the women wearing them were probably the original owners.

What was it like going to a vampire ball?

If she didn't know anything about them, she'd have thought the immortals in the room were very dazzling humans. Chloe had been around enough theater people and actors in Southern California that she recognized the "it factor" that some people naturally carried. It was hard to explain, but there was a charisma—a special sparkle—that set them apart.

Very few humans had that charisma, but every vampire she saw did. Especially the Scottish one who'd made his interest clear.

She'd felt Gavin's eyes on her the whole night. The part of her who recognized a predator saw one in the vampire with sandy-brown hair and furtive eyes.

But she wasn't afraid.

Gavin was... charming? No, he was too blunt to be charming. He didn't have any of Ben's smooth delivery or easy wit. His interest was clear and candid. She found his direct interest far more comforting than the subtle charm and manipulations of her ex. Tom had always made her wonder where she stood with him.

Gavin didn't. The first thing he'd told her when they'd started dancing was, "I find you very attractive, especially for a human."

"Thank you," she said. "I'm not sure I want a vampire to be attracted to me."

He'd nodded. "That's probably wise."

Chloe wasn't insulted by the "especially for a human" part. The more she discovered about the world Ben inhabited, the more it made sense. She'd seen dozens of vampires since she'd been here. As she danced with Gavin, he pointed them out, but within minutes Chloe hardly needed the help.

Most were beautiful, the men and the women, though they also had that "otherness" that drew the eye. Gavin was beautiful, though in a completely masculine way. His jaw was clean-shaven and his lower lip begged to be bitten.

Chloe blushed at her own thoughts.

"Tell me what you're thinking," Gavin said, pulling her closer.

Chloe shook her head, and the band switched to a waltz. Gavin didn't let her go, he just switched his steps and continued dancing.

"I want to know what put that color in your cheeks," he said.

Not on your life, vampire. "It's good to want things."

"That," he said, "you are making very clear."

Flirting wasn't her intention, but she didn't have an easy retort.

Gavin pulled her closer and leaned down to whisper in her ear. "Chloe."

Her pulse pounded. "Yes?"

"It's time."

That's right. She wasn't just fighting off an unwise attraction to a dangerous immortal creature, she was supposed to be working too. "What do we do?"

"Just follow me."

He waltzed them to the edge of the dance floor, his eyes

locked on her, steering them away from the crowd. He put his hand on her cheek and leaned closer.

"Follow me," he whispered. "Keep your eyes on mine. Let them think you're enthralled."

Not too difficult.

Her heart was pounding and her breath was short. It wasn't from the dance. When her knee wasn't bothering her, Chloe could dance all night. She kept her eyes on Gavin's, warm brown the color of dark chocolate, and allowed him to lead her to the edge of the room. She could hear whispers around them, but she didn't look away.

Mesmerized, she barely noticed when Gavin led her down a dark hallway. Her hand was in his, and his arm was around her waist. They walked side by side, past dark figures obscured by shadows.

"Look at me," he whispered. "Look only at me."

Chloe didn't want to look away. In the back of her mind, she recognized the sounds filling the hallway.

Vampires were feeding.

And it was pretty clear the humans they were feeding from liked it a lot.

The flush on her cheeks wasn't from embarrassment. Gavin's eyes dropped to her mouth. His hand gripped her waist and they kept walking. The darkness deepened. The shadows grew. Dim electric lights gave way to candles. She could smell the beeswax and smoke.

"Look at me," Gavin whispered. "Say nothing."

They paused, and Chloe kept her eyes on Gavin even when a tall woman approached them. Her hand was raised, but Gavin spoke to her in a language Chloe didn't recognize. German? Dutch, maybe? Gavin passed the woman something in his palm, and then they were moving again.

"Going right," he whispered. "Clever Chloe. You're doing so well."

"Where—"

"Here." He gently pushed Chloe against a wall—no, it was a door—and blocked her body from the rest of the hallway. "Give me just a moment, and we'll be away from the others."

Gavin was so close his shoulders blocked the light. The hallway. The darkness pressed in on her, and she was trapped. Chloe's heart began to pound, instinct bucking against her earlier calm. Her head swam, and she could feel her panic rising. "Gavin—"

"Oh damn," he growled in a low voice. "Damn it and damn him."

Chloe breathed carefully in and out. She knew Ben trusted Gavin, but what if he was wrong? What if—

"Chloe?" He bent down and pressed his cheek to hers, whispering low in her ear. "I'm sorry. Calm now. Breathe in and out. You're doing so well. I know that bastard hurt you, but I want you to listen to me, dove, you have *nothing to fear*."

Goose bumps rose along her neck and crawled down her shoulders to her arms. A warm sense of comfort filled her mind.

"You have nothing to fear," Gavin said again, reaching behind her. He had something in his palm.

Chloe could feel his lips brush her cheek. The top of her ear. From the front, it appeared he was embracing her, but Chloe could feel him fiddling with something behind her. It was the doorknob, and Chloe realized through the spell that had fallen over her that Gavin was picking the lock.

"What are you doing to me?" Her head swam, but the panic had been pushed back. She had the distinct urge to press into Gavin and take his warmth against her skin. Her arms rose, her hands sliding up his firm back. "What is this?"

"I'll explain— *Fucking* hell."

His breath was on her neck. Chloe turned her face and pressed her lips to his cheek.

"Chloe"—his voice was strained—"you need to stop."

She didn't want to stop. She pulled away from his cheek, seeking his mouth. She wanted to taste him. Bite the lips that tempted her. She pressed her body into his and felt his reaction. Felt his leg press between her thighs, holding her against the door. She was burning for him.

"Chloe, please," Gavin said with a groan. "You're going to hate me."

Of course she wouldn't. If he would just give her his mouth...

Gavin's hands worked faster. She heard a click, then in one motion, he pushed the door open and swung her into the room beyond, shutting the door and plunging them into darkness.

"Stop." He jerked away from her mouth.

Chloe blinked, but she still couldn't see a thing. Gavin flicked a lighter and illuminated the room. It looked like a library. He released Chloe and swept his arm around the room, stopping when he saw a candelabra on a side table. He picked it up and lit the candles before he flicked his lighter closed and slipped it into his pocket.

Whatever strange spell had fallen over her dissipated. Embarrassment burned her cheeks red. "I'm sorry, I don't know what I was thinking back there."

"You have nothing to apologize for," he said roughly.

"What was that?" Suspicion warred with the growing trust she'd felt earlier in the evening when he'd held her and danced with her. When she'd followed him down a dark hall with confidence. "Was that the magic Ben warned me about?"

Gavin turned to her with a grim expression on his face. "That was a lack of foresight on my part, and I apologize. I didn't anticipate your reaction to being confined like that, and I should have."

"What did you do to me?"

He opened his mouth, closed it. "You were panicking," he said slowly. "If you'd panicked before I got us away from the guards, everything would have been ruined and we both would have been exposed."

"I was panicking because—"

"I closed you in. Gave you no exit. I know, and I am sorry, Chloe."

He didn't sound that sorry. And the fact that he'd read her so easily pissed her off. "Did you use magic on me?"

"It's not magic."

She crossed her arms.

"I used a touch of amnis to calm you," Gavin said. "So you would not panic and give us away."

"And so I'd be a little more welcome to hooking up with you, huh?" Anger warred with embarrassment. She'd been kissing his neck. Rubbing against his body like a cat in heat.

He narrowed his eyes. "One, I do not 'hook up' with women. In fact, I detest that term. Two, I used amnis to calm your unconscious physical reaction, the one triggered by your past experience. Amnis does not create feelings. Everything you did in that hallway, you wanted to do, dove. Doona fool yourself."

She turned away, looking around the room. She didn't want to think about wanting Gavin. It was too soon. He was a bad choice.

He was a vampire, for heaven's sake! He probably looked at her like she was food.

"Where are we?" She walked toward the center of the room.

The arrogant look on Gavin's face told Chloe he knew she was changing the subject but he'd allow it. He followed her with the candelabra lifted high.

"We're in the study of Rothman House," he said. "The hallway leading to the ballroom runs along these outer rooms, which can all be used for guests." Gavin opened another door and led her into a room with a large billiard table in the center.

"How do you know this?" Chloe asked.

"I found old blueprints." Gavin paused in the middle of the billiard room.

"You found them?"

"More or less. They were quite old, so they will not be accurate. But it will give me a place to start." There were two doors to choose from. He closed his eyes, frowned, then opened them before he reached for the doorknob of the door on the right.

Peeking through the doorway, Chloe saw another, narrower, hall. Gavin turned right and walked to the end of the stairwell, then he opened a door on the left and walked through. There was a narrow staircase leading into more darkness. Gavin reached out, took Chloe's hand, and stepped down.

17

Ben watched Chloe and Gavin disappear into a dark hallway where Ben knew vampires would be feeding. He gripped the stem of his champagne glass, reminding himself that this was the plan. Everything was going according to plan.

"Mr. Vecchio," crooned a nearby guest. "You *must* introduce us to your friend."

Ben turned to see Emilie standing near a vampire couple. Emilie looked confused but not suspicious, so Ben smiled and walked over. The female vampire's accent was eastern European and Ben thought she was an earth vampire, but that was all. He'd met her last year but couldn't remember her name. The male was Ennis O'Brien, Cormac O'Brien's problematic little brother. He was tall and thinner than his brother, with dark Irish looks and the vivid green eyes shared by most of his clan.

Ben turned on the charm. "This gorgeous woman is Emilie Mandel." He tucked her arm into his. "A brilliant designer and good friend of mine. We didn't meet in school though." The mention of school, combined with a meaningful look at the vampires, let them both know Emilie was *not* aware of the other world she was visiting.

"She looks delightful," the female said, batting her eyes at Ben. "Emilie, my name is Natia. Ben is just too polite to tell you he can't remember."

"Of course I did," Ben said. "Emilie, I met Natia at the symphony last year when my uncle and aunt were visiting New York." That much was true.

Emilie smiled. "That sounds lovely. My grandmother loves the symphony, but we never go. I should take her this year."

"Ennis," Ben said. "Good to see you. This is a wonderful event. Did you and Cormac both sponsor it?"

"My idea." Ennis spoke in the haughty accent of New York society, which he'd been cultivating for a hundred years. "Making Cormac entertain is like pulling teeth. He's not as cognizant of our family's social responsibilities as I am."

Social responsibilities like lining your pockets? Ben didn't know how, but he'd bet that Ennis was making money on this gala. Ennis didn't participate in anything without looking for a cut.

Ben took another sip of champagne and caught Natia's eyes locked on Emilie's neck. He cleared his throat to catch Natia's attention while Emilie made conversation with Ennis about the art hanging around the gala. Ben gave Natia a reproachful shake of the head. The vampire smiled and winked.

All part of the game, her expression said. "Emilie, how did you and Benjamin meet? He's quite the celebrity tonight. Everyone in our little scene knows his uncle, but most only know Ben by reputation. He's never come to one of our parties before."

And I doubt I'll make a habit of it. Ben put his arm around Emilie. "She saw me on the street a few weeks ago and took pity on me. I bribed her with gala tickets so she'd keep seeing me."

Emilie said, "I kept him for pity, but he's also very decorative." She winked and smoothed his collar. "Not many men own custom tuxedos anymore. He's the perfect accessory with this dress. The designer in me approves."

"I have to keep my game up when my date wears vintage Chanel."

"See?" Emilie turned to Natia. "He knows vintage Chanel. How could I not keep him?"

The clutch of vampires and their human companions twittered with laughter. Ben could hear the predatory mirth behind it, but Emilie was amused.

"Benjamin, she's *delightful*," Natia said. "Emilie, feel free to examine my dress in detail." The vampire glanced at Ben. "It belonged to my grandmother originally. She had it made in France."

Ben had no doubt that Natia was the original owner, but Emilie and the vampire happily started chatting about their favorite places to shop in Paris.

"Mr. Vecchio"—Ennis lifted his champagne and sipped it —"have you visited Paris recently?"

"Not lately." Not since his uncle's only ally in Marseilles had been killed for smuggling vampire drugs. Immortal politics in France were... complicated.

"I heard your name when I was there," Ennis continued.

"Oh?"

"It seems you're building quite the reputation in the..." Ennis glanced at Emilie. "Art-collecting world. Who knows? We might have cause to work together in the future."

Oh that I should be so lucky. Ben locked his eyes on Ennis. "My partner and I have a varied clientele. I wouldn't want to commit to anything without talking to her, of course. You know Tenzin, don't you?"

Was it Ben's imagination, or did Ennis look nervous?

"Of course," he demurred. "Of course."

Moments after that, Ennis drifted into the crowd.

The gala had been subdued so far. It was a mix of humans from the art world—curators Ben recognized from the Met and MoMA, gallery owners, and a few artists—and vampires connected to the O'Briens and those visiting who needed to be impressed. The gala consisted of dinner followed by dancing. Ben could see the champagne working its magic, and buzzed humans put vampires on the prowl. The dancing was getting more risqué. The jokes louder. The predatory glances lingered longer. Some of the more conventional humans had already left.

If Ben and Tenzin hadn't needed to wait for Chloe and Gavin to search the house, he'd leave with Emilie before things got stranger, but he didn't have that luxury. He had to remain visible until they returned. Ben's absence would be suspicious if anything went wrong.

He searched the ballroom for Tenzin but didn't see her.

Typical.

Ben turned to Emilie. "Do you mind if I—"

"What did I miss?" Tenzin asked, appearing at his side. It had to have been as abrupt to Emilie as it was for Ben.

Emilie looked around. "Where did you—?"

"I needed to find a drink," Tenzin said. "I was... parched."

Ben lifted an eyebrow, but Tenzin's eyes were wide and innocent. A sure sign she'd been causing trouble.

Parched? Had she been drinking from strange humans? That wasn't typical, but Ben didn't want to examine the burning sensation he felt in his belly when he thought about Tenzin feeding, so he shoved it back.

"Did you say hello to Cormac so I don't have to?" Ben asked under his breath.

"Yes, but you should save a dance for Novia."

"Already planning on it." He heard the music change and

turned to Emilie, but a human trailing after Natia had already asked Emilie to dance. She gave Ben a little wave as she wandered off.

The band had switched from classical dances to big band as the gala went on.

"Did you see them leave?" Tenzin asked in Mandarin.

"I did. Did Gavin tell you how he—"

"He liberated a copy of the blueprints for the building after he received the invitation," Tenzin said.

"Such a responsible thief."

"Isn't he?" Tenzin continued to scan the room. "It was a good idea bringing him in to this."

"Yes."

"He might be useful in the future. He's trying to be more honest, but honesty bores him. Bored vampires are dangerous."

Ben nodded and smiled at an older vampire connected to the O'Brien clan. "I've noticed that."

The band finished the Duke Ellington standard they'd been playing and slid into the familiar notes of "La Vie en rose." Turning to Tenzin with a smile, Ben held out a hand.

She narrowed her eyes. "It's an Édith Piaf song."

"It's Louis."

"It is..." Tenzin trailed off when she heard the familiar trumpet solo. "Fine."

Ben smiled and took her hand, putting his hand at her waist, finally touching the purple silk that had taunted him all night. He swung her onto the dance floor where couples were pressed together, swaying to the music. Ben saw Emilie across the dance floor in the arms of an older gentleman Ben recognized from the European paintings collection at the Met.

"She's having a nice time," Tenzin said.

"I think so." He sank into the song, relishing the brush of Tenzin's legs against his as they moved. She was an ornery dancer, letting him lead with just enough resistance that he knew it was her choice—always her choice—to let him guide them around the dance floor. Every now and then, when they'd dance alone, she floated off the floor and he'd spin her out like a top while she laughed and laughed and laughed.

"Do you like my hair?" Tenzin said, her head cocked to the side like an inquisitive cat.

"I don't know yet." He pulled a strand from her forehead and ran it between his fingers. "I like to see it long when you fly." He ran his fingers along the velvet hair at her nape where the stylist had shorn it close to her skull. "I like this. But I'll miss your braids."

"Hmm." She looked up. "It's just hair. It grows."

"Slowly."

"Are you planning on going somewhere?"

He lifted an eyebrow. "That's always the question, isn't it?"

THE KNOT in the pit of Chloe's stomach didn't ease. She followed Gavin as he explored the richly appointed rooms of Rothman House. She couldn't figure out what it was. A house? A club? As far as she could tell, the rooms weren't laid out with any rhyme or reason.

Narrow, mazelike hallways twisted from studies to servant quarters to cozy dining rooms to music rooms. There were more entertaining spaces than bedrooms. In fact, they'd only run across three bedrooms in the whole mansion. And there was not a single window. Chloe tried not to let it creep her out.

"Gavin?" she whispered.

"Hmm?"

"Do we have any idea what we're looking for?"

He cast an annoyed look over his shoulder. "A very large painting in a very large house."

"Oh." She started walking the length of the wood-paneled room they were searching.

"Stop walking," Gavin said. "Wait in the corner by the door."

Chloe bristled. "Why?"

"Because when you walk, you make noise. We don't want to make noise. Also, in the event we're interrupted and we have to pretend to be lovers who've scampered away from the crowd, I can move like this"—in a blink, Gavin was beside her, looking down with unearthly focus—"and you cannot. So stay still."

The knot had moved from her stomach up to her throat. "Oh."

"Wait by the door."

She whispered, "Fine."

She wanted to tap her foot on the floor, but she couldn't do that either. Gavin wasn't just looking at the walls, he was tapping softly on the paneling, pulling back drapes, and searching under tables.

"Tables?" she whispered.

"I hid a stolen Van Gogh very successfully under the kitchen table in a house for several years," he said, walking back to her and reaching for her hand. "At one point, the owner joined me for dinner and we ate coq au vin on top of it."

Chloe let him lead her into the next room. It was a bedroom, and it was massive. "You enjoyed that, didn't you?"

Gavin offered her a rare smile. "Immensely."

The search continued in the bedroom. Something about it, maybe the quality of the air or the slightly misaligned furniture, told her it was a bedroom in use. "Who lives here?"

"I don't know," he said. "I have a feeling from the security"—he swung the door shut and pointed to the numerous and complicated locking mechanisms on the back of the door—"that these are guest quarters of some kind. This could be a safe house the O'Briens maintain to offer shelter to visiting immortals."

"Why all the locks?"

"Most vampires are not like Tenzin. We're vulnerable when we sleep." Gavin got on the floor and scooted under the large four-poster bed in the middle of the room. "So our rooms are designed to be impenetrable when we lock them from the inside."

"So I guess vampires don't have slumber parties," Chloe said, idly paging through a coffee table book on a high table by the door.

"That depends on what you call a slumber party." Gavin rolled out from under the bed and locked his eyes on Chloe. "Are you offering?"

"What?" Her face went hot again. "No."

"Let me know if you're curious." He came to his feet. "And if you want a job."

"Why do you want to hire me?"

"Because you're smart and beautiful. And I think..." He stopped in the middle of the room, cocking his head toward the doorway.

Chloe opened her mouth again, but Gavin was in front of her before she could speak. He whipped them around, pulling Chloe against his body and hiding them behind a tapestry hanging on one wall. She heard the sound of footsteps just as Gavin's mouth landed on hers.

Oh hell. She heard the slight whimper that escaped her throat as he kissed her.

Gavin didn't need amnis to make her head swim. Not one little bit.

She didn't want it to be good, but it was. His lips were firm and full, meeting her own in soft, hungry bites. The kiss might have been a sham, but it didn't feel like one. One hand pressed to the small of her back and the other softly gripped her neck, angling her mouth for Gavin's taking.

He was delicious. Sweet and smoky with a hint of tobacco on his tongue. Her head fell back when his mouth landed on her neck.

He wasn't going to...

Was he?

Did she want him to?

It was just for show.

What would it feel like?

The sounds of passion in the hallway filled her mind, but she realized it was her own gasp of pleasure others heard when the tapestry flipped back and Gavin lifted his head from her neck.

"Gentlemen." His voice was low and imperious. "Is there a problem?"

"I apologize for interrupting, Mr. Wallace, but you are not allowed in these rooms."

"They are for guests, are they not? Am I not a guest?"

Chloe blinked but didn't turn around. She didn't want any of the cold voices she was hearing to see her face. She stood frozen in Gavin's arms, the rumble of his brogue vibrating against her breasts. She blinked, trying to understand what it was she was seeing in the dim light of the candlelit bedroom.

"This chamber has been reserved for a specific guest, sir."

Gavin waved a hand. "Tell him I'll—"

"It's for the Lady, sir. She is quite particular about her chambers and will be unhappy if she finds you here."

"The lady?"

Chloe ignored the quiet debate behind her. Gavin was acting the offended guest and the guards were trying to cover their asses, clearly knowing they'd messed up that Gavin was even in their wing of the house. But Chloe's eyes were locked on the signature she saw just under the edge of the tapestry.

She wasn't an expert, but from the edges of the frame she could see and the size of the tapestry covering it, the painting on the wall was a very large canvas.

A canvas signed in a careful hand by one Emil Samson.

Chloe's heart raced—she wanted to shout—but there was no way of telling Gavin without giving themselves away.

"Sir, we'll escort you—"

"I'll walk behind you," he said, irritation coloring every word. "My companion has no desire to show her face to hired security. Walk ahead of me and we will follow. Do you understand?"

Chloe could tell by the pause that followed that the guards were pissed off.

"Do you understand?" Gavin asked. "Or do I need to contact Mr. O'Brien myself?"

"Very well," a guard said. "But we'll have to report—"

"Report whatever you like," Gavin cut him off. "She's just a human. You doona need her name."

The "just a human" stung that time. Gavin pressed Chloe's face into his jacket and kept his arm around her waist. She walked with him, glancing one last time at the painting behind the tapestry.

Emil Samson.

A gap-toothed imp crouched over the artist's signature, its frog-like face laughing at her as she slipped away.

BEN SAW Gavin and Chloe emerge from the hallway, followed by two of Cormac's men. Chloe's face was tucked into Gavin's neck, and he was speaking softly to her. She clutched his jacket and kept an arm around his waist. To anyone looking, they appeared to have just returned from one very passionate liaison. Gavin wore a self-satisfied smirk, and Chloe's cheeks were flushed, her mouth bitten red.

That's it. Gavin was going to die.

"Ben?" Emilie was at his side. "What's wrong?"

"Nothing."

Gavin scanned the ballroom, searching for him. When their eyes met, he gave Ben a subtle nod, but he was distracted by Chloe, who lifted her head and said something quietly in his ear.

The look on Gavin's face stopped Ben in his murderous tracks.

Well, hell. Maybe Gavin wasn't dying after all.

The look his old friend was giving the top of Chloe's head was almost tender. The hand at her waist didn't grip, but it was firm. He nodded and brushed his lips across Chloe's wiry curls in an unconscious gesture of affection, a smile lingering at the corner of his mouth.

Ben hadn't see Gavin treat a woman that way since...

Hell.

"Ben, why do you look like you want to murder Gavin?" Emilie said.

"I don't." He looked down. "I don't. Just feeling protective is all."

She smiled and her dimple peeked out. "You know, I have to say he's a little brusque, but he does seem sincere. I liked him."

"It's too soon for her," he said. "She just left a relationship that wasn't the greatest. Hence my Neanderthal attitude with her." He bent and kissed her cheek. "I promise that's all. She's an old friend. I'm worried."

Emilie shrugged. "If it's not the right time for her, he'll wait until it is. If he's not willing to wait, then he is not the right man for her."

Ben smiled. "You're so smart."

"I know. Now dance with me," Emilie said. "This night is nowhere near over."

Ben took Emilie's hand, moving toward the dance floor where he saw Gavin and Chloe headed. The song was a quiet jazz tune led by a sleepy clarinet, the perfect piece to wind down a party.

As Ben led Emilie toward Gavin, he saw Tenzin at the edge of the crowd, listening in on Cormac's conversation with one of the guards who had walked out of the hallway with Gavin. Tenzin's eyes met his for a brief second before they moved back to Cormac.

Gavin and Chloe danced nearer. Ben dipped Emilie and lifted her as she laughed.

Chloe caught his eye, and most of his concern fled.

Same Chloe. She looked slightly flustered at Gavin's proximity, but her eyes flashed when he said something she didn't like. No hint of amnis or confusion.

"Chloe found something," Gavin said as they passed.

The steps led them away, but both Ben and Emilie were listening when they came back.

"... know what I saw. I don't know why you—"

"So you're an expert on authenticating signatures, are you?"

Neither Ben nor Emilie could get a word in before the other couple danced away again. Emilie looked up at Ben, her lips pinched together, clearly trying not to laugh.

"If it was a forgery," Chloe hissed as they came within earshot again, "why hide it behind a tapestry?"

"Watch your volume," Gavin said. "If it was the original, why was it in a guest's room?"

Ben said, "I take it you found something?"

Ben had led them to an isolated corner with more humans than vampires, hoping to gain a little privacy. Gavin and Chloe circled them; both couples were still dancing slowly.

Gavin said, "She saw something while I was talking our way out of... a certain compromising position."

"Don't put it that way," Chloe said. "You're purposefully phrasing it that way to make it sound like we were..."

"We were snogging, dove." Gavin sounded far too smug about that. "Don't you remember? Do I need to remind you?"

"No!" Chloe said. "And it was for show, and I saw a painting, Ben." She looked at Emilie. "The same size as the others in the museum. Same color palette from what I could tell."

Emilie gasped.

Ben asked, "You didn't see the whole thing?"

"Well, Gavin was hiding us behind this tapestry so the guards could find us and think we were... you know. And I didn't see the whole thing, but I saw the signature. Emil Samson. Clear as day."

Ben looked at Gavin. "You didn't see it?"

"I was talking to the guards," he muttered. "Back to the wall. I dinna see it."

Ben fell silent. He didn't want to say more—not at the gala—but he could feel Emilie's excitement. She was almost vibrating with it.

"Let's go back to my place," Ben said quietly. "I want to talk this over with Tenzin."

Gavin said, "Done. Chloe should leave with me."

"What?" she whispered. "Why?"

"Because we were caught snogging in a back bedroom. If I let you leave with Ben, it would spoil the illusion."

"He's right," Ben said. "Cormac is still watching you two."

The music died down, and the crowd clapped politely as the band announced a break.

"Let's head to the loft," Ben said. "We'll get Tenzin and meet you there."

Chloe glared at Ben, but she left holding Gavin's hand. Ben looped his fingers around Emilie's and headed toward the door.

Emilie was right. The night was far from over.

18

Chloe looked at a picture of *Dawn Labyrinth* blown up to life-size and projected on the wall, examining the signature in the bottom right corner. It was grainy, but the signature was visible.

"That's it," she said. "I'm sure of it."

Tenzin stood beside her. "How sure?"

"The way he loops his *L* on Emil, it's distinctive. I've studied his other paintings and his signature didn't vary much. The *S* is a little different too. It's the same signature or a very good fake."

They both turned when the distinctive sound of a champagne bottle popped behind them.

Ben was grinning. "We did it."

Gavin wasn't smiling. "We're not positive."

"This painting"—he walked to the wall, champagne in hand —"was missing. For over seventy years, it's been a mystery. And *we found it*."

Chloe couldn't help the smile. "I mean, I can't be positive, but I'm fairly sure."

Emilie leapt to her feet and ran over to hug Chloe. "This is amazing!"

Gavin still wasn't smiling. Tenzin wasn't either.

Emilie looked around. "Why all the grim faces? Ben's right. You did it! You found *Midnight Labyrinth*."

"We may have found it, Miss Mandel," Gavin said, "but we haven't retrieved it yet."

"All in good time." Ben walked to the table where Gavin had laid out the plans he'd retrieved from Rothman House. "You said these had been altered?"

"Yes." Gavin was sketching over the plans in pencil. "This hallway here is intact, but many of the interior rooms have been expanded or combined. And this whole passageway..."

Gavin continued noting differences in the layout to Ben and Tenzin. Emilie hung on Ben's shoulder, avidly taking in every detail while Chloe watched from the couch. She was fairly sure that she wouldn't have any part of the actual theft of the painting, for which she was exceedingly grateful. This whole "job" made her nervous as hell.

Was it theft?

She knew the painting had been stolen from Emilie's family to begin with. She knew whoever owned it had likely obtained it by sketchy methods, whether it was on the black market or the grey market or the vampire market or whatever.

But...

Chloe was the type of person who'd felt guilty parking in a delivery zone when she lived in LA. She still looked twice if she jaywalked, and she'd nearly cried the one time she'd walked out of a store with a dress over her arm that set off an alarm. She'd forgotten she'd been holding it when her phone rang. The store manager had been the one comforting *her* while Chloe imagined her mother at the police station, bailing her out for shoplifting.

She got straight As and belonged to the honor society. She volunteered at the Boys & Girls Club in LA, teaching dance to little kids.

She did not go on covert intelligence-gathering missions at parties.

She did not make out with vampires she barely knew.

And she did *not* conspire to steal valuable pieces of art.

But you're not really stealing it, dove.

And why did she suddenly have Gavin Wallace's voice in her brain?

Chloe watched him in profile, wishing she could forget how it had felt when he held her. He was thrilling in a way that should scare her. He just... didn't. He didn't scare her, which made Chloe feel naive. She knew there was a lot about this strange and alluring creature she wasn't seeing. She saw the shadows in Ben's eyes. She knew that living in the world he occupied was dangerous in ways she didn't even realize.

But...

Gavin's eyes cut to her as if he could read her thoughts. He didn't smile. He didn't make a joke. He caught her gaze and held it. In the space of seconds, the vampire stripped her bare. He wanted her. She wanted him.

What are you going to do about that, Chloe?

She didn't know. She didn't know anything anymore. She closed her eyes, cutting herself off from their world. Her anxiety, which had been gradually lessening in the weeks since leaving Tom, spiked. She had a vision of herself as a bird, flitting through life in her plain brown feathers while birds of prey circled overhead.

Gavin, Ben, Tenzin and Emilie continued plotting, making plans as if the rules meant nothing.

Because they don't. Not to them.

Chloe rose and walked to the control console near the

kitchen. She scrolled through the music choices on the screen and picked a methodical piano piece by Debussy. It was the kind of measured melody that let her mind fall into a rhythm, the same way she warmed up her body by routine. Minute by minute, she relaxed. She didn't notice that the voices on the other end of the room went quiet. She didn't hear Gavin approach her but could feel his presence at her back when he did.

Gavin slipped an arm around her waist, and Chloe froze.

"Change the music. Give us something we can dance to."

"I can dance to this."

Gavin pulled her back against his chest. Chloe's pulse spiked again. The hitch in his breath told her that Gavin heard it.

"I want to see you dance," he said.

"I'm doing a show in a few months. I'll let you know when tickets are available."

He leaned down and whispered, "Is that all I can have?" Gavin took a deep breath and let it out slowly.

What could he sense that she couldn't? His senses were stronger, more perceptive. It intrigued Chloe and annoyed her at the same time.

"I don't know."

THE MUSIC HAD SWITCHED from classical to jazz, a second bottle of champagne had been popped open, and Ben was dancing with Emilie. She was incandescent with happiness. Her mood was infectious.

"I can't wait to tell my grandmother," she said. "Can you imagine? She's going to be so happy."

"Wait," he said, trying to rein in his own euphoria. "Just

wait for now. Gavin may be a cranky ass, but he's right. This job will be complicated. Let us work out who's holding it and how we're going to retrieve it before you say anything."

She nodded. "I'm still excited."

Ben bent and nipped at her ear. "Me too. You have no idea."

He spun her around, dancing through the loft, all the tables and chairs pushed to the side. She was so damn cute. Like a kid on Christmas morning, and he was the one who'd handed her all the presents. Ben felt a million feet tall. He wondered if Emilie would stay the night. Wondered if he should kick everyone out of the loft or steal her away somewhere more private. He wanted time with her. Time to explore who she was beyond the mystery of the painting and the story.

Gavin was dancing with Chloe and poking at Tenzin, chuckling when Ben opened a third bottle of champagne. The loft was filled with the sound of laughter, Billie Holliday, and shuffling feet. Even Tenzin started smiling.

But then the music switched to a dancing trumpet and Ella Fitzgerald singing about the stars above her. Gavin danced over and grabbed Emilie away from Ben. "My turn."

She giggled and swirled away from Ben. He finished his half-full glass of champagne and sauntered over to Tenzin, who was sitting on the library table.

"Get over here, Tiny. This is our song."

She was still wearing the vibrant purple dress with the hidden dagger sheaths. Her eyes were smoky grey and lazy with amusement.

"You're drunk," she said.

"Nooooo." He held out his hand and she hopped off the table. "Just... relaxed."

His tie was long gone. His cuffs were turned up. When her fingers slid across his wrist, he shivered. When his hand slid to the small of her back, she looked up. Her head angled as she examined him.

"Hello, Benjamin."

"Hey." His voice was rough. Damn champagne. "Did I tell you that you look beautiful tonight?"

"Yes."

"I decided I like the hair."

The corner of her mouth turned up. "Good for you."

"Tenzin—"

"You talk too much, Benjamin." She leaned closer, and Ben's arm pulled tight. "Just dance."

Dream a little dream.

Ben held her as they spun around the room, her body light against his. As they danced, his mind floated on a heady mix of champagne, triumph, and memory. He and Tenzin were laughing in a cargo truck driving through the Chinese country-side. They were dancing to scratched records on a steamy summer in Venice. They were sparring with daggers in a castle in Scotland.

He looked down and smiled through the haze of memories and wine. "Hey you."

She looked up, her storm-grey eyes lit with amusement. "Hey yourself."

So beautiful...

Ben slowed his steps and let himself feel the gentle curve of Tenzin's waist under his palm. He let himself imagine how easy it would be to lift her up and bury his face in the pale silk of her skin. Feel her fine, soft hair brush against his lips.

It was past midnight and he knew the wine had gone to his head, but when Tenzin was in his arms, Ben could admit what he couldn't in the light of day.

She was the darkness he wanted to fall into.

Dream a little dream of me.

He pulled her closer, and his thumb was against her wrist when he felt the single pulse of her heart. Ben looked down.

Tenzin's eyes had turned wary. "I need to go."

Ben blinked. "What? Why?"

She dropped his hand and walked toward the roof garden door. "I have to go. Tell everyone I said goodbye."

"Why are you—"

"There's something I need to do, so I won't be back today." She stepped across the threshold and away from him.

"Tenzin?" Ben followed, his feet crunching across the gravel, hurrying to keep up with her. "Tenzin!"

As Tenzin walked toward the edge, into the deepest shadows she used to hide her flight, he grabbed her wrist and pulled her back.

"*Wait.*"

She didn't pull her wrist away, but her hand came to his chest, resting there in warning.

Ben opened his mouth. Closed it. He closed his eyes and wished he hadn't drunk the last three glasses of champagne.

"What is it?" she asked in a clipped voice. "Ben, I need to—"

"Tell me to send them away," he whispered, his heart in his throat. He was in a dream. It was all a dream, and she danced with him in the moonlight and she wore a dress that made her a warrior queen. There was no one else in the darkness, and he was brave. Ben pulled her hand to his face and pressed his lips to her wrist where he'd felt her heart beat. Uncurled her fingers and leaned his cheek into her palm. He closed his eyes and let the words fall from his lips to her feet. "Tell me to send them away," he said. "I will. You know I always will."

The silence enveloped them like a cloak. He kept his eyes closed, unable to meet her eyes.

It was a dream.

Her hand slipped from his grasp.

It was all a dream.

When he opened his eyes, she was gone.

"WHERE DID TENZIN GO?" Chloe walked over to Ben, who'd abandoned the champagne glasses and was sitting at the bar drinking directly from the bottle.

"She had something to do." He turned and swung her into his arms. "What do *you* have to do? Gavin? What's that about? I wouldn't if I were you. Take my advice, gorgeous. Vampires kind of define emotionally unavailable, you know?"

"Wow." Chloe's eyes widened. "I think you're done, Benny."

"Nah, I'm good."

Ben didn't get drunk very often. Chloe was wondering what had caused him to push past celebration and into whatever mood this was. She saw Gavin's eyes turn toward them. He'd been entertaining Emilie, who was more than a little toasted herself. He'd been amusing both of them with clever jokes and stories about his bar.

"You're done." Chloe grabbed the bottle from Ben. "Don't argue. You'll be mad at yourself if you have any more."

"You are... not my mom."

"Since you told me once that your mom was a manipulative bitch, I certainly hope not."

His face fell. "That's not what I meant."

"Why don't I make you some coffee?"

"No." He wiped a hand over his face. "No, you're right. I'm done. I need water and sleep. It's been a long night."

"I agree."

Gavin wandered over. Chloe heard snoring in the background.

"That was fast," she said. "She out?"

Gavin nodded. "Shall I put her in your room, Ben?"

"Yeah," Ben slurred. "I'll sleep... futon."

Chloe frowned. "Wait, then where am I sleeping?" She was comfortably buzzed, but the couch was hard as a rock. Plus she didn't really want to be the third wheel on whatever morning Ben and Emilie had planned. Chloe groaned. "I need my own place."

"Come with me." Gavin put an arm around her waist.

"Gavin, I'm not—"

"Going to have sex with me." He casually kissed her temple. "Obviously not, dove, but I have multiple guest rooms that are all very secure and lightproof. You can take one of them tonight and let yourself sleep as long as you need to." He smirked at Ben. "Leave these two to whatever extracurricular activities they like tomorrow."

Privacy did sound appealing, but...

"I just don't want you to think—"

"I'll think nothing," he said, "except that you need a peaceful and private place to sleep."

She was wavering. Based on Gavin's car, clothes, and general demeanor, she suspected his place was probably luxurious as hell.

"I know you're friends with Ben."

"But you don't know me that well."

Chloe shook her head.

Gavin said, "Do you remember the locks on the doors at Rothman House?"

"Yeah."

"You'll have similar locks on your own door. It might be my home, but I would not be able to get into your room unless you invited me."

Chloe's cheeks reddened. "I hope you're not offended. I just—"

"Of course I'm not bloody offended." He leaned against the counter. "You're smart to protect yourself. Don't apologize for it."

"Okay, I won't." She thought about his offer. If Gavin had wanted to hurt her, he could have already done it. Added to that, she could tell he carried a healthy amount of respect for Tenzin. Would he risk pissing Tenzin off to hurt her?

Her instincts said no. Ben trusted him. Tenzin trusted him.

Gavin said, "I also keep thousand-thread-count Egyptian cotton sheets on my guest bed."

"That sounds like heaven, and I'm there." She looked at a wavering Ben and the sleeping Emilie. "If you can carry her, I'll help him downstairs."

Gavin grumbled, "When did I become the damn responsible one?" He walked to the couch and lifted Emilie. "Irritating humans."

Something about his grumpy words made Chloe smile. Gavin was a good guy despite his questionable moral compass when it came to theft.

"How much longer before dawn?" she asked.

"I have a few hours." He carried Emilie down the stairs, and Chloe forced herself to not stare at the lean muscles pressing against his shirtsleeves. He wasn't even breathing hard.

Duh, Chloe. He's a vampire.

Chloe put an arm around Ben's waist as he slid off the barstool. "Come on, big Ben."

Ben chuckled. "You haven't called me that since... you know."

Chloe's cheeks turned red. She'd forgotten about that. "Yeah, don't remind me. I was referring to your height."

"Are you sure?"

Gavin stopped and looked over his shoulder, his eyes narrowed. "Careful, Vecchio."

Ben snorted but said nothing else while Chloe helped him toward the makeshift bedroom he'd been using. She unfolded the futon and spread out the sheets. Ben sat down hard on the edge and Chloe heard the frame crack.

"Don't break the bed or you'll be on the floor," she said.

Ben yanked off his shoes and unbuttoned his shirt. "I'm an idiot."

Chloe glanced up from tucking in the corners of the fitted sheet. "You don't usually drink this much. Everything okay?"

"No." He rubbed his eyes. "I'm fine. Forget it. I don't want to talk about it."

She stood and pushed his hair back off his forehead. "We did good tonight, Benny."

He smiled. "Yeah, we did."

"We're gonna get Emilie's painting back for her."

"Emilie..." He closed his eyes. "She's really *great*, isn't she?"

"I think so."

"Me too." He grabbed her hand and kissed the back of it. "You're the best."

"I know. You're super lucky to have me as a friend." Chloe pushed him back on the pillows. "Now go to bed."

"He's not good enough for you."

She covered him with a sheet. "I'm not talking about this with you."

"He's not."

"Go to bed." Chloe walked toward the stairs only to see Gavin waiting at the bottom step. She could already hear Ben snoring, so she knew Gavin would have heard his words. "Sorry, he's...."

"Right," Gavin said quietly. "He's right. I'm probably not good enough for you."

She couldn't think of a single thing to say. She was tired and emotionally exhausted. She wasn't sure how she felt about Gavin other than irritated and attracted. Occasionally at the same time.

"Gavin." She sighed. "I'm tired."

"So we'll go." He nodded toward Emilie's room. "Your scent was all over that room, not his. Go pack a bag and we'll go to my place. We only have an hour or so before dawn. Barely enough time for me to get you settled before I need to sleep."

"Thanks." She hurried to pack a bag with the essentials, careful to bring her most boring pajamas.

Just as a precaution.

When she closed the door on a sleeping Emilie, Gavin was gone. She could hear him moving around on the floor above. By the time she walked upstairs, he'd already straightened the kitchen and put the furniture back in order.

"That was fast."

He offered her a wry smile. "Cleaning up after drunks is a life skill I've perfected. You ready?"

She held out her weekend bag. "Ready."

"Excellent. You have a key to lock up?"

She nodded. "Just head downstairs. I'll set the house security and meet you in the lobby."

"Fair enough."

Chloe pushed the buttons to set Cara into alarm mode after Gavin shut the door. She figured as much as Ben and Tenzin trusted Gavin, they still wouldn't want him knowing the code for the house.

Her eyes were barely open when she got off the elevator in the lobby. Gavin waited outside, leaning against the car and chatting with his driver. Every misgiving she'd battled through came rushing back.

What are you doing, Chloe?

She was walking into the lair—if he was a vampire, it was a lair, right?—of an immortal creature she barely knew who had a strange, hypnotic effect on her senses. She was a mess, physically and mentally. She happened to agree with Ben. Gavin was most certainly *not* good for her.

She should walk back upstairs and sleep on the couch no matter how uncomfortable it was. She should endure Ben and Emilie's morning awkwardness. She should just find a cheap hotel.

Gavin watched her through the windows, his mouth turned up at the corner.

She was being paranoid. Staying at Gavin's would be fine. He was offering a bed and privacy. He'd protected her at every turn on this crazy, tumultuous evening. He wasn't some dark creature of the night intent on her ruin.

She'd be fine.

Chloe walked out the front door and into the damp summer heat.

"Did you enjoy that mental argument with yourself?" Gavin asked.

"Yes. Both sides were persuasive, but the lightproof guest room won out in the end."

He opened the door for her. "Doona forget the Egyptian cotton sheets."

"Trust me, I haven't."

He smiled when he slid in next to her and gave the driver his address. After the human knew where to go, Gavin raised the privacy screen on the car and opened the small refrigerator to hand her a bottle of water.

"As I said before"—he opened his own bottle, but his was opaque and she saw red on the cap—"I agree with Ben. I am not good for you."

He put the bottle to his mouth and upended it, swallowing

the liquid as Chloe stared. When he finished, his tongue came out and licked the drop of red staining his bottom lip. She could see the sharp points of his fangs peeking out.

"But," he continued carefully, "though I may agree with Ben, that does not mean I'll stop."

Her heart pounded, and Gavin's predatory gaze cut toward her throat.

"Gavin?"

"A good man would stop pursuing you," he said softly. "A deserving one would wait. He'd be patient." His eyes left her throat and locked with hers. "I'm not a good man."

19

B en leaned against the counter with a bag of frozen peas on his head, waiting for the coffee to brew. The pain reliever was working, but slowly. He heard a thump in the hall, then Emilie walked up the stairs.

"Hey." She blinked. "I'm here."

Ben held out his arm and she stumbled over, tucking herself under it.

"No more champagne," she mumbled into his chest. "Ever."

"Agreed. From now on, we stick with scotch."

That earned him a feeble laugh. Emilie stepped away and rubbed her face. "Where is everyone?"

Ben ignored the stab of worry that Tenzin hadn't come home. She'd said she wouldn't. He didn't know why he was surprised.

"Tenzin's out. Chloe texted me to say she stayed at Gavin's house last night. She's planning on sleeping late, and she'll drive over with him tonight."

Emilie's eyebrows went up. "Oh really?"

"She made sure to specify his *guest room* was very nice."

"Sure it was."

Ben tossed the frozen peas on the counter and leaned back on the counter, taking in Emilie Mandel in all her morning glory. It was the first time he'd seen her so unbuttoned. Her hair was up in a loose knot. Her makeup was all gone. She'd borrowed a pair of Chloe's sleep shorts and a T-shirt, both of which were a little baggy on her. She looked messy and relaxed and undeniably beautiful.

He crooked a finger at her. "Come 'ere."

"How long until the coffee is ready?"

"A few more minutes." He tugged on the waistband of her shorts. "But I have something to wake you up."

He reached down, cupped her bottom, and lifted her up to the counter before she could protest. Then he stepped between her legs and caged her in with his arms. "Hi."

Emilie's mouth had dropped open in surprise. "You're stronger than you look."

"I don't look strong?" He closed his eyes and nuzzled into her neck, which fell at the perfect height for nuzzling. Had he been thinking about that when he designed the kitchen? Possibly. The counter was the right height for all sorts of things.

"Of course you look strong, but that was a serious Tarzan move there. I'm so impressed I can't even find it in me to protest the manhandling." She put her arms around his neck and tilted her head so he had better access. "Good morning. You're very snuggly this morning."

He loved women. They were so delicious and soft and smelled so good. "I had all sorts of plans for last night, and then..."

"Champagne happened."

"It was really good champagne."

She smiled. "And you have fun friends. I can't figure Tenzin out though."

His smile froze. "Yeah, she's... different."

"I got that feeling." Emilie kissed him softly. "I think it's great she has you. Not everyone would be so cool with a roommate out of the norm, you know?"

He desperately wanted to change the subject, so he ran his palms along the tops of her thighs.

"So, I was saying that I had plans for last night."

Her smiled turned from sweet to seductive. "Is that so?"

Ben leaned in and kissed along Emilie's collarbone, letting his tongue taste her skin. "You know, I think this coffee maker is really slow."

Emilie's hands dug into the ridged muscles at the small of his back. "You mean we'll have to entertain ourselves while it's brewing?"

"I'm afraid so."

Her voice was high and breathless. "What could we possibly do?"

Ben lifted Emilie and she wrapped her legs around his waist. "I have an idea, but we'll have to go downstairs."

"Does this idea have anything to do with the mirrors in the training area?"

He almost fell down the stairs. "It does now."

EMILIE WAS MAKING another pot of coffee in the very slow coffee maker that night when Gavin and Chloe finally arrived. Ben wasn't even going to touch all the unspoken vibes bouncing between them. He didn't want to know. Gavin was being aloof. Chloe was being perky. Perky Chloe meant she was deliberately ignoring something, but again...

He wasn't going to touch it.

Not my business.

The one who was his business landed in the roof garden a

little past ten, walking back into the apartment as if she'd never left. Tenzin glanced at Ben, looked over at Emilie, then nodded and climbed up to her loft.

Emilie noticed Tenzin walking in. "How did she...?" She glanced at the front door, then the garden doors. "I missed something."

"Stairs outside," Chloe said smoothly. "Emilie, do you think the coffee is ready yet?"

Emilie cleared the frown from her forehead and said, "Uh, sure. Let me get you a cup."

"Thanks so much." Chloe leaned over the plans Gavin had spread over the library table.

Did Ben notice a new ease between them? Probably, but he wasn't asking any questions.

Definitely not my business.

"This is the room," she said. "Think about it. We searched this library off the main hallway, then went into this room, which was like a..."

"Billiard room," Gavin said, reaching across the table to take the cup of coffee Emilie held. He set it down in front of Chloe. "We went from there to... here." He pointed at a room on the blueprints. "But this room was far, far bigger."

"I think they just combined them," Chloe said. "Look, if they took out this wall, it would be the approximate size—"

"Clever girl," he said. "You're correct. They took out this wall and made these two bedrooms into one larger room. We jumped across that hall and into the bedroom with the painting."

Ben noticed where they were pointing in relation to the plan he was forming in his mind. "This bedroom—the expanded one—did it look occupied?"

Chloe shook her head. "I don't think so."

"Good."

Emilie leaned over the table. "I feel like I'm in a movie," she said with a grin. "What are we planning?"

"*We* are planning nothing," Gavin said. "I cannot be involved in this step at all. In fact, Chloe and I are going to have to create a plausible alibi for whenever Ben and Tenzin... do what they do."

Chloe looked up. "We need an alibi?"

"We've already been seen snooping around the house," Gavin said. "In that particular room, no less. If anything is stolen from it, the O'Briens will look at me first unless I can give them reason to dismiss me." Gavin glanced at Ben. "My favors only go so far. I'm not willing to anger the O'Briens to steal a painting when I'm not making a profit."

Chloe frowned. "So if you *were* making a profit?"

Gavin raised an eyebrow and shrugged. "An entirely hypothetical scenario. I'm a legitimate businessman."

Tenzin climbed down the ladder, still playing human for Emilie. "For now. What did we decide?"

Ben tapped his chin. "We need to know more about this 'Lady.'"

Emilie asked, "Why? Does it matter? She has my grandmother's painting."

"We need to know more so we can lure her away from the house," Tenzin said.

Ben looked at Gavin. "She was at your pub."

"One of thousands," Gavin said. "You expect me to know the particulars of every single patron?"

Ben gave him a look, and Gavin smiled.

"All right. You win. She's not one of thousands. Cormac sent her an introduction."

Emilie frowned. "So she could go to your pub?"

Ben hesitated. They really needed to get Emilie away if they had any chance of strategizing openly. It would be impossible to organize an operation with Tenzin without talking about flying. Emilie wasn't ready for that. Ben wasn't ready to tell her.

"Hey, Emilie?" Chloe looked at her watch. "I'm borrowing Ben's car tonight to run an errand in Harlem. Did you want me to drop you at home while I'm heading up there? It's not that much farther."

Bless you, Chloe.

But Emilie wasn't an idiot. She turned to Ben. "Trying to get rid of me?"

He opened his mouth, but Tenzin was the one who answered.

"We need to plan, and you need plausible deniability," she said. "On the off chance anything goes wrong, you can honestly say you didn't know anything about what we're doing. It's not just you." Tenzin nodded at Chloe and Gavin. "We're kicking them out too."

Gavin turned. "You think so?"

"I know so," Tenzin said. She rolled up the map. "You've done your part. Chloe, are you comfortable staying at Gavin's house for a few more nights until this is all settled?"

A look passed between Gavin and Chloe that Ben couldn't read.

"Yeah," Chloe said quietly. "Sure."

"And thank *you*, Tenzin, for offering my house," Gavin said. "That does seem to be a habit with your group of friends, doesn't it?"

Tenzin shrugged. "Don't have houses in convenient places then. Or decorate worse."

Chloe said, "If I'm intruding—"

"Of course you're not." Gavin cut her off. "I told you earlier that you're welcome to stay as long as you like. And tomorrow night you're starting work at the pub. If you're staying with me, I can give you a lift."

Chloe opened her mouth to protest, but Gavin cut her off before she could argue.

"They have their plans," he said. "I have mine. We need an alibi, and the pub will provide it. I'll tell you more in the car when we're taking Emilie home." He cocked his arm in Emilie's direction. "Shall we?"

Emilie glanced at Ben. "Can you... uh, help me get my stuff together downstairs?"

"Of course." He took her hand and led her away from the others. He stepped down two stairs and paused while she hopped on his back with a giggle. "I wish you didn't have to go, but..."

"I get it." She kissed his neck. "Is it wrong that I'm so excited about this? I'm sending you to commit a crime."

"It's not a crime when the painting belongs to you in the first place." He reached his bedroom door and kicked it open. "Whoever this woman is, she either stole it herself or bought it from someone who did. There's a reason it's not displayed with the others. She knows it doesn't belong to her."

Emilie slid off his back and walked around the room, picking up her few things that were scattered around. Dress. Earrings. He tossed her the lacy bra sitting on an end table.

"I'm going to miss you," he said.

She smiled. "I'm just heading uptown."

"I know, but it was kind of nice having an Emilie all to myself for the day."

She paused, looking at the ground. "I wish..."

Ben stepped closer. "What?"

Emilie shook her head. "Nothing. Being silly. I better get home. My grandmother will be wondering at this point." She held out her things. "I don't suppose you have a bag I could borrow?"

He went to the closet and brought out a backpack. "Don't

tell your grandparents anything at this point. I'm not sure what our timeline is, but it could be a while, depending on what we need to do."

She nodded as she folded her dress and placed it in the backpack along with a few other things. "Tell Chloe I'll get her stuff back to her soon."

"I wouldn't worry. She's got a ton of clothes."

"Still."

"Hey." He tapped her chin to make her look up. "Everything all right?"

Her eyes were wide. "Yeah. I just wish I could stay longer."

"When this is all over, we should plan a weekend away. Maybe go upstate or down south. Somewhere out of the city."

She smiled. "That sounds nice. I have a brother who lives in Savannah."

"You have a brother?" He frowned. He didn't remember her mentioning a brother.

"Not really." Her cheeks went red. "He's one of those friends that feels like a brother. We knew each other in school. It's not important." She stood on her tiptoes to kiss him. "I guess this is goodbye."

"For now." He wrapped an arm around her and lifted her up to deepen the kiss. Their tongues danced in new familiarity. She put her hand on his cheek and sighed, releasing a breathy moan against his lips.

"I could kiss you for hours."

Ben nipped at her bottom lip. "Soon." Reluctantly, he set her down and grabbed the backpack and her hand. Leading her upstairs, he thought about what it might be like to have her in the apartment. What if he told her the whole truth? Would she react as well as Chloe? It was too soon—way too soon. But he couldn't help but let his mind wander ahead.

Ben kissed her goodbye at the door, leaving her in Chloe

and Gavin's care. When he turned around, Tenzin was stretched out in the air, hovering over the map of Rothman House, staring at the blueprints.

They both spoke at the same time. "I have a plan."

~

"THAT WON'T WORK," she said.

"Why not? You can carry that much weight, can't you?"

"Of course I can." Tenzin munched on a small bowl of almonds. "It's not the weight. If it's framed like the others, it's probably no more than a hundred pounds. The weight isn't the issue. It's the size."

"They moved it into the house. It has to be small enough to get out. The dimensions aren't—"

"The dimensions aren't small enough for me to fly it off the top of the roof without anyone noticing." She stood and leaned over the blueprints. "You're right. The problem isn't getting in, it's getting the painting out. That said, just getting it up to the roof and flying away isn't an option. This is not a piece of jewelry or a Fabergé egg. I can't just—"

"A Fabergé egg?"

Tenzin looked up. "What?"

"Do you have a Fabergé egg?"

Her eyes darted away. "Maybe."

"Maybe? You're not going to give me a straight answer about a *Fabergé egg?*"

Tenzin opened her mouth. "Uh... no." She looked back down. "It's a guest house, so the security isn't top-notch, but the O'Briens do have wind vampires patrolling the roof. They'll notice another wind vampire. Especially one trying to take off with a large painting. The dimensions are awkward."

"You are maddening." He sat down and crossed his arms.

"Fine. The roof is not an option. There's no way to sneak it out the front door. The back is guarded more heavily than the front. So none of my ideas—"

"Who says we can't take it out the front door?"

Ben frowned. "They're big doors, Tenzin, but I do think the staff will notice someone walking out with a giant piece of art."

"Of course they will," she said. "But if we do this right, not only will they let us in the front door, they'll help us carry the painting out."

THREE DAYS LATER, Gavin called Ben.

"I have an in," he said. "She's a wine collector."

"And you sell whiskey."

Gavin made a small huffing sound on the other end of the line. "I'm a multifaceted creature, Benjamin. I have a wine cellar that rivals the finest in Paris. I also happen to have just obtained a case of 1980 La Romanée-Conti."

"Is that supposed to mean something to me?"

"It would if you collected wine." Gavin's voice lowered. "I'm dropping hints and massaging egos at the moment. This woman is... eccentric. Not mad like yours, mind you, but a definite eccentric. I can tell Cormac is getting fed up with her, but her reputation in France can't be ignored."

"What is she?"

"She's a patron. One of her sycophants called her a muse, if you can believe it. She's rich and she funds new businesses, supports artists, has some winemaking enterprises here and there. Supposedly she's working with a partner on a blood-wine that will blow all current competitors out of the water, so everyone is pandering."

"Have you ever heard of this woman before?"

"That's part of the mystique. She's a shadow. No one even knows her name. Everyone, even that grumpy Irish bastard, calls her the Lady."

Ben tried to imagine Cormac O'Brien deferring to a French aristocrat and almost burst out laughing.

"Is she an earth vampire?"

"No," Gavin said. "Wind like me. At least that's the rumor. I've never seen her fly."

"Damn." Wind vampires tended toward paranoia, which meant her rooms at Rothman House might have been reinforced. "Gavin, have you apologized for trespassing at the party?"

"Not yet, but I let Cormac know I'd like to. Simple mistake. Carried away by bloodlust. The usual excuses. Cormac doesn't seem overly offended, but that's where the wine comes in."

"How?"

"I'm trying to arrange a tasting for her," Gavin said. "Dinner and a couple of bottles of the 1980 La Romanée-Conti as an apology for trespassing on her territory. I figure a reasonable promise of groveling and ten-thousand-dollar wine should lure her out of the house. I can't give you an exact night though. Does your... activity contain a certain margin for flexibility?"

"It will if it needs to."

"Good."

Ben cleared his throat. "How's Chloe doing?"

"She's fantastic. I'd say she was born to sell drinks, but that would insult her dancing."

Chloe had been staying at Gavin's for the past four nights, but she still came over during the day to grab things and practice with Tenzin. She didn't share a whit of what she and Gavin were up to—if they were up to anything—but she seemed happy and content to stay at the vampire's place for a while.

Gavin did have an enormous house. It was possible he was simply being a benevolent host with no ulterior motive.

Possible. Not probable.

"Be careful with her," Ben said quietly.

Gavin paused at the other end of the line. "I'll leave that alone and try not to be offended you said it. I know she's important to you. She's brilliant at the bar and doing extremely well. Most of my servers are a bit younger, and she's a natural leader. I can see her managing very quickly if it suits her plans."

"Don't get too attached. Tenzin is already bitching that she's not always around."

"Well, Chloe disna belong to Tenzin, does she?" Gavin growled. "She's an assistant, not a bloody servant."

Ben's eyebrows went up at the hostility in Gavin's tone. "Fine. I'll pass along the message. And you pass along whenever you get word from Her Lady of Eccentricity, okay?"

"Done. I'd like this finished as quickly and as cleanly as possible."

"Trust me. I feel exactly the same way."

20

Chloe wiped down the bar, absently watching the door for any sign of Gavin. While she cleaned, she poured drinks and kept an eye on the younger servers at the Bat and Barrel. It was the nicest pub she'd ever worked at, and she enjoyed herself. The patrons were far more civilized than she expected.

Most nights seemed to swing about half and half between vampires and humans. More humans earlier in the evening. More vampires later. Gavin had told her the pub was a mecca and neutral ground for "day people" like herself. Humans who worked in the vampire world could come and be among others like themselves. Vampires traveling through town could get a safe and easy drink from one of the servers with a red pin on their collar, and everyone could taste the finest whiskeys and wines.

No arguments. No sketchy dealings. Absolutely no violence.

Yep, pretty much the most mellow place Chloe had ever worked, including the family-owned Italian place in Little Italy.

Gavin walked through the door dressed in an impeccable grey suit. Since he'd left the house that evening wearing a concert tee and a kilt that made her mouth water, she knew something was up.

"Hi," she said as Gavin approached the bar. "That's a fancy suit. What's up?"

"The wine tasting for Cormac and our French guest is at midnight," he said in a low voice. "You might want to call your roommates and let them know you'll be late."

"Aren't you my roommate now?"

His eyebrow lifted. "Have you decided to take me up on my offer?"

Chloe's cheeks heated. "No."

"You mean not yet?"

"Gavin—"

"Call please." He lifted her hand and kissed the knuckles. "For me, dove. I have to prepare the cellar tasting room and contact the chef."

"You got it."

Gavin backed away. "So you like the suit?"

She shrugged. "I liked the kilt better."

His smile was wicked. "They always do."

She raised a hand and flicked her fingers away in an irritated gesture, but she couldn't stop the smile on her face.

Chloe noticed other servers glancing at them. She knew the other employees assumed that she'd formed some kind of relationship with Gavin, but she didn't really care. They could think whatever they wanted. And since they thought she was with Gavin, no one—human or vampire—hit on her, which was a relief.

She pulled out her phone and called Ben, conscious of the many ears at the bar.

"Hey, Chloe. What's up?"

"I think I'm going to be late tonight."

Ben fell immediately silent.

"Going to be helping Gavin with a wine tasting," Chloe said quietly. "Supposed to be around midnight. So... yeah. I'll probably be late. You might want to go ahead without me."

"Understood," Ben said. "They're supposed to be there at midnight?"

"Uh-huh."

"Thanks, Chloe."

"No problem. I'll see you later."

She hung up and slid her phone in her apron. Then she turned to the young female vampire who'd sat down at the bar. "Can I help you?"

The vampire glanced at Chloe's collar, then away. "Just a glass of wine. Costa de Prata, please."

Chloe recognized the name of a popular blood-wine, so she retrieved the black-glass goblets they used for the deep red drink.

She had no idea what Ben and Tenzin had planned, but whatever it was, it was happening at midnight.

BEN HUNG up the phone and shouted, "It's tonight!"

Tenzin stuck her head out of the loft. "Finally." She flew down. "Are you ready?"

He downed the last of his espresso in one swallow. "You need to help me with the first part, then you can head to Rothman House and start your entry. Keep in mind they won't be leaving the house until just before midnight. After that, we want to work quickly. Meet me over at DePaul's?"

"I'll see you there." Tenzin changed into black leggings and a black fitted tunic and was out the roof garden door before he finished rinsing out his coffee cup.

Ben walked to the closet and got out the brown uniform he'd

procured the week before. He changed quickly—stopping in the bathroom to apply a large temporary tattoo to the left side of his neck—and walked to the elevator, taking it directly down to the garage. He didn't take his car, instead he tied the coveralls around the white T-shirt he wore and walked out onto Mercer Street, just another delivery guy finishing up his shift. He made his way north, heading for the Village and a quiet shop with no phone number on the window.

TENZIN WAITED on the roof of the building opposite Rothman House. She watched until 11:45 precisely, when a black car pulled up to the front of the house and a woman dressed in black—from lace veil to black stockings—descended the steps of the old house and entered the idling car. At 11:47, it pulled away from the curb. At 11:50, Tenzin was hopping from shadow to shadow, making her way to the guarded roof of Rothman House.

Don't kill anyone, Tenzin. It's just a painting.

It was good advice. No one should ever be killed for a painting. Their value was far too subject to market trends and had little inherent worth.

She needed to remain unseen. There was no way of rendering vampires unconscious without breaking their necks, and she really didn't want to cause that much commotion. She looked for the tiny window she'd picked as an entrance the week before, waited for the guard to cross to the other side of the building, then she flew to the window, quickly cut the glass, and slid inside.

It was 12:01.

CHLOE STOOD SILENTLY at the edge of the room. Gavin's tasting room was not on the typical employee tour, nor was it open to the public. It was located in the basement of the building. Red brick lined the walls, giving it an old-world feel, but the tasting room itself was surrounded by glass with a sealed door and strict temperature controls. It looked as if a laboratory had been plopped into the middle of a 1930s gangster movie.

The party inside was just as incongruous.

Gavin spoke to them from within the tasting room, discreetly showing off the features of the basement from the extensive racks to the hand-polished dining table where servers in white uniforms were laying out a tasting menu that made Chloe's mouth water. She could smell everything going in, but once the food and vampires were locked in the tasting room, all scent and sound was cut off.

She waited at the doorway on Gavin's instruction. There wasn't much to do, but it would be natural for an employee to be waiting at Gavin's beck and call, and Gavin wanted to make sure Chloe was seen by anyone who might harbor suspicions later.

Chloe still hadn't seen the elusive Lady of Normandy. She seemed to live behind her veil. A pale white hand was the only physical trait she could see of the woman. If she were closer, Chloe would be able to see more, but from a distance, the vampire's features remained elusive.

The last of the tasting menu was laid out, Gavin's greeting came to a close, and he brought out the bottle of wine—*the ten-thousand-dollar bottle of wine*—that was the reason for the tasting.

Chloe glanced at her watch. It was 12:15.

∽

Ben pounded on the door of Rothman House, clipboard in hand. It took a few minutes to get an answer, but eventually a tall South Asian man in a dark suit came to the door. His hair was silver and swept back from a regal forehead when he looked down his nose at Benjamin.

"May I help you, sir?" The butler spoke in a crisp British accent. "I believe you may have the wrong address, but I'd be happy to direct you."

Ben made a show of tugging on his hat and looking at his clipboard as he flicked the toothpick between his lips. "I don't know, man. I been doing deliveries in this neighborhood all day. I think I know where I'm going, you know?" He wore his father's accent, Puerto Rico by way of the Bronx, and laid it on thick. "This the right address?" He flipped the clipboard to the butler, who inspected it carefully.

"That *is* the correct address, but I was not informed of any deliveries this evening. If you could give me a moment to contact—"

"They tell you about every little thing they order?" Ben asked. "They ain't like other rich people I met then, are they?" He laughed. "They buy a mansion and don't even remember the next day. No worries. You don't owe anything on it. Some kind of art, I think. I just need a signature."

The man had a mobile phone in his hand and was dialing. "Nevertheless, it's *highly* irregular for my employer to not inform me of a delivery. If you could just give me a few moments to verify—"

"Verify? You kidding me?" He wasn't worried about the phone. He'd given Gavin a jammer days ago. There wasn't a mobile or satellite phone on the planet that was reaching the tasting room in the basement of the pub.

"It will only take a few minutes," the butler said.

"Listen, Jeeves—or whatever your name is—this is our last

stop and we been working all day, you get me?" Ben said, letting an edge of temper fray his voice. He grabbed the toothpick from his mouth and let his hands start talking as his voice rose. "I got one more painting to deliver and this is it. I don't even care if it's going to the right place at this point. You say this is the right address on my paperwork? Then this place is where it's going." Without waiting for an objection, Ben walked to the dark brown delivery van he'd "borrowed" from DePaul's and opened the back end. He slid out the crate with the blank canvas and walked back up the stairs.

"I say!" the butler sputtered. "I have not been informed of a delivery this evening. I refuse to—"

"Hold on! This thing ain't made of feathers, is it?" Ben muscled his way into the entryway using the crate to push the butler back. He set the crate down and pulled out his clipboard again. "Okay, let's take a look at the information I got."

The butler's phone chimed. He picked it up with relief, but his expression soured. He hit a number and spoke tersely.

"It is a misdirected delivery. I am quite capable of handling the matter. I do not need a nanny, if you please." The butler paused. "Do what you need to do."

Ben knew as he waited in the entryway that security would be checking the truck. They wouldn't find anything amiss. Not the registration, which tied it to DePaul and Sons art delivery, not the stack of proofs of delivery he'd mocked up and signed, and not his own license with the name and license number of an ordinary deliveryman from the Bronx.

He glanced at his watch. It was 12:16.

TENZIN HEARD the commotion in the hallway. She used Ben's voice to mentally map her escape route. She had a total of five turns to make carrying the painting. She just prayed Ben attracted enough attention at the entryway to clear the hallway of curious humans and vampires.

As was usually the case, breaking in was never a problem. She was small, she could fly, and humans rarely looked up. It was getting out with a large painting that would be the challenge.

She paused at the locked door and listened.

Quiet. The scent of lavender, roses, and bergamot came from the other side. It was fresh but not present. She pulled out her lockpicks and went to work on the door. There were three locking mechanisms, all with different keys. It took her a bit longer than anticipated, but she could still hear Ben in the entryway. As long as the painting wasn't bolted to the wall, she had plenty of time.

She cracked open the door and ducked inside. The room was empty. The clock on the wall read 12:20.

CHLOE WAS STARING AT GAVIN. It was hard not to. There was something quintessentially sexy about watching the man drink. He rarely smiled. When he did, it was only a slight lift at the corner of his mouth. He'd poured the wine with the elegance of an expert sommelier. As he'd passed the glasses filled with ruby-red liquid around the room, he'd kept up a steady stream of banter. She couldn't hear him, but she could see his expression. He was wry. He was charming. He was flirtatious. He was serious.

At one point, he glanced over the rim of his wineglass and caught Chloe staring. His eyes locked with hers for a moment before she looked away. She crossed her arms and glanced at her watch.

It read 12:25.

THE PAINTING HADN'T BEEN LOCKED to the wood paneling, and it was easy to remove. It rested against the wall, waiting for her to carry it out. She took off the backpack Ben had packed for her, put on the coveralls, and shoved the cap reading "DePaul and Sons" on her head. The canvas was in a slimline floating frame so as not to detract from the truly odd art on the canvas. Before she removed it from the room, Tenzin took a moment to study it.

She really didn't understand surrealism.

But she *did* understand why this painting wasn't hanging with the others in the museum. She threw a clean drop cloth over the painting, left the black backpack in the corner of the room, and lifted the canvas by the middle stretcher bars. Then she walked out the door, hooking the edge with her toe to close it on the way out. She made the first turn carrying her awkward cargo and came face-to-face with an empty hallway. She could hear Ben in the distance, his voice growing louder.

The clock hanging on the wall ticked to 12:26.

BEN LIFTED the clipboard for the fifth time. "I don't care what you say, it says here that this painting was bought by an anonymous buyer at this address, paid for in full, and ordered to be delivered to this address tonight. You want me to get in trouble with my boss? You want me to call him right now?" Ben smacked his forehead. "What am I thinking? The guy's already asleep because it's *past fucking midnight already!* Will you just sign the paper and sort it out with your boss tomorrow?"

The butler was still sputtering, thrown off by the small crowd of household staff that had gathered around. Thankfully all were human, Ben noticed. Apparently Rothman House was only guarded by vampires, not staffed by them. It was what he'd been counting on.

"Andrew, will you please take this... box outside." The butler gestured toward a tall blond man who'd been hanging in the background. "Just take it outside and put it back on the truck so we can all go to bed."

"Whoa, whoa!" Ben yelled. "I don't think so." He puffed up his chest. "You going to sign for the painting?"

Andrew looked confused. "What?"

"You sign for the painting—you take responsibility for it—you can do anything you want. But if no one here is signing for the thing, then you better keep your mitts off. You know how much this lady paid for this piece?" Quiet from the surrounding crowd. "Yeah, me neither. But I do know I don't deliver thrift store junk, if you know what I mean." Ben glanced at the hallway clock. She had three minutes. "Listen, Jeeves, can you just sign for the—"

"I'm not signing for anything until I hear from my employer or Mr. O'Brien."

"I don't know anything about a Mr. O'Brien." Ben glanced at his paperwork. "Is that who lives here? Would he buy something all anonymous? That don't make sense."

He noticed a young woman in a uniform looking at him under his cap. He puffed up his chest and smirked. "How you doing, baby? You working here all night?"

She rolled her eyes at him and turned away.

"Hey, give me your number," he said to her back. "We'll hang out later."

"I say, Mr.... Whoever you are." The butler was livid. "That is quite enough."

All the employees started speaking at the same time. Some were laughing and others were incensed about Ben hitting on their coworker. As the volume rose, a black shadow flickered in the corner of his vision as Tenzin slid into the room, touching humans gently to move them out of the way. Everyone was paying attention to Ben, and no one even noticed the small woman sliding along the edges of the crowd.

His phone chimed at precisely 12:30.

Thank you, Cara.

Ben held up his clipboard as he pulled out his phone. "Shut up, shut up, will ya!" He made a big show of checking his phone, looking back at the paperwork, then his phone again. "That asshole! Can you believe this shit?" He felt the Samson painting slide behind the crate. The back panel slid forward and the painting notched into place, protected by the drop cloth covering the surface.

"What?" the butler shouted over the hubbub.

"My dispatcher just texted me. He gave me the wrong address. Owner's waiting up around the block. I can't believe this shit."

A groan came from the collected crowd, and the butler's expression was a mix of annoyance and relief.

"Hey, I'm sorry, Jeeves." Ben held out his hand, but the butler ignored it. "I got the right address. You got the right address. This yahoo from Boston don't know his ass from his elbow in this neighborhood, if you know what I mean."

Tenzin lifted the back end of the crate as Ben opened the door and tried to push the angry employees away.

"I'll get outta your hair now. Again, I'm sorry my dispatcher's an idiot."

"The nerve," the butler said. "His mistake does not excuse your rudeness."

"Eh, call my boss and complain in the morning," Ben muttered. "I just want to get outta here, am I right?"

Tenzin and Ben lifted the crate and walked out the door, nearly jogging to the truck as angry employees poured out the doorway and stood on the stoop, chattering while the butler tried to calm them down. Ben and Tenzin loaded the crate with the blank canvas and the Samson painting in the back of the truck. Tenzin jumped in back with the crate, and Ben jogged to the front, waving his clipboard at the irate employees of Rothman House.

At 12:33, *Midnight Labyrinth* was theirs.

21

Ben stared at the painting hanging over Mrs. Vandine's mantel. It was exactly as Emilie had described it, but far more gruesome than he'd imagined. A woman stood at the middle of a labyrinth, tall hedges surrounding her. She faced the painter, and all around her, creatures both macabre and fanciful flitted and danced. They played in the labyrinth and filled the sky where a moon hung full and bright. Clawed hands reached up from the ground and scratched her legs. Devils peeked out from the green while needle-toothed fairies flew overhead. A squat imp followed the woman, lapping at her feet, which were soaked in blood.

But the woman stood placidly in the midst of the horror, smiling with a very long and very sharp set of fangs. In her hands hung two white rabbits, their throats bloody, and the vampire's lips were crimson red.

She was entrancing—ethereal and deadly at once. She didn't look a whit like his partner, but something about her eyes reminded him of Tenzin. She was a survivor, and part of her enjoyed the fight.

Ben couldn't stop staring. It was possible Emil Samson had

wanted to depict the woman becoming a monster to fight monsters. It was possible that, like the imps and demons, the vampire was just another creature of the imagination he'd included in the work.

It was also very possible Samson knew about vampires, because those were some pretty accurate-looking fangs.

"It's a masterpiece," Mrs. Vandine said. "And yet so disturbing."

"It was a disturbing time." Emilie slipped an arm around her grandmother's waist. "It's technically brilliant. Look at his use of color. For a painting to be so vibrant and yet so dark is phenomenal. And his brushwork?" She sighed and put her head on her grandmother's shoulder. "I just wish we could display them together. She needs context."

"Will you hang it like that?" Ben asked. "On its own?"

"Of course," Mrs. Vandine said. "As my granddaughter said, it is a disturbing painting because it was a disturbing time. It's macabre, yes, but beautiful. And most importantly, it is my uncle's work. One of his finest pieces." She walked over to Ben and kissed both his cheeks. "How can I ever thank you for bringing it back to me?"

Ben's heart swelled. He'd tracked down priceless art and found lost artifacts for his clients, but turning them over to their owners never felt like this. He'd tried to imagine what it would be like to restore a piece to a family like Emil Samson's, a family who had lost so much and clung to the few memories that remained.

It was so much better than he'd imagined.

"I'm just glad she's home," Ben said. "Even if she took a few detours since the war."

So far, he'd heard nothing about the theft, but it was daytime. He'd taken the painting directly to a storage locker he kept in Brooklyn and dropped it off in the crate while Tenzin flew home. Then he'd driven the delivery truck back to DePaul and Sons to clean every trace of himself and Tenzin from it before he walked home. Not once had he spotted a tail.

That morning, he'd woken, driven his truck down to the locker to pick up the painting, then taken it to Emilie and her grandmother. They had been beside themselves, and Ben once again felt a million feet tall.

Mrs. Vandine went to the kitchen to make coffee while Emilie came to stand beside him. She hugged him around the waist and leaned into his chest.

"Do I want to know?" she asked.

"Doesn't matter if you do or not," Ben said. "I'm not telling you."

"Plausible deniability?"

He nodded. "There shouldn't be any trail that could lead anyone to you. If anyone suspected me—which I don't think they will—they'd think I was retrieving it for one of my private clients, not for my..." Ben looked down with a raised eyebrow.

Emilie smiled. "For your... girlfriend? Maybe?"

He nodded, unable to stop the huge grin. "Exactly. There's nothing that would lead them here. As far as you are concerned, you are the only owners of *Midnight Labyrinth*. The insurance papers I mocked up show a record of ownership as far back as the 1950s, which was around the time your great-uncle's work was gaining value in the European market. So it would make sense your grandparents started including it on the insurance at that time."

"Good." Emilie rested her head against his chest. "And you're safe?"

"I'll be fine. Don't worry about me."

"And Gavin and Chloe? Tenzin?"

"Emilie." He tilted her chin up and kissed her. "I told you: don't worry about me. Stay with your grandmother tonight.

Enjoy the painting. For the first time in seventy years, it's exactly where it's supposed to be."

~

HE DROVE HOME a few hours later, leaving Emilie with her grandmother to share memories and talk about their family. They had no desire to sell the painting, so as far as they were concerned, the insurance paperwork was incidental. But it was important to Ben. Not only had he created a trail of ownership for them, he'd done it in a way that vampires would never be able to detect. Only a very few of them were computer literate. Though they depended on computers and automated systems like everyone else in the modern world, most had no idea how that complicated electronic infrastructure worked.

He arrived home exhausted and fell promptly into his own bed, barely sparing a wave for Tenzin and Chloe, who were practicing in the sparring area.

Ben dreamt of running. It was nighttime, and he could feel the gravel beneath his feet as he dodged scaffolding and ducked into tunnels. He was running through a stone labyrinth covered in vines. The vines grew thicker and shot out to slice his face. His feet began to drag in the mud.

He could see the way out in the distance, but the narrow light grew smaller as he ran toward it. Hands reached from the ground to trip him. Something with claws landed on his back. He heard swooping sounds overhead and cackling from devilish throats. Hissing whispers echoed down dark corridors.

He ran past them, turning each time a hedge rose to block his way, but a sick feeling in the pit of his stomach told him the maze wasn't pushing him out but closing him in.

The lanes grew narrower.

He tripped and fell. Tasted blood in his mouth.

The laughter was higher. Sharper.

Claws dug into his scalp, drawing his head back, exposing his throat—

BEN WOKE in a cold sweat to the incessant ringing of his phone. He reached for it.

"Hello?"

"Was it you?"

He blinked and tried to clear the nightmare from his mind. "Who—?"

"Don't fucking play with me, Benjamin!" Novia O'Brien's voice was ice-cold. "You were the one asking about DePaul's."

"Novia?" He cleared his throat. "What are you talking about? Did something happen to DePaul's?" His waking confusion must have added to his denial, because he could hear her pause.

"Nothing happened to DePaul's."

"Okay." He sniffed and rubbed his eyes. "That's good. They seemed like nice guys. What's going on?"

"You haven't heard anything?"

"What would I hear?" he asked. "I was sleeping. Spent the day with my girl and her grandma. So what's going on?"

She went silent, like she was listening to someone in the background.

"Novia?"

"I need to go."

She hung up, leaving Ben rubbing his eyes and wondering what move to make. How much did Novia know? Had it been a mistake to use DePaul's? Should he call Gavin and Chloe? That was probably the worst thing he could do. Offer to help?

Possibly.

He sat up in bed, debated, then yelled, "Tenzin!"

A moment later, she walked in. "You called me, so I didn't knock. I'm assuming you don't care that you're shirtless."

"Novia O'Brien just called me. Asked me if I had anything to do with it."

Tenzin's eyebrows went up and she sat on the end of his bed. "Anything to do with what?"

"Which is exactly what I told her." He crossed his arms over his chest. He needed coffee. His brain was still in a fog. "She narrowed in on the DePaul's connection."

"Because you asked about them?"

"Yes."

"I wouldn't make too much of it," Tenzin said. "Every vampire in the city uses them for sensitive deliveries. All the DePaul's connection tells her is that it's another vampire, and she knew that already."

"Someone at the house could identify me. My disguise was minimal."

"Ben, we talked about this. Humans do not have good visual memory. The people at the house were noticing your body odor, your accent, the tattoo, and your mannerisms. They will not connect the well-groomed Benjamin Vecchio with the rude deliveryman. You avoided the cameras I showed you?"

He nodded. "Used the hat when I couldn't dodge them."

"As did I. So..." Tenzin shrugged. "They can question, but I don't see them pushing too hard. Cormac won't want to piss Giovanni off. And if this vampire has any sort of reputation, it's most likely known she deals in stolen art. She's no innocent. A certain margin of loss is expected in the game."

Ben nodded, but he still felt uneasy. He didn't like that Novia had called him nearly as soon as she'd woken for the evening. That meant that she had a gut instinct about him, and he didn't want her exploring it too much.

He took a deep breath. "Did you look at it?"

"The painting?"

Ben nodded.

"Yes," she said. "It was beautiful. It's no wonder his work is trending right now."

"And the woman?"

Tenzin smiled. "She's definitely a vampire."

"That's what I thought too. It could just be fantasy."

"No." Tenzin shook her head soundly. "You recognized the expression, didn't you?"

He did. Bloodlust. Vampires in the throes of bloodlust had a certain blank expression behind their eyes. That's what he'd recognized in *Midnight Labyrinth*. It was what most of his nightmares were about.

"Do you think I should I call Gavin and Chloe?" he asked.

"Were you planning on calling Gavin and Chloe?"

"No. I think they're both working tonight."

"Then leave it. Chloe was here during the day—if anyone cares to look—and she went back to Gavin's in the early afternoon. It's her normal routine as far as any of the O'Briens know. Nothing is out of the ordinary."

"Okay." Ben nodded. "Got it."

There was a long pause, and Ben realized it was the first time he and Tenzin had been really alone since the morning of the gala when he'd made his awkward, drunken confession. He hated feeling like anything hung between them.

"So," he started, "we're pretending the thing that happened the other night didn't happen, right?"

Tenzin looked genuinely confused. "What thing?"

She'd probably discounted it five minutes after she left while he'd been stewing on it for days.

"Never mind. It's nothing."

"Okay." She rose. "Do you want food? I'll make food. I want

noodles." She walked out the door, leaving Ben in bed. He glanced at his phone, but it was past ten o'clock. Too late to call Emilie, but not too late to text.

Hope you had a nice day, he texted. *Miss you being here. Come over tomorrow?*

She texted back a few minutes later. *Probably, but behind at work. Maybe late?*

Sure.

Good night. I'm turning in early. Grandmother is still glowing.

Ben smiled. *Tell her I said hi.*

I will.

He flipped back the covers and pulled on the pair of well-worn jeans he'd left on the floor that afternoon. Then he slipped his phone in his pocket and walked upstairs, wondering what Novia O'Brien was up to at that moment.

CHLOE WAS POLISHING glasses and watching Gavin as he conversed with Cormac O'Brien and his daughter with the bright red curls who only looked about five years younger than he did. She was having a hard time getting used to that part. Vampire families were not bound by age. Sometimes sires looked older than their "children," but just as often they looked younger. It was... interesting.

Gavin was casual, his hands in his pockets, leaning against the high bar top as the other vampires spoke to him. By their posture and expression, she was guessing they were asking about the theft.

Gavin wandered back to the bar a few minutes later while Chloe watched Cormac and his daughter leave through the front door.

"Nothing to worry about," he said.

"Good." She watched the door swing closed. "Do you think I should dye my hair a fun color?"

He almost looked offended. "What?"

"I love Novia's hair. It's so cool."

Gavin grimaced. "Bloody nonsense."

"I think mine is too wiry anyway. Too fine." She picked up another glass. "She has the right texture to dye it. Mine would probably get damaged."

"The right texture?" Gavin reached over, put his hand on the back of her neck to play with the tight curls at her nape. "I doona know a thing about women's hair, but yours is perfect." He dropped his hand. "It's your hair, so do what you want with it, but if you're welcoming opinions, then I vote you keep it as it is."

He leaned over, kissed her temple, then walked down the hall to his office.

It was a very Gavin gesture. Flirtatious, but just so much. He never let Chloe forget that he was very, very male and very, very attracted to her. But since she'd been staying at his house, he was oddly reserved about making any further moves. She'd expected him to steal kisses in the hallway or try to push her boundaries.

He didn't. So why did Chloe still feel pursued?

She finished filling an order for a group of day people, then walked back to Gavin's office. She still wanted to find out what Cormac and his daughter wanted. She tapped on the door and waited.

"Come."

Poking her head in, she saw he had an old-fashioned ledger out on his desk. "You know, they have software applications for that now. You could use Cara."

"Like I want to bloody recite every single figure to do with running this damn bar," he muttered. "No thank you. I'm fast with this method, and I don't have to worry about little shits like Ben hacking into my business."

Chloe smiled and closed the door behind her. "Speaking of Ben..."

He raised an eyebrow and said, "Very quiet, Chloe."

"Was their visit...?"

"Cormac and Novia were visiting in order to ascertain if I had any information that might lead to the recovery of a certain work of art that was taken from one of their guest houses last night."

"Oh?" Chloe sat across from him. "What was it?"

"They seemed reluctant to say."

"Is that so?"

"Apparently it was located in the room where we were"—he let the smile spread on his face—"enjoying ourselves the other night."

"Do you have to make it sound so illicit? We were kissing, Gavin. Kissing. That was all."

"I think you greatly underestimate how delightful that inter-lude was."

No she didn't. She had dreams about that kiss.

"So are we... suspects?"

His expression was angelic. "How could we be? We were here all last night, which was apparently when the sordid theft took place."

She mouthed, *Sordid?*

"Very sordid," he whispered. "Like our kiss."

"You have a one-track mind."

22

Ben spent the rest of the evening being very boring. He called his aunt and uncle. He organized his records. He read a new book on Persian antiquities a collector had recommended. He went to bed.

He woke the next morning and tried to call Emilie before he went to go running with Zoots, but it went to voice mail. She'd probably already left for work. He left a message, then walked to the subway. After his run, he needed to go up to Hudson Heights. He'd found another insurance paper he'd forgotten to put in the portfolio. Emilie might be at work, but her grandparents were retired. He'd drop it off with her before he forgot.

Running and climbing with Zoots proved to be the perfect cure for the dark and twisted dream he'd woken from. The gravel crunched beneath his feet. He fell twice but managed to climb the new wall on his third attempt—without cheating—prompting Zoots to applaud when he reached the top. He was dripping sweat as he walked to the subway, but he didn't want to head home when he was already halfway to Emilie's. Ben grabbed the towel from his backpack and caught the northbound train.

The ride was long and boring, but at least the train was on time. Ben got off at the 190th Street Station and made his way down the tree-lined streets. The summer heat was baking the pavement, and he was grateful for the shade.

He buzzed the apartment when he reached the building on Fort Washington Avenue, but no one answered. A resident opened the door right after and Ben grabbed it. He walked up to the second floor and knocked at 202.

No answer.

Ben frowned. He tried calling Emilie again, but it still went straight to voice mail. Should he leave the insurance paperwork under the door? "Hey, Emilie," he said after the beep, "I'm at your place and no one's home. Do you want me to..." He heard a door open next door. "Call me back when you get this." He hung up the phone and walked toward the older woman who was struggling with a trash bag. "Hey there." He reached for the bag. "Let me help you with this."

"Oh, thank you." She adjusted her large glasses. "It's so nice to have young people around. Everyone in this building is old like me." She smiled broadly. "But we're spry. Are you the new renter? I'm Mrs. Clark. It'll be nice to have someone young. Not that I'm going to use you for labor. I have a grandson for that—good boy, he lives in Harlem—but every now and then..."

"New renter?" Ben smiled and walked to the shoot. "I think you're thinking of someone else. I'm visiting my girlfriend. You know, the family next door to you. The Vandines. I'm dating Emilie."

The old woman squinted behind her glasses. "The Vandines?"

"Yes." He raised his voice. "I'm dating—"

"I'm not hard of hearing, young man." Mrs. Clark tapped her ear. "I have my batteries in. But Mrs. Vandine passed away two years ago. What are you talking about?"

Ben felt a cold knot form in the pit of his stomach. "What?"

"*Two* years ago?" She cocked her head. "Maybe it's been three. I do lose track of time."

"No, I saw her yesterday. You must be thinking of..." Who? Emilie's great-grandmother was dead. The old woman couldn't be thinking about her.

"I know who the Vandines are, young man. I've lived here for fifty years."

Ben looked around the hall, checked the door numbers. His heart began to race. "I'm dating their granddaughter, Emilie."

"Who?"

"Emilie." He reached into his backpack and removed the lockpicks he kept in the side pocket. "Emilie Mandel," he said to himself. "She's Emilie Mandel."

Mrs. Clark shook her head slowly. "I don't think the Vandines had a granddaughter. A grandson, yes. He's the one who takes care of the place."

Ben didn't wait for another sentence. He pulled out his lockpicks and went to work on the door to the apartment.

"What are you doing?" she asked.

"Just... I'm worried something is wrong," he lied. "With my girlfriend's grandmother. She's not answering the door." The lock clicked open and the door swung in.

Ben walked into the living room and stopped in his tracks.

The painting over the mantel was gone, though all the furniture remained as it had been. Ben walked through the living area and into the kitchen. It was scrubbed clean, though it had a homey array of decorations and appliances on the worn counters. He walked back to the hallway and into the first bedroom on the right, the one where Emilie had shown him the trunk with so many clippings featuring Emil Samson's work. Posters and postcards. Yellowed pages from newspapers and old pictures.

The bedroom was stripped clean.

The trunk sat at the foot of the bed, but when he threw it open, he was staring at the worn, curling paper lining the bottom.

No pictures.

No clippings.

Nothing.

Mrs. Clark had followed Ben into the apartment. She spoke from the doorway. "Their son rents it out to people from the internet. It's a beautiful place, isn't it? He left all their furniture here. His mother's china and everything! I don't know how he can sleep at night with strangers eating off his mother's china, but I'm more traditional, I think."

Ben stared at the empty trunk. Anger and inevitability warred in his head. "They're gone."

"I think they left last night. Were you interested in renting it?" She turned to leave. "I can get you the number if you—"

"Wait." The cold lump that had formed in his stomach spread like black ice through his veins. "The people who were here weren't the Vandines?"

"Are you feeling all right?" She frowned at him. "Didn't I tell you Mrs. Vandine passed two years ago?"

He had to be sure. "And they didn't have a granddaughter?"

The old woman shook her head, but all Ben could see was the tearful girl on the museum bench, fighting back tears in front of her dead uncle's paintings.

Running away.

Luring him in.

Giovanni's laughter on the phone.

"You do have a type, don't you?"

Emilie smiling at him in the sunlight, dressed in a yellow sundress outside his regular haunt.

So what are the chances... in a city this big?

What were the chances that he'd randomly run into Emilie Mandel, a girl who pushed every one of his buttons, twice in the space of a week? A girl with a brilliant laugh and a smart mouth. A girl thrown in his path, tied to an art mystery with a sympathetic grandmother and a noble mission to retrieve a work of art stolen from her family by the Nazis.

A mystery tailor-made to tempt him.

So what are the chances?

"I don't believe in chance," Ben muttered.

Mrs. Clark said, "What?"

Ben forced himself to keep talking. "The people renting this place, did you get their names?"

Her brown eyes were wide. "Didn't you say you were dating their granddaughter? You don't know their names?"

The ice in his stomach moved up to his chest and began to burn. He forced a smile to his face. "A misunderstanding, ma'am. Did you say you got their names?"

"She called herself Mimi. I thought it was cute. I never saw the son."

"The son?"

"Yes." She nodded. "She had her son with her, but he was an odd man."

"And when did they move in?"

"Three... four months ago, maybe? It was a long rental." She wrinkled her nose. "You're really not supposed to rent like that in this building, but most of the people have been so nice I didn't want to say anything. But this family..."

"What?" Ben walked to the hallway and offered his arm to Mrs. Clark. "Was there something unusual about them?"

Ben began walking Mrs. Clark to the door. He'd come back to search the apartment later if he needed to, but instinct told him whoever Emilie and her "grandmother" had been, they were good enough not to have left anything behind.

Mrs. Clark said, "I thought it was just the older woman, Mimi, and her son. And the son was strange. Had an accent, but I'm not sure from where. The girl I only saw a few times. I thought she was visiting the son. She didn't live with them, I can tell you that."

His chest might have been burning, but his voice was calm. "I'd like the number of the owner, the grandson you mentioned, if you still have it."

"Of course." She patted his arm. "What a thing! To move on and forget to tell your own boyfriend. Who would do something like that? I don't know if she's the right girl for a thoughtful young man like you."

Ben walked the old woman to her apartment and opened the door for her, pulling out his phone as soon as she walked in to look for the landlord's number. He tapped on Emilie's name and didn't blink when he heard her voice on the recording.

"I will find you," he said in a low voice. "You have no idea what you've done."

23

Tenzin was frying eggs and rice when Ben came home. He slammed the door and sat at the counter. He didn't say a word, but she could read his face better than any human she'd ever known. She'd studied his expressions and mannerisms as if he was her own personal map, her guide to the foreign world she'd woken in five years before.

Ben was angry.

No, he was livid.

When Ben was truly angry, he did the opposite of most humans. Most humans yelled or exploded outward. With Ben, the explosion was inward and it quickly turned from hot to cold.

Giovanni's influence? Maybe. But she suspected that part of Ben had been forged long before his fire vampire uncle had found and adopted him. She paused for a moment, then went back to frying the rice.

"Tell me when you're ready," she said quietly.

He didn't wait long. "We didn't steal the painting back. We just stole it."

Tenzin looked up and she was...

Not surprised.

"So the woman—"

"I don't know what her real name is, but the apartment is empty. It was a furnished rental."

Tenzin nodded. "And the grandmother?"

"Gone."

"The painting?"

"Gone."

Tenzin flipped over the scrambled eggs. "The clippings you showed me? The copies and pictures you took?"

"Forged, probably," Ben said. "It's not that hard to forge things. You and I both know that. The clippings she could have collected or faked. The pictures could have been anyone."

Tenzin turned the rice and added a few more drops of sesame oil.

"You're not shocked," Ben said.

"No."

"Why didn't you say anything?"

She drew in a breath and let it out slowly. "I didn't know for sure. She might have been legitimate. It was doubtful, but possible."

"But you didn't feel the need to tell me you were suspicious?" His voice was flat and cold enough to concern her.

"Would you have listened?" she asked.

"If you told me you thought the woman was conning me? Yes, I would have listened." He carefully gripped the counter. "What the hell, Tenzin?"

She raised her cooking chopsticks. "It wasn't about the woman."

"What are you talking about?"

"It wasn't. About. The woman," she said again, looking him in the eye. "You might—might!—have listened if it was just the woman. But you weren't obsessed with the woman."

Ben was silent.

"You wanted to find that painting," she said. "You were addicted to the mystery, and you wanted to take it. Having Emilie in the background just gave you an excuse. It made you a knight in armor instead of a thief."

He curled his lip. "She lied to me. She played me."

She nodded. "And she was quite good too. Did you have sex with her?"

"None of your business," he said through gritted teeth.

"That means yes." Tenzin went back to frying the rice. "That always makes it worse somehow, doesn't it? I don't know why, but it does."

"Tenzin—"

"Do you want me to kill her?"

Ben blinked. "What?"

Tenzin looked up to meet his eyes. "Think very carefully, Benjamin. Because I will."

"No." The ice had cracked. "I don't want you to kill Emilie. Or whatever her name is. I'm sure it's not Emilie."

"Okay."

"Jesus, Tenzin. I just want the painting back."

"I know. Because it was never about the woman." Tenzin grabbed a plate and served him food. Food always made him more levelheaded. "It was about the painting. The anger you're feeling is about her fooling you. It is about your pride."

Ben glared at the eggs and rice, but he picked up his chopsticks and started eating. "It's not just about my pride, Tenzin."

"No?"

"We stole a valuable painting—a painting with a vampire in it—from one of Cormac O'Brien's guests."

"Yes, we did."

He took a deep breath. "Should I call Gio?"

"Why? Do you think we can't get it back?" She leaned

across the counter and smiled. "This is the fun part, Benjamin. This is the revenge."

~

AT NIGHTFALL, Tenzin left Ben fiddling with his computer while she took off into the night. She landed on top of Cormac O'Brien's building and waited for the guard to find her.

"I need a word with him," she said. "When he has a minute."

The guard said, "He's busy tonight."

"He'll want to talk with me." She perched on top of a water tower and waited for Cormac to show. It only took ten minutes.

The earth vampire was wearing a pair of jeans and a black T-shirt that night. No glasses. No pipe. The affectations were gone and the look in his eye was brutal. He waved the guards away, leaving them alone on the roof.

"Good evening, Cormac."

"Tenzin."

"How are you this evening?"

"Cut the shit." He put his hands in his pockets. "You know, when I allowed you to set up house in my city, I knew you'd cause problems. It wasn't a question. The only real question was if the benefit of you owing me a few favors and increasing trade would be enough to offset the annoyance of having you around."

It's amusing that you thought you had a choice in the matter. Tenzin didn't say it aloud. She liked Cormac most of the time. "You probably overestimated how much I was going to increase trade."

"That fucking human of yours had something to do with this," Cormac spit out. "And he involved my own daughter this time, Tenzin. So stop pissing me off."

She floated down to stand in front of him. She looked up

and met his eyes. "I'm not going to tell you anything when you think you know everything."

He crossed his arms over his chest. "Then why are you here?"

"To remind you that everyone starts somewhere and some lessons are harder than others."

"I don't need any of your Zen bullshit tonight. I have a guest who is furious, Tenzin. A woman who was in serious negotiations with me about a distribution agreement that could change the future of my clan. A guest I made assurances to when I guaranteed the safety of her personal art collection she brought to the city as a gesture of good will."

"She should have kept the second painting at the museum then," Tenzin said. "Their security is a lot tighter than yours."

Cormac exploded. "*Do you want me to fucking kill you both?*"

In the blink of an eye, Tenzin flew into his face and grabbed him by the throat, digging her nails into his windpipe and cutting off his speech.

"You could try," she said in a singsong voice. "But you know how that would end, my friend."

He curled his lip, but she saw him grabbing control of his temper.

"Here is what will happen," she said quietly, still holding his throat. "You will buy me a little time. Just a little. I don't need much. Is that understood?"

He nodded his head slightly, but she didn't release him.

"After that time, you will have *Midnight Labyrinth* back and there will be no further questions." She released him. "Understood?"

Cormac rubbed his throat. "Keep your human away from my daughter."

"For the last time, Ben is not my human. And your daughter

could find far less honorable people to socialize with, believe me."

"Three days," he said.

She waved a hand. "More than enough time. It only took me thirty minutes to steal it." Tenzin saw Cormac start to boil again. "Consider this a favor. You really do need to work on your security." She stepped to the edge of the building, ready to fly to her next meeting. Cormac would be fine. Pissed off, but fine.

Which was... his usual state of being, if she thought about it. So really, no harm done.

"You know why she couldn't keep it at the museum," he said. "Don't you?"

"I know." Tenzin stepped up on the ledge.

"Things are volatile in France. She has enemies."

"Clearly. They went to a lot of trouble to obtain that painting. If she wanted to be safe, she should have destroyed it."

Cormac's voice softened. "It was her brother's work. Would you?"

Interesting. So that part of the story was true.

"Who suggested she bring her art collection here?" Tenzin stared down at her feet as they inched over the ledge.

Cormac was silent behind her.

"Was it Ennis?" she asked.

"He has connections at the museum. He'd heard about the surrealist exhibition and knew the Lady—"

"I don't need to know any of this to get the painting back," she said. "But think about how long it took you to answer me."

There was another long pause before Cormac spoke. "He's my brother."

Tenzin turned back to him. "I used to have brothers too. Three days, Cormac O'Brien. Goodbye."

She took some time to check in at DePaul and Sons. She liked the old man and there was no need for him to feel any blowback from their actions. If there was, she'd have to speak to Cormac again. She opened the alley door and walked in.

A Caucasian man in his thirties looked up from his workbench. "Oh! You're back early."

"Is my frame ready?"

"I'm afraid not," he said.

Tenzin glanced around the shop as he spoke.

"My father just doesn't work as fast as he used to," the young man said in a lower voice. "Are you sure I can't refer you to a proper framing shop? We know several who deal with customers like yourself who need privacy."

"I'd rather keep my business here," she said. "I don't mind waiting."

"Of course." He stood. "Would you like to see the progress?"

An older man stuck his head into the hall. "Bill, were you... Oh! Hello again."

"Hello. I came to check on my piece, but I'm happy to wait." Reassured that nothing was amiss with the old man and his son, Tenzin walked back to the door. "Please call my assistant when the frame is finished."

"Of course. Are you sure we can't—"

Tenzin walked out the door before he could finish. Which was fine. DePaul and Sons was a valuable business for just that reason. They accepted the unusual with no questions asked, but they wouldn't be moving this stolen piece. No, whoever Emilie was working with would have other channels. Tenzin walked farther into the shadowy alley and took to the air again.

Her last stop of the night was Gavin Wallace. Tenzin found

the wind vampire on his roof, sitting in the low light of the pool area, reading the newspaper while Chloe snoozed on a lounge chair next to him. Tenzin sat on his other side and waited for him to acknowledge her.

After a few minutes, he set the paper aside. "Can I get you a drink?"

"I appreciate that about you," Tenzin said.

"What's that?"

"You honor hospitality," she said. "Even when a visit isn't in your plans—even if you don't particularly like a person—you honor the ritual of hospitality."

"Fuck's sake," he muttered. "I'm just offering you a drink; it's not a sacred ritual."

"It was," she said. "For a long time."

"What is your purpose here, Tenzin? Normally I'd say this is far too soon to socialize after a job, but as Ben seems determined to make us all friends, there appears to be no avoiding it."

Tenzin glanced over at Chloe, but the girl was still sleeping soundly.

She looked back at Gavin. "You're taking my advice."

"I don't know what you're talking about."

"Fine." She kicked her legs up on the lounge chair and crossed her ankles. "I like her. I consider her a friend."

"Yes, so do I."

"Do you understand her situation?"

"Probably more than you."

Tenzin turned to meet his eyes. "Do you think so?"

Gavin looked away. "You didn't come here to talk about Chloe."

"No, I came here to talk about Ben."

"He having pangs of conscience?" Gavin curled his lip. "If he is, tell him he can assuage them by paying me back for that bottle of wine."

"I'll pay you for the wine."

Gavin narrowed his eyes. "Why are you paying for Ben's wine?"

Tenzin let out a long breath. "Do you remember the first time someone used you to steal something?"

The Scotsman let out a long and delightfully colorful string of curses. Tenzin had to smile. Scottish curses truly were amazing. She needed to go back to the Highlands for a visit.

"That girl," Gavin muttered after he'd vented his ire. "That fucking girl. I knew something was off with her."

"I did too, but..."

A long silence filled the air between them.

"She was actually quite good," Gavin admitted.

"Yes, I thought the same thing."

"Dinna come on too strong."

"Running away after the first meeting was a brilliant move," Tenzin said. "She could not have drawn him in faster after that."

"You saw them at the gala. She sold it. Ben might not like to admit it after this, but she had some genuine emotion for him. There was chemistry and you canna fake that."

"The best jobs are that way." Tenzin swung her legs over the lounge chair and sat up straight. "But now he knows her."

"Yes," Gavin said, sitting up straight. "And she knows him. She *knew* him."

"Yes."

"You think this was personal."

"I do," Tenzin said.

"That girl was human," he continued. "Someone trained her. Hired her. But why go to all the trouble to have Ben steal the painting? If you're skilled enough to run that job, you'd be skilled enough to get the painting yourself. Why use Ben?"

"To tarnish his reputation? Make him leave New York?"

Gavin raised his eyebrows. "Or make you leave."

That was a valid point. If Ben left New York, Tenzin would leave with him.

Tenzin was having fun brainstorming with Gavin. The vampire was far less cranky when he was discussing illegal activities than when he was discussing his legitimate business. "Who do you think benefits from us leaving?"

Gavin said, "I can think of an earth vampire who'd be more than happy for you *not* to have his brother's ear."

"Ennis?"

Gavin nodded.

"That's a possibility."

Silence fell between them.

Finally Gavin said, "He'll be brooding over this for a good long while, won't he?"

"I think getting the painting back will help." She sighed. "I'm going to end up owing you another favor."

Gavin smiled again. "I canna object to that."

"I like you more when your Scottish comes out."

Gavin's smile turned to a scowl. "What do you need?"

"Ask around," Tenzin said. "I want to know who the real thief is. Ben was content with one painting, but I'm fairly sure whoever is behind this will want all three, so keep an eye on the museum."

Gavin nodded. "I have a few contacts."

"They'll have to move it, but Ben and I can look into that."

"They won't use DePaul's."

"Not now; too much attention. They'll have other resources."

Gavin asked, "You have no idea who might be behind the girl?"

Tenzin cocked her head. "I have suspicions. They picked her, which means they know him. They know his weaknesses.

What he's drawn to. Some of that is obvious because of his age, but some of it..."

"Is personal."

Tenzin nodded.

"Does our Ben have enemies already? He is precocious, isn't he?"

"One in particular I'm thinking of. Luckily, his friends still outnumber the enemies. For now."

"Ebbs and flows." Gavin glanced at Chloe. "We leave her out of this bit."

"Agreed. She doesn't have the stomach for revenge. Not right now."

"Does Ben?"

"Ben?" Tenzin smiled. "You'll have to ask Chloe's ex-boyfriend sometime."

Gavin leaned back on the lounger. "I believe I will."

24

B en Vecchio walked into the diner in Queens and spotted Valerie Beekman immediately. She was sitting in a corner smoking a cigarette beside the No SMOKING sign, along with all the other late-night visitors to the diner just off the highway. The booths were cracked and fixed with duct tape. Half the neon lights flickered.

But perversely, the diner smelled fantastic. Gravy and chicken-fried steak drifted from the kitchen along with the scent of freshly brewing coffee.

Valerie Beekman hadn't seen him yet. He looked for the exits. One in the hallway by the bathrooms, but it was on the opposite side of the diner. The door he'd walked in. A fire exit near Valerie's booth. That was the one she'd go for.

If she even tried to run.

He walked forward and shook his head at the waitress before she could speak to him. There was enough noise in the diner that his quarry didn't look up. She didn't look up until he was three feet away and standing between her and the fire exit.

"Hey, Grandma."

The older woman looked up and a smile slowly spread over

her face. "You're a sharp one. I told her she was playing with fire."

Ben sat down when it became apparent Valerie wouldn't run. He hadn't thought she would. The age wasn't part of the costume. She had to be in her eighties if she was a day. The old con woman knew her limits. She wouldn't be outrunning him.

"How'd you find me?" The French was gone, and her native Queens accent shone through.

Ben said, "Your car."

Valerie frowned. "My car?"

"GPS units are handy when you drive upstate to visit your granddaughter in school and need directions. Their online security sucks though."

"Told her..." She smirked. "Playing with fire."

"Who is she?"

Valerie took another drag of her cigarette. "Don't know."

"You took a job for four months and didn't know who you were working with?"

"I have no illusions." She stubbed out a cigarette and lit another. "Do you know how many people want to hire an eighty-two-year-old woman? I'm not picky these days."

Fair enough. He couldn't imagine she had a wealth of jobs available, though he had no doubt she'd ruled back in the day. Valerie would have been a stunner in her prime. Plus she was smart.

"Your accent work is impressive. I've known a few French people over the years, and you nailed it."

"Thanks." She took a drag on the cigarette. "That was my claim to fame. My Italian"—she slipped into an accent Ben knew backward and forward—"is even better than my French. Don't you think?"

If Ben didn't know any better, he would have sworn up and down she was an upper-class woman from Genoa. He didn't want to be impressed, but he was. The woman might have conned him, but she had class and skill.

"I ran your bank numbers," he said. "You're doing better than average and drawing the max in social security."

"You better believe I am."

"So why are you still working?"

The old woman shrugged. "I get bored. What's life without a little job on the side?"

"A little job like art theft?"

"It's always been my favorite," Valerie said. "Usually things don't get violent, and I like pretty stuff."

"Yeah, you and my partner." Ben drummed his fingers on the table. "You've done pretty well for yourself, Valerie. Only two convictions and one stretch at Beacon. Not a bad career."

"You do know your shit." She lifted an eyebrow, clearly impressed. "And all my kids are still talking to me."

"Well, you're ahead of my mother on that one."

Valerie took another drag and nodded at Ben. "That figures. You grow up in this business and you know how it goes, young man. The girl had you. Lesson learned. You'll be more cautious next time."

"That's not how this goes," Ben said.

The old woman stubbed out her cigarette in the cut glass ashtray. "That's how it's gotta go."

"Not this time."

"You think you're special or something?"

"My auntie tells me I'm a goddamn treasure."

Valerie laughed, but it died on her lips when she saw his face. "Listen, kid, I know you're upset about the job, but—"

"I am not upset." Ben leaned forward. "I'm *focused*. Does your daughter know how you pay for Autumn's tuition, Valerie? How about your son-in-law? Cops don't like being married to criminals."

"My daughter is not a criminal." The old woman's voice turned hard. "She never had anything to do with—"

"Sure she didn't. But he's always wondered, hasn't he? They almost split when he found out about you."

Her wrinkled lips twisted in anger. "He knows I did my time."

"What was your spin, Val? Poor single mom down on her luck and forced into check fraud? Been straight for nearly sixty years, huh?" Ben's voice went cold. "You've been lying to him for thirty. You think he's gonna take that? Your daughter will probably get through the divorce okay, but you think a cop is gonna let his precious daughter keep spending her summer at grandma's place on Long Island if he knows you hang with criminals?"

"I do not let *any* of that shit touch my family," Valerie spit out. "Who the fuck do you think you are?"

"I'm the kid who's going to fuck up your nice life if you don't tell me who the girl is."

She lit another cigarette, but this time her hand was trembling. "I told you, I don't know."

"Not good enough."

"I heard the younger guy call her 'angel' once!" Valerie hissed. "She worked for him. I don't know if it's a nickname or a name."

"Tell me about the other guy."

"I'm pretty sure he really was French. Strange. He mentioned you a few times—didn't like you much—but he was..." Her eyes drifted off. "Really... nice."

"Nice?" Something about her eyes stirred Ben's memory. "What was his name, Val?"

"Don't know." She furrowed her brow and shook her head. "I can't remember details. I barely saw him anyway. The two of them, they always talked in the other room. I know he mentioned another name, but I don't think it was his. Ellis. Emmet or something."

Ennis O'Brien. Ben wasn't surprised to hear Ennis's name. Maybe Ennis paid for something—used his connections to bring the Labyrinth Trilogy to the United States—but the vampire wasn't a con. Someone else put this together. Someone who knew Ben's weaknesses. Someone... with a grudge?

Pretty sure he really was French.

Didn't like you much...

This was bringing back far too many memories of Scotland. Ben leaned forward. "The Frenchman. Did you ever see him during the day?"

She frowned. "Yeah, of course."

"Are you sure?"

"I think..." Her eyes swam again. "Yes, he was very nice."

Ben muttered a curse, but at least he was sure the other person in the scam—the "son" that the neighbor had mentioned —was immortal. Valerie couldn't tell him anything useful about him, which meant the vampire had wiped her memory with amnis.

"The other name he mentioned, was it Ennis?" Ben asked.

"No." Valerie blinked. "Yes."

"It was Ennis?"

"I think so." Her eyes cleared. "What is going on here?" She looked at her coffee cup. "Did you drug me?"

"I didn't do anything to you. When did they take the painting?"

"Two nights ago. It was gone an hour after you left the place."

So the night he'd been texting Emilie, she'd already ripped him off. He was tempted to get pissed off again, but that wasn't a productive use of time.

"What did the strange one look like? The man."

Valerie shrugged. "Good-looking. Longish brown hair. Brown eyes. He dressed European. All smiles and charm. Pale." Her eyes narrowed. "Really pale. He must have been using something. He must have given me something that made my memory all cloudy."

"Sure." Ben grabbed a golf pencil wedged in the corner of the booth and quickly sketched a face on the napkin. "I'm sure he gave you something."

She stubbed out her second cigarette and lit another. "I ain't senile, kid."

"Not saying you are." He finished the sketch and turned it around. "This the guy?"

Valerie's eyes went wide. "How'd you know?"

It was all the confirmation Ben needed. "Go upstate to visit your daughter," he said. "Maybe don't come back to the city. Ever."

"Who are these people?"

Ben stood. "Way more dangerous than your average lowlifes, Valerie. You want to keep that good streak going? Get out of town."

WHEN HE GOT BACK to the loft, Tenzin was already there with Gavin.

"René DuPont," Ben said. "He's the vampire Emilie is working with. And I think Ennis—"

"Ennis O'Brien is in on it?" Gavin asked. "You would be correct, my friend."

"René?" Tenzin turned to Gavin. "That would be the Frenchman I was talking about."

"The one who tried to kill Ben last year? That would explain the personal aspect."

Ben asked, "How did you know about Ennis?"

"Besides being suspicious of a tricky minge?" Gavin asked. "Tenzin asked me to keep my ears open. There was gossip about Ennis meeting with a Frenchman—also an earth vampire—and trying to avoid attention. All sorts of our kind chattering about it though. Ennis canna keep a secret to save his life."

"In this case," Tenzin said, "I believe that may be exactly right."

Ben took a deep breath and let it out slowly. "I'm sorry, Gavin."

"For what? Tenzin's already offered to pay me for the wine."

"For getting you involved in all this."

"Not your fault. This happens to all of us at one point or another." Gavin smiled ruefully. "It's almost an honor to see you taken for once. Your life has been far too charmed thus far."

"Sure," Ben said. "Whatever you say." His life had been shit before his uncle found him, and that shit just kept rearing its ugly head. His mother was right. You couldn't trust anyone.

"So who is this René DuPont?" Gavin asked.

"A vampire we angered in Scotland," Tenzin said. "He's an interesting fellow. Related to Carwyn's clan."

"The black sheep of that virtuous crowd, I'm guessing," Gavin said. "And he's teamed up with Ennis O'Brien to rip off Cormac O'Brien? That seems an unlikely play."

Tenzin said, "Ennis is an interesting development. I can't decide if I'm surprised or not. In a way, I am."

"I'm not," Ben said. "Didn't Gavin say that this Lady of Normandy was negotiating a deal with Cormac? If it was successful, Cormac would cement his leadership of the clan. Right now he's de facto. If he signed a distribution deal for blood-wine that brought in enough money and settled their businesses on the right side of the law, then he'd be undisputed."

Tenzin said, "Ennis doesn't want that to happen."

"Does he want to take over?" Ben asked.

"No. He doesn't want to lead. He just doesn't want Cormac to lead."

"Why not?"

"Because then Cormac will have to kill him," Tenzin said. "Once Cormac is truly the leader of the clan, he won't be able to ignore Ennis's messes. He'll kill him. Ennis would partner with his worst enemy to save his own neck."

"You really think Cormac would kill him?" Gavin scowled. "It's his brother."

"So?" Tenzin looked genuinely confused.

Ben said, "So maybe... Ennis knows this Lady is coming to New York to negotiate with Cormac. They've probably been in talks for months."

"Ennis isn't happy," Tenzin said. "But René... Why is he involved? Do you think Ennis is paying him?"

"Ennis is a cheap bastard," Gavin said. "For all his extravagance, I don't see him paying anyone. Not out of his own funds."

Ben said, "René only works if the price is right. Someone in France wants this vampire exposed or vulnerable. Ennis told me at the gala he'd just been to France. Even said he'd heard my name."

"France is a mess since Jean Desmarais was killed. It could be that this Lady of Normandy has her own enemies. Stealing the painting is about hurting her. Someone in France hires René to steal the *Midnight Labyrinth*, and René sees an opportunity when he meets Ennis O'Brien. Paintings are easier to steal when they're being moved. René is savvy enough to use Ennis."

Tenzin nodded. "Ennis uses his connections through Historic New York to plan this surrealist exhibit and convince this vampire to contribute her artwork to the exhibit."

"And she accepts as a gesture of goodwill," Gavin said.

"But *Midnight Labyrinth* isn't on display," Tenzin said. "So

René drops a pretty girl in Ben's lap, and she leads him on a merry chase to find her lost treasure."

Ben curled his lip as Gavin and Tenzin shared a look. "Don't say it," he muttered.

Gavin grinned. "It really was beautifully planned."

"It was, but I still don't like it," Tenzin said. "If Cormac had just killed Ennis the first time I told him he needed to, this would never have happened."

Ben rubbed his temples where a headache was forming. "To be fair, you suggest killing people a lot, Tenzin. I'm not saying you're wrong, I'm just saying that sometimes it seems excessive. That might have been Cormac's reason for not taking your advice."

"I doona give two shites about O'Brien politics," Gavin said. "It's none of my business. What I do know is that this French bastard pissed off a very prominent blood-wine producer by taking her painting."

"You do remember that you helped in the theft, right?" Ben asked.

"Not as far as she knows. But if I can help get it back to her"—the Scotsman's smile turned wicked—"I imagine I'll be able to sign a very favorable deal. And that's always worth my time."

Ben shook his head. "Always a profit angle."

"Well, yes. Some of us aren't charitable humans." Gavin walked to the fridge and grabbed a cold beer. "So we know that René DuPont has the painting and he wants to move it back to France. So what is his next play? He'll try to move the painting, yes?"

Tenzin shook her head. "Not yet."

"Why not?"

Ben said, "If this is René, then he'll want all three paintings."

"Maybe he was only contracted for one."

"Doesn't matter," Tenzin said. "He'll want all three."

"How do you—"

"I'd want all three," Ben said. "If I could get them. Wouldn't you?"

Gavin pursed his lips. "Fine. Yes. It's neater. And it's a really excellent series. I have a house outside Barcelona that would... Well, never mind. So René will be looking to steal the other two paintings, but they're at the museum."

"Far better security at MoMA," Tenzin said. "I checked."

"Of course you did," Ben said. "So... we have to steal them before René does."

"We don't have to steal them," Tenzin said. "Not exactly. We just have to make sure they don't get stolen."

Gavin and Ben both looked at her.

"So yes," she said. "The easiest way to make sure of that is to take them ourselves."

"Exactly," Ben said. "So how do we break in?"

They all turned when they heard a key in the door.

Chloe walked in. "Hey."

Ben stared at her. He'd forgotten Chloe didn't work at the bar that night. Shit.

She frowned. "What's going on?"

"Nothing."

All three of them said it at once.

All three of them were lying.

Chloe dropped her backpack by the door. "Really?"

"What?" Ben was using his innocent look.

"Do you honestly believe that face is going to work?" she

asked. "I've seen it for too many years. I repeat: what's going on?"

Gavin said, "I thought you were working at the pub tonight, dove."

Chloe didn't mind *dove* when Gavin was being sweet, but it pissed her off when he was being secretive.

She put her hands on her hips. "Well, *sugar-buns*, I don't work at the pub on Thursday nights. I work here with Tenzin. I'll forgive you all for forgetting that because you're involved in plotting a dastardly plan. Now, what is going on?"

Tenzin was the one who broke the silence.

"Emilie wasn't really Ben's girlfriend. She was a con artist who fooled him into stealing *Midnight Labyrinth* for her, which she then handed over to René DuPont, who is Ben's nemesis, and now we have to get it back so Gavin can sign a favorable blood-wine deal with the Lady of Normandy, who is the rightful owner of the painting." Tenzin flew over and handed Chloe a stack of mail. "These are mostly bills. Can you pay them tonight?"

So many thoughts. So very many thoughts.

Gavin opened his mouth, but Chloe raised a hand and he shut it.

"So Emilie was a con artist and not who she said she was."

"Her real name is probably not Emilie."

"I guessed that part," Chloe said.

Gavin spoke up. "*Sugar-buns?*"

Chloe's eyes swung back to him and she shrugged.

"You haven't even checked my *buns* to see if they're to your liking." His eyes heated. "But feel free. In fact, you're welcome to check anything you like. If you're looking for descriptors, I'd be happy to provide you a more accurate list."

Chloe looked at him. "Seriously?"

"Yes, I'm quite serious about that."

Ben started, "What Tenzin was trying to say—"

"Is that Emilie lied about Nazis stealing her family's art," Chloe said.

"Yes."

"The basic story she told us is correct," Tenzin said. "I have reason to believe that the Lady of Normandy is actually Emil Samson's sister, Adele. She must have become a vampire before her brother was killed. She had a child, but that child died during the war. Her husband died as well. The whole family died. Except for Adele."

"Her whole family was killed." The black mourning garb of the vampire made a lot more sense when Chloe saw it in that light. "And Emilie—or whatever her name is—knew just enough of that story to lie to Ben? You mean she faked all those clippings and photographs and postcards at the apartment. Her grandmother—"

"*Not* her grandmother. Someone hired her. Emilie wasn't working alone."

"But she used Adele's real story and Emil's death to... steal Adele's own painting from her?"

"Yes," Ben said.

"That *bitch!*"

Ben and Gavin's eyes both went wide.

"She used a tragedy to lie to us so we would help her steal from the real owner, the artist's own sister?"

Gavin said, "Apparently yes."

"I hate her so much right now." She glanced at Ben. "Who is René DuPont? Was that the old lady?"

"No, the old lady was Valerie Beekman from Queens. Pretty sure she's headed upstate to visit her daughter after our talk earlier tonight."

"Well, she's a liar too." Chloe got more and more incensed

as she thought about it. "So this chick used you to steal a painting for her?"

"Yes."

"She just... *used* you. Like a tool!"

Gavin started laughing, and Ben grimaced. "That's not exactly the way I'd put it, but—"

"Tenzin called this René guy your nemesis. I didn't know that was actually a thing." She glanced at Gavin. "And you! You're helping so you can sign a good wine distribution deal?"

"You've seen the bills for the Costa de Prata."

"And I've seen what you charge for it," Chloe said. "You're doing just fine."

"I don't want to interrupt your tirade," Tenzin said, "because it's really quite good. But are you going to pay those bills tonight?"

"Yes, Tenzin. Just give me a chance to deal with..." Chloe waved a hand at Ben and Gavin. "All this."

Gavin asked, "What's wrong with using this opportunity to make a better deal with a producer?" He sidled over to Chloe and tucked a tight coil of hair behind her ear. "You smell delicious tonight. Have you eaten anything? Shall we order some food?"

He was incorrigible.

"I'm fine," she said. "Stop trying to charm me."

"I could but I won't, because I enjoy it too much."

"Self-indulgent vampire," she muttered.

"I know. I really am," he said. "You should move in with me and keep me accountable for all my sins."

Chloe's cheeks heated at the thought of Gavin's sins. "I am not your mother."

"I should hope not." He raised an eyebrow. "But you're welcome to be my keeper."

"You don't want that either." She lowered her voice to a

whisper. "Stop trying to distract me, and tell me what's going on."

Gavin's charming facade slipped. "I doona want you involved."

"I'm already involved. I need you to keep me informed."

The corner of his mouth twitched, but he nodded. "We think René is going to try to steal the other two paintings. He'll want the complete set, whether he's been hired for it or not."

"The other two are at MoMA."

"I know. Ben and Tenzin were just—"

"Wait." She pulled out her phone and scrolled through her email. She'd gotten something from the museum newsletter. Something about the surrealist exhibit... "They *are* at MoMA, but they won't be there for long. The exhibit's last night is tomorrow. Friday night. They just sent out a reminder today for museum members."

Ben said, "That's when they'll go for it. It'll be over the weekend. Probably Saturday night."

"Why?" Chloe asked.

"Because things are always easiest to steal when they're being moved," Gavin said. "Everything is in flux. The museum will be open over the weekend. People complain about noise and Americans are ridiculously accommodating, so the museum staff will be working at night."

Ben was looking at his phone. "There's an exhibition of Picasso's pen-and-ink drawings scheduled to open less than two weeks after the surrealist exhibit closes."

Gavin said, "Pen-and-ink means books. Sketchpads. Those need cases. Tables. Flat surfaces for display. They're going to break the surrealists down and move them as quickly as possible. They'll have a lot of shuffling to do."

"Can we take advantage of that?" Ben asked. "Tenzin said museum security is tight."

"There are protocols for breaking down a museum exhibit," Gavin said, "but they can be rushed. And every one is a little different. Mistakes are unavoidable. Some of the paintings and sculptures will be moved back to other parts of the museum. Some will go into storage. Others will be delivered back to donors. With everything in transit..."

"The two other Labyrinth paintings will be vulnerable," Tenzin said. "They're two paintings among dozens, most of which are far more valuable. Samson's not unknown, but he's not Magritte or Dali."

"Exactly," Gavin said. "We have to get into the museum Saturday night." He looked at Tenzin. "Any ideas?"

"Oh..." Tenzin smiled. "One or two."

25

Ben drank a beer on Tom's couch, watching the man tape the ribs Ben had just broken. Tom might have been an abusive asshole, but he had decent taste in beer. Ben pressed his swollen knuckles to the cold glass bottle.

Fighting hurt. Which was why most movie fight scenes were complete bullshit. He should have used the marble paperweight again. His hands were too valuable to break. This was why Ben avoided violence when he could. Adrenaline was the antithesis of thinking.

Tom winced as he twisted his torso to secure the tape. "Are you done?"

"With what?"

"With me?"

The man had two black eyes and a broken lip. Three ribs were fractured and his hands and throat were bruised. Ben had refrained from doing more damage to Tom's skull. He didn't want to have to take the man to the emergency room.

Tom stared at him through two black eyes.

Two black eyes.

Cut lips.

Broken ribs.

Bruised windpipe.

They were the same injuries Chloe had born months ago when she first came to Ben's apartment in the middle of the night.

Was it enough?

"Be wise, Benjamin Vecchio. For though a sword must be drawn to protect the needy, and anger is necessary for survival, a lack of discipline leads only to death in the spirit."

The doctor's words came back to him.

Was it enough?

It had to be. He'd received no pleasure from beating Tom. As Arjan Singh had predicted, there was only a dulling of his spirit, a cold, ruthless shell that coated his skin like an animal's carapace and grew thicker with every bruise he left on the man.

Ben had satisfied the relentless drive to make Tom pay, but it gave him little satisfaction. It wasn't about that. It was about evening the scales. Tom was a bully and a criminal. Chloe would never forget being helpless under his fists. Tom needed to know what it was like to feel helpless too. Had the bully learned a lesson?

Maybe. Only time would tell.

"It's enough," Ben said. "As long as you never lay another hand on a woman."

The man nodded.

"I want to hear it, Tom."

"I will never lay another hand on a woman," Tom said.

"You'll stay in the city so I can keep an eye on you. I left my card. If you move, you will email me. If you don't, I'll find you. Do you believe me?"

The second time Ben had visited Tom, he'd been holed up at a hotel.

The third time he'd met Ben with a gun.

Neither option had deterred Ben. After the third visit, Tom didn't try to fight.

"I will find you," Ben said more softly. "Do you believe me?"

"Yes."

"If you try to run, I'll send my partner after you. She's not as even-tempered as I am." Ben finished his beer and stood. "You don't want my partner coming after you, Tom."

"I understand," the man said through gritted teeth.

"Are you going to try to contact Chloe again?"

"I don't know anyone named Chloe."

"No, you don't." Ben walked to the door, opened it, and closed it behind him.

He was done.

GAVIN WAS WAITING for him on the sidewalk, looking up at the lights of Tom's apartment.

"She'd never know," he said.

"She'd figure it out." Ben flexed his sore hands. "Come on, Gavin."

Gavin didn't move.

"She doesn't want this. She's not impressed by macho behavior or strutting. She'd be pissed at me if she knew I was still coming here. You don't need to make her angry at you too. I'm done."

"And I have not even begun," Gavin said. "I want him dead."

"It's not about you." Ben bumped his shoulder with Gavin's. "She didn't want him dead."

Gavin looked away from the windows and met Ben's eyes. The rage took Ben by surprise. Gavin's fangs were elongated. The air around him stirred, as if he'd lost an edge of control over his amnis. Ben had known Gavin had feelings for Chloe, but this level of anger indicated a far greater attachment than he realized.

"It's not about you," Ben repeated. "It's about Chloe. And she wants to put this behind her. I returned to him every bruise and every break he dealt her. So we need to let it go. I'll keep tabs and make sure he's not a threat to anyone else. Anything more than that is indulgence."

Something passed over Gavin's face. Recognition? Awareness? The air around him stilled and his fangs fell back. The anger retreated and the laconic humor returned. "Christ, you sound so much like Giovanni when you're lecturing me. It's enough to make me boak the blood I drank for dinner."

"Thanks." The cold carapace of violence thinned. "I can think of a lot worse comparisons than me to my uncle right now."

"Are you still brooding about the girl?" Gavin rolled his eyes. "Everyone takes their turn as a mark, Ben. I've been fooled. I doubt Tenzin would admit it, but so has she. There's always someone just as smart as we are, looking for a crack in the armor."

"You admitting you have cracks?"

"Everyone has cracks." Gavin's face was deadly serious. "Anyone that tells you different is a lying shit."

They walked in silence for four more blocks.

"Do you think Tenzin's plan will work?"

"Yes, because we're vampires and both she and I can use amnis. Humans on their own?" Gavin shook his head. "Not on your life. If you tried to pull this off on your own, you'd be in a jail cell."

"Thanks."

Gavin cracked a smile. "What do the kids say these days? I'm keeping it real."

GAVIN AND BEN arrived back at the apartment to hear the sounds of thumping and grunting on the floor below. Ben ran down the steps to see Chloe lying on the ground, arms spread wide, staring up at the ceiling.

"What's going on?"

Chloe panted. "That's. Totally. Unfair."

"What?" Ben ran to her and looked up.

Tenzin was hovering over Chloe, nearly in the rafters. "Fighting with vampires is not fair," she said. "You need to find our weaknesses or you'll have no chance of surviving."

Gavin walked in behind Ben. He must have stopped in the kitchen, because he was holding a beer. "What's going on?"

Chloe glanced over, her eyes darted down. "Speaking of unfair."

Gavin looked amused. "All's fair."

Ben frowned and looked down. "What is she talking about?"

Gavin kicked up a knee, and Ben noticed he was wearing a kilt that night.

"And?"

"Kilts are catnip these days," Gavin said. "Bloody cable television is doing half my work for me."

Ben glanced down. "Well, you do have great legs, Gavin. Very shapely."

"Thank you. I work out."

"Really?" Ben asked.

"No, you idiot. I'm a vampire." Gavin unlaced his combat boots at the edge of the mat and set his beer down. "Come now, dove, you can't lie there all night and try to sneak a look up my kilt." He walked over and held out a hand to Chloe. "Up you go."

She let him help her up and stretched her shoulders. "You're doing it on purpose."

"What, love?"

"Wearing more kilts." She turned and Gavin rubbed her shoulders. "You know I like them."

"Of course it's on purpose." He ran his hands down her back, but it wasn't a seductive move. It was... comforting. Almost routine. A man rubbing his woman's back after she'd had a long day.

Ben looked up at Tenzin, who was watching them with a smile. He nodded toward Gavin and Chloe. Tenzin just shrugged.

"You're not done," Tenzin said. "I want you to practice that throw on someone taller."

"What throw?" Ben asked.

"Judo," Gavin said. "Tenzin's been practicing judo with Chloe. My suggestion."

"Judo?" Ben should have thought of judo. It was his aunt's martial art of choice.

Gavin nodded. "It's a good choice for beginners. And especially good for Chloe with her build."

Chloe smiled. "What Gavin means is I have thunder thighs."

"What I mean is you're a fucking brilliant athlete with a mass of power in your legs, hips, and abdominals," he growled. "Which means you need to be utilizing techniques that make the most of those strengths, not focusing on the fancy footwork and swordplay these two practice. Tenzin can fly." He pointed at Ben. "That one has abnormally long arms for his height."

Ben frowned. "They're not abnormal." Were they?

"It gives him a massive reach for hand-to-hand combat and swords. But you will do better with judo." He unbuckled his belt and tossed it near his boots. "Try me."

Chloe's eyes went wide. "What? No."

"Why not?" Gavin said with a wink. "Worried you'll be overwhelmed if you see what's going on underneath, dove?"

"You're ridiculous. And no, because you're way bigger than me."

It was true. Gavin wasn't a massive man. Probably five foot ten inches or so. He was well-built and leanly muscled. But Chloe was tiny. She was a full foot shorter than Ben, even if she was strong.

"Throwing a larger opponent is the point," Tenzin said. "Most of your opponents will be bigger than you. You can't fly to get away."

"Thanks for the reminder," Chloe grumbled, squaring off against Gavin.

Ben could see her nerves start to build.

"Focus on what we talked about," Tenzin said. "See the geometry of his body and yours. Find your center of gravity."

Chloe let out a breath and looked Gavin up and down.

"I love it when you do that," he muttered.

"I'm not trying to flirt."

"So you say."

In a burst of speed, Chloe stepped forward and planted her right foot by Gavin's. She locked his arm in hers and pulled him off-balance at the same time she twisted and planted her hip against his pelvis, then she bent down and tossed him over her right shoulder. In seconds, she was straddling his chest with both thighs, holding him against the mat.

Gavin groaned.

Her eyes went wide. "Did I hurt you?"

"No. That was perfectly executed. Well done."

"So why are you groaning?"

Chloe tried to move, but Gavin grabbed her wrists.

"Fucking hell," he said. "That was incredibly sexy."

Chloe was breathing in short bursts. "What?"

"So damn sexy."

The color rose on Chloe's cheeks. "I wasn't doing it to turn you on."

"I know."

I do not need to see this. Ben inched toward the stairwell.

Nope.

Ben could accept Gavin having the hots for Chloe in theory, but he didn't need to witness it.

"You were so damn good." Gavin twisted his wrists out of her grip and sat up with preternatural grace, scooting Chloe down so she straddled his hips. "You took your time analyzing my stance, but once you'd decided, you moved so fast."

"It's a little like dance. Slow training, then a burst of speed at execution."

"Exactly." Gavin's eyes were locked on Chloe. "Tenzin, get the fuck out of here."

Ben glanced back. Tenzin was still hovering near the rafters.

"She's not my ex-girlfriend," Tenzin said. "I find this fascinating."

"Get the fuck out of here!"

Ben was already up the stairs.

"THIS ISN'T A GOOD IDEA," Chloe said. She couldn't take her eyes off Gavin's mouth. His lips, flushed and glistening. His fangs peeked out to rest on the full swell of his bottom lip. He was so aroused, so tempting, and he smelled so good. "Gavin?"

"I do many things that are very bad ideas." He leaned forward and inhaled the scent of her neck. "I've learned to live with the consequences."

Her head fell back. What was she thinking? His touch was intoxicating. If she hadn't already experienced the buzzing warmth of amnis on her skin, she'd think he had her under some kind of spell. But there was no spell. No magic. The heightened awareness was from his scent and his touch, not from any mental manipulation.

"Gavin?"

"Yes." His lips never landed. They skimmed up her neck and over the line of her jaw. She leaned into him, and he twisted her arms behind her, locking her wrists in one hand while he slid fingertips up her arm. Goose bumps rose on her body. Shivers overtook her. Her pulse was pounding, and she could feel the rock-solid muscles of his thighs as she leaned into them. Their torsos were pressed together. Her breasts against his chest. Pelvises locked. It was the most intimate pose a man had ever held her in.

She was exposed, but she didn't feel any fear. No panic.

It was Gavin.

How many nights had she slept in his house, vulnerable in slumber and safe in the morning? How many nights had he read a book silently as she practiced yoga or ballet, wordlessly watching over her until she felt strong and confident again?

"What am I to you?" she whispered.

Gavin slowly lifted his head. "What?"

"I don't know what I am to you." Chloe swallowed the lump in her throat. "I want you. You want me. That's obvious. But what am I to you, Gavin Wallace? A wounded bird to protect? An amusement to pass the time?"

He shook his head and released her wrists. "You're neither of those things."

"What then?"

Gavin took a breath and let it out slowly. He leaned back, propping himself on his arms but keeping Chloe locked to him with her thighs straddling his hips and his knees caging her. "What do you think you are?"

Chloe opened her mouth, but nothing came out.

A wry smile from Gavin. "That's a problem then."

"I don't—"

"You're a woman worth knowing, Chloe Reardon."

"What does that mean?"

"Just that." He lifted his hand and cupped her chin in his palm. "If you take nothing else from me, take this. You're worth knowing. You're worth discovering. You're worth..." He smiled, and it was so gentle it brought tears to her eyes. "Damn it, she was right."

"What?"

"I'll tell you someday." Gavin smiled and leaned forward, pressing a kiss to her lips. Once. Twice. The third time he licked his tongue out and tasted her. "But not yet."

Wait for me. Her heart said it even if her mouth didn't. *Wait for me to find myself in this odd night world. Wait for me to discover who I'm supposed to be.*

"Should I stay here tonight?" Chloe said.

"Why?" Gavin continued to watch her, letting his eyes roam over her face. It felt as intimate as the brush of his fingers. "You can stay here if you like, but your room will always be ready in my home. I was thinking you'd like a soak in the tub with all the wrestling you did today."

Unexpected emotion clutched her throat. "A soak sounds good."

"Then it's settled." He lifted her by the hips as if she weighed nothing. Gavin moved around the practice area, gathering his things. "You'll stay at my place tonight. None of the plans for tomorrow have to start before dusk, do they?"

Chloe usually thought of Gavin as being so human. He was

unfailingly careful at the pub and wore humanity like a comfortable suit. It was rare for him to exhibit the "vampire stuff" to Chloe. The effortless strength was unnerving. The speed made her dizzy.

"What?" She blinked to clear her vision.

"The plans for tomorrow night," he said. "Breaking into the museum? All that starts after dusk, yes?"

"For you. Tenzin is heading over to the museum tonight to do her thing. Ben and I will head over in the late afternoon. The museum is open until nine."

"Excellent." He paused in front of her. "Was there anything else you needed to do here before we left?"

"I... uh, I need to pay some bills for Tenzin and rework some stuff in the house calendar."

"A couple of hours?"

She nodded.

Gavin said, "Then I'll head to the pub to check in with Audra. Call my office there if you finish early."

"Okay."

He slid his hand along the curve of her waist to the small of her back and pulled Chloe in for a kiss against her temple. "Well done, dove. You're a natural with the standing throws. I'll see you later."

Before she could say another word, he flew away.

Flew. Away.

"He flies." Chloe knew that. She knew it in her head. But she didn't know if she'd ever seen it before. "He flies. Because he's a wind vampire. So he flies."

TENZIN WAS LISTENING at the stairwell with a smile on her face. She heard, rather than saw, Gavin flying up the stairwell, through the apartment, and out the french doors leading to the roof.

Clever, clever vampire.

Tenzin made a mental note to never underestimate Gavin Wallace. The vampire was savvy enough to play the long game.

Ben was in the kitchen heating up some frozen curry she'd made two nights before. He was stirring a pot on the stove, and his hand was sunk in a bag of frozen peas.

Tenzin said, "You know, I do cook with those."

"Not with these you don't."

"Gavin and Chloe—"

"I don't want to talk about it."

Tenzin frowned. "Are you jealous?"

"No. I just don't want to talk about it."

"Because Gavin is your friend and he's likely going to have sex with a woman you have also had sex with?"

Ben closed his eyes and looked up to the ceiling. If Tenzin didn't know better, she'd say he was praying.

"Tenzin." He sounded as if he was in pain. "Enough."

"I don't understand why you don't want to talk about it if you're not jealous."

"Because it's none of my business."

She burst into laughter. "Of course it's your business! She is your friend and so is he. If they formed a connection, it would change your relationship to both. It is most definitely your business." Tenzin walked away, shaking her head. "Americans are so strange. How could the romantic connections of friends not be your business?"

"Because..." Ben frowned. "Actually, you're right. If they got together, it would definitely change our friendship."

"See?"

"Dammit, Tenzin." Ben picked up the frozen peas and

pressed them to his forehead. "You have boundary issues, and now you're spreading them to me."

"What?" She widened her eyes.

"Don't give me the innocent look." He put down the peas and stirred the curry. "Will you make some rice please?"

"Yes." She pulled on two oven mitts to protect the rice cooker from her amnis. "Did you hear him align their schedules before he left her here?"

"Not listening to you."

"He has taken my advice far more quickly than I imagined he would." Tenzin set the rice cooker on the counter and plugged it in. It was awkward with the oven mitts, but not impossible. "Chloe was an unpredictable factor. Still, I am surprised at the swiftness with which he's adapting."

"Can we talk about breaking into the museum tomorrow? How much René hates me? Root canals? Anything besides this?"

"What are root canals?" She grabbed the bag of rice from the pantry. "Did you see that he flew in front of her? He's conditioning her to his true nature. That was very clever."

Ben let out a short sigh and gave Tenzin a reluctant smile. "Your focus is both admirable and irritating as hell."

"Thank you." She grabbed the frozen peas. "Now stop using my vegetables for first aid."

26

Ben and Chloe strolled into the Museum of Modern Art at six forty-five the next night with sketchpads under their arms. The museum stayed open until nine that night. They had time. They strolled through the sculpture garden before it got too dark, waiting for crowds to clear. They pulled up chairs near the fountain and waited for the crowds to clear as they pulled out their sketchbooks and started to draw the colorful figures standing silently on the other side of the fountain.

Ben glanced over at Chloe's page. "Stick figures?"

"I told you I can't draw."

"Didn't you go to art school or something?"

"Yeah. For dance." Chloe flipped the page. "Not drawing. I like art. I can't make it."

"Dance is art." Ben took his time. He could draw decently—another one of the lessons his uncle had forced on him—but it was an acquired skill, not a natural talent. "And drawing well is practical for me. I can't always count on having a camera with me in my work. Sometimes cataloguing has to be done by sketch."

Chloe looked at the grouping he'd done on his page. "You're

better than all right. You have shadows and stuff." She cocked her head. "You're pretty good, actually. You never draw for fun?"

"Drawing isn't fun," he said. "Like I said, it's practical."

"Huh. You're good at it."

"Well thank you." He flipped the page and glanced around the garden. "People are leaving."

"It's dinnertime."

Ben closed his book. "I want a drink. You?"

"Oh definitely. Fifth-floor terrace?"

Ben nodded. "We'll take the elevator up to six and then walk down."

"There's a shop on the sixth floor outside the special-exhibit gallery."

"Perfect."

Tucking their sketchbooks back under their arms, Ben and Chloe headed back inside and toward the elevators.

More and more people were drifting out of the museum, but a few were still entering. People in suits. Singles more than groups. Most likely those who waited to visit until after seven o'clock were locals just off work or students like the ones Ben and Chloe were posing as.

Chloe asked in a low voice, "Can our friends take elevators?"

Ben nodded. "They can, but it's tricky. Older elevators are easier. Gio avoids new ones. He can't touch anything near the control panel, but he's more... sparky than Gavin or Tenzin."

"Why?"

He smiled at her. "How many elements are there?"

"Four. Or five sometimes."

He pushed the button for the elevator when they reached it. "Which element seems the most sparky?"

Chloe mouthed, *Fire?* with wide eyes.

Ben nodded.

"He always seemed so calm and rational," she said. "I mean, after I got over the movie-star looks, I always thought of your uncle as super boring. No offense."

"None taken," Ben said, stepping into the elevator and holding the door for Chloe and another couple of student-types. "I think he'd consider that a compliment. He works very hard to live a quiet life."

"Your aunt, on the other hand, is awesome, and I want to be her when I grow up."

Ben smiled. "I kinda want to be her when I grow up too."

They got off on the sixth floor and wandered over to the shop to look at the books, trinkets, and toys that made up the museum merchandise. Ben glanced over his shoulder and watched the comings and goings of the crew, noting the service elevator and the hallway where they disappeared carrying cords and benches.

They had white partitions up to block the entrance and exit of the special-exhibitions hall, but he could hear more workmen in the background and the low voice of someone giving directions.

No art. Not yet. They wouldn't be carting Dalis, Magrittes, and Kahlos through the hallways. Not during open hours anyway.

Chloe paged through a book. "Anything interesting?"

"No, it's exactly as expected."

"Any sign of Tenzin?"

Ben glanced toward the large air-conditioning vent in the corner. "She'll be around somewhere. Hiding out. By the time we're ready to move, she'll have the whole ventilation system and service area mapped out."

Chloe took a deep breath. "This feels super weird."

Ben put an arm around her and bent down. "Remember,

we're not stealing anything," he whispered in her ear. "All we have to do is make sure Samson's paintings get back to where they belong."

Chloe nodded and put the book down. They lingered in the small shop long enough that Ben had a fairly good idea who was coming and going and what kind of employee badges they would need. He grabbed Chloe's hand, and they headed down the stairs and toward the café that overlooked the sculpture garden.

"And... it's closed," Chloe said.

"Damn." He looked around. "Does that mean I'm allowed to bring out the flask I snuck in in my messenger bag?"

She laughed. "You did not."

"I absolutely did." He hooked his arm in hers. "But for now why don't we go be studious and kill some time?"

They sketched and walked around the museum until eight thirty. Their reservation was at eight forty-five. Glancing at the windows as they walked down the stairs, he saw the sun had finally set.

The vampires would be waking, and Ben and Chloe were fair game.

Gavin would be at the museum soon, as would René DuPont, if Ben's theory was correct. Tonight was the night everyone would be making their move. The exhibit was being taken down, the paintings shipped back to the generous donors of Historic New York, and René would try to intercept them.

Would Emilie be with him?

Ben couldn't decide whether he wanted to confront her or not. He couldn't decide if he ever wanted to see Emilie again.

Had it all been a lie? If it wasn't, did that make it better or worse? He'd become too accustomed to kindness in the years since he'd been with his uncle. He'd let down his guard.

A mistake.

Betrayal was a fact of life. Most relationships were an exchange. *You give me this; I give you that.* The currency varied but the rules remained the same. Emotions were a tool, and loyalty could be stolen like anything else.

Ben and Chloe walked down to the restaurant in the lobby and through the doors. It was Saturday night, but Gavin had managed to secure a reservation in Ben's name. They sat, ordered drinks, and stared out the windows while the glittering lights of the sculpture garden glowed brighter as darkness settled on the city.

"What now?" she asked quietly.

"Now we wait for Gavin. He said he'd be here and he'd find us a way back in the museum."

He glanced at the bar, then back at the menu. "The salmon or the lamb?"

She shook her head. "I don't know how you can eat right now."

"I can always eat." He closed the menu. "Slow-cooked lamb for me, and we should start with the tuna tartare. Try the mushrooms and polenta. It's going to be a long night."

HALFWAY THROUGH THEIR APPETIZER, Chloe saw Ben's eyes narrow on someone entering the restaurant. When she glanced over her shoulder, she saw Gavin walking in wearing one of his impeccable suits. He scanned the bar with purpose, his eyes narrowing on an attractive Caucasian woman who was drinking alone. She appeared to be in her late thirties or early forties. Sleek brown hair. Stylish suit. She looked smart. Professional. Gavin walked up and took the barstool beside her.

"They match," Chloe muttered.

Ben said, "What?"

"Nothing." She turned around. "Who is she?"

"I don't know. I'm pretty sure they've met before though, judging from her reaction."

When Chloe looked again, Gavin was leaning into the woman, smiling and flirting openly. His hand pressed into the small of her back when he lifted her hand to kiss her knuckles as she laughed.

Chloe wasn't prepared for the stab of jealousy. It pierced her stomach hard and fast, burning when she saw him lean in and whisper in the woman's ear. She turned back to the table, stunned by her reaction.

"It's fake, Chloe."

"They know each other."

"His job was to find a way back into the museum after closing," Ben said. "He found one. She's a curator. I recognize the ID."

"It's fine."

It wasn't fine.

Ben kept glancing over Chloe's shoulder. "Finish your food. This is going to be faster than I expected given her body language. She's not interested in dinner."

Chloe turned to peek. The woman pressed her breasts against Gavin's side and leaned close to whisper in his ear. His eyebrows went up, and she laughed. The corner of his mouth turned up, and he nodded.

Just then, his eyes lifted and locked with Chloe's.

The woman at his side continued to whisper in his ear, but Gavin kept his eyes on Chloe's until she couldn't take anymore. She turned around, her stomach in knots, her hands twisted in her lap.

"I'll take care of the bill," Ben said, pulling out his wallet. "I don't want us to leave together. Head to the bathroom hallway and wait there. Check your phone until you see them leaving the restaurant, then follow them out. I'll catch up with you."

Chloe nodded, her mind cataloguing the steps Ben had told her and not thinking about Gavin's behavior. Her feelings for Gavin were complicated, but her jealousy wasn't.

Get over it, Chloe. He's playing his part.

Or was he? He'd certainly been hands-off with her lately. She might have been staying at his place, but some nights she barely saw him. He was at the pub or meeting with... whomever he met with. What did she really know about Gavin, anyway?

Ben rose and grabbed his messenger bag. "Chloe, you ready?"

Chloe nodded and made her way to the hallway, walking by Gavin and the woman, pointedly not looking at them as she passed. She leaned against the hall and pulled out her phone, pretending to check her email while still keeping an eye on the happy couple at the bar.

Chloe couldn't look at them, so she watched their shoes.

The woman had pretty feet. Slender, pale, unmarred feet clad in elegant designer heels. They were nothing at all like the bruised and callused feet Chloe had. Dancers were hard on their feet. More than one of her instructors had had foot surgery before fifty.

Chloe walked around Gavin's house barefoot. Did he mind? Had he noticed her hard, bruised little feet? Did he compare them to other, elegant feet he'd seen?

She shouldn't care. It pissed her off that she did.

Chloe knew she was nothing like the sophisticated woman at the bar. She was herself. She'd only ever wanted to be herself.

She was Chloe Reardon, who ignored the jabs of all the girls who told her she didn't have a "ballet body." She was the one who forced her teachers to take notice. She'd defied her parents and crossed the country to make her dreams come true when no one believed in her. She was the pauper who worked three jobs so she could dance in brilliant shows that paid nothing. She was the woman who hadn't cried, even faced with her worst nightmare of never dancing again.

She was the woman who'd walked away from Tom, refusing to be crushed. And she was the woman who was learning to fight back.

Chloe's head came up, her chin lifted, and she examined the woman at the bar with new eyes.

Soft. She was *soft*. Chloe wouldn't trade places with that woman for all Tenzin's gold.

The woman turned and picked up her purse before she walked in Chloe's direction, heading toward the bathrooms. Chloe caught Gavin's eye, then she looked down at her phone again. It wouldn't be good to draw attention. The woman brushed past Chloe, wafting sweet perfume.

Chloe kept an eye on the clock. It was likely they would leave after the woman finished in the restroom. Chloe heard a heavy step coming toward her. She looked up and met Gavin's eyes a second before he backed her farther down the hall, gripped the back of her neck, and lifted her mouth to plunder.

Gavin's kiss invaded her senses. His right hand gripped the nape of her neck and his left braced against the wall, caging her in as his tongue plunged into her mouth. She opened her lips instinctively, meeting his desire with her own. Her fists clutched the lapels of his jacket when he pressed her against the wall. His knee shoved between her thighs as he took her mouth and wiped every thought from her mind. His lips were firm, almost hard, and the hand at the back of her neck angled her mouth to his with an unyielding grip.

It was hard and hot and fast. The kiss only lasted seconds before he pulled away and whispered in her ear.

"Fuck me, but the look in your eyes just now." His teeth sank into her earlobe and she gasped.

"Gavin—"

"One day soon, Chloe Reardon." Just as quickly, he was gone.

Gavin left her standing with her mouth open and her blood running rampant as he moved to the end of the hall, straightening his cuffs and rubbing a thumb over his mouth. His tongue came out and flicked against his skin, as if he was tasting the last of their kiss.

The museum curator came out only seconds later, and Chloe saw the mask fall into place. Gavin was all charming smiles. He cocked his arm out, and the woman put her pretty little hand in the crook of his elbow. They walked out of the restaurant chatting, and Chloe followed them.

It was only seconds after they left the restaurant that Chloe saw the effect of Gavin's amnis. They turned right and walked down 53rd Street. The curator leaned into his side. He put his arm around her, put his hand on the back of her neck. Chloe saw the thumb that had just brushed his lips press into the woman's neck and knew that Gavin's elemental energy was flooding her senses.

Ben fell into step beside her. "Stay close."

They picked up the pace. No one stopped them when the woman walked to the glass double doors down the block and pulled out her keycard. She opened the door, and Gavin held it open for her to walk through. Then he nodded at Chloe and Ben. Ben put a hand on Chloe's back and urged her forward. They slipped into the long hallway, staying close enough to Gavin and the woman to give the appearance that they were all together. The woman didn't turn, not even when she opened the next door and Gavin let them in again.

Gavin paused and put a hand on Ben's shoulder. "You have the uniforms?"

Ben nodded.

"Then you should be clear from here. I'll be accompanying Dr. Walker up to the sixth floor to see the surrealist exhibit that she was so enthusiastic about. If I see you—"

"We're invisible." Ben slapped him on the shoulder. "Go."

Gavin shot one last look at Chloe before he walked back to the woman and took her hand before she could regain her senses.

"You ready?" Ben asked.

Chloe nodded and they walked into the coat check. Ben handed her a staff uniform and one of the photo IDs he'd mocked up the night before.

"From what I saw upstairs, these are the right ones," Ben said. "I have more in the bag if we need others. If they're scanned, we're in trouble, but they'll be good enough for the eyeball test."

"Got it." Was she actually doing this? This was crazy! She was breaking into the Museum of Modern Art to... make sure no one stole a couple of paintings that belonged to the vampire they'd just stolen a different painting from a couple of nights before.

How did my life get so weird?

Chloe walked to the corner and turned her back, stripping off her clothes and putting on the uniform before she thought too much.

This was nuts and they were all going to jail.

Tenzin waited for the lights to dim before she tested the vent register over the air duct in the secluded hallway on the sixth floor. She'd spent the day crawling through the ventilation system of the museum. It was surprisingly enjoyable. She'd been able to eavesdrop on numerous conversations, had been privy to far more staff gossip than anticipated, and even scared a couple trying to have exhibitionist sex in the third-floor stairwell.

Honestly. Humans.

She really hadn't considered lurking in museum ventilation systems as an interesting pastime prior to this job, but she decided to investigate the Metropolitan Museum next. That was far bigger than MoMA. She could probably spend days in there.

It had been silent for over an hour when she pushed open the register. She slipped out of the duct and dropped to the ground a moment before Ben rounded the corner.

"How did you—"

"This is the only register large enough for a person on the sixth floor that's also in a hallway," Ben said. "Here's your uniform and ID. Chloe is already in the exhibit. They put her to work right away. Didn't even bat an eye. You should blend in too." He turned to face the wall.

"You've seen me naked before."

"Tenzin, just change."

She shrugged and pulled off her clothes, stowing her own stuff in the open duct. "Is Gavin here?"

"He chatted up the curator in the bar. That's how we managed to get in. They're wandering around too. Her name is Dr. Susan Walker. If anyone asks about you, just say Dr. Walker or Susan asked you to help."

"Okay. Have you seen Emilie or René?"

"Not yet."

"It's possible they might do exactly what we did to grab *Midnight Labyrinth*."

Ben asked, "Intercept the delivery? I thought about that."

"Might be good for someone to stake out the loading area."

"We don't know if the shipment was set to go out tonight," Ben said.

"It *needs* to go out tonight." Tenzin tucked in the stiff white shirt and turned around. "I'm decent, you Puritan."

Ben turned to face her. "We can't wait. Whatever the schedule says, the Samson paintings go back to Rothman House tonight. If we run into trouble, we'll need Gavin to use amnis on Dr. Walker."

Tenzin nodded.

They walked out of the hallway and over to the special-exhibit gallery. The partitions had been taken away, and the lights were turned up while cases were being constructed and paintings and sculptures were being crated.

They were in the room adjacent to the Samson paintings when Tenzin heard her voice.

"I'm not sure what the problem is. These paintings were scheduled to go to the restoration room directly from the exhibit."

Tenzin looked at Ben, and he'd heard the voice too. He really had exceptional ears for a human. His jaw clenched and his eyes were ice-cold.

"Not here," Tenzin said quietly, picking up the pace.

"Okay," a man's voice said. "So what's the problem?"

"The problem is... I have to check with, uh, Dr. Walker." Chloe was valiantly bullshitting her way through an excuse.

"Dr. Walker is here tonight?" the man said. "What's she doing here?"

"It doesn't matter," Emilie said. "I have a work order."

"But..." Chloe scrambled. "I think there's been a mistake. I mean... do they look like they need to be restored? Sure, they're old, but they seem to be in pretty good shape, so I'm not sure why they'd need to be restored. We should check with a curator, don't you think?"

Ben and Tenzin rounded the corner right as Chloe was running out of steam.

"Oh... Te—iffany!" Chloe said when she spotted them. "Tiffany, did you hear anything about the Samsons going to Restoration?"

"No." Tenzin walked up and crossed her arms, immediately going on the offensive with Emilie, who visibly paled as Tenzin approached. "These aren't in the museum's permanent collection; it's not our job to restore them. Who are you?"

Emilie was wearing a white coat and gloves. Her hair was piled up into a bun with pencils sticking out of it. Her ID said her name was Sarah Miller and she was with the art restoration department.

Despite the increased heart rate Tenzin could hear, the human played it cool. "My name is Sarah Miller, and I work in the restoration department. And you are?"

"My name is Shu Chen."

Emilie's eyes went wide. "I thought your friend called you Tiffany."

"Yeah, that's my nickname." Tenzin said nothing else. Let Emilie be the one to call *liar*.

Flustered, Emilie held up her paperwork. "Be that as it may, I think you'll find this work order specifies both *Twilight Labyrinth* and *Dawn Labyrinth* are slated to go to Restoration tonight."

The French accent was gone and a British accent had taken its place. Americans were foolish about British accents. For some reason, they conferred authority. It was an odd quirk of American culture Tenzin had noticed in Los Angeles, but it held true in New York.

"No, they're not," Tenzin said. "I was talking with Dr.

Walker earlier. She said they were being shipped back to the donor tonight. Immediately, in fact. They need to be delivered as soon as possible."

"Oh really?" Emilie asked. "Do you have paperwork?"

There was little Tenzin could to do to expose Emilie without giving her own facade away. Chloe had covered for them surprisingly well but had melted back and was trying to avoid notice. Tenzin couldn't get a read on Ben. He was behind her, probably seething silently.

The museum employee standing between them looked annoyed, confused, and impatient. He clearly had better things to do than referee an argument between a grunt and a nerd.

Before Tenzin could say another word, Ben jumped in. "I think it's obvious we just need to talk to Dr. Walker about this." He ignored all the women and spoke to the employee in a one-of-the-boys voice. "It's so easy for wires to get crossed on this kind of stuff, am I right?"

The employee looked relieved. "Curators. They're particular about how stuff gets organized, you know?"

"Exactly," Ben said, nudging Tenzin aside. "Let's get the okay from Dr. Walker before we do anything. Have her sign off on any changes, okay?" He turned to Emilie. "I'm pretty sure we'd piss of a lot of *really important people* if these paintings ended up in the wrong place."

"That's what I'm saying," the man said. "I'm gonna go find her. See what she wants to do."

The employee walked off, leaving Chloe, Tenzin, Ben, and Emilie standing next to the Samson paintings. Tenzin didn't need to be a vampire to feel the energy in the room.

"Hi there, sweetheart," Ben said in a low voice. "Did you miss me?"

27

"**D**on't make this personal," Emilie said, her British accent still in place. "It's business, and you know it."

"Was it business when you slept with me?"

"Are we bringing that up?" Emilie glanced at Chloe. "Well then, no. That was just a side benefit. Don't tell me you're complaining."

"I don't like it when people lie to me."

Emilie glanced at Tenzin. "I don't either."

"Are you actually trying to—"

"Why are you bickering?" Tenzin broke in. "This is ridiculous. Girl, in a few minutes that man is going to come back with the curator, who is currently under our control. You have failed. Leave now."

Ben tried not to smile. Leave it to Tenzin to cut to the chase.

Emilie smirked. "She may be under your man's control, but she's working for *my* boss."

"Your boss?" Tenzin asked. She turned and looked around the room. "I don't see anyone who..." She froze, and Ben turned to look.

At the end of the gallery, walking with a jaunty step, was

René DuPont. He smiled at Tenzin as if he was seeing an old friend, ignored Ben, and continued his stroll. They were surrounded by oblivious humans, and he knew he was safe.

He hadn't changed a whit since Ben had first met him in London. His hair was immaculate, and the suit he was wearing spoke of both success and style. René DuPont was an elegant predator and a more than decent thief. The fact that he annoyed the shit out of Ben and had a hard-on for Tenzin only made him that much more obnoxious.

"Mr. Vecchio." He side-eyed Ben. "My lady." He bowed toward Tenzin. "It will never be anything less than a pleasure to see you. You look... *magnifique.*"

"Thank you," Tenzin said.

Ben said, "Why are you thanking him?"

"You told me I needed to work on being gracious when people compliment me."

"Not with *him.*"

"Oh, such resentment!" René said. "I love it. Have I inconvenienced you, Benjamin?" He cocked his head and looked at Emilie. "Has she? I so wish I could have been there when you discovered that it was all a lie." He turned to Tenzin. "Was his disappointment delicious?"

Tenzin narrowed her eyes. "You're very strange."

Ben had locked down his emotions so he didn't strangle Emilie. René's taunts hardly made it through. "Was it *delicious* to walk in here tonight and find out you're not going to make off with the other two Labyrinth paintings?"

René pouted. "Well, I haven't given up hope yet. And after all"—his pout turned to a sneer—"I stole the one that matters, didn't I?" He turned his attention to Tenzin. "You must tell me why you are still toying with this one. He is so far beneath your notice, I cannot even comprehend it."

"Was this what all the apple jokes were about?" Tenzin asked.

"Apple jokes?" Ben said.

"I'll tell you later."

Chloe tried to slip away, but Emilie shot a hand out and stopped her. Chloe wrested her arm away and grabbed Emilie's hand.

"I don't think so, bitch," Chloe said through gritted teeth. "How many fingers do you want me to break?" Emilie squeaked, and Chloe dropped her hand. "Try touching me again. Just try it."

René tutted. "So much aggression. So much drama." He shrugged as oblivious humans bustled around them. "This is all so unnecessary."

Tenzin watched René, her head cocked to the side as if she were examining an interesting specimen under a microscope. "You like to hear yourself talk."

Ben muttered, "Yeah, he does."

"And you think you're safe here because you're surrounded by humans."

René's eye twinkled. "Aren't I? You can't fly away in the middle of the museum, can you?"

"No," Tenzin said. She paused, then her right hand shot out and she punched René in the throat. Her left fist cut up and landed directly on René's nose, spraying blood all over the pristine white gallery. "I can do that though."

René fell to the ground, clutching his throat and nose while Emilie screamed.

As soon as Emilie screamed, Chloe turned and walked away. *Shit. Shit. Shit.* She was going to get arrested.

Tenzin had drawn the attention of the room, and every employee dropped what they were doing and rushed toward the Samson room. Everyone started shouting at once. Hubbub meant distraction, and distraction meant things could go missing.

Chloe ducked into a corner in the next gallery to catch her breath.

What would Ben do?

Remember, we're not stealing anything. All we have to do is make sure Samson's paintings get back to where they belong.

The curator with Gavin could tell the employees to put the Labyrinth paintings on a truck and get them delivered where they were supposed to be. Gavin had the curator under his amnis, which meant Chloe needed to find Gavin and find him fast.

She heard someone running after her. She spun and planted her feet with her fists raised.

"Chloe!" It was Ben. He had his arm around Emilie and a hand over her mouth.

"What are you doing?" Chloe hissed.

"I couldn't just leave her there. Where's Gavin?"

"That's who I'm looking for." She turned right, then left. Hit a dead end. The gallery was a maze. Was it designed to mimic the labyrinth in the painting? She walked back to the previous gallery with Ben still walking behind her.

Emilie had moved beyond shock and was struggling to get free. Without missing a beat, Ben hoisted her over his shoulder. Emilie started to yell as soon as his hand wasn't over her mouth.

"You bastard! Put me down!"

"Who told you I'm a bastard?" Ben said. "Was it René? I warn you, he doesn't like me much. Though technically, he's right. I am a bastard."

Chloe rolled her eyes. "Stop being clever. Is there any way to shut her up?"

"Not without hurting her," Ben said.

And Chloe knew there was no way Ben would be hitting a woman who wasn't out for his blood.

"Everyone is shouting at the other end of the gallery," Ben said. "They're not paying attention to her."

Ben was right. The crowd near the entrance of the exhibit was shouting one over the other.

"What on earth are they arguing about?" Chloe asked. "How does she do these things?"

"You're telling me this man, Dr. DuPre, has been harassing you?" The foreman of the maintenance crew stood over René with his arms crossed.

Tenzin's eyes were wide and innocent. She mumbled, "He propositioned me while I was working."

It was the absolute truth. Of course, it had been over a year ago and in Scotland while they were both trying to steal a historic sword, but the human hadn't asked for details.

The foreman glared at René. "Guys like this... Did you report him? This has to be documented, ma'am."

"He told me he's the director." Were her fangs showing? Damn things. They could be truly inconvenient at times like this. "Who would listen to me? I'm new."

"This is the Museum of Modern Art, Miss Chen. We take that shit seriously around here," the human said.

She let out a breath. "That's such a relief. Thank you."

René's eyes were shooting daggers at her. Tenzin could also tell he was fighting laughter.

He wasn't completely evil, no matter what Ben thought.

René DuPont was a little too much like Tenzin, a vampire with a flexible sense of morality. He would use any excuse and any method to get what he wanted, but he tried to avoid violence. After all, René was also very vain. The difference between them was she didn't need other people's money and she had Ben to use as a moral compass since her own was faulty.

From the back of the crowd, a voice popped up. "Where's Dr. Walker? I saw her walking around earlier. She'll know what to do."

Tenzin saw the two crated Samson paintings sitting propped against a wall as everyone gathered around the bleeding René. She'd broken his nose, which had made a mess, but it was probably healed already. Of course it had healed incorrectly, based on the angle, so René would need to break it again.

Not Tenzin's problem.

"Where is Dr. Walker?" the maintenance foreman asked. "And who is this guy? He's a director? I've been working here fifteen years; I never seen this guy before."

"I've never seen him either," another voice chimed in. "Who is he?"

Still another voice said, "Shouldn't someone call security?"

"Yeah, call security on his ass."

The foreman's eyes narrowed on René. "Mister, I'm gonna need to see your ID."

Tenzin melted back into the crowd. She waited for a few minutes, but the focus seemed to have shifted from her altercation with René to the question of his identity. She picked up the papers Emilie had dropped and walked over to the wall where the two paintings rested. Without a word, she tucked the work order between her lips and picked up the first crate. She couldn't carry them both without arousing suspicion. A human of her size wouldn't be strong enough. She'd walked partway down the gallery when she heard someone following her. She dropped the painting and spun around.

It was a dark-haired young man with light brown skin and beautiful mahogany eyes. He was carrying the other crate under his arm.

Tenzin grabbed the work order from her mouth. "Is that the other Labyrinth painting?"

"Yeah." He glanced over his shoulder and set down the crate. "I thought I could help."

"Why?"

The young man nodded toward the shouting crowd. "I don't want to be anywhere near that mess, you know? I just started here, and I don't need to be caught in any drama. You were taking these down to shipping, right?"

Tenzin nodded.

"Cool." He lifted the second crate. "I'm happy to help. I know just where to go. Just helped carry a Magritte down there for some local donor. Crazy, huh? That thing is probably worth more than my parents' house."

"I know," Tenzin muttered, picking up the first crate. "It's criminal. A completely manufactured market for things with little to no intrinsic value."

"What?"

She turned and offered a closed-mouth smile. "I'll let you go first. I always get lost."

Chloe found Gavin trying to fend off Dr. Walker's advances near the sixth-floor shop. She was hanging on him, trying to shove her hand in the back pocket of his trousers.

"I really think you should sit down, Susan," Gavin said, his voice strained. "You're clearly not feeling well."

"Don't wanna," she purred. "Let's go to my office."

Chloe stopped and glared at him. "Go a little overboard on the amnis?"

"She has a weak mind and little willpower," he grumbled, propping Dr. Walker in a corner.

"She didn't ask to be drugged, Gavin."

"Can we debate this later?" He spied Ben walking down the hall and cocked his head. "What is that?"

Ben turned. "Emilie."

"Let me down!"

"Hello, little betrayer." Gavin cocked his head to the side. "Her face is turning an alarming shade of red." Gavin walked over and held out his arms. "Give her to me."

"No!" Emilie said, starting to kick again. "He's a—"

"Vampire," Gavin said. "Yes, that's the point." He pressed both his palms to Emilie's neck and she immediately stilled. "Now, little girl, you're going to go take a nap with this lovely academic with no head for immortal power."

Chloe frowned. "Wait, do some people have natural resistance to amnis?"

Ben nodded as he handed Emilie to Gavin. "We're all susceptible, but to different degrees. My resistance is pretty strong. Tenzin said yours is too."

"How does Tenzin know that?" Chloe asked.

"Uh... with her, it's sometimes better not to know."

Gavin walked around the corner with Emilie in his arms. "There's a rather convenient bench over there." He lifted Dr. Walker over his shoulder.

"Whoo!" She reached down and grabbed two handfuls of Gavin's ass. "Now we're having fun!"

Chloe slapped a hand over her mouth but a snort still escaped. The look on Gavin's face was priceless.

"You'll pay for that later," Gavin said, leveling his eyes on her.

"Sure thing, sugar-buns."

Gavin disappeared and reappeared a moment later. "They're both asleep and will be for some time," he said. "Now, where are the paintings?"

~

THE NICE YOUNG human was leading Tenzin down another dimly lit corridor. If he weren't so chatty, she'd probably think he was up to no good.

"I wonder what's going to happen to that guy, you know?"

"Who?" Tenzin asked. This appeared to be a maintenance tunnel of some kind. Large air-conditioning units hummed loudly.

"The guy who was harassing you," the young human said.

"Oh." Should she be more angry? "Yes. *Yes.* He was awful. And should be beaten publicly."

The young human stopped and turned to her with wide eyes. "Wow. That's harsh. I mean... I thought he'd just get fired or something."

That's right. Public beatings for antisocial behavior had been outlawed long ago in this culture.

"I was joking." Tenzin smiled but couldn't open her mouth. It probably appeared more strained than jovial. "He should not be beaten. That was a joke."

The human nodded but looked a little nervous. "Right."

"Is the shipping room much farther?"

"Yeah." He turned around and started walking again. "Let's just... get these delivered. Quickly."

~

Emilie was out of the picture.

René was being publicly humiliated.

The Samson paintings were... not in the gallery where they'd left them.

Neither was Tenzin.

Ben took stock of the current situation while they rushed down the stairs. Leave it to Tenzin to go off plan.

"She always has to make someone bleed," he muttered. "Is it too much to ask that one job—one single job—not involve bloodshed?"

"What are we doing?" Chloe asked, panting and trying to keep up with Ben.

Gavin said, "That's an excellent question."

"We're finding Tenzin and making sure the paintings get shipped out to the O'Briens tonight," Ben said. "That's all we have to do. Just make sure they get to where they were already supposed to go."

"And then find the other painting?" Gavin said. "We're not forgetting about that, are we?"

"No, I'm not forgetting about that."

Chloe said, "Who has the other painting?"

"René, most likely," Gavin said.

Ben pushed open the door to the subbasement. "And where's René?"

"Still bleeding?" Chloe asked.

Gavin laughed. "Tenzin?"

"Every single time," Ben said through gritted teeth.

Gavin and Chloe followed Ben as he strode down the hallways and toward the shipping department. If Tenzin had the paintings, she'd take them to the shipping room. All they had to do was make sure they weren't intercepted.

"Should someone stay with Emilie?" Chloe asked. "What if she wakes up and gets away?"

Ben shrugged. "She doesn't know where the painting is. René does." He turned right and almost collided with Tenzin and a young man who was walking at her side. His hackles rose. "Who are you?"

The man's eyes went wide. "A-Anthony. Who are you?"

"They're from the restoration department." Tenzin put her palm on the back of the man's hand. "It's fine."

His eyes drifted to the side. "Oh. Right."

"They are supposed to be here. They work here," Tenzin said in a low voice.

"Right."

"And you need to go help upstairs."

He nodded, and without another look at Ben, Chloe, and Gavin, the museum employee walked past them and down the hall toward the elevators.

Chloe said, "That is creepy as hell."

Tenzin smiled. "I know. What are you doing here?"

"Looking for you," Ben said. "And the paintings."

Chloe said, "It is really inconvenient that you all can't use cell phones."

"Tell me about it," Ben muttered.

Tenzin said, "The paintings are on their way back to Rothman House. They were scheduled to go out tomorrow, but I convinced the driver to deliver them tonight."

"Are you sure?" Ben asked. "Did you check the delivery address?"

"Yes."

"And you're sure?"

"The nice young man you scared away scanned something on the crates. And then the computer printed out a label. And on the label was the address of Rothman House. The driver took it and drove away. I'm not sure how much more sure I can be."

Gavin said, "Should one of us go with the truck?"

Tenzin cocked her head. "It wouldn't be a *bad* idea."

Ben and Gavin exchanged a look.

"I'll find the truck and escort the two paintings back to the O'Briens," Gavin said. "You three deal with your French friend."

CHLOE AND BEN went back up to the sixth floor just in time to see René being escorted to the stairs by security.

René saw Ben and Chloe standing on the edge of the crowd, smiled, and said, "And yet I still have what I came for."

One security guard shoved him in the back. "What did you come for, asshole? Pissing me off? Get your ass out of here."

Ben debated whether to follow them or track down Emilie.

"Leave him for Tenzin." Chloe tugged on his arm.

"Right."

René narrowed his eyes as they walked away.

Ben ignored him. "Tenzin's waiting for him outside."

Chloe said, "Should we go... help?"

Ben smiled. "Help Tenzin?" In a city like New York, René was cut off from most of his elemental strength since he was an earth vampire. Tenzin would have no problem picking him up. "Nah," Ben said. "She'll be fine."

They walked back to the hallway behind the special-exhibitions gallery where Gavin had left Emilie and the museum curator.

Dr. Walker was sleeping soundly.

Emilie was gone.

28

Tenzin dropped a kicking René on top of a landing she liked in Midtown. It was an office building on West 47th Street, and the only one who used the balcony on the fifteenth floor was an executive who smoked too much and left cigarette butts all over the tile. It was messy but deserted.

René DuPont looked suitably grim when she dropped him on the balcony. She'd picked him up a block from the museum trying to hail a yellow cab, an attractive human woman under his arm.

"It really is admirable how fast you work," Tenzin said. "You were going back to her place after, what? Five minutes of conversation?"

"It's my preferred method of lodging in Manhattan." René stood and brushed off his suit. "Hotels are so anonymous."

"But using random humans for food and lodging isn't?"

"She would have had a marvelous time." René smiled. "I always make sure of that. You should find out sometime."

Tenzin perched on the edge of the railing. "Do you truly find me sexually attractive, or is it part of the game?"

"Of course I do. You're quite beautiful, frighteningly intelligent, and immensely powerful. We both find you attractive. I'm simply willing to act on it and have the stamina to keep up with you."

"It's interesting that you think that." She ignored the dig at Benjamin. For someone who purported to care nothing for a weak human beneath his notice, René noticed Ben an awful lot. He'd cooked up an elaborate scheme to have Ben steal a painting for him when it would have been far easier to steal it himself.

René walked over to her. "Are you saying you *don't* find me sexually attractive?"

She cocked her head. "You're not *un*attractive."

"That's not what I asked."

"You can keep talking." She leaned forward and whispered in his ear, "But I'm not going to forget about *Midnight Labyrinth*."

"My lady," René purred. "Oil paint. Canvas. These are worthless things, are they not?"

"Not to my Benjamin."

He smiled. "Then he should have kept the painting instead of being taken in by my little trap."

"We wondered if the woman worked for you or Ennis. I voted for Ennis. Ben voted for you."

"The O'Brien doesn't have enough imagination to train a girl like that. She works for me. My angel is quite good, isn't she?"

"She's not bad," Tenzin said. "But you're going to tell me where the painting is now."

He pressed a hand over his heart. "You wound me. Can you not accept that you lost this round?"

Tenzin leapt on him, knocking him to the ground and baring her fangs as she gripped his throat and dug her nails into the soft flesh. She held him down and ignored the evidence of his arousal.

"I don't lose, René." She drew a sharpened fingernail across his neck, cutting the skin and filling the night wind with the scent of his blood. "Ever. That's why I'm still alive."

René's fangs fell and his lips flushed. "I'm not going to tell you where it is."

"Then I'm going to throw you over the railing," Tenzin said. "We're at fifteen stories. You won't die unless something happens to decapitate you on the way down. But you'll break every bone in your body and become a smudge on a Midtown sidewalk. That will take a very, very long time to heal, assuming you manage to find shelter before the sun kills you."

He grinned. "Would you change your mind if I told you I don't have it anymore?"

"Did you give it to Ennis?"

René just kept smiling.

"No." She stared at him. "You were waiting for the set. Were you hired to steal all of them or just the one?"

"I can't tell you all my secrets," he said. "I do have to consider my reputation for discretion. I was hired for a job, and I did it. This isn't personal; this is business."

"Of course it's not personal. You have no loyalties." Tenzin cocked her head. "Oh!"

"What?"

She smiled at René. "I know where it is."

A flicker of doubt in his eyes. "You couldn't possibly."

"I do." She picked him up by the shirtfront and flew over the edge of the balcony. "Of course, I'm going to have to get rid of you for a little while to make sure you don't interfere. Just remember..." She kissed him long and full on the mouth. "It's not business; it's personal."

René's eyes went wide with shock a second before she dropped him.

BEN WAS BACK at the loft, banging away on his computer when he heard her land on the roof.

Chloe was on her phone, trying to connect with the delivery company or Gavin's home system or anything that might let them know where the Scotsman was and if the remaining two Samson paintings had arrived safely at Rothman House.

Tenzin walked through the french doors. "Have you found her apartment yet?"

"Not yet." His fingers flew over the keys. "Working on it. I should have had Gavin quiz her before he put her to sleep."

"Try the name Angelique."

His eyebrows went up. "Why?"

"René called her his angel." Without another word, she was back out the door and had flown away.

HE'D LANDED on a car because that's where she dropped him. He was broken, but by the time Tenzin flew back to 47th Street, René had put himself together again, leaving a few gaping and horrified humans on the sidewalk and one tourist wearing a T-shirt that said I LOVE NYC—with a bright red apple on it—who fainted dead away.

An apple? *The Big Apple.* Oh, that's what the jokes had been about.

René was far too impressed with his own cleverness.

Tenzin followed from a distance. She'd seen his eyes before she dropped him. René believed her when she said she knew where the painting was.

She didn't.

She did, but she didn't.

He'd left the painting with his human. The one who'd played Ben. Tenzin was guessing her name was Angelique, but even with that information, it could be ages before Ben found her through the computer. There were likely hundreds of Angeliques in New York, and they didn't have ages. René was a professional. He'd cut his losses and get the painting back to France to assuage his buyer. He already had a carrier. He'd already taken care of the details. So the only hope Tenzin had of finding it before it left the city was to follow René and beat him to Emilie's apartment. Tenzin just hoped he hadn't set the girl up in a condo building with hundreds of residents. She could search, but it would still take time.

Her hopes lifted when the vampire headed downtown.

René limped toward Grand Central Station, losing the few gawkers he'd accumulated amid the rush of Saturday-night traffic headed toward the last commuter trains out of Manhattan. A line of cabbies waited outside the station. Tenzin hovered in the shadows, watching as René waved a handful of cash at a driver. The vampire was stumbling a bit—luckily, so were the drunks—and Tenzin suspected the cabbie was being hired for far more than his wheels. René would need blood, but he'd wait until he arrived at his destination safely.

If she was lucky and he didn't lose control.

The driver was no slouch, and soon Tenzin was playing a game of three-card monte from the sky, trying to keep her eye on the single cab she needed to follow in the madness of Midtown streets.

The taxi went south, and Tenzin almost lost it in the bustle of Park Avenue, but the traffic thinned near Gramercy Park and she kept her eyes locked on the bright blue sign decorating the top. The car turned left on East 14th Street, then right again on

2nd, heading toward the East Village. The cab slowed, took another left onto 12th, and slowed to a crawl. After a few minutes, it double-parked in front of a redbrick building, and René got out on the driver's side. He walked to the window, reached in, and grabbed the driver's hand.

Tenzin didn't stop to watch. Wherever the painting was, it was on that block. She would start with the building on the north side of the street, right where René's cab had parked. The south was occupied by a large school under renovation, but the north side was an apartment building. Tenzin flew to the back of the building first. One by one, she checked the windows. Each apartment had two windows, one blocked by the fire escape. She started at the top, moving quickly.

One was occupied by a couple having sex.

Another by a family who were all asleep.

A terrier waited on the third floor, staring at her accusingly. She bared her fangs and the small canine began barking.

She flew down to the second story. The corner apartment on the left side was lit by a single light that appeared to be from an interior bathroom or kitchen. At the window, Tenzin caught a familiar scent trail.

Hello, Emilie.

Tenzin took out her glass cutter and removed a section large enough to fit the painting. She didn't want any stray shards damaging the canvas on the way out. Then she softly pushed the glass into the apartment where it fell on a threadbare sofa. She flew in, listened for a moment, then rushed down the hall to the bedroom where Emilie—or whoever she was—was trying to climb out the fire escape.

Tenzin grabbed Emilie and threw her to the ground, driving the wind out of the human's lungs.

"You're a fool," Tenzin said. "Did you think you could escape me?"

Gavin showed up at the loft an hour after midnight, breezing by Chloe with a kiss on her temple and zeroing in on Ben.

"Does she have it?"

Ben was following a rabbit trail of immigration entries and credit card receipts narrowing in on a neighborhood in the East Village and didn't immediately respond.

"Chloe?" Gavin turned. "Has Tenzin been here?"

"Did the paintings get back to Rothman House?"

"Yes," he said. "They're fine. Tenzin?"

Ben heard them, but they were like a buzzing in the background.

Almost have you... I almost have you.

"She flew in a few minutes ago, then flew out again. Told Ben to look for the name Angelique. Does that sound familiar?"

Angelique was her name, or at least the name on the French passport she was using. But one of Angelique's hotel reservations in Gramercy Park had been paid by a traveler's check issued to an Emily—Emily Brandon—so Ben had tracked that name through credit records and come up with several hits, but only one that regularly made purchases in Lower Manhattan.

Gavin said, "There was a report of a man in a black overcoat that fell out of the sky on 47th Street. I doona suppose Tenzin mentioned anything about that?"

That caught Ben's attention. "He fell out of the sky?"

"And landed on a car," Gavin said through gritted teeth. "Ambulances were dispatched, but by the time they arrived, the body was gone. Witnesses claim the man lay in the wreck for a few minutes, then suddenly crawled out and headed east."

Chloe's eyes were wide. "Nope. She didn't mention anything about that."

Ben said, "He landed on a car?"

Gavin nodded. "She threw a thief off a bloody roof, Ben. Now, you know I have an odd affection for the woman, but—"

"She didn't throw him off a roof," Ben said, looking back to his computer. "She threw him on a car."

Gavin scowled. "And?"

"He's a vampire. He'll survive falling from the sky if he lands on a car."

"That's not the point! She tried to kill him because he stole something that was not even hers. René DuPont wasna violent. He dinna threaten her or anyone under her aegis. But she still tried to kill him."

"If she was trying to kill him, he'd be dead," Chloe said quietly. She looked at Ben. "Right?"

Ben nodded. "She needed him alive. But he needed to *think* she wanted him dead."

"Bloody *why*, Benjamin?" Gavin was fuming. "That mad—"

"She didn't want him looking for a tail," Ben said. "René knows where the painting is. She needed to follow him, and she didn't want him watching for a tail."

EMILIE WAS STARTING to lose color, so Tenzin eased up and the woman gasped.

"I'm just doing my job." The British accent was back. "You know—"

"You lied to him," she said. "You made him fall a little in love with you. Not all the way, but it was beginning."

To her credit, the human didn't hide her eyes.

"You'll probably lie to him if he ever asks you," Tenzin said, "but I know you have feelings for him."

"Is it possible *not* to?" Emilie asked.

"I don't know." Her grip tightened again. "You're the one

who betrayed him. Give me a reason to let you live."

"I'll take you to the painting," she choked out.

"I'm taking the painting anyway. I know it's here."

The woman started to cry. "Please."

"Please what?"

"I don't want to die."

Tenzin leaned down. "You play games with monsters," she whispered, "then you ask for mercy when you are caught?"

"You're not... not a monster," Emilie choked out.

"Oh, little girl, I very much am." She eased up on Emilie's windpipe.

"You're not." Emilie gasped. "You l-love him. I've seen the way you look at him."

Tenzin sat up, a smile lingering on her lips. "If you believe that, then you should know that makes me the most dangerous kind of monster." She squeezed hard, then released Emilie's throat, leaving bruises so the young woman wouldn't forget. "A monster with something to protect."

Tenzin heard the front door crash open, and she grabbed Emilie's throat again. But it wasn't René. Ben rushed into the room, his hair as wild as his eyes.

She blinked. "That was fast."

"You always underestimate what can be done on the computer." Ben glanced down at Emilie struggling in Tenzin's hold. "Don't."

"Why not?" she asked.

When Ben looked at Emilie, his beautiful face was shuttered. His eyes shone a little less. Her shining boy wasn't as shining as he had been. The girl had marred a little of his light. Tenzin's hold on the human's throat tightened. She was so slender. Like a bird. Snap! She'd be gone. And she'd never mar any of his light again.

Ben snapped his fingers until Tenzin looked at him. "She's

not worth it."

Tenzin glanced down. Emilie was crying, and her face was getting pale as Tenzin cut off her circulation. In a moment, she would pass out. If Tenzin didn't let go of her hold, she would be dead.

"Please, Tiny." He sighed. "I don't need that on my conscience."

Tenzin released Emilie and floated away, leaning against the far wall while the human sat up and scooted to the corner, gasping and rubbing her throat.

"Where's René?" Tenzin asked.

"Gavin interrupted his dinner with the cabbie. He's keeping him outside."

Tenzin glanced down. There was a closet beside her. She slid the door open.

How unimaginative.

"Is that...?" Ben walked over and opened the large black portfolio case sitting in the closet. "This is *Midnight Labyrinth*. They took the frame off, but this is it."

The painting had been sitting in the girl's bedroom closet.

Tenzin looked at the girl. "You didn't even try to disguise it?"

Emilie was sniffing back tears. "He said no one would find me here."

"Well, he was wrong," Tenzin said. "He's smart, but not as smart as he thinks he is."

Ben picked up the portfolio case and walked over to Tenzin. "Let's go."

He glanced at Emilie.

She watched him with tears in her eyes. "Ben, I'm so—"

"Not interested," he said, taking Tenzin's hand. "Stay out of my city, and stay away from me."

∾

BEN FELT like he could breathe again when they walked out the grey door on 12th Street. Gavin and Chloe were leaning against a red sedan. René DuPont was nowhere in sight.

"Where did he go?" Tenzin asked.

"I let him run away, you madwoman," Gavin said. "He's just a thief. I dinna want you throwing him off any more buildings."

Tenzin shrugged. "I threw him on a car. I knew he'd be fine."

"Yes, but the cab driver could have died, couldn't he?" Gavin said.

Ben's eyes went wide. "Did someone—?"

"I called an ambulance," Chloe said. "Gavin hid the wounds with some of his blood—that's a handy trick, by the way—and then I called an ambulance. They'll probably be confused by the blood loss when he gets to the hospital, but the EMTs said his heartbeat was steady. I got his card." Chloe held it up. "So Tenzin can make sure to pay for his hospital bill."

"See?" Tenzin hovered a foot over the sidewalk. "No harm done then. Chloe, you are an excellent assistant."

"Please don't make me call ambulances for people again."

"No guarantees."

Ben held out the portfolio case. "Here. The last thing I need is a third person stealing this. Take it home, and we'll figure out what to do with it tomorrow night."

"As you like." Tenzin grabbed the portfolio case, then melted into the darkness and flew away.

Gavin said, "I might have a... judicious way to return the painting to its rightful owner."

"I thought you might," Ben said.

"Tomorrow?"

"Please."

Gavin turned his attention to Chloe. "As for you, time to go home?"

She stepped toward him and smoothed her hands over his lapels. "I think... I'm going home with Ben."

Gavin was silent for a long time. "For now."

"For now."

He took her hand and lifted it to his mouth, pressing a kiss to the center of her palm. Then he leaned over and whispered something in Chloe's ear.

"I know," she said.

Gavin said, "I'll see you at work tomorrow, dove."

She nodded. "I'll be there."

Gavin took a step back, then another. He released Chloe's hand. Then he turned, walked down the street, and disappeared into the night.

Chloe walked over to Ben and put her arm through his. "Home?"

"Home." They started walking north to 14th Street, where Ben knew there would be more cabs. "So are you going to tell me what he said?"

"Nope."

"Mean."

"Like you don't have secrets," Chloe said. "I hope it doesn't take forever to get a car."

"It's Saturday night and the bars just closed," Ben said. "We'll probably be walking awhile."

"So the vampires get to make their dramatic exits, and the humans get stuck walking home?"

"Yeah," Ben said. "That's generally the way these things go."

29

The second official time Ben went to Rothman House, he was greeted at the front door by the very same butler whom he'd offended a few days before. The man gave no indication of knowing who he was. Ignorance or a good poker face? Sometimes it was hard to tell with experienced day people.

"Mr. Benjamin Vecchio and Ms. Chloe Reardon." The butler announced their names at the entrance to the drawing room where Cormac O'Brien, Gavin Wallace, and Adele Samson, the Lady of Normandy, sat waiting for them. Cormac and Gavin rose. Adele didn't.

Her face was unveiled, and the Labyrinth Trilogy hung behind her.

Ben stared at them, finally seeing the story in its entirety. The pale woman entering the labyrinth at dusk, her hair tied back neatly and her dress unmarred. The creature with the bloodstained lips fighting off the demons at midnight. The exhausted woman at dawn, stumbling out of the labyrinth with bloody feet and tangled hair, a monster of her own creation. Every shadow and twisted vine told a story. Every demon had blood on their claws.

"They're perfect." Ben tore his gaze away from the macabre and beautiful artwork and turned it toward Adele, who was very clearly the woman modeled in the painting. "Your brother was very talented, Ms. Samson."

"Thank you." Adele's voice was entrancing. "It's been so long since anyone called me by that name, it sounds foreign."

"But I hope not unpleasant."

"No." Her face was utterly placid. "Not unpleasant at all."

He examined *Midnight Labyrinth*. Emil Samson had perfectly rendered Adele's luminous skin, her pointed fangs, and the craving in her eyes. "Your brother knew about you, didn't he?"

She smiled, and it was beautiful and frightening at once. "Not everything, but enough. Unfortunately, my transformation wasn't enough to save my family."

Her eyes were golden brown with an edge of blood-red burgundy that made them completely otherworldly. Ben had never seen eyes quite the same color and wondered if that was part of the reason she wore a veil. Her nose was too prominent to be called beautiful, but she was striking—a dramatic model for any artist. Ben had little trouble understanding why some called her a muse.

"I understand that you and your partner specialize in retrieval," Adele said. "Mr. Wallace was kind enough to explain the situation to me, but he declined to tell me why I should not reward you. I did not hire you, yet you have returned *Midnight Labyrinth* to me, no doubt at some expense and trouble to yourself. I do not like to be beholden to another, Mr. Vecchio."

"There is no debt," Ben said. "And there never will be. Since the moment I first saw the paintings, I only wanted them together and with their rightful owner." It had been a carefully constructed response. Not a lie, but not the whole truth either.

"Now they are, and it is an honor to see them. That is all the payment I need."

From the look in Adele's eyes, she knew there was more going on, but she nodded, content to let the details remain ambiguous. "You understand, of course, why *Midnight Labyrinth* cannot be displayed."

"The resemblance is... unmistakable. If you have any kind of public life in France—"

"I do. I'm sure I won't always, but for now I do. If that was taken away, my business would suffer and my competitors would be emboldened at a very... delicate time."

"Then we have the privilege and honor of enjoying your brother's genius privately," Ben said.

Adele examined him carefully, came to some conclusion, then nodded. "You will pass along my thanks to your partner."

"I will."

"I was hoping to meet her tonight."

"She's horribly bad at being social." Ben gave her his most charming smile. "So I brought our assistant, Chloe."

Chloe nodded, having been instructed not to shake hands. "It's so nice to meet you. I've loved Emil Samson as an artist for a long time. I'm incredibly honored to meet you."

"You work with Mr. Wallace also, do you not?"

"I help out at the pub, yes."

"I thought you looked familiar."

Gavin finally spoke. "Chloe is also a very talented dancer, my lady. She's working with a new choreographer on a modern ballet scheduled for production next spring." He walked over and handed Chloe a glass of wine, ushering her into the chaise at Adele's right hand. "Perhaps the next time you visit New York, you'll be able to see her perform."

"I am a great lover and patron of the arts," Adele said. "It is how I believe my brother would have wanted me to spend my eternity. I would be most interested in hearing more about your show."

Ben let Gavin and Chloe talk to Adele about the ballet as Cormac sidled up next to him.

"No Tenzin tonight?"

"You know how she is."

"I do." Cormac sipped a glass filled with amber liquor. "Your explanation to Adele was very... politic."

"I try."

A flash of anger in Cormac's eyes. "Don't test me, boy."

Ben's smile faded. "I'm not trying to test you. I never was. I'm trying to do the right thing."

"Just remember, there's nothing more dangerous than a man who knows half the truth."

Ben blinked. "That was almost wise, Cormac."

The vampire downed the rest of his whiskey. "Now you're trying to piss me off."

"No, it was." Ben glanced down at the glass. "Can I get a drink?"

"No."

"Why not?"

"Because I don't like you."

"How's Ennis these days?" Ben asked. Since Cormac already didn't like him, he might as well go for broke. "I haven't heard much about him."

Cormac's face went eerily still. "That's because he's dead."

Ben felt the cold radiating from the vampire. "I'm sorry."

"So am I."

"ALL IN ALL," Emmanuel said, "you'll make a very tidy profit."

"How much?"

"With the pieces you bought and the current market frenzy, I'd anticipate your profit at around two million euros."

For oil paint and canvas? Tenzin shook her head. The world truly was an odd place.

Emmanuel was still talking. "The prices of the Samsons have gone through the roof. I don't know how you anticipated it, but I'd love to share the tip with my other clients. Perhaps those more interested in long-term growth."

Tenzin tapped her chin. "Give the paintings one more month. I think the price will peak at that point and then arrange to sell them. After that, you can tell anyone you want."

"As always, you're an extremely savvy buyer, my dear."

"Fine." She'd already become bored with the conversation. "Convert the money to gold when you're finished, then send it to me."

"Are you sure you don't want to hear about the other opportunity I mention—"

"Goodbye." She hung up the call. He was so chatty.

BEN SAT on the couch in the loft with a glass of bourbon warming in his hand. He was... drunk. Not as bad as champagne drunk, but moving well past buzzed. He stared at the wall of weapons that decorated his home. Weapons from China and Iran. Weapons from Chile and Kenya and Romania.

He took a long sip of bourbon. "My uncle's house is full of books."

"I remember." Chloe spoke from the kitchen. She'd been mellow all night, glowing and happy since their reception at Rothman House. Both Adele and Cormac had been enchanted with her, though Gavin had clearly staked a claim. They talked about dance and theater. Gavin had smiled more than Ben could ever remember seeing.

Ben was happy for her. He was happy she was happy. Chloe was an amazing person who deserved to be happy. She deserved to have people appreciate her. She deserved to be a star if she wanted to be.

He'd never felt more conflicted about bringing her into his world.

"My uncle's house is full of books," he said. "And my house is full of weapons."

Chloe took a deep breath. "It is. But they're... historic weapons. They're like art."

"Every single one of those weapons has probably killed someone," he said. "Have you ever thought about that when you walk through a museum with an arms and armory display? Every one of those historic swords has probably killed someone. Maybe a lot of people. And if they haven't, that's what they were designed to do. Art designed to kill things."

"No, I haven't thought about that," Chloe said. "But you're right."

"I was designed to kill things." He finished his drink and set the glass down on the table. "You know that, right? My aunt taught me the fastest way to kill someone with a sword when I was fifteen. We used dead pigs because they're the closest to human flesh and bone."

"Ben—"

"That wasn't even the beginning. Not really. She taught me to steal first."

"Your aunt?"

"No, my mom." He desperately needed another drink.

Which meant he really didn't need another drink. Not if he didn't want to end up like his dad.

Chloe asked, "Your mom taught you to steal?"

"And pickpocket. I was good at it." He brought his hand up and waved. "Long fingers. I bought the groceries. She paid the rent with what she stole, and I bought the groceries with what I could get."

"So if you didn't pick pockets—"

"We didn't eat." He closed his eyes and rested his head on the back of the sofa. "Don't worry. I didn't go hungry very often."

Chloe said nothing. What could she say? He'd dumped all his baggage on her when she'd been having a nice night.

He was a shit friend.

"How did I get here?" he murmured.

Chloe sat next to him on the couch. "We took a cab."

"You know what I mean."

"I do," she said. "And I don't. This is all new to me, Ben. It still feels fantastic and forbidden. Like I'm in a special club. You've been living this life for longer than you've known me."

"I've been putting up with this... *bullshit*"—he spat out the word—"for thirteen years now. I'm tired of it. Walking on eggshells. Watching every word. Weighing every move."

"Sounds exhausting."

"It is." Ben stretched out, putting his head in Chloe's lap after she scooted down the couch. "I don't like fighting."

"I know you don't." She stroked his hair. "In school, you were always the guy with the joke. Make 'em laugh when tempers and egos get hot. Do you know how many kids probably *didn't* get beat up because of you?"

"No." He closed his eyes. "I never thought about it."

She kept stroking his hair, lulling him into relaxation as he drifted in an alcohol haze.

"You talk about being designed to kill things," Chloe said, "but that's not what I see. Maybe life has thrown that at you—

put you in horrible situations where you had to fight to survive—but that just made you less violent, not more."

"I know things..." He closed his eyes and saw vomit and gore. He saw headless bodies and blood. *So much blood.* "I just know things I wish I didn't, Chloe. And you will too. Not now, but you will. Please don't hate me. I'm really afraid you'll hate me."

"If I promise I won't, will you believe me?"

It was a valid question. "I'll try."

"Then I promise I won't hate you, Ben Vecchio." She bent down and kissed his cheek. "I don't think I could ever hate you. You saved my life."

"You saved yourself. You were the one who walked away."

"Yeah, I did," she said. "But I could only walk away from Tom because I knew you'd give me a safe place to land. That's what you do, Ben. You help people."

Ben felt the rush of guilt rise up and choke him. "I was trying to do the right thing."

"With Emilie?"

He hated that name now. Hated her. Hated feeling like a complete fool. "Yeah."

"I know you were trying to do that right thing," Chloe said. "I think everyone knows that."

"But I fucked everything up."

"And then you fixed it."

"With Tenzin." He rubbed his eyes. "Once again, she bails me out of trouble."

Chloe took a deep breath. "From what I hear, half the time you're the one bailing her out."

"Half's probably... a really high estimate."

"It doesn't matter. Know why?"

"Why?"

She put her hand on his cheek. "Because no one is keeping score. That's not what friends do. That's not how it works." She lifted his head and stood up, propping a pillow under him before she rose. "I'm exhausted, Benny. Bed for me. You gonna be okay?"

"Yeah." He closed his eyes. "Just gonna sleep here, I think."

"You need a new couch."

"I know." He tried to get comfortable. "This one sucks, but it looks cool."

He heard her laugh as she walked downstairs, turning off the lights behind her.

Ben lay in the dark, thinking about Chloe's words.

"...no one is keeping score. That's not how it works."

Right.

That was always how it worked, whether people wanted to admit it or not.

BEN WOKE when she flew him up to her loft. She'd grabbed him under the armpits and was dragging him because he was completely dead weight, but she laid him down gently.

"Tenzin?"

"Go back to sleep."

"But why—?"

"I don't sleep," she said, arranging pillows around him. "And you're inebriated. Stay on your side. I will watch you to make sure you don't get sick."

He wasn't drunk. In fact, he was mostly sober since he'd slept a few hours. But he wasn't going to tell Tenzin that. Ben rolled over and turned into pillows that smelled like her. Cardamom and honey.

The bitterness that rested on the tip of his tongue melted away at her scent, and he stretched his arm out. "Come here."

Her voice was soft. "I'm reading."

"Then read next to me," he said with his eyes closed.

Tenzin said nothing, but she went and lay next to him, resting her head on Ben's arm.

"Read to me," he said.

"I'm in the middle of the story. If I read to you, you'll be lost."

"So start over."

"Selfish."

"If it's a really good story," Ben murmured, "you won't mind reading it again."

Tenzin paused for a moment, and he heard her turning the pages.

"'There was once a witch who desired to know everything,'" she read. "'But the wiser a witch is, the harder she knocks her head against the wall when she comes to it. Her name was Watho, and she had a wolf in her mind. She cared for nothing in itself, only for knowing it. She was not naturally cruel, but the wolf had made her cruel.'"

Ben drifted to sleep as Tenzin read. He dreamt of full moons and labyrinths made of tangled branches that grabbed his legs and shredded his skin, leaving him bloody. He dreamt of the burning sun and heat so intense it seared the flesh from his body. He heard the rumbles of wolves and thunderstorms. Felt the brush of flower petals against his skin.

When he woke in the blue light of early morning, Tenzin was lying with her back to him, still reading aloud in a soft voice:

"'No, no,' persisted Nycteris, 'we must go now. And you must learn to be strong in the dark as well as in the day, else you will always be only half brave. I have begun already—not to fight your sun, but to try to get at peace with him and understand what he really is and what he means with me—whether to hurt me or to make the best of me. You must do the same with my darkness.'"

It was dawn and the sun was rising, but no light reached the loft where they hid. Ben reached over and ran a finger up Tenzin's spine, playing with the velvet hair that lay against her nape.

Tenzin stopped reading. She lay completely still as Ben touched her, her amnis prickling against his fingertips.

"'To be trusted,'" he whispered, "'is a greater compliment than being loved.'"

"Wrong book."

"Right author." He was only half awake; his eyes fluttered open, then closed again. "What did you call me once? Your shining boy?"

"Yes, I called you that."

"Not so shiny anymore."

"No, you're not."

Ben's hand froze when he felt Tenzin's amnis reach toward him. It was a tentative touch, like the lick of summer wind against his skin.

"I have been a hero and a villain in the same moment," she said. "If you live long enough, you'll understand what that means." She reached back and lifted Ben's arm, drawing it over her waist. "Sleep, my Benjamin. I'll stay with you until nightfall."

Ben tucked Tenzin against his chest and relaxed into the pillow, letting himself fall back into darkness as daylight breached the horizon.

EPILOGUE

B en stood at the counter and sorted through the mail, ignoring the huffing and loud flip of pages coming from Tenzin's loft.

If she starts throwing my books again...

More huffing. More page flipping.

Ben's irritation mounted with every passive-aggressive huff.

Chloe looked up from where she was working at the research table. She had her laptop open, but she glanced between the loft and the kitchen, her eyes getting wider as the tension in the room built.

"You know, I think I'm going to go into the pub early tonight." She stood and closed her laptop. "I think Gavin wanted to do inventory tonight, so... yeah. That sounds like a really good idea." Then she muttered under her breath, "Please don't let there be bloodshed."

Tenzin shouted, "There wouldn't be any bloodshed if Ben would just be reasonable!"

"Damn it," Chloe hissed. "It is freakish how good her ears are."

"Gavin's are probably just as good," Ben said. "Might want to keep that in mind."

Without another word, Chloe fled the loft.

"I do not care how many times you suggest it," he said calmly. "I am not going to Puerto Rico."

Tenzin flew out of the loft and hovered over him, tossing the glossy travel magazine to the ground. "Pirate. Treasure! How hard is that to understand?"

"Not interested," Ben said.

"How can you not be interested in Spanish treasure?"

"There are a hundred easier ways to get gold than running around after fictional treasure."

Tenzin glared at him. "Who said it's fictional?"

"Me."

"Is this because of your grandmother?"

Ben's mouth fell open. "How did you... No, I don't care. And it's not— *This has nothing to do with my family, Tenzin!*"

"I went with you on the stupid painting thing—even though art is a completely fabricated market that depends on—"

"—on the whims of a handful of self-important collectors," Ben repeated the tired phrase. "Yes, I've heard that argument from you before. I'd still rather chase a lost Renoir than Spanish pirate treasure."

"But this is gold, Benjamin. *Gold.* With actual monetary value in the millions of dollars."

And it's pretty and shiny, he mouthed.

"Yes, it *is* pretty and shiny!"

He slammed down the stack of mail, no longer trying to feign disinterest. "You are suggesting we follow a treasure map, Tenzin. A treasure map to some caves on an island in the middle of the Atlantic Ocean. *A treasure map.*"

She crossed her arms. "And?"

"Do you not hear how insane that sounds? It's a treasure map!"

"That your uncle has authenticated."

"All that means is that it was produced during that era; it does not mean that whoever drew the map was sane. Or that he or she possessed any treasure. Or that if there *was* a treasure that it's still there and hasn't been looted!"

She hovered over him, her mouth set in a grim line. "I am going to Puerto Rico. You know you're going to come with me, or I'm liable to cause an international incident." With that, Tenzin flew back to her loft and pulled up the rope ladder.

Every curse his father had ever taught him flew through his mind. "*So pendejo!*"

"I know what that means!" she yelled from the loft. "I'm still going."

Ben grabbed his phone and wished he could still punch in numbers, because punching anything sounded really satisfying in that moment. Giovanni's phone rang three times before his uncle picked up.

"Hello, Benjamin."

"I cannot believe you told her about that damn map."

"I didn't think she'd become so enamored with the idea," his uncle said with a laugh. "I've told her about other treasure maps in the past and she's been completely uninterested. There's no predicting her."

Tenzin shouted, "Tell him to send us the map!"

"I'm not sending you the map," Giovanni said. "Tell Tenzin the map doesn't belong to me. It belongs to a cartography collector, and he would never allow me to loan it to someone."

"Sorry, Tiny, we can't get the map," Ben said. "Guess we're not going."

Tenzin said, "Send us a copy of the map!" at the same time Giovanni said, "I suppose I could make you a copy."

Ben closed his eyes, drew in a long breath, and let it out.

"Fine," he said. "Send us a copy. I guess we're going to Puerto Rico."

THE END

Sign up for my newsletter
to receive news about the next novel in the
Elemental Legacy series and other works of fiction.

IF YOU NEED HELP...

Get help now.
Call the National Domestic Violence Hotline to get
information, to talk, or to find resources in your area.

1-800-799-SAFE
1-855-812-1011 (VP)
1-800-787-3224 (TTY)

No names.
No fees.
No judgement.
Just help.

GET HELP WITHOUT SAYING A WORD.
Online chat is available 24/7.
www.thehotline.org

AFTERWORD

The book referenced in the very last chapter of *Midnight Labyrinth* is *The Day Boy and the Night Girl* by Scottish fantasy writer George MacDonald. When I started reading MacDonald's *The Princess and the Goblin* as a child, I had no idea he was a pioneer in fantasy literature. I just knew I liked stories with princesses who did things and that MacDonald and his collection of fairy tales fed my imagination.

The Day Boy and the Night Girl is a wonderful story with themes exploring light and dark that have carried into my work to this day and seemed particularly fitting for Ben and Tenzin. I highly recommend it.

"Seeing is not believing—it is only seeing."
G.M.

ACKNOWLEDGMENTS

First off, I want to thank every one of my longtime readers who were wonderful and weird enough to think: "Hmm, five-thousand-year-old vampire and twenty-five-year-old human dude partnering up to hunt for treasure and stuff? Yeah, I can dig it." THANK YOU for getting why I love these characters so much and for being willing to jump onto this ride for a while. Thank you also for your patience. The Elemental series started out with four books, but it soon grew to be a world that encompassed so many different storylines. It feels great to start fresh with these characters.

And to all you new readers who also thought that *Midnight Labyrinth* sounded like your jam, thank you too! I hope you'll check out some of the other books I've written in this world, but if you want to just stick with Ben and Tenzin, that's cool too. Welcome!

This book is a little bit of a love letter to New York City. Though I didn't grow up there, NYC has always welcomed me. I've never felt like a tourist. Some of that is thanks to all the wonderful friends I've made who live there, but some of that is just the character of that crazy, diverse, all-hours-a-day city.

New York, I love your energy. I love your style. I love your noisy streets and your quiet corners. When I thought about settling Ben and Tenzin in a new place, you were the first and only choice.

I want to thank my friends who offered particular insight to the city, particularly Denise Cataudella; and my one and only Scottish Profanity Beta, Cat Bowen. Many thanks to the keen eyes of RJ Blain and Mel Sterling, as well as so many other encouraging author friends. Amy Cissell, Colleen Vanderlinden, April White, Grace Draven, Penny Reid, and so many others. Thanks for being part of this fabulous indie publishing tribe. You are my people.

Thanks to my marvelous editing team, Heather Kinne, Anne Victory, and Linda. Thanks for all the work you do to help me get better with every book. You are so very appreciated.

Thanks to my assistants, Jenn and Gen. You are marvelous and I'm getting you matching capes.

Thanks to the staff and artists at Damonza.com who are both consummate professionals and extraordinary artists. You captured my vision for this book cover and were such a pleasure to work with.

Thanks to my family, especially Colin and David, my two best guys. Thanks to my mom and dad, who make so many things possible. Thanks to my canine assistants, Mac and Charlie, for having the generosity to let me feed you, clean up after you, and occasionally snuggle.

Thanks to God, who makes *all* things possible, especially the peace that passes understanding.

~

Life is unpredictable, but I'm happy to be going along on this ride with people I love and admire. Thanks for joining me.

ABOUT THE AUTHOR

ELIZABETH HUNTER is a contemporary fantasy, paranormal romance, and paranormal mystery writer. She is a graduate of the University of Houston Honors College and a former English teacher. She currently lives in Central California with her son, two dogs, and many plants, eagerly awaiting some guy from Ethiopia she's going to marry as soon as his visa comes through.

She's also the best-selling author of the Elemental Mysteries, Elemental World, and Elemental Legacy series, the Cambio Springs Mysteries, the Irin Chronicles, and other works of fiction. Her books have sold over a million copies worldwide.

For more information:
ElizabethHunterWrites.com
Elizabeth@ElizabethHunterWrites.com

ALSO BY ELIZABETH HUNTER

The Elemental Legacy

Shadows and Gold

Imitation and Alchemy

Omens and Artifacts

Midnight Labyrinth (November 2017)

The Elemental Mysteries

A Hidden Fire

This Same Earth

The Force of Wind

A Fall of Water

Lost Letters & Christmas Lights (novella)

The Elemental World

Building From Ashes

Waterlocked

Blood and Sand

The Bronze Blade

The Scarlet Deep

Beneath a Waning Moon

A Stone-Kissed Sea

The Irin Chronicles

The Scribe

The Singer

The Secret

On a Clear Winter Night (short story)

The Staff and the Blade

The Silent

The Storm (Winter 2017)

The Cambio Springs Series

Shifting Dreams

Long Ride Home (short story)

Desert Bound

Five Mornings (short story)

Waking Hearts

Contemporary Romance

The Genius and the Muse

CPSIA information can be obtained
at www.ICGtesting.com
Printed in the USA
LVHW112354130120
643456LV00001BA/96/P